Praise for Martin Edwards

"Martin Edwards is a true master of British crime writing."
—Richard Osman

"Martin Edwards has earned distinction in every area of the crime-fiction field."
—*Ellery Queen's Mystery Magazine*

"Crime fiction is blessed to have Martin Edwards."
—*New York Times*

"Martin knows more about crime fiction than anyone else working in the field today. He's always been a fan of the genre, and his passion shines through in his work: the fiction, the nonfiction, and the short stories. In his editing, he's brought new writers and forgotten favorites to discerning readers."
—Ann Cleeves

"Martin's fiction alone makes him a truly worthy winner of the Diamond Dagger. His editorial excellence, his erudition, his enthusiasm for and contributions to the genre, his support of other writers, and his warmhearted friendship are the icing on the cake."
—Lee Child

"Martin is not only one of the finest crime writers of his generation. He is the heir to Julian Symons and H. R. F. Keating as the leading authority on our genre, fostering and promoting it with unflagging enthusiasm, to the benefit of us all."
—Peter Lovesey

"Martin Edwards is not only a fine writer, but he is also ridiculously knowledgeable about the field of crime and suspense fiction."
—Ian Rankin

THE PUZZLE OF BLACKSTONE LODGE

The Third Rachel Savernake Golden Age Mystery

Longlisted for the CWA Historical Dagger Award

"Martin Edwards celebrates and satirizes the genre with wit and affection... He leaves you wanting more."

—*The Times*

"For his latest classic mystery, Martin Edwards serves up an engaging mix of ingredients familiar to fans of golden age crime... The plot is intricate but never less than compelling. Martin Edwards holds his own with the best of classic crime."

—*Daily Mail*

"Fabulous locked-room mystery... Full of suspense, this entertaining and engaging read is a classic whodunit."

—*My Weekly*

"The third Rachel Savernake investigation is perfect for those who love a locked-room mystery. It has a wonderful Golden Age of crime feel to it."

—*Belfast Telegraph*

"An irresistible Gothic thriller...Edwards's book keeps you gripped to the very end; you find yourself caring about the characters and their fates."

—*Yorkshire Life*

"A satisfying puzzle for established genre fans and a good starting point for readers looking to dip their toes into Agatha Christie–adjacent fare."

—*Publishers Weekly*

"A triple-decker banquet honoring the Golden Age of mysteries and bidding fair to continue it to the present."

—*Kirkus Reviews*

MORTMAIN HALL

The Second Rachel Savernake Golden Age Mystery

★ "[A] triumph, from its tantalizing opening, in which an unnamed dying man begins to explain an unspecified perfect crime, through its scrupulously fair final reveal...impressively channels Agatha Christie."

—*Publishers Weekly*, Starred Review

"Maintains a cracking pace. Elegant period escapism."

—*Mail on Sunday*

"A classic whodunit."

—*Daily Express*

"Rachel Savernake is on spectacular form...a Miss Marple for the twenty-first century."

—*Daily Mail*

"Martin Edwards is a guru of the Golden Age. His work pays homage to the intricate puppetry and byzantine plotting popular in the period."

—*The Times*

GALLOWS COURT

The First Rachel Savernake Golden Age Mystery

2018 Dagger in the Library Winner

2019 eDunnit Award shortlist, Best Novel

2019 CWA Historical Dagger Award nominee

"Martin Edwards's *Gallows Court* seems awfully bloodthirsty for a traditionally designed mystery set in foggy old London in 1930... Fans of clean-cut heroes will be rooting for Jacob, although some of us would rather see devilish Rachel clean his clock. Either that or commit a clever, more refined murder of her own."

—*New York Times Book Review*

★ "Highly atmospheric, spine-tingling fun… The way that Edwards keeps deepening the creepiness of this mystery until the very end is utterly stunning."

—*Booklist*, Starred Review

★ "Exceptional series launch from Edgar-winner Edwards… The labyrinthine plot is one of Edwards's best, and he does a masterly job of maintaining suspense, besides getting the reader to invest in the fate of the two main characters."

—*Publishers Weekly*, Starred Review

"Superb—a pitch-perfect blend of Golden Age charm and sinister modern suspense, with a main character to die for. This is the book Edwards was born to write."

—Lee Child, #1 *New York Times* bestselling author

THE STORY OF CLASSIC CRIME IN 100 BOOKS

2018 Macavity Award winner for Best Nonfiction

2018 Anthony Award nominee for Best Critical/Nonfiction

2018 Agatha Award nominee for Best Nonfiction

★ "This is an exemplary reference book sure to lead readers to gems of mystery and detective fiction."

—*Publishers Weekly*, Starred Review

THE GIRL THEY ALL FORGOT

The Eighth Lake District Mystery

"There's intrigue… Edwards juggles all the subplots with a master's hand and even produces a pair of utterly surprising candidates for the title role. Welcome back, Cold Case Review Team. Please don't wait seven years for the next update."

—*Kirkus Reviews*

"Edwards makes engagement easy through crisp prose and thoughtful characterizations. This skillful combination of procedural and whodunit will prompt newcomers to seek out earlier series entries."

—*Publishers Weekly*

"Life is certainly nasty, brutish, and short—least for most of the characters in Edwards's much-awaited new installment, set on the edge of England's Lake District."

—*First Clue*

"Edwards deftly weaves the multiple plots into a cohesive, quirky story with a smart heroine, fascinating insights into Lake District history, and a stunning conclusion."

—*Booklist*

"Readers who appreciate an atmospheric story with a strong sense of place will be satisfied."

—*Library Journal*

THE DUNGEON HOUSE

The Seventh Lake District Mystery

"Readers who enjoy British procedurals will find this multidimensional, multigenerational case very satisfying."

—*Booklist*

THE FROZEN SHROUD

The Sixth Lake District Mystery

"Martin Edwards uses the lovely landscape of the Lake District to fine effect...clean prose and an engaging love for the territory."

—*Chicago Tribune*

THE HANGING WOOD
The Fifth Lake District Mystery

★ "With an unforgettable ending, this outstanding cold case will attract Lynda La Plante and Mo Hayder fans."
—*Library Journal*, Starred Review

THE SERPENT POOL
The Fourth Lake District Mystery

★"An excellent choice for discerning readers who want an unusual and challenging puzzle mystery that will keep them guessing until the final pages. Wow!"
—*Library Journal*, Starred Review

THE ARSENIC LABYRINTH
The Third Lake District Mystery

"A beautifully crafted book."
—Ann Cleeves, CWA Gold Dagger winner

THE CIPHER GARDEN
The Second Lake District Mystery

"Fans of the British village mystery who are very particular about setting should trek to *The Cipher Garden*."
—*New York Times*

THE COFFIN TRAIL

The First Lake District Mystery

"A wonderful, absorbing read: a crime deeply rooted in the past, a beautifully evoked sense of the Lake District…"

—Peter Robinson, *New York Times* bestselling author

Other Awards

2019 CWA Short Story Dagger shortlist for "Strangers in a Pub" (*Ten Year Stretch*)

Poirot Award 2017

Edgar Awards for Best Biographical/Critical for *The Golden Age of Murder* and *The Life of Crime*

CWA Red Herring Award 2011

CWA Margery Allingham Prize 2014

George N. Dove award for outstanding scholarship 2023

Edward D. Hoch Golden Derringer award for lifetime achievement in the field of short fiction 2023

Also by Martin Edwards

THE HOUSE ON GRAVEYARD LANE

A RACHEL SAVERNAKE
GOLDEN AGE MYSTERY

MARTIN EDWARDS

Winner of the CWA Diamond Dagger 2020

Poisoned Pen
PRESS

Published by Poisoned Pen Press, an imprint of Sourcebooks
P.O. Box 4410, Naperville, Illinois 60567-4410
(630) 961-3900
sourcebooks.com

First published as *Sepulchre Street* in the UK in 2023 by Head
of Zeus, part of Bloomsbury Publishing Plc.

Cataloging-in-Publication is on file with the Library of Congress.

Printed and bound in the United States of America.
VP 10 9 8 7 6 5 4 3 2 1

For Elizabeth Kiss, Andrew Copson, and Martin O'Neill,
my colleagues in Team Balliol, who made Christmas
University Challenge 2022 such a memorable experience.

MAJOR WHITLOW'S SKETCH MAP OF RYE
(NOT TO SCALE)

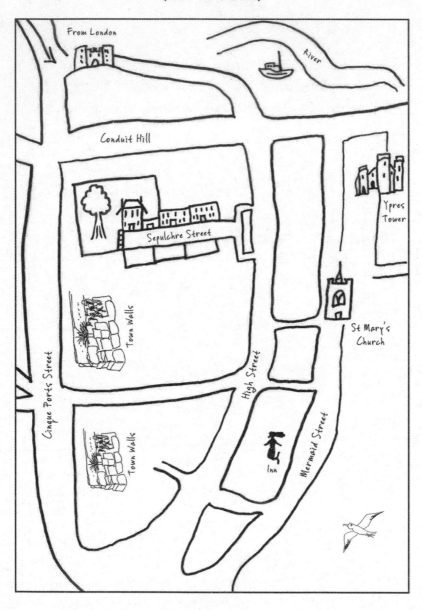

Chapter 1

"I want you to solve my murder," said the woman in white.

Rachel Savernake gave a sardonic smile. "Quite a challenge."

"Rumour has it that you seldom refuse a dare."

"True," Rachel said. "But I anticipate difficulties. You're flesh and blood, an artist who lives and breathes. Not a ghost."

"Not yet."

In the dim glow of a solitary wall candle, Damaris Gethin's appearance was spectral. Her face was as pale as the cotton dress clinging to her slender, boyish frame. A white cap adorned with black ribbon sat on short hair dyed silver. Her skin was stretched tight over sunken cheekbones and her lips were thin and bloodless. She kept clenching and unclenching her small fists, as if to suppress emotion. A strange glint lit her eyes.

"I have a confession to make, Miss Savernake."

"I'm not a priest."

"More like a she-devil, perhaps? The truth is, I had an ulterior motive for inviting you to my new exhibition. I hear you're insatiably curious about crime."

"One of my many weaknesses."

"You're an art lover with a taste for the avant-garde. Because you are rich, the clammy fingers of the Slump haven't touched you. So I hoped you would accept my invitation."

"To a private view at the Hades Gallery. How could I resist?"

"The name suits this place, don't you agree?"

The two women were standing apart from the small knot of guests, in a dingy corner of a cavernous space with a high brick ceiling and no windows. The other visitors kept screwing up their eyes, adjusting to the Stygian gloom, trying to make sense of the figures on display. The Hades was less like a gallery than an eerie subterranean grotto, home to a strange kind of waxworks.

Rachel said, "You'll have heard that I admire your work. I love the way you shock the critics and test the boundaries of good taste. People call you the Queen of Surrealism. Britain's most subversive exponent of modern art."

"You flatter me, Miss Savernake."

"Not at all. Two years ago, you were the talk of the town. By the time I arrived in London, you'd vanished from sight. Yet you were only in your mid-thirties, far too young to retire. Out of the blue, you summon me to an exhibition with an irresistible title. *Artist in Crime.*"

"I like to tantalise. Hence my question. Will you solve my murder?"

"Tell me more. Does an enemy want you dead? Have you been threatened? Is that why—"

A thunderous roar drowned her words. Candles flickered and the whole gallery seemed to shudder with dread. People gasped and looked up in terror, as if fearing the roof would fall in and bury them alive.

A moment later, the cacophony subsided. An unseen train driver had stamped on his brakes. The Hades Gallery occupied a tunnel beneath the railway track close to London Bridge railway station.

"Threatened? No, I'm reconciled to my fate." The woman in white glanced at her hands, unclenching them with a visible effort. "Naturally, I feel a certain tension as the minutes tick by. My spine prickles as I anticipate…what is to come. Yet at the same time I feel oddly elated."

"I'm intrigued."

"Mysteries fascinate you, don't they?" Damaris Gethin shifted from one foot to another. "You're a puzzle in your own right. I tried to find out everything about you, but you remain mysterious."

"I value my privacy."

"You guard it like a tigress." She hesitated. "We have something in common, Miss Savernake. People fear us because we are women they find impossible to understand."

Rachel said nothing.

"You've been mixed up in more than one strange murder. You're outrageously rich and your late father was a hanging judge. Beyond that, nobody knows much about Rachel Savernake. Not in the art world, not in society at large. Not even that young journalist who hangs on your coattails."

"Jacob Flint?" Rachel frowned. "I caught sight of him across the room, just as you buttonholed me."

"Forgive my rudeness. I wanted to make sure that we could speak tête-à-tête before you were caught up in the social cobweb. Mr. Flint doesn't know I invited you here."

"Jacob is a crime reporter, not an art critic. He thinks a Miro is for checking your reflection. Have you asked him to investigate this murder of yours?"

Damaris Gethin shook her head. "It's your help that I seek. Not his."

"Then why is he here?"

"He and his newspaper went to great lengths to secure an

invitation once they got wind that Mrs. de Villiers's name was on the list of guests. In the end it was simpler to agree than to provoke the press with a refusal."

"He's interested in Kiki de Villiers?" Rachel murmured.

"You didn't know?"

"I'm not his keeper."

"His fascination with the lady isn't romantic. Not unless he has ideas far above his station. If an admirer is neither a millionaire nor a member of the landed gentry, the lovely Kiki won't give him the time of day."

"Why has the *Clarion* sent a crime reporter chasing after her?"

"Perhaps she's stolen a policeman's helmet for a bet. Or does he have a weakness for stories of scandal in high society?"

"With Jacob Flint," Rachel said, "anything is possible."

"People say the same about you, Miss Savernake." A thin, humourless smile. "Captain Roderick Malam described you in those very terms, the last time I spoke to him."

"You and he are still in touch?"

Damaris Gethin's expression was unreadable. "You're aware that he and I have…a little shared history? Of course you are. Once a detective, always a detective."

"I am not a detective."

With a dismissive twitch of the hand, the artist said, "A student of criminology, then."

"If you like."

"When Roddy Malam took a shine to you, presumably you looked into his background. You must have lost count of the lovers who came and went before he turned his attention to you."

"He and I were never lovers."

"I suspect you still fascinate him," Damaris Gethin said. "Oh, please don't accuse me of jealousy. On the contrary, I admire his taste, and I'd be glad to tell him so when he arrives. Roddy is never punctual, as no doubt you've discovered, but he'll be here any moment now. Provided he's not broken his neck racing at Brooklands."

"You invited him to this exhibition?"

"He forgot to mention it?" Damaris Gethin was becoming fidgety. "I suppose he didn't want to parade the fact that he and I are still on speaking terms. Like so many men, he is wonderfully naïve. He will presume that I wouldn't ask you to come here. Simply because he thinks I still yearn for him myself."

Rachel shook her head. "I haven't seen or heard from Captain Malam for quite some time. In small doses, he amused me. Anything more would give me severe indigestion."

The artist laughed, a hollow sound. "Take a tip from me. Don't underestimate Roddy. He is persistent and devilishly persuasive."

"I can take care of myself."

"So I gather, Miss Savernake. That is one of the reasons why I place my faith in you."

"To solve a murder that hasn't been committed?"

"I hear you have a craving for justice."

"On my own terms."

"That is good enough for me." Damaris Gethin was breathing faster. "Your late father was notoriously fond of donning the black cap. There was scurrilous gossip that he loved to exercise the power of life and death. It excited him to send men to the gallows. Guilty or innocent."

"I am very different from Judge Savernake."

"People find you menacing. I've heard whispers that you inherited his ruthlessness."

Rachel's face was a mask. "So you are to be murdered in mysterious circumstances?"

"In a manner of speaking."

"Do you propose to give me any clues?"

"If you deserve your reputation, you will discover them for yourself."

"What exactly do you want of me?"

In the flickering light, the woman's pallor made her look more than ever like a phantom.

"When the time comes, Miss Savernake, I rely on you to do whatever is necessary. I ask nothing more. My only question is this: Do you accept my challenge?"

Rachel breathed out.

"How could I say no?"

Chapter 2

"Mr. Flint, I presume?"

Jacob put his champagne flute down on a table. In between sips, he'd been scanning the room in search of Mrs. de Villiers. The candles illuminating the gallery were few and far between. Tobacco smoke clouded his vision and made his sinuses sting.

He stared into a face familiar from photographs and film reels. The man's chiselled features were well-scrubbed and his light-brown hair combed to perfection. A briar pipe was clamped between his lips. He looked as if he'd stepped into his dinner suit after a cold, bracing shower. Was that a whiff of carbolic soap on his skin? A yellowing bruise marked his left cheek, but he radiated robust masculinity. His pedigree showed in his erect posture, in the expert knotting of his bow tie, in every syllable of his patrician drawl. He might have had a tattoo stamped on his forehead proclaiming *Eton and Sandhurst*.

"Captain Malam?"

"Got it in one, young man. Saw your picture once in that rag you write for. You were on the spot during that malarkey in the godforsaken wilds of Yorkshire last autumn, weren't you? Blackstone-something-or-other?" Malam crushed Jacob's hand in a grip so powerful it almost brought tears to his eyes. "I bet

Miss Rachel Savernake gave you a helping hand. She's mentioned your name in despatches."

"Oh really?"

He freed Jacob's hand from the vice. "You seek her help during your trickiest investigations."

"We're acquainted, yes."

Jacob preferred to think of Rachel as a friend, yet each time she seemed about to drop her guard, she thought better of it. Already it was mid-March and he'd hardly seen her since Christmas.

"What brings you here?"

Jacob had foreseen this question. Telling the truth was impossible, but his answer was smooth and well-rehearsed. "The *Clarion's* art correspondent is indisposed, and I was happy to step in. I don't know much about art..."

"But you know what you don't like, eh?" Malam drew on his pipe and blew a smoke ring. "Funny business, this."

"Yes?"

"Lord knows what Damaris is playing at. We're...old pals, but she and I never saw eye to eye about art. Between you and me, her stuff strikes me as ludicrous, if not indecent. Make no bones about it, she called me a Philistine. Damned unfair. Personally, I'm a Landseer man. *Monarch of the Glen*, now that's what I call painting. Can't make head nor tail of this nonsense."

"She drops a hint in the title of her exhibition."

"*Artist in Crime*?" Malam's nose wrinkled, as if at a bad smell.

Jacob waved at a figure on a plinth a few feet away. "See·that waxwork of the fellow with a saw in one hand and bloodstains on his fingers? It's a caricature of Dr. Crippen."

"Scrawny little beggar, isn't he? Such a crazed look behind those pebble glasses. You may be right. Except he's not a wax model. When I blew a smoke ring, the blighter twitched. For a moment I thought he was going to sneeze."

Jacob concentrated on the Crippen figure. Malam's eyes were sharp. The model's occasional movements were almost imperceptible, but he wasn't able to keep perfectly still.

"There's a female figure close to the entrance. I thought she was made of wax too. Come to think of it, she reminds me of pictures I once saw in a book. Images of Elizabeth Báthory."

"Never heard of her," Malam said.

"A Hungarian countess who killed a great many women. So the story goes, she bathed in the blood of virgins in order to stay young."

"Typical Damaris. Macabre sense of humour. Loves to make people jump out of their skins. She's always so contrary. When we were…seeing each other, I never could tell when she was joking." He shot a quick glance at Jacob. "Mind you, Rachel's as bad, don't you agree?"

Jacob made an indeterminate noise, like a lawyer dodging a yes or no answer. He could guess why Malam had accosted him. The man wanted to pump him for information about Rachel. A waste of time. She demanded total discretion from everyone admitted to her small circle.

As for the captain, he was a popular man about town, a pukka sahib and a believer in noblesse oblige. Jacob had no idea why Rachel was interested in him. If there was more to the fellow than met the eye, what was it? He was supposed to be as astute in business as he was daring on a sports field. If his wealth hadn't evaporated during the worldwide aftershocks of the Wall Street crash, he must have his wits about him. Hardly a conventional flannelled fool or muddied oaf.

Malam leaned forward. "What do you make of her?"

The captain had a name for bravery, up to and beyond the point of recklessness. Jacob wondered if that taste for danger explained his appeal to Rachel. After leaving Sandhurst, Malam had served in France with the Royal Engineers at the tail end of the Great War. He'd earned a Military Cross for conspicuous gallantry under enemy fire. After the Armistice he'd given up soldiering for hedonistic pleasures and had roared through the Twenties as one of the country's most admired amateur sportsmen. At the Winter Games in St. Moritz, he'd narrowly missed winning a medal for skeleton sledding. Last year, after cartwheeling off the racing track at Crystal Palace, he'd insisted on climbing back into his damaged Bentley, finishing in sixth place to more rapturous applause than greeted the winner.

Groping for a suitably bland response, Jacob said, "A remarkable lady."

A flunkey dressed in a police constable's uniform and bearing a silver tray handed a fizzing glass to each of them.

Malam said, "Go on."

"Quite good-looking." Jacob was determined to give nothing away. "Formidably intelligent. And of course, very well-off."

He took a gulp of champagne as Malam stroked his impeccably shaved chin.

"Indeed. Curious *ménage* at that house of hers in the square. Only three servants, when she could staff a whole palace. It's no secret that she's as rich as Croesus. Damned peculiar, don't you think?"

"Rachel Savernake grew up with the Truemans. They lived together on a small island off the Cumberland coast."

"She doesn't strike me as the sentimental type who can't bear to put an old retainer out to grass. Can't say I care for those Trueman people. Let alone their attitude. Sullen and overfamiliar by turns. Beats me why she wants to spend so much of her time cooped up with them." He paused. "Anyone would think they have some kind of hold on her."

Lifting his glass, Jacob swallowed more champagne.

Malam eyed him. "As for this hobby of murder, that may be how you put food on your own table, old boy, but for an attractive young woman, it strikes me as positively unhealthy."

"You're planning to take her mind off it?"

"Between you and me, I hope to whisk her over to Monaco for the Grand Prix. A change of air will do her the world of good. Bring some roses to those fair cheeks, eh? She can meet some of the other Bentley Boys."

"I'm sure she'll love that," Jacob muttered.

"Astonishing that she's never once set foot on the Continent. Such a waste. No sense in frittering away your youth like some sort of recluse. Rachel Savernake needs to smell the sea breezes. Make up for lost time."

Jacob, whose own experience of crossing the Channel was confined to a return ferry trip to Boulogne, was distracted by a gust of a perfume so fruity that it made his head swim. The intoxicating aroma accompanied the arrival of an elegant woman with luxuriant red hair. The blue of her eyes dazzled, their beauty oddly enhanced by a tiny imperfection, a keyhole-shaped mark in the left iris. Her dress was all sinuous curves, the skirt comprising layers of translucent tulle complemented by colourful embroidered flowers. Jacob blinked, hardly daring to believe his good luck. As if to answer an unspoken prayer, his quarry had presented herself at Malam's side.

Kiki de Villiers. At last.

———

Rachel noticed a man with horn-rimmed spectacles and a small goatee beard detaching himself from a group of bemused guests studying the exhibits. He'd spotted Damaris Gethin, and taken a step in their direction. As Damaris glanced over her shoulder, he seemed to have a sudden change of heart. He turned on his heel and plunged into conversation with a tall, handsome woman in a blue dress.

"You know him?" Damaris asked.

Rachel shook her head.

"That is Evan Tucker."

"The composer?"

"Yes." Damaris began to sing softly: "*Where there's a heart-ache, there must be a heart.*"

"A very popular ditty."

"At one time of day. His star has waned." Damaris sang a line from the chorus of another song. "*Don't say I didn't tell you so.*"

"I suppose his brand of sentimentality fell out of fashion."

"Yes, and poor Evan lacks another string to his bow. His lyrics are as sweet as honey—but sicklier. He can't act like Ivor Novello and he lacks Noël Coward's wit. You can smell the jealousy on him; it reeks like a sour cologne."

"Yet you were friends."

"What makes you think so?"

"You did invite him here."

"I invited you and Mr. Flint as well, yet we've never even met," Damaris said sharply.

"A moment ago, he was about to approach you. When he realised we were in conversation, he thought better of it. As if he'd wanted a word with you in private."

"Once upon a time, we moved in similar circles." Damaris gave a dismissive shrug.

"Oh, yes?"

"He was renowned for throwing parties with no expense spared. The rich and famous flocked to The Risings. His house in Kent; you may have heard of it?"

Rachel shook her head. "His guests included artists as well as fellow musicians?"

"Certainly. Not to mention authors, actors, anyone who took his fancy. And plenty of lovely young women."

"You speak in the past tense. Isn't he in the mood for parties these days?"

"I'm afraid the smart set are no longer in the mood for someone so thin-skinned and insecure. Evan can't cope with the fact his glutinous tripe has fallen out of fashion." Damaris gave Rachel a searching look. "Do I sound harsh?"

"Refreshingly honest, perhaps."

Damaris laughed. "For as long as the Twenties kept roaring, people were happy to trek out to Romney Marsh. Now, gay shindigs in the backwaters have lost their lustre. Nobody wants to chum up with a has-been."

Rachel glanced towards the composer. If his ears were burning, there was no sign of it. He was still talking to the woman in the blue dress.

"That woman is his neighbour," Damaris said. "She also happens to be the widow of Giles Malam."

"The captain's brother?"

"The doctor, that's right."

There was a scornful edge to her voice. Giles Malam had died before Rachel met his brother Roddy, but she recalled the captain mentioning that his sister-in-law was a formidable woman. It may not have been a compliment.

"Why did you ask Evan?" Rachel murmured. "Did you invite him as a kindness? To help him get back in the social whirl?"

The artist gave a wry smile. "I doubt he'd see it like that. I suspect he came here to feed his fragile ego. His taste in art is passé. He swoons over the paintings of the late Henry Scott Tuke."

Damaris gave her a sharp look to see if the name meant anything to Rachel, who inclined her head.

"Even worse, he clings to the notion that art is distinct from theatre."

Rachel raised her eyebrows. "Unlike you?"

"If those self-styled authorities on cultural affairs are to be believed, a painting is not a performance." At once, Damaris was speaking with a zealot's fervour. "But you will agree with me, Miss Savernake, that their vision of the world is not only outmoded—it's utterly banal. Think of the Cabaret Voltaire, and what the Dadaists achieved! When the futurists..."

The artist's words trailed away as she became conscious of Rachel's intense scrutiny, her eyes sweeping over the plain cotton dress, the simple cap, the deathly pale face. It was as if she were examining a laboratory specimen.

"What is it?" she demanded.

"The penny has finally dropped," Rachel said. "You're part of the exhibition yourself, aren't you? Just as much as your models, the people pretending to be wax models?"

Damaris mimed applause. "Well done! Or should I say, well deduced? I knew you were the perfect choice to solve my puzzle. Naturally, you know who I am?"

"You remind me of a character in a painting. Or a figure in Madame Tussaud's."

A nod of encouragement. "You're getting warm."

"Marie Antoinette?"

"It's true what people say. You are a good detective."

Rachel didn't speak. She was contemplating the wildness in Damaris Gethin's smile.

"Yes, I am the Queen of France, on the day of her execution."

The artist drew a breath.

"And now, if you'll excuse me, I must walk to the scaffold."

Chapter 3

"Roderick, *chéri*! Wonderful to see you again!"

In the flesh, Kiki de Villiers was even more glamorous than in the photographs that sold so many popular magazines. Her graceful physique and nimble movements made her seem like an exotic bird. The French accent enhanced her allure, as much as that rich floral fragrance. Narcisse Noir, Jacob said to himself, her favourite.

Her dress was the latest creation of Madeleine Vionnet. Jacob was no expert on women's clothes or scents, but clippings in the *Clarion*'s file on Kiki de Villiers mentioned her favourite fashion designer and choice of perfume almost as regularly as those sapphire eyes and her penchant for rouging her cheeks with the petals of a geranium.

She gave Malam a loud, lavish kiss which left a vermilion stain on the captain's starched collar.

"Kiki, my dear, how splendid! I didn't know Damaris had invited you."

Jacob had racked his brains about how to scrape an acquaintance with the woman. A stroke of luck that she and Malam were friends. The Great and the Good, eh? It's not what you know, but who you know.

Mrs. de Villiers savoured her champagne. "You have a stake in the Hades Gallery, don't you? Did you not run an eye over the guest list?"

"Damaris did persuade me to invest in this place when it was first set up, but I never got involved with the details." The captain allowed himself a roguish wink. "You know me. One of life's sleeping partners."

Kiki de Villiers's smile dazzled; her teeth were as superb as her perfectly proportioned figure. "You Englishmen are so mischievous! Sleeping partner, indeed!"

Jacob coughed. He never liked to be left out of a conversation for long.

The captain shot him a glance. "Ah, yes, must remember my manners. This is Flint from Fleet Street. Newspaper wallah, writes for the *Clarion*. Flint, this lady needs no introduction from me, I'm sure. These days, she's never out of the popular prints. Mrs. Yvette de Villiers, known to her friends as Kiki."

"You're a columnist, Mr. Flint?"

When she gazed straight at him, Jacob's knees were in danger of buckling. Impossible to deny the power of her charm when she chose to exert it. Had he misjudged the woman, formed a prejudice born of ignorance? In person, she was much more than just a pretty face. The smell of Narcisse Noir was intoxicating. And how else could you describe her eyes? Sapphire captured their beauty to perfection.

"I... um... yes..."

She gave a graceful wave towards the exhibition. "Such a privilege to be invited here. In my humble opinion, Damaris Gethin is a genius."

Another full-beam smile. Jacob realised she had bestowed a gift upon him, granting a quotation for a column in the *Clarion*. As he stammered his thanks, she flicked a stray hair with a *think nothing of it* gesture and returned her attention to Captain Malam.

"I *suppose* I understand her purpose," she said. "It is as if Damaris has created her own private waxworks. Her own miniature Chamber of Horrors."

Malam made a sceptical noise.

"Didn't you recognise Landru, the Bluebeard of Gambais, alongside Robespierre, another of my fellow countrymen?"

"A mystery to me, I'm afraid," Malam said.

"Forgive me, but I was never sure you and Damaris were entirely suited to each other. The upstanding English gentleman and the bohemian artist."

"Bohemianism is one thing. Raging headaches and erratic behaviour were quite another."

"You poor dear. No wonder you were tempted away by that pretty young filly with curly blonde hair." Mischief gave a sly twinkle to those gorgeous blue eyes. "Daughter of the head of the stock exchange, wasn't she? How is the charming little thing, by the way?"

Malam shrugged. "Seen nothing of that particular young lady for ages."

"Ah, yes, you keep venturing into…pastures new." Her soft laugh was musical, but Jacob detected a bite in her words. "That nasty bruise on your handsome cheek. Don't tell me you've fallen foul of a jealous husband?"

"A disgruntled investor, as it happens." He gave a mocking laugh. "I warned the fellow fair and square. A loss is only a loss if you sell up at the wrong time. But he didn't have the guts to stay the course. Poor beggar was left with not much more than the clothes he stands up in."

"You need to take care. Once people have nothing left to lose…"

A smile played on Malam's lips as he stroked his injured cheek. "This is nothing. Barely a fleabite."

"Even so. We live in dangerous times."

"What could be more exciting?" he asked. "Life is a gamble. Surely you agree? We can't run scared of our own shadows or scuttle off in a funk at the first hint of trouble."

Kiki de Villiers smiled. The conversation swirled with undercurrents, but Jacob felt several fathoms out of his depth.

Malam swallowed some champagne and surveyed the gallery. His gaze settled on a bespectacled man with a goatee beard standing next to a dark-haired woman. They were contemplating one of the exhibits. Up on the pedestal was Lizzie Borden, the supposed axe murderer from Fall River, Massachusetts. She was clad in a bloodstained smock and clutched a hatchet which bore ominous smears. As the bearded man caught Malam's eye, he gave a shy smile and beckoned him over.

The captain turned his attention back to Kiki de Villiers.

"Oh, well, good to see you again, my dear. Better circulate, I suppose." He glanced at Jacob. "Evening, Flint."

He strode towards the bearded man and his companion. Jacob was conscious of Mrs. de Villiers following Malam's progress. He fancied she was holding her breath. The dark woman was attractive if rather gaunt. A strong jawline that suggested she'd brook no nonsense. Was Kiki jealous because the captain was interested in another woman?

The bearded man gave Malam a welcoming clap on the shoulder. The woman turned away from the captain, only to lose her footing. Malam shot out an arm to prevent her falling to the floor. She regained her balance and gave him a brisk nod before returning her attention to Lizzie Borden.

Jacob was aware of Kiki de Villiers' heady perfume. She seemed to have forgotten he was there, so closely was she studying Malam and his companions. He felt dizzy. Perhaps it was this strange sense of being in the underworld. Maybe he shouldn't have risked that last glass of champagne. He still wasn't accustomed to the high life. Given the chance of a free drink, his instinct was to gulp it down, with no questions asked.

"Who is the fellow greeting the captain like a long-lost brother?" he asked.

"Evan Tucker."

Jacob racked his brains. "Rings a faint bell..."

"He writes songs. Tuneful ditties, utterly forgettable."

He indicated the dark-haired woman. "And that lady is Mrs. Tucker?"

"Dear me, no." His question prompted a mischievous giggle. "That is Roderick's sister-in-law."

"Oh, yes?"

"His late brother was a doctor." For a fleeting moment, Kiki looked pensive. "She is a nurse. Goes by her maiden name, Wardle, if I remember rightly."

The hint of snobbish disapproval amused Jacob. Was she implying that the woman was some kind of fortune hunter? There could be no better example of the pot calling the kettle black. But it was no concern of his. He took a deep breath. Time to take the plunge.

"Actually, I'm so glad to have bumped into you. I wonder if you'd be willing..."

She raised a beautifully manicured hand. A diamond bracelet glittered on her wrist. "Ah, it's been a delight to chat with you, Mr....Flint, was it? Truly, an absolute pleasure."

"Mrs. de Villiers," he said urgently, "I must ask..."

"Some other time, young man. I'm sure you have enough copy now. If you'll excuse me, I ought to circulate."

Without so much as a parting glance, she tripped away from

him. The crowd swallowed her up before Jacob could persuade her to continue the conversation. He dug his fingernails into his palm. He'd never admit it to a living soul, but in her presence, he'd felt overawed. As a result, he'd missed a golden opportunity to question her.

Failure stabbed him. If his hunch was right, Kiki de Villiers's life was in danger, but he'd done nothing to save her. Or persuade her to confess her true identity.

———

"Good evening, Jacob," Rachel whispered in his ear. "Do you come here often?"

He spun round. "I didn't expect to see you here."

"An art lover at a private view hosted by the Queen of Surrealism?" She shook her head. "Goodness me, even you might have managed to put two and two together. Or do you only have eyes for Kiki de Villiers?"

"What do you mean?"

"Even in this poor light, I can see you're blushing. You looked so miserable after she deserted you. No need to feel embarrassed. You're young and single, and she is a notorious beauty. No harm in aiming high. Just beware of vertigo."

"You're making fun of me."

Rachel sighed. "I shouldn't enjoy it as much as I do."

"Apology accepted," he retorted; it never took him long to regain his equilibrium. "So you saw me chatting to her?"

"And Roddy Malam. Once he moved away and left the field clear, you appeared desperate to keep her locked in conversation. Not that I was surprised."

"Why not?"

"Damaris Gethin mentioned that you'd cadged an invitation tonight in the hope of bumping into the lady."

"The *Clarion*'s society pages are short of stories."

"Is that so?" She furrowed her brow. "Or is there something else?"

A bell rang, saving him from the need to reply. Two of the servants who were masquerading as policemen began to clear a space, shooing people to the right and left. Jacob and Rachel found themselves at the head of the crowd.

In front of them stood a scaffold. Steps from the left of the gallery led upwards. On the top, to the right, was erected a tall guillotine made of coarse-grained oak. The side of the machine faced Jacob. Shining in the candlelight, the angled blade had a wicked cutting edge.

"Rachel!"

Malam hissed her name as he arrived at her side. His conversation with Evan Tucker hadn't lasted long, Jacob thought. There was no sign of the songwriter or the captain's sister-in-law. Malam rewarded Jacob's affable smile with a grimace. Presumably he wanted Rachel to himself. She put a finger to her lips.

"Shhhh. Here she comes."

Silence fell as the white-clad figure of Damaris Gethin emerged from the gloom, gliding over the stone floor like a wraith. She climbed the four steps leading to the top of the scaffold. Jacob watched as she glanced up at the blade and then at a large wicker basket by her feet.

"Good evening, ladies and gentlemen. Welcome to the Hades Gallery."

As she paused, a smattering of applause broke out, dying away the instant she raised her hand.

"Quiet, please. I won't detain you long, but I ask you all to keep absolutely still. No one must move or say a word."

She took a moment to survey the guests, as if to make sure there were no signs of dissent.

"The title of my exhibition is *Artist in Crime*. Around this space you can see my latest creations. Men, women, and artefacts associated with violent and bloody death. Killers, victims, a hangman or two. A gibbet, a guillotine, an electric chair. Guilt and innocence, cheek by jowl. My purpose is simple. I hope to capture a subject that has come to preoccupy me. No, that's wrong. To obsess me beyond all reason."

Jacob glanced at Rachel. She was gazing up at the woman on the scaffold. Her expression was rapt. Next to her stood Captain Malam, his face a picture of bafflement.

"Murder, ladies and gentlemen! Our fascination with the ultimate crime is a bond. In one way or another, that bond unites many of my guests here tonight. Hence my desire to have you all here as witnesses."

The tremor in her voice was unmistakable. Again she paused, as if summoning her last reserves of energy.

Under his breath, Malam muttered, "Witnesses? She's barking mad."

The woman on the scaffold gazed down at the onlookers. "Of course, there are limits to verisimilitude. You will see that tonight I am here in the guise of Marie Antoinette. Whatever people say about her, she didn't die a shameful death. As she pointed out herself, shame is for criminals. Unquestionably she had her faults, but I believe she suffered a grievous wrong, inflicted by people who were selfish and cruel. Ladies and gentlemen, I sympathise. I can assure you, I know how it feels."

One of the spectators sniggered, only to be hushed by the people around him.

"Every artist cares about their legacy." Her voice sounded scratchy, as if her throat had dried. "In my case, it is simple. I want justice to be done. One person in this room understands what I mean."

Jacob was conscious of Rachel stiffening beside him.

Damaris Gethin bent down with a swift, decisive movement to place her head in the circular collar of the guillotine.

She snapped her fingers and the candles were snuffed out in unison, plunging the gallery into darkness.

There was a loud click and the sound of something falling into place.

Jacob's heart thumped in his chest. Vague murmurs of alarm came from his fellow spectators.

A scream of fear tore through the air. There was a terrible crashing noise, but this time the racket didn't come from a train. It was so close, so frighteningly close.

People cried out in anguish. Some impulse made Jacob seize hold of Rachel's cold hand.

He felt sick in his stomach. His head was swimming. Even before the candles were lit once more, he knew that Damaris Gethin was dead.

He was a witness, just as she'd proclaimed. A witness to the Queen of Surrealism's execution.

Chapter 4

"We stood there and watched her kill herself." Half an hour later, Jacob was still numbed by the horror of what he'd seen. "I simply can't believe it."

"You have the evidence of your own eyes," Rachel said.

"In the darkness, I could scarcely see the guillotine fall."

They were standing in the cold night air on the cobbles outside the Hades Gallery. There was a straggle of bemused individuals along the street, people so stunned by the nightmare vision of Damaris Gethin's dead body that they could barely speak, let alone bring themselves to leave the scene of the tragedy.

Inside, the police were continuing to interview people one by one. Their questions had struck Jacob as cursory, as if the officers were as dazed as everyone else by the death of Damaris Gethin. They'd certainly seemed star-struck by Kiki de Villiers. She was the first to be interviewed, the first to be allowed to leave. It was a wonder the constable who spoke to her didn't beg for an autograph.

Not that Jacob could complain. As soon as he'd confessed to being a journalist with the *Clarion*, they'd bustled him out of the gallery before he could make a nuisance of himself. He'd rushed to a telephone to call the office with the news. Rather than race off to Fleet Street, he'd come back and waited for Rachel to emerge. If anyone could make sense of the inexplicable, it was Rachel Savernake.

"You saw what the blade did to her," she said.

He shuddered. "Such a horrific accident."

"An accident? What makes you think that?"

"Nobody would do that to themselves."

"I disagree. All of us die sooner or later. Every single day, people die in circumstances far more pitiful and painful. Not to mention protracted beyond endurance."

"But the guillotine…"

"It has the merit of being quick and decisive. Merciful and humane, some would say."

"Humane!"

"Absolutely. According to advocates of the National Razor, at any rate. Their proud boast is that the prisoner feels no pain."

"Ridiculous. They're guessing. How can they possibly know for certain?"

A pause.

"True."

"No woman in her right mind would ever choose that way out."

"You may think so, but Damaris Gethin loved to shock. I'm certain she had a very different point of view."

"A warped perspective," he said bitterly.

"Death by guillotine is appalling, but consider things rationally. Is it really more horrific than the claustrophobia of the gas oven or the giddy terrors of the cliff-edge leap? Those familiar methods of ending it all are conventional. And Damaris Gethin loathed the commonplace."

"You talked to her. Did she seem unhinged?"

"Unhinged, no. Disturbed, yes. Profoundly so."

"Did she give any indication of what she planned to do?"

Rachel sighed. "She deceived me. Or rather, I allowed myself to be nudged down a false trail."

"How do you mean?"

"I presumed that someone meant to kill her. I kept my eyes peeled for a crime that was never going to happen."

"Suicide is a crime."

"I've never understood why."

"It's a sin. Make a mess of it, and you can be sent to jail."

Rachel glowered. Feeling as if the temperature had suddenly dropped a couple of degrees, he changed tack.

"Maybe there's another explanation."

"Such as?"

"What if she was playing a role for the purposes of the exhibition? Let's say that someone took advantage of the prearranged opportunity to commit a murder." Jacob was thinking on his feet. "Wasn't she renowned for testing the boundaries of good taste?"

Rachel nodded. "Go on."

"She dreamed up this weird notion of pretending to be Marie Antoinette and reenacting her final moments. The woman was obsessed with murder, she said so herself. If she confided in someone who wanted her dead, perhaps she gave them an idea."

"When I say she was disturbed, don't misunderstand me. Within her own terms, she was utterly rational."

"Then surely she was murdered. How could anyone actually put their head down and somehow execute themselves?"

"It was over in an instant."

"Don't forget her ghastly scream!"

A train roared above them. Rachel said softly, "I doubt any of us will ever forget it."

"It's the stuff of nightmares. I mean, she seemed calm enough while she was addressing us. Nervy, yes, but she's an artist, not an orator. Would anyone bent on taking their own life succumb to terror at the very last moment?"

"Is it really so unreasonable?"

He rubbed his chin. "What if, when the candles were put out, someone seized their chance and ran up the steps to the scaffold? If this person took her unawares, he might have forced her head down and then…"

"The killer ran away again? Escaped scot-free, without anyone noticing?"

"It's not impossible."

"A premeditated crime, would you say, or an inspired piece of improvisation?"

Jacob pondered. "Premeditated, is my guess."

"Really? While I was waiting for the police to interview me, I wandered around the gallery and listened to the gossip of the gallery staff."

"They looked as dumbstruck as everyone else."

"Exactly. Nobody knew what Damaris had in mind."

"You think so?"

"If they did, their acting skills would put Henry Irvine to shame." Rachel shook her head. "Before the doors were opened to guests tonight, Damaris instructed them to put out the candles the instant she snapped her fingers. The servants were stationed in position, ready for the signal. Nobody was sure how long she would speak for. How could someone plan her murder without leaving far too much to chance?"

"All right. The killer is a quick-thinking opportunist. When everything went dark…"

"How did he work the guillotine?"

"It beats me."

"And you call yourself a newshound? You need to practise your eavesdropping skills. The guillotine was custom-made to Damaris's precise specification. One of the servants said that both blade and neck collar were operated by switches close to the blade."

"Electric switches? Not the traditional lever?"

"No. The Hades Gallery opened for the first time last year. The gloomy ambience was a choice, not a necessity. There's no shortage of modern utilities. Damaris Gethin wanted candles to light her exhibition because they provided the sinister atmosphere she was determined to evoke. The guillotine was designed to work with twentieth-century efficiency."

"Even if you're right and she contrived her own death, surely there was a chance that something would go wrong?"

"Nothing in life is free of risk. Damaris went to extreme lengths to minimise the likelihood of a mishap. The traditional revolutionary guillotine is not designed for *felo de se.*"

Jacob spread his arms. "I'll take your word for it. I never studied how the wretched thing does its deadly work."

"You never know when snippets of trivial information may come in handy. Our own hangmen are so parochial. They could learn a thing or two from the French."

"What do you mean?"

"The guillotine, as developed during the last century, is a mechanical marvel. First, the condemned person's neck is locked into the collar, or lunette. Next, the executioner pulls the *déclic*, a handle which releases the *mouton*, the weight attached to the blade. And then..."

"All right, all right. I can see it'd be tricky for someone else to do all that on the spur of the moment. What do you think happened?"

"I believe Damaris Gethin planned her own death, paying

meticulous attention to detail. She was a daring artist, but she was also highly practical; you see that in so much of her work. She believed art shouldn't be static, but brimming with life and movement."

"So she turned her own death into a performance?"

"Exactly. She staged her own execution. A dramatic finale fit for a queen, in keeping with her whole philosophy."

"How did she do it?"

"The guillotine had several refinements, all to her precise specifications. They made it easy for her to press a button as soon as she'd placed her head securely in the lunette, causing the collar to lock around her neck. Another button operated the blade. One of the gallery staff said she practised endlessly with mannequins, making sure they were beheaded with clean strikes of the blade. He presumed she was rehearsing for some kind of gruesome display tonight. So she was, except that it wasn't a dummy that she decapitated."

Under the street lamp, Jacob's face had a greenish hue. "It doesn't bear thinking about."

"Buck up. There will be hell to pay with that editor of yours if you don't write two columns of eyewitness testimony before the night is out."

"Hell?" His tired eyes turned to the entrance of the Hades Gallery. The police had shut the double doors and put a constable on guard. Inside they were still questioning people. "I'd say we spent an evening there. Damaris Gethin chose the ideal name for the gallery. Who needs fire and brimstone, when you have an artist so deranged?"

"She wasn't deranged," Rachel murmured. "Not in any conventional sense. Yes, the balance of her mind was disturbed, but she knew what she was doing."

"Is that what you told the police?"

"They only asked me what I'd seen. When I simpered and said I was an art lover, they lost interest."

"It'll be different when the names of the invited guests are studied at Scotland Yard."

Rachel smiled. "I've seen nothing of Inspector Oakes since we met at Blackstone Fell."

"If you're right about the guillotining, this is a straightforward case of suicide. Unlikely to reach the Yard's top detective."

"Time will tell."

Jacob stared at her. "There's more to this than meets the eye, isn't there?"

"What makes you say that?"

"You maintain that she killed herself, but you haven't explained why she'd want to end it all. Her death doesn't make sense."

"In her mind, it did."

"It's ridiculous! A successful woman with everything to live for. She had money, fame..." He folded his arms, making no attempt to hide his exasperation.

"As you know, I have a weakness for mystery," Rachel sounded uncharacteristically meek. "At the moment, the truth is this. I haven't the faintest idea why Damaris Gethin died."

————

For a minute or so, neither Jacob nor Rachel spoke. The moon was high above the railway. There were few clouds and the temperature was close to freezing. Jacob rubbed his hands, trying to keep warm.

"I'd better file my story."

The main door of the Hades opened and two burly men emerged, carrying a stretcher. Jacob whipped off his hat as a mark of respect as the remains of Damaris Gethin, covered by a fawn blanket, were loaded into the ambulance.

Malam's sister-in-law, clad in an overcoat of maroon wool, followed the attendants out of the gallery and then strode towards a line of cars parked on the approach to the station.

Jacob muttered to Rachel, "Did you see her examining the corpse?"

Without waiting for a reply, he loped after the woman.

"Excuse me!" he called. "Can I have a word?"

Nurse Wardle spun round, almost tripping over. She subjected him to a fierce stare. "Who are you?"

"My name is Flint. I'm a reporter for the *Clarion*."

"I want nothing to do with the newspapers." She spoke in a faint rural burr. "Not after what just happened."

"I saw you inspecting the body…"

She took a stride towards him. "You're accusing me of being a nosey parker?"

Jacob changed tack.

"No, no, I only meant…"

"I'm a trained nurse. When I saw that terrible…incident, I rushed forward to see if there was anything I could do. Any decent citizen in my shoes would do the same."

"Absolutely! I simply…"

"Of course, it was a waste of time." Her tone was biting. "If your readers itch for gory details, tell them that the guillotine severed her neck cleanly with a single blow. The blade was very sharp."

"Was the deceased a friend of yours?"

"Damaris Gethin?" Just for a moment, she seemed to falter. "We were acquainted, but I didn't know her well."

"Yet she invited you here tonight?"

"I did her a good turn once, and I suppose she was grateful. Why on earth she'd do something so dreadful, I haven't the foggiest." Her voice faltered. "Anyway, I can't stand here chattering. I really must go home."

"Was she the neurotic type?" Jacob asked. "Would you describe her as suicidal?"

She glared at him. He had no doubt that her anger was genuine, but her hands were trembling, the only hint of the horror they'd witnessed.

"How dare you! Mind your own business!"

She moved away towards the cars. Jacob supposed that one of them belonged to her.

"If I could just ask..." he began.

Glancing back over her shoulder, she seemed to be trying to control her temper. "I live in Kent. It's a long way home, and I'm as stunned as everyone else by what we've witnessed. I've seen some appalling sights during my time as a nurse, but...nothing compared to that."

At that moment, Evan Tucker came out of the gallery. He spotted Nurse Wardle and gave her a quick nod.

"Here's my neighbour," she said. "He's giving me a lift. Goodbye, Mr. Flint. I have nothing more to say to you."

She turned her back on him. Tucker quickened his pace and took her arm.

Jacob returned to Rachel's side. She regarded him with bleak amusement.

"Sent off with a flea in your ear?"

"She took umbrage when I asked if Damaris Gethin was neurotic or suicidal."

Rachel sighed. "Please don't tell me you accused her of tampering with the body."

"Certainly not! I was curious, that's all. She was the first to bend down over Damaris Gethin after...the blade fell."

"That's right. I watched everything that happened in the immediate aftermath." She smiled. "While you kept your eyes tight shut."

"Only for a few seconds," he said. "Not a full minute, anyway. All right. What did you see?"

"She announced that she was a nurse and everyone stepped back to let her through. She examined the corpse for a moment or two, just long enough to confirm the obvious, that life was extinct. I'm positive that nothing untoward took place."

"You're absolutely sure?"

"Yes. I suppose she was trying in vain to help. My bet is, she wanted to make some kind of sense of what she'd just seen. There's no doubt in my mind that she was appalled. Shaking with the shock of it."

"She happens to be the sister-in-law of your chum."

"My chum?"

"Captain Malam. You're pally with him, aren't you?"

"I find him interesting."

"In what way?" A snarky note entered Jacob's voice.

"Oh, there's more to him than cricket and car racing. Tell me about the conversations you had. With the captain, Mrs. de Villiers, and the nurse."

"What do you want to know?"

"Everything. You have a first-class memory. Be as precise as you can about what they said and did, before time passes and little details begin to fade."

He couldn't help feeling flattered. Words of praise from Rachel meant a good deal; mockery came easily to her, but she wasn't one to scatter compliments. And she was right: he was blessed with excellent powers of recall as well as a vivid imagination.

"I gather the captain has taken a shine to you."

"Can you blame him?" Rachel asked.

"No, no. I mean…" He shifted from one foot to another. "It's just that he talked about taking you to Monte Carlo, to watch him racing."

"Did he now? Why not begin at the beginning? Let's get things in order. I'd like to know everything that was said to you by everyone you spoke to. Word for word, so far as you can."

Jacob took a breath and launched into an account of his conversations. He enjoyed the way Rachel hung on his every syllable.

"Excellent," she said at the end. "Clear and cogent."

He managed not to preen. "I've just had an idea! Captain Malam served in the Royal Engineers, didn't he? He's obviously got a practical turn of mind. What if he monkeyed about with—"

"You're trotting down a blind alley, Jacob," she interrupted. "Haven't we already agreed that Damaris Gethin operated the guillotine?"

"All right," he said sulkily. "What do you make of it all? Come to that, why are you so taken by Malam? I wouldn't have thought he was your type."

"What is my type?" she asked.

Her tone was cool rather than vexed, but he realised he was venturing into dangerous territory. Time to scurry back onto safe ground.

"Sorry." He yawned. "It's been a long evening. And truly extraordinary."

"Yes," she said. "We both need to sleep on it. Think about everything that's happened when our minds are fresh. We should talk again, Jacob."

"I'd like that."

"You'll be busy working tomorrow. Come to Gaunt House at seven. Hetty will cook one of your favourite dinners."

"Perfect."

"And I shall have a question for you."

He managed a weary smile. "Might have known there'd be a catch. What is it?"

"I'm longing to know why you're so fascinated by Mrs. de Villiers."

Chapter 5

Roderick Malam was one of the last guests to emerge from the Hades Gallery. Everyone else had gone home to see if they could sleep without nightmares, but Rachel was still loitering on the street corner. When he spotted her, he approached with such purposeful strides he might have been on parade.

"Thanks for waiting for me."

"I whiled away the time talking to Jacob Flint. He's raced off to Fleet Street in his shiny new car. He'll be the first to tell the world what happened to Damaris Gethin."

"Newspapermen." The captain filled his pipe. "Parasites, frankly. They make money from the misery of the people who supply their headlines."

"And we all rush to devour their stories," Rachel said. "Poor Jacob was under the impression that someone had murdered Damaris."

"Murdered her?" He frowned. "Stuff and nonsense. How could anyone else have harmed her? Surely it's impossible?"

"So I explained to Jacob."

"I've no idea why you bother with a fellow like that. Working on Grub Street will turn any man into a cheap sensation seeker."

"You think so?"

"It's morally wrong to turn a tragedy into a melodrama, don't you agree?"

She gazed at him. "I find moral rights and wrongs rather complicated."

Malam grunted. "Anyway, he's off beam as far as Damaris is concerned. I get the impression the police are satisfied."

"You do?"

"Their fingerprint chappie dusted the buttons that work the lunette and the guillotine blade. I gather there was only one mark on each. Bound to be Damaris's finger or thumb."

"I'm sure that's right."

"Nobody else can possibly have been involved. The gallery staff who dressed up as bobbies for the exhibition are as shaken as the rest of us. Damaris always kept her cards close to her chest, so nobody had the foggiest about what she intended to do. It's a shocking case of *self*-murder."

"Agreed. All of which begs one question. Why did she do it?"

He shook his head. "Not much point trying to find rhyme or reason, my dear. The poor woman was highly strung. Desperately so. A classic study in neurasthenia, if you ask me."

"You think so?"

"Beyond a doubt. Take it from me, when the mind plays tricks, life can seem very cruel. I've lost count of the number of poor wretches I've seen who suffer from shell shock."

"Damaris was never in the trenches."

"No, but there was something deeply depressing about her art. No wonder she started having headaches and being overcome with nausea."

"She was ill?"

He made an impatient gesture with his hand. "I'm talking about the days when I knew her. A lot of the trouble was in her head. I used to tell her she needed to buck up. Don't mourn what might have been. Live for the moment. But she refused to listen. It was as if she couldn't make sense of life."

"Nor can plenty of other people. They don't all decapitate themselves."

"If you ask me, she simply found the wretchedness of life too much to bear. So she decided to end it in the way she knew best. As part of some sort of weird artistic performance."

"I suppose," Rachel said, "you knew her much more…intimately than most."

"I'm not sure anyone knew her intimately," he said. "Other than in the purely physical sense."

"Ah."

"Believe me, my dear, she bore no comparison to you. Damaris was no great beauty, but she could be glorious company when she was so inclined. When we first met, I was bowled over by her intelligence and wit. But intelligence in a woman is a mixed blessing, frankly."

"I expect you're right," Rachel said.

"Nobody admires a woman with spirit more than myself, but Damaris always yearned for something that was out of reach."

"What was that?"

"I'm not sure." For a moment, he looked uncomfortable, as if she'd touched a nerve. "Damaris never found true happiness. If you want the evidence, look at those bizarre works of art. Absurd. And frankly tragic."

"You and she were lovers."

He took a breath. "I won't deny it. Why should I? She was an extraordinary woman who cast a spell over the men she met."

"And you were spellbound?"

A self-deprecating laugh. "You know what simple souls men are, Rachel."

"How long were you...?"

He frowned. "I hate to talk about these things. It hardly seems decent. But since you ask, we were close for a while. Three or four months, give or take. It soon became clear that we were unsuited to each other."

"Temperamentally?"

"In every way." He breathed out. "I found her passion exhilarating, but within a short time it became wearing. She was so *intense*. Especially about her art. If inspiration deserted her, candidly, she was hell to live with."

"So she lost her way as an artist?"

"You know something about art, my dear. She hasn't produced anything for a couple of years, has she?"

"True." Rachel considered. "Tonight's exhibition was her first in a long while."

"And its sole purpose was to bring the curtain down on her career."

"You believe she lost her creative drive because she was depressed?"

"I'm afraid so. You know that fellow Churchill? I've bumped into him once or twice. Suffers fits of melancholy, calls it the black dog. The chap has a vivid turn of phrase, even if he's hopelessly unreliable. When the black dog was on Damaris, there was no living with her. Once the first flush of infatuation began to fade, I realised we could never bring each other lasting happiness. It was impossible."

"And Damaris Gethin felt the same? She never wanted to settle down? Or have a child?"

For a few moments, Malam looked troubled. He seemed to be weighing things up.

"I'm not a mind reader, my dear. I couldn't make sense of her, but it was crystal clear that we were incompatible. As for things that mattered, we had nothing in common. She was scornful of cricket and racing and shooting, all the pastimes I love. Business didn't interest her, either."

Rachel tutted. "Oh, dear."

He gave her a sharp glance. "Damaris wasn't short of money, but she didn't give a fig for it. In her opinion, it was simply a means to an end."

"You didn't persuade her to invest in one of your companies?"

"Actually, the boot was on the other foot. Shortly after we met, she persuaded me to buy the lease on this gallery. Purely as a business proposition, you understand. I could never make sense of Damaris's work, but there's a market for it. You're a damned sensible young woman—yet even you pay hand over fist for modern so-called artworks. I wouldn't give them house room, but the bankers thought the Hades would turn a tidy profit, so I put up some cash."

"You have such a wonderful head for these things," Rachel said. "I'm afraid high finance is gobbledegook to me."

"It's not an exact science. I got it badly wrong with the Hades. The place turned out to be a white elephant. Because she stopped working, there were no exhibitions. In the end, I asked Damaris to take the lease off my hands. Free, gratis, and for nothing."

"Generous of you."

He shrugged. "She'd been unwell, and I wanted to do her a good turn. Although we'd stopped seeing each other, she had no friends capable of helping her through. I wasn't keen on the company she kept. Her arty pals were a rotten bunch. Bolsheviks and pansies, mostly."

"Goodness me," Rachel said.

He warmed to his theme. "Some of those beggars made my flesh creep."

"What about Evan Tucker?"

He blinked. "Tucker?"

"The songwriter, yes. I noticed the two of you talking in the gallery."

Captain Malam hesitated. "Truth to tell, I feel rather sorry for the poor fellow. He's not exactly on his uppers, but he's lost his touch as a tunesmith. People don't hum his melodies any more."

"Is he afflicted by the same loss of energy as Damaris Gethin?"

"They are two very different people." He sighed. "It's a sign of the troubled times we live in. This wretched Slump is disastrous for everyone."

"All bad things come to an end."

He laughed. "You're right. Must look on the bright side."

"Evan Tucker's companion was rather chic. I adored her blue gown. Designed by Lanvin, if I'm any judge."

Malam considered her. "You're incurably nosey, Rachel."

"A horrid failing, I admit. But I do like to have my weaknesses indulged."

"As a matter of fact, Phoebe Wardle is my sister-in-law. I told you, my late brother was a sawbones. Unfortunately he over-indulged in his favourite medicine. Whisky, that is. His liver packed up a couple of years ago."

"How sad. He was older than you?"

"By seven years. Our father was a surgeon and wanted Giles to follow in his footsteps. The poor devil wasn't cut out for it. He made a hash of an operation and a woman died. Long story short, he finished up as a lowly country quack. He once said he envied me. Taking risks, living for the moment. So he found solace in the bottle."

"Hard for his widow."

"Yes, can't have been easy, even for a woman as strong-minded as Phoebe."

"She kept her maiden name?"

"Phoebe is fiercely independent. She met Giles after being engaged to nurse one of his patients, an elderly spinster."

"You introduced her to Evan Tucker?"

"Oh, no, he's a neighbour of hers. Out in the sticks, as the Yanks say."

"Where do they live?"

"Romney Marsh. Giles had a small clinic down the road from Tucker's country house."

"Oh, yes, The Risings, isn't it?"

He considered her. "You're very well informed, Rachel."

"Damaris mentioned his parties to me."

A frown. "Did she now?"

"I lead a quiet existence. Perhaps that's why I'm so interested in other people's thrilling lives."

"I'm not sure Evan Tucker gets many thrills these days," Malam said drily. "It's quite a while since people flocked to his parties."

"What about your sister-in-law?"

Rachel had the impression that he was choosing his words with care. "I can't imagine she was fond of Tucker's crowd. Phoebe is rather straitlaced, I'm afraid."

"Immune to your charms, in other words?"

He winced. "I'd forgotten that your tongue can sting."

"Forgive me, I'm only teasing. However, she is a fine-looking woman."

"Steady on, Rachel. I mean, dash it all. You're talking about the wife of my brother."

"But he died some time ago."

He changed the subject. "I was surprised to see her tonight. I gather Evan Tucker brought her as a treat. Since Giles died, she's become reclusive, stuck out there in the wetlands of Kent. I'm afraid Giles drank away most of their money."

"But she keeps the clinic going?"

He frowned. "She must find it a desperate struggle to make ends meet."

"What about you? Have you ever been a guest at Evan Tucker's parties?"

"From time to time."

She gave a mischievous smile. "Were they very scandalous?"

He tapped the side of his nose. "Mum's the word, Rachel. Tucker's guests were a pretty fast set. In my line of country, one often spends time with folk one would never count as bosom friends."

"You mean, when looking for people who might seek your investment advice?"

He raised his eyebrows. "You make me sound awfully cold-blooded. And you're putting me through a hell of a catechism, my dear. Dash it all, a fellow has expenses. Racing cars don't come cheap, you know. They have to be paid for somehow."

"So you are forced to endure the social whirl?"

He grinned. "That's about the size of it."

A car horn pipped behind them. A Rolls-Royce Phantom eased along the road and stopped close by.

Rachel said, "There is Trueman. He's come to take me home."

Malam seized hold of her hand. "Tonight has been a ghastly experience for you, my dear. During the war, I saw some rotten things, but..."

"You were close to Damaris Gethin once upon a time."

"And now, at last, she's at peace," he said heavily. "I hate to think of you being upset. You know, I'm racing in Monte shortly. Perhaps it would take your mind off things if..."

"Don't worry about me." Rachel withdrew her hand. "I'm made of strong stuff."

"May I see you again?"

She hesitated. "I don't..."

"Please, Rachel." He leaned towards her. "Despite this evening's tragedy, it's been marvellous to see you again."

"All right. Drop in for coffee at Gaunt House tomorrow. Eleven o'clock sharp."

Before he could reply, she'd hurried to the car. A hefty man in a chauffeur's uniform got out and held open the door for her. Malam took one step forward before the chauffeur caught his eye.

Malam stopped in mid-stride and stared at the big man. After a moment's irresolution, he marched off to where his Bentley was parked. Rachel watched him drive off and then said to Trueman, "Before we leave, I have a little job for you."

———

"How can you be sure that someone didn't murder Damaris Gethin?" Martha Trueman asked.

Four people were gathered in the elegant sitting room of Gaunt House in the heart of the capital. Clifford Trueman had slung his chauffeur's jacket over the back of his chair and was sitting in shirtsleeves, a half-empty tankard of beer in front of him. His sister Martha was, like Rachel, drinking gin and tonic; Trueman's wife Hetty was content to sip from a cup of cocoa.

"I'd stake my life on it," Rachel said. "Nobody else could have killed her."

"Some murderers achieve the impossible," Martha said. "A stabbed corpse is left on a beach, surrounded by unmarked sand. A murder victim is found in a room which nobody could have entered. Remember those men who vanished from Blackstone Lodge…"

"Trust me, Martha. The death of Damaris Gethin is very different. Sometimes the obvious answer is the right one."

"But the woman *told* you she was going to be murdered!" Hetty said.

"Maybe someone had warned her. Sent her a message, perhaps." Martha spoke in a hushed tone. *"You will die tonight!"*

Rachel shook her head. "Damaris fed me a red herring. She couldn't risk my thwarting her plan. So she threw me off balance. Even when she stood on that scaffold, I found myself scanning the room, wondering if someone might fire a shot or lunge at her with a knife. If I'd realised…"

"You can't reproach yourself," Hetty said.

"I don't," Rachel said. "She was intent on taking her own life."

"Then what did she mean when she asked you to find whoever murdered her?" Martha asked.

"To do what she did," Rachel said, "she must have been profoundly disturbed. Captain Malam said as much. Whatever his faults, he certainly isn't stupid. In this case, I'm sure he's right."

"For once," Clifford Trueman said.

Rachel allowed herself a smile. "You don't like him, do you?"

"No."

"Cliff doesn't care for anyone who takes a shine to you," his sister said. "He scarcely trusts poor Jacob Flint, even after everything the pair of you have been through together."

Rachel put down her glass. "Damaris said that murder obsessed her. In her eyes, whoever drove her to such desperation bore the responsibility for her death. For her, that person was as guilty as any conventional murderer. That's what her exhibition was about. And she asked me to solve the crime."

"She wanted you to find whoever drove her to kill herself?" Martha asked.

"Exactly," Rachel said.

"Why you?" Hetty demanded.

"Rachel is well known in the art world these days," Martha said. "Even though she keeps herself to herself, word has got around. She's a collector with deep pockets, and there aren't many left now that economies all over the world are in chaos."

Hetty snorted. "That doesn't explain it."

"It explains why she felt she could attract Rachel's attention by inviting her to the exhibition. Perhaps she heard whispers about what happened at Gallows Court."

"Nobody knows the full story."

"But people gossip. However much we live behind closed doors."

"My guess," Rachel said, "is that Damaris Gethin had no one else to turn to. That's why she decided to gamble on me."

"She knew Malam," Trueman growled. "Why not him?"

"Their relationship was over. As far as I can tell, they remained on civilised terms, but they were chalk and cheese. She realised that he's not a man to be relied upon."

"Glad to hear you say that."

Rachel laughed. "Surely you didn't believe I'd succumb to his charms?"

"You seemed to take quite a fancy to him."

"He intrigued me, that's all." She pretended to yawn. "But not for long."

"You get bored so easily," Hetty said.

"Don't I deserve a little excitement every now and then? Thanks to Damaris Gethin, I've been presented with a riddle I can sink my teeth into."

"You didn't even know the woman."

"And she didn't know me. Despite that, she took the risk of placing her faith in me."

"That was her choice. You don't owe her anything."

"No." Rachel smiled. "But she was clever enough to realise that I find it impossible to resist a challenge."

Martha leaned towards her. "You're going to accept?"

"Yes. She was a wonderful artist, and her death was truly shocking. I want to find out who caused her to destroy herself."

Chapter 6

"Horror in Hades!"

The senior correspondents of the *Clarion* were having their regular morning conference. Walter Gomersall held up the front page for the assembled reporters to admire before turning to Jacob.

"Damned good work, lad. You were in the right place at the right time. We'll make a newspaperman out of you yet."

From the grizzled editor, this counted as high praise. A murmur of approval came from those present. Jacob tried to look self-deprecating, with limited success.

"I was lucky."

"It wasn't luck." The calm voice belonged to Trewythian, the *Clarion*'s recently appointed astrologer. "Did you consult that natal chart you had me draw up? Remember what the stars foretold for you this week? *A night to remember.*"

This phrase prompted some ribald remarks at Jacob's expense which had most of the journalists in stitches. Trewythian remained unmoved, wearing the sorrowful expression of a teacher contemplating an unruly classroom.

"Mock if you wish, gentlemen. Let me assure you, our readers are desperate to discover what the future holds. Who else can tell them but the stars?"

"I wonder if they warned Damaris Gethin?" Toby Lever, the chief sports writer, was invariably irreverent, unless discussing the serious business of England's fortunes on the cricket field. *"Don't lose your head!?"*

This was a cue for further tasteless merriment, quelled only by Gomersall's raised hand. "That will do, gentlemen. If none of you has any further sensations to present, you'd better make yourselves scarce until you've found some. Flint, Trewythian, can we have a word?"

As the other reporters filed out, Toby Lever winked at the astrologer. "Hey, Percy, what are the chances of Sheffield Wednesday winning at the Arsenal?"

Trewythian sighed. "A prophet has no honour in his own country."

When the door closed behind Toby Lever, Gomersall said, "They will have their little joke. Take no notice."

Trewythian stretched in his chair. "The sceptics don't worry me. Their prejudices belong to the past. What matters is the future."

"Luckily for us," Jacob said in a breezy tone, "you know all about that."

Horoscopes had come into vogue in popular newspapers the previous year, when an astrologer called Naylor prophesied that the newborn Princess Margaret would have an eventful life. He'd followed up this startling revelation by predicting the R-101 airship disaster. Never mind the cynics who pointed out that he'd simply said a British aircraft would be in danger during a period *after* the actual tragedy. Fleet Street cared nothing for pedantic quibbles. All that mattered was circulation, circulation, circulation. Dazzled by Naylor's brilliance, editors went in search of astrologers as if hunting big game.

"Aye, well," Gomersall said. "You've increased our daily figures by ten thousand inside a month. I just hope you foresee the day when we pinch the rest of the *Express*'s readers."

Trewythian was a prize recruit. He'd borrowed his pseudonym from a fifteenth-century fortune-teller. His real name was Percy Jones and because his elderly parents had spent their lives in domestic service, he knew the stately homes of England like the back of his hand. His brother Eric worked as a waiter at the Hotel Resplendent in Piccadilly. By seasoning his horoscopes with sly hints about the private lives of the rich and famous, Trewythian had made a name for himself. Given that the *Clarion*'s veteran society columnist, Griselda Farquharson, was recovering from a heart attack, the weekly half-page devoted to Trewythian's horoscopes killed two birds with one stone.

"Trust me," the astrologer said. "It's only a matter of time."

He didn't specify how much time, Jacob noticed, but his answer seemed to satisfy Gomersall. The editor had spent much of last year pursuing a crusade against fraudulent mediums and the more dubious practices of spiritualism. Yet this same gruff, hard-headed Lancastrian had embraced the popular craze for horoscopes with an evangelist's zeal. It was still early days, Jacob told himself. Wait until Trewythian gave Gomersall a tip for the Grand National and the horse fell at Becher's Brook.

"So you managed to speak to Mrs. de Villiers?" the editor asked.

"You've seen the quote in my report." Jacob hoped he didn't sound too smug. Yes, he'd failed in his original mission, but he'd got away with it.

"*In my opinion, Damaris Gethin is a genius.*" Gomersall grunted. "For the life of me, I never understood what people saw in her stuff. Call that art? No rhyme or reason to it."

The thought flitted through Jacob's mind that there wasn't so much to choose between the Dadaism of Damaris and the pontifications of Percy. In their own ways, surrealist art and horoscopes both represented escapes from the rational. But he knew better than to say this out loud.

"She turned her own death into a performance."

"Sure it was suicide? Or an accident? Nobody else had a hand in it?"

"Quite sure." Having slept on it, Jacob was convinced that Rachel was right. As usual. "She rigged up the guillotine so she could kill herself at the flick of a switch."

"No question of jiggery-pokery? Not another of your weird impossible crimes?"

Jacob shook his head. "Not this time."

"All right. Where does this leave us with Kiki de Villiers?"

"I was hoping for a longer conversation once Damaris Gethin had opened the exhibition." Jacob had spent an age preparing and practising his explanation for failing to pin her down. "Unfortunately, the tragedy denied me the opportunity."

"Slippery as an eel, that one." Gomersall gave a heavy sigh. "So the plain truth is, we are no forrader?"

"As regards connecting Kiki de Villiers with Marcel Ambrose?" Jacob considered making optimistic noises, but one look at Gomersall's frown made him think better of it. "I'm afraid not."

Gomersall turned to Trewythian. "Any forecast about when the man will be back in Britain? If he isn't here already?"

Trewythian's expression was grave. "I have nothing else for you at the moment."

"All right. Well, young Flint, what next?"

"I'll have a word with one of my sources." This was Jacob's favourite means of buying time whenever his editor pressed him to come up with a new headline. "I'll report back as soon as I have something definite. Leave it with me."

Gomersall grunted. He knew when he was being fobbed off, but the Damaris Gethin scoop had earned Jacob goodwill.

"Keep me posted."

It was a dismissal. Outside the door of the conference room, Trewythian said, "Best of luck, old fellow. And do watch your step. You're a true Aries, after all."

"Is that right?"

Trewythian nodded sadly. "You have a spirit of adventure, but you're apt to be hot-headed. The stars are saying that your life is at risk."

———

Breakfast at Gaunt House was a leisurely affair. As Rachel finished her coffee, she looked across the big kitchen table at Trueman, who was buttering the last slice of toast.

"The list of people at the Hades Gallery. Do you have it handy?"

Trueman's jacket was slung over the back of the chair. He reached into a pocket and fished out a sheet of paper.

"What's that?" Martha asked.

"Before we left the Hades last night," Rachel said, "I sent Trueman on a little errand. I asked him to use his powers of persuasion to get some names and addresses. I saw the gallery manager give a list to one of the police officers conducting the interviews. Everyone present when Damaris killed herself was on the list."

Martha laughed. "Powers of persuasion? You didn't threaten the poor chap with physical violence, did you, Cliff?"

"Heaven forbid," Rachel said.

Trueman was expressionless. "Told the manager I'd come

straight from Scotland Yard. Representing the commissioner himself. Said we needed the original document, quick sharp. He handed it over without a peep."

Martha laughed. "You silver-tongued devil."

She turned to Rachel. "Why do you want the list?"

"I wonder if it casts light on two questions that are nagging at me. Who exactly did Damaris Gethin invite to witness her death—and why?"

————

The office of Major Grenville Fitzroy Whitlow, DSO, was to be found at one end of a corridor running along the top floor of an inconspicuous eighteenth-century mansion on Whitehall. The corridor was reached by four flights of stairs, which ran up from an unmarked door at the side of the building. An internal staircase accessing the lower floors was concealed behind a false bookcase and only for use in an emergency. No more than half a dozen of the senior civil servants who occupied the honeycomb of rooms beneath the Top Corridor were aware of its existence, far less of the work done there.

The major was frowning at a typed report when his telephone rang. He lifted the receiver with a steel claw. He'd lost his right hand as a result of being blown up during the war.

"Whitlow."

"Spare me a minute, would you?"

"Right away, sir."

Replacing the receiver on its cradle, the major slipped the document into a buff folder which he placed within a cabinet made of steel. He locked the cabinet and then, on stepping out of the room, the door of his office. This was one of the most secure buildings in London, with two police constables patrolling outside twenty-four hours a day, but although Major Whitlow had no qualms about taking chances, he only did so when he saw no alternative.

He walked down the Top Corridor, his movements stiff—the legacy of severe war wounds—but vigorous and disciplined. At the end of the passage he halted in front of a heavy oak door without a nameplate. He struck it twice with the claw. A deep, resonant voice commanded him to enter.

Sir Hector Jarvis's office was three times the size of Whitlow's sparsely furnished eyrie and had the comfortable ambience of a discreet gentleman's club. The almond aroma of Moroccan cigars hung in the air. The walls were panelled in mahogany and adorned by a large portrait of the King. Sir Hector didn't sit behind a desk but in a capacious leather armchair. He was a large, corpulent man of sixty who bore a disconcerting resemblance to G. K. Chesterton.

"Take a pew, Whitlow." Sir Hector pushed a box across the occasional table by the side of his chair. "Smoke?"

"Thank you, sir, but no."

"Wanted to see what you make of this business at the art gallery last night." Sir Hector cast a disapproving glance at the pile of popular newspapers in front of him. "This exhibition called *Artist in Crime*. The woman who chopped off her own head. I see Mrs. de Villiers was among the witnesses to this bizarre spectacle."

"Correct, sir. She was an invited guest."

"Anything more to it than meets the eye?" Sir Hector peered at the major through his pince-nez. "I take it the lady isn't personally implicated?"

"For all her faults, sir, we have no evidence to suggest any homicidal tendencies on Mrs. de Villiers's part. The report from Scotland Yard leaves no room for doubt. Gethin operated the guillotine herself. It was physically impossible for anyone else to have done so."

"No trick machinery, no scope for operation by remote control?"

"None whatsoever."

"Extraordinary way to top yourself. Was the woman insane?"

Major Whitlow's face gave nothing away. "She was an artist, sir. An exponent of surrealism."

"Very well." Sir Hector clicked his tongue. "All the same, it's damned peculiar. Mrs. de Villiers was a friend of hers?"

"They moved in similar circles, which probably explains why the lady was invited to attend. More than that, we don't know at this stage."

"How many people were present?"

"She'd invited around twenty guests. A mixed bunch. Art critics, dealers, and sundry Bohemians."

"Anybody other than Mrs. de Villiers who is connected to… our Very Important Person?"

"Not as far as I'm aware, but enquiries are continuing. The models who pretended to be notorious murderers from the past in the exhibition all seem to be impoverished actors. They were recruited via an agency to take part in the artistic performance, as directed by Miss Gethin."

Another tongue click. "As if there isn't enough crime in the world, without people turning it into a peep show for sybarites."

"Indeed, sir. As you will appreciate, in the current economic climate, any out-of-work thespian will bite the hand off someone who is willing to pay through the nose for an evening's work, however eccentric or dubious. Their backgrounds are being checked, but at the moment none of them seem to have criminal connections."

"What about the employees of the gallery?"

"They acted as waiters. Miss Gethin instructed them to dress up as police officers, in keeping with the exhibition's theme."

"Anyone with a criminal record?"

"Nobody, as I understand it. Again, with unemployment so high, it's easy to recruit good staff if you have cash in the bank. And Damaris Gethin wasn't short of money, despite not having sold a single new work of art in the past two years."

"Why was that? Fallen out of favour with the cognoscenti?"

"Apparently she hadn't worked for some time. She's supposed to have been suffering from some kind of depression, which may explain why she resorted to...such drastic measures."

"Hmmm. Anything else I need to know about the people who were present last night?"

The steel claw pointed to the newspapers. The *Clarion* was at the top of the pile. "You'll have noted that Jacob Flint, the journalist, was there."

Sir Hector pursed his lips. "Which begs an obvious question. What was a crime reporter doing at an exhibition of so-called modern art?"

"The woman who reports on social tittle-tattle for his rag is indisposed. When interviewed, he claimed he was simply standing in for her."

"Plausible?"

"Not remotely. Flint knows as much about modern art as I do. I'm quite sure there was an ulterior motive for his presence."

"Such as?"

"The guest list also included Miss Rachel Savernake."

"Ah, yes." Sir Hector peered at Whitlow through the pince-nez as if to detect an otherwise imperceptible tightening of the major's jaw. "I am well aware that you and she have crossed swords in the past."

"Yes, sir."

"Water under the bridge, Whitlow. You've made a fresh start here. We must look forward, not back."

"Understood, sir."

"Miss Savernake spends a good deal of her fortune on avant-garde art, I hear. Presumably that's why she was invited."

"So she told the officer. She said she'd never met Damaris Gethin before last night."

"Any reason to doubt her word?"

"In my experience," Whitlow said, "Miss Rachel Savernake is, whatever else may be said about her, not a liar. Except *in extremis*. She is intelligent enough to stick to telling the truth whenever she can. Having said that, she is highly selective with it."

"There you are, then. She's an art fiend, and Jacob Flint has a soft spot for her. Hence why he seized the chance to attend the exhibition."

"Possibly, sir. Captain Roderick Malam was also there. Apparently, he was once close to the Gethin woman. When giving his statement, he mentioned that he's become friendly with Miss Savernake."

"In search of yet another conquest, eh?" Sir Hector pushed the newspapers to one side. "We mustn't allow this incident with the guillotine to blow us off course, Whitlow. Our priority is to deal with the de Villiers woman."

"Indubitably, sir. On this occasion, it looks as if she was simply an innocent bystander."

Sir Hector drummed his fingers on the desk. "That's as may be, Whitlow, but this latest piece of nonsense is another reminder of the kind of person she is. You put it admirably the other day. She attracts scandal like sweat attracts mosquitoes."

"Quite, sir."

"When we spoke last week, I told you that I wasn't persuaded the time had come to take decisive measures." Sir Hector looked straight into his subordinate's cold eyes. After holding his gaze for several moments, he was the first to look away. "This department is much smaller than your old outfit across the road. We're all batting on the same side, safeguarding the national interest, but our concerns are both specialised and sophisticated. Takes time, even for an experienced chap with an outstanding record of service like yourself, to get up to speed. As I explained when you joined us, we do things differently here."

The major's glance strayed to the portrait on the wall. "Understood, sir."

"All that still holds true. In itself, this ludicrous incident at the Hades Gallery is neither here nor there. Except for the deceased, of course. On this occasion, Mrs. de Villiers hasn't done anything herself to…make waves. But we simply can't go on like this, turning a blind eye to her antics, waiting for calamity to strike." Sir Hector paused. "There has been a further development. If we sit on our hands, we can expect the balloon to go up in a matter of days."

"Yes?"

Sir Hector lowered his voice. "I have been informed that our Very Important Person is keen to pay a visit to Rye."

"To call on Mrs. de Villiers?"

"At her hideaway in Sepulchre Street, yes."

"Has he…?"

"You may take it that he has been spoken to by the Great and the Good," Sir Hector snapped. "I'm afraid that at present he is disregarding all advice."

"Unfortunate," Whitlow murmured.

"I'd call it catastrophic."

"You think that…"

"I think that things are getting out of control! His behaviour is quite intolerable." With a heavy sigh, as if the time for tongue-clicking had passed, Sir Hector said, "We simply cannot permit the present state of affairs—so to speak—to continue."

"No, sir."

"Rye isn't London. A small and attractive town, a magnet for visitors, even out of season. It is utterly inconceivable that a Very Important Person can travel around without a care in the world and expect to remain anonymous. Unnoticed and untroubled by the hoi polloi."

He paused. The major held his tongue.

"This morning, I have discussed the situation with the Great and the Good." Sir Hector cleared his throat. "It is still conceivable that sanity will prevail as far as our Very Important Person is concerned. It may also be that this man Ambrose will do our work for us. But we simply can't rely on either eventuality."

A faint gleam lit the major's eyes. He waited.

"Indeed not, sir."

"The upshot is that you have authority to put your proposal into effect."

"Thank you, sir."

"I need hardly remind you," Sir Hector said as the major rose, "the vital importance of this matter. If news were to leak out about…Mrs. de Villiers's activities, the very future of this country would be in peril."

Chapter 7

Clifford Trueman sat at the kitchen table, scribbling brief notes on the list of names he'd obtained from the Hades Gallery in his crabbed, unsophisticated hand. Like the rest of his family, he'd had a limited formal education. During their long years on the island of Gaunt, they'd taught themselves as well as each other. The same was true of Rachel. She'd spent thousands of hours devouring the books in Judge Savernake's library, one of the finest in private hands.

"What do you make of it?" she asked.

"If we don't count the art critics or dealers," he said, "or the gallery staff or the people who acted as the wax models, that leaves just six guests at the Hades Gallery."

"So few? How interesting."

"You and Jacob, plus Malam, his sister-in-law, the songsmith Tucker, and Kiki de Villiers."

"A very select gathering," Martha said. "So there were no other artists?"

"Not one," her brother said.

"Isn't that surprising?"

"No," Rachel said. "Damaris Gethin didn't belong to a clique. She was a notoriously prickly character, scornful about most of her peers. As for the critics and dealers, we daren't ignore them. Let me see who was there."

As she peeked over his shoulder, Trueman asked, "Recognise any of the names?"

"Yes," she murmured. "For all the attention it attracts, surrealist art is a small world. Three of those dealers come from the Continent; so do a couple of the critics. There are natives of Austria, Germany, and Spain on the list. Each of them has an impeccable reputation."

"Suspicious in itself," he muttered.

She laughed. "How very cynical."

"Realistic, you mean."

"True. There are a handful of critics, mostly people who write for the art magazines rather than national newspapers. Jacob is the only representative of the popular press."

"If a reviewer was brutal about Damaris Gethin's work," Trueman suggested, "that might have driven her to despair."

Rachel made a sceptical noise. "Unlikely. If creative artists decapitated themselves every time some critic treated them unfairly, soon there wouldn't be anyone left."

"All right, what about the gallery staff and the models?"

"We can take nothing for granted, but I doubt they are involved."

"Narrows the field."

"Yes, but remember this. Damaris Gethin set a challenge that she wanted me to solve. She hoped I'd do justice on her behalf."

"Whatever that means."

"I can't believe that she'd force me to look for a needle in a haystack. She had to strike a balance. The puzzle must intrigue me, but not prove so difficult that I give up on it."

"You never give up," Trueman said.

"You know me as well as anyone alive, but until last night

Damaris Gethin had never met me. She was willing to gamble, but she couldn't risk her death going unavenged."

"You think that's what she meant by doing justice? Vengeance?"

"Yes."

"So she appointed you as her avenger? Even though you have no idea what you're avenging?"

Rachel nodded.

He looked at her. "And you're prepared to take that on?"

She returned his gaze.

"Why not?"

———

"You'll love Monte," Captain Malam said. "Marvellous spot. I've travelled far and wide and, take it from me, you simply can't beat the Riviera."

"All I know about the place is what I've seen in that new film," Rachel said.

The two of them were in the drawing room of Gaunt House. Their coffee cups were almost empty but a subtle tang of blueberry from the Arabica beans lingered in the air.

"The musical?" he asked.

"Starring Jack Buchanan, yes. And Jeanette MacDonald singing that lovely song."

She moved over to the piano stool and played a few bars of "Beyond the Blue Horizon" on the Steinway.

The captain rewarded her with a burst of applause. "Bravo! I never knew you could play so delightfully."

She gave a little bow. "I can't claim to be a Harriet Cohen."

"You're far too modest, my dear."

"I love music almost as much as I love art. But perhaps I should change my tune."

She started playing "The Man Who Broke the Bank at Monte Carlo," crooning her own version of the words. *"Don't you hear those girls declare / The captain is a millionaire?"*

Malam laughed. "You just wait and see. Given my rotten luck at the tables, I'll be a pauper in next to no time."

Smiling sweetly, she closed the piano lid. "Now you're being too modest, Roddy. More coffee?"

"No, thanks." He glanced at his watch. "I really must dash."

"So soon? Oh, do stay for a few more minutes. I feel we have such a lot to talk about."

"I'd love to." He stood up. "Next time we meet, I promise."

"What a shame. You've only just got here."

"Believe me, Rachel, it's a real tonic to see you again. Especially since I'd got the impression you were bored with me."

"Perish the thought!"

"I don't mind admitting, I was pretty downcast when you didn't return my calls. Thought I'd somehow put my foot in it. I even wondered if your maid had forgotten to tell you that I'd rung. Then when I wrote to you here and received no reply…"

Rachel bowed her head. "I'm so sorry if I behaved badly."

"Don't give it another thought."

Her expression was soulful. "I don't mean to seem stand-offish, truly I don't. You mustn't pay too much attention to my moods. I'm not like Damaris Gethin, I promise."

"You certainly aren't," he said fervently.

"No neuroses," Rachel insisted. "No headaches, no bouts of nausea."

Malam gave a rather nervous smile. "Of course not."

"It's because of my upbringing, you see. On that lonely island. I'm accustomed to being on my own."

He waved a hand. "No harm done, my dear."

"You're very magnanimous. When I'm in the company of such a dashing man about town, I feel rather gauche."

Malam's pale blue eyes gazed into hers. "Gauche is one adjective I'd never apply to you, Rachel. Elegant, yes. Enigmatic, perhaps. Beautiful, certainly."

"Now you're making me blush, Roddy."

"I'd love to get to know you better."

"How kind you are." She reached out to touch the bruise on his cheek with her fingertip. "You poor thing. Does this hurt? Don't tell me someone walloped you!"

"It's nothing," he said shortly. "I walked into a door, that's all there was to it."

"You really should be more careful, Roddy."

"People have been telling me that ever since I was in short trousers." He gave his watch another quick glance. "Right, I need to be on my way. Business matters to attend to. Damned nuisance, but must keep the wheels of commerce turning, you know. I'll be glad to get across the Channel and finally relax."

"You won't have too much time to relax if you're driving in the Grand Prix."

"What?" For a moment he seemed disconcerted. "Oh, no, I suppose not. But don't worry. We'll have plenty of time to amuse ourselves together. Take my word for it. There's endless scope for fun and games in Monte."

"I can't wait," Rachel breathed.

———

"Well?" Martha asked, the moment the door closed behind Malam. "How did you get on?"

"The captain has invited me to fly over to Monte Carlo. He wants me to marvel at his prowess behind the wheel of a racing car before squandering our money at the tables."

"How glamorous. Will you find room on the plane for your devoted maid?"

"Don't get your hopes up."

Martha pouted. "I'm surprised at you. Don't you want a chaperone?"

"That's not the question. I'm not convinced his heart was in it."

"How do you mean?"

"Somehow the invitation didn't ring true. The whole thing sounded like a charade."

"How strange."

"Very. Not that I'm desolated. I've no intention of letting him whisk me off to the Continent or anywhere else."

"What do you think he's up to?"

"Not sure," Rachel confessed. "He said all the right things, yet he was surprisingly eager to make his escape."

"Is he playing a game? Indulging in reprisals because you didn't respond to his phone calls or that letter?"

"Then why bother to turn up here this morning? It would have been simpler to snub me by pretending to forget our appointment."

"Sounds to me like a mean trick. He wants to get your hopes up, before letting you down. And then he can waltz off to Monte Carlo with some floozy in tow. Proving that there are plenty more fish in the sea."

Rachel ran a hand through her hair. "When he talked about playing roulette at the casino, I wondered if it was a prelude to offering me another exclusive opportunity to put fifty thousand pounds into some hopeless business venture."

"And?"

"For once he didn't even try to persuade me to make any investments. One thing interested me. He told me an obvious lie."

"What about?"

"You saw the bruise on his cheek when you let him into the house?"

Martha touched her own scars. Half hidden by her chestnut hair, they were the fading legacy of an attack when she was a young girl. A man had thrown acid at her face. "Yes, I notice these things."

"According to Jacob, Malam told Mrs. de Villiers that he'd had an argument with someone. An investor he'd shortchanged punched him in the face. But he pretended that he'd walked into a door. Not that he bothered to make his story plausible."

"Maybe he was embarrassed. Doesn't want his lady love to know that his get-rich-quick schemes are anything less than guaranteed winners."

"He may have lied to Mrs. de Villiers too. But I doubt it. And given that amateur boxing is one of his sports, whoever struck him meant business. My guess is that the captain knew I wouldn't believe him. He simply wanted to tantalise me— heaven knows why."

"Did you find out any more about what happened at the Hades Gallery?"

Rachel shook her head. "Nothing. In fact, I wonder if that's the reason why he rushed off."

"To avoid discussing the death of Damaris Gethin?"

"Or to dodge any questions about our fellow guests."

"Why do…?" Martha began.

A distant, muffled boom interrupted her. The women stared at each other.

"What was that?"

"It sounded," Rachel said, "like a bomb exploding."

———

Rushing out of the house with Martha close behind, Rachel smelled smoke in the air, tasted its bitter poison on her tongue. There was a hubbub of voices and sounds of unmistakable distress, but the square was deserted. She hurried round the corner. The noise and the smoke were coming from a narrow mews that ran off a side street.

She began to run. Her strides were long but Martha, equally fit, kept pace with her. Growing up and roaming around on the rugged, inhospitable terrain of Gaunt had given them the stamina and staying power of trained athletes. They reached the entrance to the mews and came face to face with the chaos of destruction. The blast had blown out several windows in the surrounding buildings. Shards of glass were scattered over the cobbles and so were lumps of broken metal, twisted and sharp.

A girl was sobbing and someone was trying to hush a small, frightened child. The air was thick with noxious fumes. People were gathering around the smouldering wreckage of a large car.

"Captain Malam's Bentley," Martha's voice said in her ear.

"Yes."

"Is he...?"

"Alive?" Rachel pointed. "There he is, on the far side of the car. Trying to damp down the blaze with his jacket."

"Someone must have tried to blow the fellow to high heaven," a man standing in front of them said to his neighbour.

"Recognise him?" his companion said. "That's Roddy Malam. The daredevil, you know?"

"Is this some kind of stunt?"

"Hardly. It's a miracle he's still in one piece."

"Remarkable man."

Rachel elbowed her way through the crowd and cupped her hands round her mouth so that she could be heard amid the confusion.

"Are you all right?"

Malam snuffed out a dying flame before looking up at her. His face was blackened and blood was leaking from his shirt. It looked as though a piece of the vehicle had struck his shoulder, like flying shrapnel.

"Rachel!"

"Did someone try to kill you?"

"If so, they didn't succeed," he said grimly. "Looks like I've used up another of my nine lives."

She moved towards him. "What happened?"

"I've parked the Bentley here whenever I visit Gaunt House. Out of harm's way, or so I used to think. As I walked back into the mews, the car blew up. A few seconds later and... Lord, it doesn't bear thinking about."

"A bomb?"

"What else?" he said roughly. "It was like being back in the trenches. A long time ago, but you never forget."

Rachel dodged around the car, and came close enough to whisper in his ear. "Who can have done this, Roddy?"

He avoided her eye. "In my time I've crossed a number of people. Who knows?"

"I think you do."

A sheepish grunt. "Perhaps I can make an educated guess."

"Who hates you enough to blow you to smithereens?"

He hesitated. "I'll talk to the police when they arrive. I don't want to run around accusing all and sundry. Get sued for slander if I don't look out."

Rachel fixed her gaze on the captain's injured cheek. "Someone wants you dead, it seems. Was your car bombed by the same person who left that bruise on your cheek?"

"I told you, I walked into a door."

"And you lied."

"Can't get much past you, can I?"

"Don't bother to try. Who was it?"

"How can I be sure?"

A bell clanged in the distance; the noise growing louder with each passing second.

"Here comes the fire engine," someone cried. "Make way!"

"We'll come to the bomb in a moment. Who hit you?"

He rubbed his shoulder and grimaced at the pain. "All right, you win."

"What is his name?"

A sigh. "Butterworth."

"Who is he?"

"Ned Butterworth used to be a sapper. He served under me in France. Fine soldier. Loyal and brave."

"Did you quarrel?"

"The other night, he turned up outside my front door. Drunk as a lord. He accosted me, and we came to blows."

"Is this about something that happened in the war?"

"Not at all. I had enormous respect for him, and I like to think he felt the same about me."

The crowd scattered as the fire engine thundered round the corner and into the mews. A police car wasn't far behind.

"Sorry, Rachel," he said. "They'll need to talk to me."

She waved towards the mayhem. "Did Butterworth blow up your car?"

"I can't be sure. But I can't think of anyone else who would have the right know-how."

"And he does?"

"During the war, he was the bravest bomb disposal man I ever saw. He must have followed me here. It's the only thing that makes sense."

"Why would Butterworth want you dead?"

Captain Malam let out a defeated groan. "All right, if you insist on the gory details. The poor fool lost his shirt in a company I promoted. I was trying to help him, but it went badly wrong. He chucked everything down the drain instead of waiting for the business to turn the corner. Now he lives on charity and is pretty much destitute. After his health broke down, his wife ran off. He blames me for everything that has gone wrong. His life is in ruins, and it's all my fault."

———

"What do you make of it?" Martha asked.

They were back in the kitchen of Gaunt House. Hetty was preparing lunch while Trueman continued to ponder the list of guests invited to *Artist in Crime*.

"Roddy Malam is a tricky customer," Rachel said. "I doubt he's telling me everything he knows."

"If this man Butterworth was a sapper in the army, he'd be trained in bomb disposal." Martha paused. "Chances are, he'd also have the expertise to *build* a bomb."

"Precisely."

"You think the captain is lying about Butterworth?"

"No," Rachel admitted. "What he said about the man's hatred of him had the ring of truth. But it's not the full story, I'd swear to that."

"I don't care for the captain," Hetty said, "but you could have brought him back here for lunch. Nourishing broth, just the thing after a nasty shock."

Rachel inhaled the aroma coming from the stove and gave an appreciative murmur. "His loss is our gain. The police wasted no time in whisking him away. Once the officers have questioned him about the bomb, the medics will need to examine him. Looks like the damage to his shoulder is only a flesh wound, but if he'd been inside the Bentley when it exploded..."

"His luck was in," Hetty said.

"One of these days, it will run out."

Martha leaned over the table. "You think his life is still at risk?"

"Blowing a car to bits is a statement of intent. Someone who goes that far to commit murder won't give up easily."

"Thank heaven that innocent passers-by weren't maimed or killed," Martha said.

"Yes, the mews is often busy, so that was another stroke of good fortune. I suppose the bomber may simply have aimed to frighten the captain, but chances are that it was a deliberate attempt on his life. What I can't see is any link between this bomb and the death of Damaris Gethin."

"Surely the two incidents are unrelated?"

"In the public imagination, Roddy Malam is a national hero. For all his popularity, he leads a complicated life. He courts danger in everything he does. Butterworth isn't the only person to lose a packet by following his investment advice. Perhaps the connecting link is simply a matter of character. At one time he was on good terms with Sapper Butterworth, only to become his mortal enemy. Damaris Gethin was once his lover. What if he made the same mistake with her?"

"She was the one who died," Martha said. "Not him."

"True." Rachel shook her head. "I'm missing something. Quite a lot of things, I expect. I'll leave Roddy Malam's wounds to heal for a while. It's time to look at the other names on Cliff's list. Starting with Evan Tucker."

Chapter 8

As the Rolls-Royce Phantom moved through afternoon traffic under overcast skies, Rachel Savernake hummed "London Life," the last of Evan Tucker's songs to achieve any sort of popular success. Trueman eased the car smoothly to a standstill a short distance from the corner of Charing Cross Road and Denmark Street.

"All right for you?"

"Perfect." She smiled dreamily. "My very first visit to Tin Pan Alley."

"Isn't that in New York?"

"Denmark Street is our answer to it. Do you know how the street got its nickname?"

A grunt. "I expect you're about to tell me."

"So the story goes, it comes from the racket made by cheap upright pianos. People said they sounded like tin pans banging in an alleyway."

"Ah, you learn something every day. Shall I pick you up when you've done with him?"

"If Tucker doesn't send me away with a flea in my ear, you go back to the house and I'll make my own way home. You can help

Martha to follow up the other names on the Hades guest list in the meantime."

She jumped out of the car. Drizzle splashed on her cheeks, but her spine tingled with anticipation. At times like this it felt wonderful to be alive. She was about to make a fresh move in her favourite sport, a game that beat chess and crossword puzzles hands down. Solving a strange mystery about murder.

Lithe as Lina Radke, she shimmied through the crowd of shoppers making for the Tottenham Court Road underground station and turned into Denmark Street. Her destination proved to be an unremarkable three-storey building in the middle of a terrace. Half a dozen telephone calls that morning had established that Evan Tucker leased a flat near Holborn and rented an office from a firm of music publishers. He often turned up here on weekday afternoons, Tuesday to Friday. Presumably he hoped to rekindle his career by composing another song that caught the attention of a fickle public.

The bell was answered by a young Chinese woman who directed her up a rickety flight of wooden stairs. Rachel took them two at a time. A narrow corridor ran off an uncarpeted landing on the first floor. The frosted glass of the door at the far end bore Evan Tucker's name in flaking gilt letters. Inside, someone was pounding away on a piano. Tucker was no Paderewski. That joke about tin pans wasn't far from the truth.

The moment she knocked, the tune came to an abrupt halt.

"What is it?" a voice demanded.

Rachel detected a mixture of petulance and frustration. The muse has deserted him, she thought, and he blames interruptions rather than the fading of a modest talent.

Closing her eyes, she imagined herself as a gushing ingénue. She'd chosen the champagne coat and lace Fiesole dress to suit the part she was about to play. Now to fix on a smile intended to melt the iciest heart.

"Mr. Tucker? How wonderful!" she trilled.

"I'm busy. What do you want?"

"A thousand apologies for interrupting a maestro at work! If you'd be kind enough to let me in, I'd love to explain."

A long, low sigh was followed by footsteps. The door opened to reveal Evan Tucker. He was roughly the same height and build as Captain Malam, but the stoop of his shoulders diminished him and the horn-rimmed spectacles and furrowed brow made him look much older. Dark bags hung under his eyes, and Rachel doubted that he'd slept a wink since Damaris Gethin had beheaded herself in front of him. His tie was at half mast and his rumpled suit was spattered with cigarette ash. He had the demeanour of a man who yearned to shrink until he became invisible and nobody bothered him again.

"Well?"

Rachel glanced around the small room. The shuttered windows allowed barely a chink of natural light. A naked bulb shone through the gloom, and the air was sour with smoke and a whiff of gin. The furnishings comprised a piano, a stool, and a small desk cluttered with manuscripts of unfinished compositions. A single shelf was littered with gramophone records, a pile of dog-eared sheet music, and an overflowing ashtray. A chipped tumbler and a half-empty bottle of Gordon's stood on the linoleum floor beside the piano.

"So this is your sanctuary! Where your creative juices flow!" Rachel clapped her hands in a show of excitement. "May I?"

She stepped past him before he had a chance to say no. Slipping off her coat, she threw it over the desk and sat down on the stool.

"I'm not looking for a singer." His Welsh accent had a faint, melodious lilt, but he sounded weary and defeated. "Talk to an agent; there's one across the street. Better still, try your luck in the West End. Times are hard, mind. The Slump has hit everyone hard. There's not much work going, even for a pretty slip of a girl."

"Oh, goodness me, that isn't why I'm here." She turned to the piano and began to play. "Remember this?"

Behind the spectacles, pale blue eyes blinked. "Of course. 'Don't Count the Days.'"

"Splendid! Such a relief that my tinkling hasn't mangled your chords out of all recognition. I can't compete with Pauline Alpert, but I get by."

"One of my less well-known songs," he murmured.

"I adore every single one of them!" she gushed. "Your work is an inspiration. Deeply romantic and yet so heart-rending. I've followed your career with admiration. Such a privilege to meet you at last, Mr. Tucker."

"Well..."

From Tucker's bemusement, she guessed that it was years since anyone had lavished such praise on him. Perhaps she'd overdone it, but sometimes the value of subtlety was exaggerated. So often the crudest methods worked best. Especially with men whose egos were fragile. Already she detected an easing of the tension in his bent shoulders. Was that the ghost of a smile playing on his dry lips?

"Are you an autograph hunter, Miss...?"

She flashed her perfect teeth in a beam of delight. "I do have an album containing favourite signatures, yes. But that wasn't the main purpose of my visit. My name is Savernake, by the way. Rachel Savernake."

"Rachel Savernake," he repeated. "Sounds familiar. In fact, there's something about the look of you..."

"That's generous of you, Mr. Tucker, but I doubt that a musical giant has heard of someone as obscure as little me. As it happens, I've tried my hand at writing songs, and I was hoping for a little advice on my latest compositions."

She began to play a melody of her own devising, faintly reminiscent of "My Blue Heaven."

"I hope you don't feel I'm being too forward," she said, "but if you ever felt you wanted to collaborate, that would be a dream come—"

"Miss Savernake," he interrupted. "I'm obliged by your interest in my work, but this business is brutal enough towards professional composers with catalogues built over a decade. Let alone if you're a novice."

With a pout, she brought the tune to a discordant end. "Oh, dear, how awfully depressing. But I suppose you're right. If even someone with your gifts loses heart…"

"Believe me, Miss Savernake." He made no attempt to sugarcoat his bitterness. "Once upon a time, the leper colony of St. Giles occupied this stretch of central London. Frankly, there are times when I feel like a twentieth-century leper. A relic of the past. Yesterday's composer. Nobody sings my songs any more."

"No, no! I can't believe it!"

She hummed a snatch of a tune before proceeding to sing the chorus: "Where there's a heartache, there must be a heart."

His teeth gnawed at his lower lip. "Ah, my finest achievement."

"There will be more!" she assured him. "Look at your countryman, Ivor Novello. If he can—"

"Novello and I both come from Wales," Tucker snapped, "so people bracket us together. They couldn't be further from the truth."

"Really?"

"Oh, yes. Novello is a city slicker from Cardiff, one of the handsomest fellows around. Myself, I'm a country lad. Born and bred on Anglesey. My parents never spoke English at home in Moelfre. I'll never be a sophisticate or a performer like Ivor."

Rachel gave a sympathetic murmur.

"They reckon that every dog has his day. Well, mine has come and gone. I'm just a writer, and now the words and music don't flow as they did in the old days. Coward talks smugly about the potency of cheap music, but when I sit down at the piano now, I'm impotent. The truth is, I've written myself to a standstill. I'm past it. Finished."

"Nonsense!"

He screwed up his face, as if dredging the recesses of memory. "Rachel Savernake, you say? I remember now. Your name cropped up in conversation. You're a pal of Captain Malam, aren't you?"

"Fancy you remembering that!" she said gaily.

"A judge's daughter, isn't that right?"

Rachel ignored the question. She never talked about Judge Savernake, and she didn't intend to start now. As far as she was concerned, the old devil was dead and gone. Not a soul had shed a tear at his passing. Now the preliminaries were over, and Tucker was starting to unbend, she was ready to get down to business.

"Am I mistaken?" she asked. "Or did I see you at the Hades Gallery last night?"

"Good God, yes." His voice was hoarse. "What a nightmarish evening!"

"Nightmarish, yes," Rachel said softly. "You never said a truer word."

He peered at her like a doctor trying to make a diagnosis. "So you were there too? You saw what happened?"

"I'm afraid so." Rachel hung her head. "That poor woman

must have been in appalling distress to end it all in such a desperate fashion."

Tucker closed his eyes. "I never saw anything like it in my life. What on earth possessed her to…?"

"Indeed," Rachel murmured. "One simply can't help wondering. What do you make of it?"

"I…I really can't imagine. Of all things…to kill yourself with the aid of a guillotine! It's beyond belief."

Rachel lowered her voice to a whisper. "Did she confide in you?"

"Me?" He looked startled. "Good God, no. We weren't on intimate terms."

"Yet you were old friends?"

Tucker hesitated. "I wouldn't say so. Not at all. Actually, we were just…acquaintances."

"She invited you to her private view. A select gathering."

A touch of colour came to his pasty cheeks. "You were a guest as well. And I presume that you weren't a bosom friend, either."

"You're right, of course. As it happens, I've always admired her work. Such a pity that she has been…professionally inactive of late. Do you happen to know why?"

A flush came to his cheeks. "Not in the mood, I suppose. Did Roddy Malam take you along to the Hades?"

"No. As a matter of fact, until last night we hadn't seen each other for a little while."

"Ah." He took off his spectacles, and Rachel detected a glimmer of calculation in his eyes. "Not had a tiff, have you?"

"Gosh, no. Captain Malam is so busy, so much in demand, I don't expect him to waste precious time with the likes of me."

"Did Damaris Gethin invite you, then?"

"Yes."

He raised his eyebrows. "You and she were close?"

"We'd never met until last night." Rachel looked sheepish. "However, she had discovered my guilty secret."

Tucker moved towards her, leaning against the piano. The reek of gin and tobacco was overpowering.

"Such a charming young lady with a guilty secret?"

"More than one, I'm afraid," she breathed. "You see, I love to collect modern art. And I have an absolute passion for the surrealists."

He ran a hand over his head. "Expensive hobby, Miss Savernake."

"Yes, I feel positively embarrassed about my good fortune. You see, I came into a large inheritance. A sheer fluke. How much nobler to earn from the sweat of one's own brow. As you still do."

"Me?"

The sudden edge to his manner interested her. "I'd love to make a living from my own compositions. Or failing that, to take some part in the world of music. Even if simply by encouraging those whose creative gifts are more sophisticated than my own."

He gave her a puzzled glance. "As a songwriter's muse?"

"I'd like to help."

She played a few bars of another melody she'd composed for her own pleasure. He drummed his fingers on the top of the piano in time to the music.

"Not bad, Miss Savernake. A touch derivative, but quite accomplished for an amateur."

"How kind of you."

"I'm sure you'll make good use of your inheritance. You strike me as a generous soul."

His smile made Rachel exult inwardly. It hadn't taken long even for this melancholy fellow to thaw. The transformation from petulance to geniality was complete. Talking about money, in her experience, often had that effect.

"Of course," he said, "it's a truth universally acknowledged that a single young woman in possession of a good fortune must be in want of sound financial advice."

She rewarded his wit with a giggle. His left hand lay on the edge of the piano, and she gave it a gentle pat.

He coughed and moved his hand away. "We live in straitened times, Miss Savernake."

"Please don't stand on ceremony. I'd be honoured if you call me Rachel."

"Thank you, Rachel. I wonder, has Roddy been helping with your investments, by any chance?"

"Captain Malam has been kind enough to offer me expert guidance whenever I need it."

"Decent of him. Shows you the type of fellow he is." Tucker leaned forward. "Have you followed his advice?"

She sighed. "I'm a novice in matters of business, Mr. Tucker. The technicalities of family trusts are double Dutch to me. The lawyers take such a long time to disentangle the complexities and allow me to spend more of my fortune. I'll make sure to take advantage of the captain's wisdom and experience."

"Very sensible. He's a good friend to have. Well-connected." He paused. "Always willing to help someone out if they get into a ticklish situation."

Rachel was conscious of a glint in his eye. It was as if he were teasing her, inviting her to confide in him.

"The two of you are old chums?" she asked.

"We first bumped into each other years ago. Fine man, Roddy. Remarkably accomplished. A genuine swashbuckler."

"You admire him?"

He gave her a quizzical look. "Doesn't everyone?"

"Oh, absolutely," she said.

"He has achieved so much."

"How true." Had she slipped up by allowing a trickle of scepticism to seep through her mask of innocence? She wasted no time in changing the subject. "As for Damaris Gethin, how did the two of you meet?"

"You know how it is." He made a vague gesture with his hand. "People in the public eye tend to cross each other's paths. London is a teeming city, but cultured society is a small world. Damaris and I met at a fancy dress party at the Albert Hall one New Year's Eve. As a matter of fact, I was the person who introduced her to Roddy."

"Is that so?"

"Yes. I invited them both to a party at my home in the country, and before I knew it, romance was brewing." He sighed. "Not that it lasted."

"Why did they break up?"

"Who knows what goes on between a couple behind closed doors?" he said vaguely. "I suppose they simply decided they weren't compatible. She was always rather...fey. As time passed, the swings of her mood became more extreme."

"Was she in poor health?"

"Not to my knowledge," he said quickly. "But then, I wasn't privy to her medical affairs. Certainly she was a nervy type. The blunt truth is that she and Captain Malam could hardly have been more different. She is—was—a famous artist, even if her work strikes me as ridiculous. He's a man of action."

"Yet opposites attract," she murmured.

"I wonder why you are so interested, Rachel? No need to be jealous of Damaris Gethin, I assure you. Even before last night's tragedy, she and Roddy had gone their separate ways."

"Forgive me," Rachel said. "It was just idle curiosity. I've led such a sheltered existence, I long to hear about how the other half live."

"Sheltered?"

She blushed. "Until recently, that is. Coming to London has opened my eyes to—so many marvellous new experiences."

"I can imagine," he said slyly.

"Your country house sounds gorgeous. It's not in Wales?"

"Good Lord, no. Years since I last visited the land of my fathers. I rent a tiny flat not far from here. Some afternoons, I labour here at the piano, the rest of the time I escape to The Risings. Barely two hours' drive from here, but rural Kent feels like a different world."

"The garden of England!" Rachel cried. "How delightful."

"Do you know Romney Marsh? An ancient lagoon, reclaimed over the centuries."

"Sounds quite magical."

Her enthusiasm pleased him. "Absolutely. Have you read *The Ingoldsby Legends*?"

"Of course!"

"They describe Romney Marsh as the Fifth Continent, and the name stuck. The Marsh isn't to everyone's taste, but it suits me."

Rachel pondered. "Didn't Roddy's brother live in that neck of the woods? The doctor who died, poor fellow?"

"Giles Malam, yes, God rest his soul. He lived barely a mile from The Risings, close enough to make us neighbours. His widow, Phoebe, is still there. As a matter of fact, she was at the Hades last night."

"Now you come to mention it," Rachel said, "didn't I see you talking to her? A lady with dark hair?"

"Handsome woman," Tucker said vaguely. "She keeps her late husband's clinic going. Tiny place, but she is devoted to her patients."

Rachel's expression became coy. "Are you and she…?"

"Good heavens, no." He coloured. "We're just neighbours."

"So you asked her along to the exhibition?"

"Damaris invited her too. Candidly, neither of us care for her so-called art, but we were curious. She doesn't drive, so I gave her a lift." He tutted. "Little did we guess what the Hades Gallery had in store for us. If ever a place lived up to its name…"

"So Damaris Gethin knew Roddy's sister-in-law?" Rachel asked. "I suppose he introduced them?"

"Presumably." He spoke in an offhand way, but Rachel suspected he was being evasive. "Why do you ask?"

She tittered as an alarm bell rang in her mind. Better not push her luck too far. Even the sweetest ingénue couldn't get away with an endlessly prolonged inquisition.

"Surely Roddy has told you one of my other guilty secrets?" she said. "I'm incurably nosey."

Evan Tucker considered her. "Every now and then, I host parties at The Risings. Perhaps that was when she and Phoebe met."

"Sounds wonderfully glamorous," she said, striking a wistful note.

He relaxed into a smile. "Perhaps one of these days you might like to venture out to Romney Marsh?"

Rachel gave a joyful clap of her hands. "Oh, I'd love to!"

"You'll be most welcome."

"How exciting!" She lowered her eyes. "I hope you won't think me too forward if…"

"If what?"

"No, no, it seems so presumptuous."

"Tell me," he said gently.

"I'm not sure dear Roddy quite realises, but the truth is, I'm a creature of impulse."

"Nothing wrong with that."

"Once or twice lately, it has got me into…rather a lot of trouble."

He moved closer to her, and she could smell the gin on his breath. "You know what they say. A trouble shared…"

"How true." She smiled. "You can see I'm one of your staunchest admirers. Would it seem too bold of me if I were to pay you a visit?"

Evan Tucker gave a crooked smile.

"It would be an honour."

Chapter 9

"A Corpse Reviver?" Jacob Flint asked.

"Don't mind if I do, Mr. Flint," Sammy Postles said. "They know how to mix a decent drink in this place."

The two men were in the American Bar of the Savoy. Of all the snouts who supplied Jacob with snippets of information, none had such an exotic taste in alcohol as Sammy Postles. Most were content with a week's beer money, but Sammy had a taste for the high life. These days, the closest he came to it was sampling hot grogs at the Café Royal or cocktails at the Savoy.

"Cheers, Sammy."

"Bottoms up, Mr. Flint."

They chinked glasses and headed for a small table at the rear of the room, beside an aerial photograph of the Thames covering one wall. Jacob was content with a Perrier water. A busy evening lay ahead, starting with cocktails and dinner at Gaunt House. Sammy didn't need to keep a clear head, and it was obvious that he had no intention of doing so. Four in the afternoon, and already his breath reeked of alcohol.

Once upon a time, Sammy had been a promising footballer with Tottenham Hotspur, a darling of the crowds at White Hart Lane. An ankle broken in a bad tackle had finished his playing career, and nowadays he haunted the capital's demi-monde, sailing ever closer to the wind in order to fund his drinking habits. His older brother, Joe, had worked in Soho as an odd-job man for years and was another valuable source of information. Over the past year or two Sammy had needed to pull a few strings to escape winding up in a police cell, but with his good humour and extensive contacts with the criminal classes, he more than earned his Corpse Revivers. Even at the prices they charged in the American Bar.

"That's better," he said, draining his glass and then taking a look at the cocktail list on the table. "Blimey, they know how to make something special out of two measures of cognac plus Calvados and vermouth."

"I'll take your word for it."

Sammy leaned forward. "Want to know the best way to drink a cocktail?"

"Tell me."

"Quickly, while it's still laughing at you."

Jacob didn't need a further hint to pay another visit to the bar. Sammy raised his glass again.

"You're a real gent, Mr. Flint."

Sammy had recently passed thirty, and the handsome young right winger now possessed the puffy features of a hardened drinker. Yet although his suit was almost as shiny as Jacob's, there was no mistaking its origins in Savile Row. In these smart surroundings, in a room shaped like a grand piano and exquisitely furnished, Sammy seemed at ease. A man who still took the good things in life as his due, even though Lady Luck had deserted him long ago.

In the next hour or two the American Bar would fill with well-dressed couples who fancied a drink before going to the theatre, but for now the place was quiet except for the pianist rehearsing an excerpt from "Rhapsody in Blue."

"You was asking after Monsieur Ambrose." Sammy pronounced the title *Mon-sewer*, which to Jacob seemed fair enough.

"Are the rumours true? Is he definitely back in England?"

Sammy nodded. "Arrived by ferry the night before last, or so I hear. Kept everything hush-hush, but you know how it is, Mr. Flint. Word gets out. You can't trust people to keep their mouths shut nowadays, I'm afraid."

"Thank the Lord for small mercies," Jacob said.

Sammy chortled. "You're a card, Mr. Flint; I'll say that for you."

"What's he getting up to now he's back? Revisiting old stamping grounds?"

"You bet." Sammy made a performance of looking over his shoulder to make sure nobody was listening. "Shouldn't be surprised if he showed up at Chez Laurent before either of us are much older. I heard a whisper that Laurent isn't the real owner, after all. He just holds it as Ambrose's proxy. Ambrose certainly haunted the place in days gone by. Before he..."

"Faked his own death?"

Sammy put his finger to his lips. "I didn't say that, Mr. Flint. Closed mouths catch no flies, know what I mean?"

Jacob took a sip of Perrier. Closed mouths were no use to him, with or without flies.

"Ambrose vanished before I came to London. Before Wall Street came tumbling down. The world has changed since he was last in England."

Sammy savoured his cocktail. "One thing won't have changed, if you ask me." He looked at his glass in a meaningful way.

"I'll get another round in a moment," Jacob said. "What were you saying?"

"Marcel Ambrose is murder to cross. You've talked to my brother. He can tell you tales that would make your hair curl. Joe has seen Ambrose shoot a man in the stomach to win a bet and slash a stranger's throat for giving one of his fancy women a cheeky wink."

For the first time in their acquaintance, Sammy's voice trembled with apprehension. He gulped down the rest of his Corpse Reviver and emitted a loud belch.

"I don't know what you're up to that involves him, but you need to watch your step. If I was you, Mr. Flint, I'd take an interest in somebody else. Someone who doesn't enjoy hurting people so much. Forget we ever had this conversation. If you poke your nose into Ambrose's business, God help you. People who fall foul of that evil bastard seldom live to tell the tale."

————

Adeline Laporte stood on the rocky heights of the Citadel, in the shadow of the old Ypres Tower, a surviving fragment of the ancient defences of Rye. The town was a Cinque Port deserted by the sea and built on a sandstone pyramid rising sharply above the flat, green grazing land. Adeline had read that, centuries ago, her fellow countrymen often raided this stretch of the south coast. The French invaders were repelled but, much later, after the massacre of St. Bartholomew, Huguenots fled across the Channel to seek refuge here. Some settled on the outskirts, in the well-named parish of Rye Foreign. And now Mrs. Kiki de Villiers and her maid occupied one of the finest houses in town. How amusing. Perhaps this proved something that Adeline believed with a passion. Everything comes to those who wait.

She watched the sun setting over the salt marsh, listened to the cries of the herring gulls. The beauty of nature soothed her like a balm. She'd spent her life cramped up in cities, but since encountering Rye, she'd fallen in love with this quaint corner of East Sussex. The sheer sense of space helped to calm her nerves after the shock of that telephone call earlier in the afternoon.

Snug as she felt in the fur-trimmed ocelot coat, she couldn't restrain a shiver of apprehension as she replayed the brief conversation in her mind. Would she ever be able to escape from danger, to feel safe from the threat of retribution?

She checked her silver watch, a present from Madame. Such a wonderfully generous woman. A truly free spirit, and so beautiful. Adeline doted on her. Madame would be home soon, and it was time to return to Sepulchre Street. She set off past the church and its strange brick cistern, making her way through narrow, winding streets full of curious, timber-framed buildings, happily conscious of admiring glances from men who passed by. One cheeky youth wolf-whistled at her.

How many of them mistook the humble maid who grew up in poverty and never even knew her father for a woman of wealth and glamour? The thought made her skip along the pavement like a delighted child. Madame was not by nature discreet, but Rye was their bolthole, and hardly anyone knew about the home they shared here. In this gorgeous town, with its red-tiled roofs and grey walls, they were free to be themselves.

And when Madame went on her travels, there were plenty of opportunities for Adeline to fill her shoes. She loved pretending to be Madame. No longer merely a devoted servant, but a woman blessed with money and fame.

Madame was so kind to indulge these fancies. They had been together a long time, and they understood each other. Adeline liked to think that as regards appearance, it was quite easy to confuse the pair of them, and not just because Madame allowed her to borrow her clothes. Adeline was a couple of inches shorter and her eyes were hazel not blue, but they both had well-developed figures and high cheekbones. A childhood attack of chicken pox had left Adeline's complexion pockmarked, but she was expert at using make-up to disguise the scars. Her hair was mousy, and she'd always envied Madame's red tresses, prompting a generous gift of this wonderful new wig, so that the resemblance was now uncanny. It was almost as if she, Adeline, could *be* Kiki de Villiers, and take her place as the talk of the town. The sheer thrill of it made her tingle with excitement.

Her destination was tucked away in a quiet neighbourhood on the outskirts of the town. Sepulchre Street was broad but no more than eighty yards long, a cul-de-sac with a mossy stone wall at the end and no convenient passageways offering shortcuts to other parts of town. Large warehouse buildings stood on either side, but were derelict. As a result, there was seldom anyone to be seen.

The wall at the bottom of the street enclosed the rambling grounds of Sepulchre House, a Georgian building in red brick which stood at the right-hand side at the far end. There was no other private residence in Sepulchre Street, which was known locally as Graveyard Lane. Other than the name, the stone wall was the only surviving reminder of the street's history, all that remained of an ancient friary which occupied this patch of land prior to the Reformation.

Sepulchre. A place where the dead were laid to rest. There was a legend about a friar called Cantator, a member of the choir, whose love for a girl of the town led to him breaking his vow of chastity. For punishment, he was buried alive. People said his mournful voice could still be heard singing in Turkey Cock Lane. The very thought of it made Adeline shiver. But now her fears were forgotten. This place was the closest she had known to a genuine home.

Next to the house was a large garage. The building had been converted from a long-vanished cobbler's shop. Madame had taken it into her head to buy a sporty little Peugeot and that wretched man Malam had taught her to drive. His daredevil antics had entranced her for a few weeks, which seemed to Adeline like an eternity; she'd never trusted the man and she'd rejoiced when the *affaire* fizzled out. Madame drove like she did everything in her life, with gusto and taking no heed of the dangers. Much as Adeline loved her, she hated being her passenger. Madame didn't take the car up to London but liked to drive out into the countryside. Adeline had only accompanied her once and that was enough. She'd found the experience terrifying.

As she walked down the street, Adeline saw her mistress emerge from the garage and shut the wooden door. She was back! Hurrying down the street, Adeline made sure she could open the front door while Madame fiddled in a capacious handbag for her keys. Her reward was a dazzling smile that gave her a physical thrill of pleasure.

"Thank you so much, Adeline. Always there in the right place at the right time. I can rely on you, can't I?"

"You're looking radiant today, Madame."

Her mistress lowered her voice. "Are we alone?"

"Yes, the gardener finished work a couple of hours ago, and I sent the Rowbottoms home."

The Rowbottoms were a married couple who had looked after the house for years. They'd come with the property when Edwin de Villiers purchased it for his wife eighteen months ago. He'd bought it at an auction and never so much as crossed the threshold before illness reduced him to an enfeebled invalid. Now he was conveniently out of sight and out of mind. The Rowbottoms lived out, sharing a poky terraced house in Rope Walk with the wife's parents and an elderly maiden aunt. This arrangement suited everyone and guaranteed the privacy of Sepulchre House at night.

At first Madame had scarcely bothered with Rye, but lately she'd begun to spend more time here and less amid the bright lights of London. She'd talked idly about inviting her famous lover for a weekend in Sepulchre House, but Adeline was sceptical. Of all Madame's romantic liaisons, this one was undoubtedly the most hopeless. Adeline was confident that soon Madame would realise who cared for her most. The one person she could trust with her life. Naturally, she knew better than to say so out loud. She'd pretended to share her mistress's girlish excitement at the prospect of transforming the place into a love nest fit for...well, You-Know-Who. To her glee, the plan hadn't been mentioned for several days. Adeline didn't care on whose side ardour had cooled fastest, as long as it had cooled.

Kiki exhaled. "You read about our little excitement at the Hades Gallery last night?"

When they were alone together, her accent was hardly noticeable. Only in the company of people whom she wished to impress with her exoticism did she sound like a native of Lille.

"Of course. The newspapers are full of it. How frightful that you should be invited to an exhibition in order to witness the death of a madwoman!"

The words came in a rush, but Adeline's English was almost as perfect as that of her mistress. Long ago they had agreed not to converse in French. A symbolic gesture, but important. The past was dead and gone. Neither of them wanted to revisit it. All that mattered, in Adeline's mind, was their future together.

"Extraordinary. I've never seen anything like it." Kiki spoke in tones of wonder rather than horror. "I suppose she was insane, but what nerve, to put an end to yourself in such a spectacular fashion. Poor Damaris wasn't an artist so much as an actress."

Adeline helped her off with her coat, closing her eyes as she inhaled again the heady fragrance of Narcisse Noir. They went into the sitting room.

"Wonderful to be back," Kiki said, making herself comfortable in her favourite chair. "After yesterday's melodrama, I crave peace and quiet."

The maid coughed. "As it happens, Madame..."

"Yes?" Kiki said briskly.

"There is something you need to know."

The sapphire eyes examined her. "Is something wrong, Adeline? You're nervy, I can always tell. Calm yourself, please. What is the matter?"

Adeline bit her lip. "Earlier today I received a telephone call."

Her cheeks felt hot. Her mistress had insisted that they must break off all contact with their comrades from the old days. An iron rule. And Adeline had obeyed. With a single exception.

Kiki's expression tightened. "Who called?"

"I owe you an apology, Madame. The call was from Stilts."

"Stilts?" Kiki demanded. "How on earth did she know the right number to ring?"

A chill went down the maid's spine. If only the floor would open and swallow her up.

"My apologies are sincere, Madame. You know I would never want to disobey you."

"But you have disobeyed!" Kiki swore in French. "How could you be so foolish? Do you want us both to die?"

Adeline was conscious of tears pricking her eyes. "I told nobody else, Madame, I swear it. But... Stilts and I were so close. She was almost like a sister to me."

"You and I are closer," her mistress said frostily. "Or so you have always claimed."

"Oh, yes, yes, believe me! But I couldn't simply vanish into thin air without a word and never contact her again."

There was a short pause. Adeline guessed that Madame was counting to ten.

"You told nobody else, you say?"

"On my mother's life, Madame."

"You hardly knew your mother. She gave you up for a handful of francs. You hated her."

"Please, please, I beg you to believe me. Even with Stilts, I have not seen her or spoken to her for more than a year."

"Then how did she know to ring here?"

"Oh." Adeline blushed. "Well, I did call her when we were about to move. Just to let her know."

"And you told her that I'd acquired a pied-à-terre in Sussex?" Kiki let out a little cry of disgust. "Despite my insistence that nobody should know? Above all, nobody from the old days?"

Adeline hung her head. "I feel so wretched. It was a terrible mistake, so very stupid of me."

"Yes, idiotic!"

"Please, Madame, what can I do to atone?"

A pause, followed by a heavy sigh. "What's done is done. Tell me. What did Stilts have to say?"

"Marcel Ambrose is back in Britain."

There was a long silence. Madame was taking deep breaths, gathering her strength after sustaining a blow that would reduce a lesser woman to gibbering hysteria.

"Is she sure?"

"I'm afraid there is no doubt. He is sure that it is safe for him to return."

Kiki de Villiers swore again.

"I am so sorry, Madame."

"This complicates everything."

She was speaking to herself. Adeline wasn't sure what her mistress meant, but she did know that she had to make a full confession.

"And there is more."

A low groan. "What else?"

"Stilts has heard that he is asking after you. Wants to know where you are, who you are with. Everything about what you've been doing since he last saw you."

"How did she learn this?"

Adeline spread her arms. "The grapevine, you know? Stilts is popular. Her life is very different now, but she keeps in touch with old friends. Especially those from Soho. As a result she is always very…well informed."

"Precisely the reason you should have kept your mouth shut."

"Madame, I am mortified by my own folly. Will you ever forgive me?"

Kiki de Villiers breathed out. "I suppose forewarned is forearmed."

"Yes!" A pause. "But what do you think we should do?"

"I presume that Stilts hasn't spoken to Ambrose?"

"Certainly not. She is terrified of him. I said she should make herself scarce for as long as he remains in this country."

"Is he likely to go back to France in the near future?"

Adeline hesitated. "Stilts has no idea. If the police find evidence that he…"

"Ambrose makes mistakes, but he isn't a fool. He will keep one step ahead of the boys in blue."

"What will you do?"

There was a long pause. Kiki de Villiers's head was bowed. She was lost in thought. Finally she straightened her shoulders.

"I must change my plans."

The maid couldn't stop trembling. "I am frightened."

Kiki laid a hand on her arm. "You must be brave, Adeline."

"You know how vile he is, Madame!"

"And so do you."

She rolled up the left sleeve of the maid's dress to reveal a livid scar. Kiki de Villiers contemplated it for a moment before bending down to kiss it. The maid closed her eyes.

"I promise you this, Adeline," her mistress whispered. "We will never go back to the life we knew. Never again will we be slaves to that evil creature, Marcel Ambrose. This I swear to you."

———

"Yes, I'm quite alone," Kiki de Villiers said into the telephone twenty minutes later. "I've sent Adeline out to the shop. We must change our arrangements. Everything must happen this weekend."

She listened for a few moments before saying, "Marcel Ambrose is back in England. There's no time to lose."

The person at the other end of the line spoke for a full minute. Kiki squeezed the telephone receiver in her hand, waiting for another chance to speak.

"Don't you see, *chérie*? This changes nothing, it's just a matter of shifting our timetable. I hate waiting anyway, so really this is a blessing in disguise."

The other person made sceptical noises, but Kiki was not a woman who took no for an answer.

"So that's settled, then," she said at length.

There was a brief hesitation and then the voice in her ear murmured, "Yes."

"Marvellous," Kiki said. "Everything will work out perfectly. Trust me."

As she put down the receiver, she told herself that she'd got her own way again. In the end, she always did.

Chapter 10

"So the great songwriter succumbed to your charms," Martha said as Hetty poured Lapsang Souchong in the conservatory of Gaunt House. "Will you be safe if you venture out to The Risings? Do you need a chaperone?"

Rachel smiled. "Evan Tucker has no designs on my virtue."

Hetty looked round. "You don't know what some men are like. You can't learn everything from reading books."

"Don't forget that I've had my share of experiences with predators," Rachel said sharply. "Evan Tucker isn't interested in my physical assets, but my bank balance is a different matter."

Martha nodded. "Maintaining a country pile isn't easy these days. The upkeep must cost a fortune. If his songs are no longer selling and funds are running low, he may be getting desperate."

"Exactly. I'll never be his muse, but I bet he'd like to lay his hands on some of my money. Incidentally, I've got a job for you. I'd like you to speak to that nice surgeon of yours, Mr. Spruce."

Over the winter, Martha had undergone experimental surgery to repair some of the damage the acid had done to her face. Spruce was at the head of his profession, and he favoured a step-by-step approach. It would take time, but so far he had done a remarkable job.

"You have his home number. He's a busy man, but can you track him down? On the off-chance that he can tell us something more about why Giles Malam's career hit the buffers."

As Martha nodded, the door swung open and Cliff Trueman marched in.

"Any news of Sapper Butterworth?" Rachel asked.

"The police picked him up without any fuss. As soon as Malam told them what he told you, they descended on his lodgings in Farringdon. Within an hour of the bomb exploding he was being questioned."

"Did you manage to get his address?"

"Greenhill Rents, off Cowcross Street. Not the poshest neighbourhood."

"Well done. Has he been charged?"

"Not yet, but he doesn't have much of an alibi."

"He's in trouble, then."

"So it seems. According to Butterworth, his landlady took a phone message for him this morning. He's trying to earn a crust as a salesman, but he's not much good at it, so he's drifted around from job to job. Lately he's found a new line. Braces and garters. The caller said he represented a consortium of tailors and wanted to discuss a big new order with him. The address the man gave was the mews where the bomb went off. The time he was bidden for was half an hour before the explosion."

"Does he have a car?"

"No, a Flying Squirrel."

"Don't be silly, Cliff!" Hetty exclaimed.

Her husband exchanged a grin with Rachel.

"The Scott Company manufactures motorcycles called Flying Squirrels," Rachel said.

Hetty made a noise of disgust. "Now I've heard everything."

"If he was on a motorbike, he could have planted the bomb and then dashed back home, with nobody any the wiser," Martha said.

"Except that he claims he never made it," Trueman replied. "According to Butterworth, in his haste to get to this meeting, he fell downstairs as he was leaving his room and hit his head on the tiles at the bottom. Knocked himself out and when he came round, he felt so sick and dizzy that he couldn't face riding his bike. So he stayed at home and missed the appointment."

"Convenient," Rachel said.

"Very. The man he was supposed to meet called himself Taylor. Made a joke of it, in fact, according to the landlady."

"Is it possible she got confused?"

"I'm told she's as sharp as a knife, but so far, the police haven't found anyone at the mews who knows anything about a local tailor."

"How pleasingly mysterious. Can anyone corroborate Butterworth's story?"

"No. His arm is in a sling and when the police got a doctor to examine him, it was confirmed that he'd broken a bone. Plus he's got a few cuts and bruises. Nothing serious; he'll be as right as rain in no time. The coppers reckon that he could have got to the mews and back before doing a bit of damage to himself to give his alibi some substance."

"Sounds reasonable."

"The drawback is this. They have no witnesses. So far, they can't find a single person at the scene of the crime who saw anyone matching Butterworth's description. Or spotted a Flying Squirrel."

"Enquiries are continuing?" Rachel asked.

"Yes, but he'll be released shortly unless anything comes up to pin him to the scene."

"So soon?"

"He's represented by a very smart lawyer."

Martha said, "How did you find all this out so quickly?"

"A stroke of luck. I found out the duty sergeant is a chap called Heaselgrave. An uncommon name, which rang a bell. We were both invalided out from the Western Front at much the same time. To cut a long story short, the sergeant's gained the impression that I'm an outdoor clerk employed by Butterworth's solicitor."

His sister laughed. "You're developing a crafty streak in your old age."

"He's always had it," Hetty said. "You just didn't notice."

Trueman ignored them. "Heaselgrave thinks Butterworth is as guilty as sin. Like everyone else, he admires Captain Malam. War hero, and all that. So he wants the bomber behind bars pretty damned quick. All the same, he can't help feeling sorry for the suspect."

"Because of the army connection?" Martha asked.

"Exactly. Heaselgrave had shell shock, same as me. So did Malam's enemy. Ned Butterworth reckons that he's never felt right since the war."

"Plenty of men are in the same boat, so it's plausible enough."

"And irritatingly difficult to disprove," Rachel said.

Martha sipped her tea. "What if he planted the bomb and then forgot about it?"

"It's possible."

"Would a man suffering from shell shock want to keep messing around with bombs?" Hetty demanded.

"Stranger things have happened," Rachel said. "Tell me about Butterworth's solicitor."

"He's one of the city's top criminal defence briefs. Name of Rhodes-Denton. Known as the one-armed lawyer. Lost the other arm in a car smash before the war."

Rachel frowned. "I've heard the name. He's highly reputable."

"That's right. I gather he makes a joke about his own straight talking. *Not like other solicitors, saying: 'On the one hand, this, on the other hand, that...'* The police are wary of Rhodes-Denton. He's not crooked. Heaselgrave told me I'd fallen on my feet, finding a job with him. What I find peculiar is this: How did a brief of that calibre come to act for Butterworth?"

Rachel pursed her lips. "You're right. It's very odd."

"Why?" Hetty asked.

Martha said patiently, "How can a shell-shocked sapper with no money afford an expensive lawyer?"

"Good question," Trueman said. "Wish I knew the answer."

Rachel nodded. "Unless the police come up with cast-iron evidence, Rhodes-Denton will put them under so much pressure they will have to let Butterworth go home. Perhaps tomorrow you might look the man up. Reminisce about the old times in France and see what you can prise out of him."

————

"Time to sing for your supper, Jacob." Rachel stretched languidly in her armchair. "We could discuss Captain Malam and the mystery of who blew up his Bentley until we were blue in the face. I'm puzzled by something else. What on earth were you doing at the Hades Gallery? Other than making eyes at the lovely Kiki de Villiers, of course."

"I wasn't making eyes at her!" Jacob exclaimed.

They were in company with Martha, who was curled up on the settee in the newly extended drawing room, one wall of which now slid away to reveal a further sitting area, complete with well-stocked bar. The house next door had come onto the market after the elderly husband and wife who owned it died in rapid succession. Rachel had purchased the property and engaged an architect and a team of contractors to connect the two buildings to her own specifications. At a time when work was short and money tight, she'd made sure that an ambitious programme of work was completed at lightning speed yet with maximum attention to detail. As a result her home had been transformed, with alterations from top to bottom. There was now a well-ventilated sauna in the basement next to the gymnasium, while a small photographer's darkroom had metamorphosed into a scientific laboratory.

"Don't blush, Jacob; no need to be embarrassed." Martha giggled. "You understand how inquisitive we are. Don't hold back; tell us everything."

He pretended to yawn. "You do love teasing me."

"Sorry," Martha said. "You're a rising star of the fourth estate, and I ought to show you more respect. Will you be mollified if I tell you my brother is making a cocktail in your honour while Hetty cooks dinner?"

Jacob glanced at Trueman, who stood behind the bar counter, cocktail shaker in hand. Over the past six months he had become a dab hand at mixology. Harry Craddock's recipe book was his bible.

"Really?"

"Especially for you," Rachel said. "Come on, Cliff, shake that shaker as hard as you can. Don't just rock it. You're trying to wake it up, not send it to sleep."

Jacob peered across the room as Trueman went about his work. "What are you doing with the egg yolk?"

"Patience," Martha said. "We know you don't have healthy

tastes in eating or drinking. Don't fret about the egg; keep your mind on the grenadine, curaçao, and brandy."

Trueman brought four cocktails over on a silver tray. The glasses were stemmed, with wide, shallow bowls. He handed round the drinks before sitting down next to his sister.

Jacob took a sip. "Silky smooth. What is it, exactly?"

"You won't taste better even at the Savoy," Martha said. "You don't know what it's called?"

"Not a clue."

"The Bosom Caresser."

Jacob made a choking sound.

"Are you all right?" Martha lifted her glass. "To the memory of Marie Antoinette!"

"What?"

"So the story goes, the original coupe glasses were formed from a mould of Marie Antoinette's breast."

He was struggling to recover his composure. "I don't know what to say."

She gave him a demure smile. "You're always on the lookout for interesting titbits."

"Stop distracting the poor man," Rachel said. "Jacob, the floor is yours. No half-truths or evasions. We want to hear all about you and Kiki de Villiers. Come on, spit it out."

"I've been sworn to secrecy."

"We won't breathe a word."

He caught Rachel's eye. She was in an excellent humour, causing him to wonder if she had the glimmerings of an idea about why Damaris Gethin had killed herself. The bombing of Malam's car hadn't dampened her gaiety, but he knew how fast her mood could change. He was also aware that he'd gain nothing by trying to fob her off or change the subject. She was implacable.

"Very well, I give in."

"Quite right."

"How much do you know about Mrs. de Villiers?"

"Since I came to London, her name has kept cropping up in the society columns. She has a rich and elderly husband, but there's never any sign of him whenever she attends a fancy party or a West End premiere. Activities which seem to occupy most of her waking moments. She's famed for her charm as well as her good looks. One of Fleet Street's more fanciful scribes likened her to a bird of paradise. She didn't interest me. Is there more to her than meets the eye? Should I have dug deeper?"

Jacob nodded. If an oddity connected with a mystery or crime caught Rachel's imagination, she wouldn't rest until she'd satisfied her curiosity. She hated to be bored and could afford to go to extraordinary lengths to indulge her fancies. If you had something to hide, it was best to give her a very wide berth.

He cleared his throat. "I'll begin at the beginning."

"Splendid. Don't stint on the detail. Remember, Hetty's casseroles always take ages to cook."

"Kiki is a nickname. Before her marriage to Edwin de Villiers, she was Mrs. Yvette Pearson. Her previous husband, Alfred Pearson, owned a smelting works in Birmingham, though I've discovered that when they met in London, she was calling herself Yvette Charvet. The marriage didn't last long. Pearson suffered a massive heart attack in the middle of an acrimonious annual general meeting and died in front of his fellow directors and shareholders. Kiki deserted the Midlands and came back here. She didn't remain a widow for long. Before the year was out, she'd married de Villiers."

"How old was Pearson?"

"Late sixties. In case you're wondering, there's no suggestion of anything untoward about his death. The age gap doesn't seem to have worried her any more than the fact she was marrying a man with a history of heart trouble. Today she gives her age as twenty-nine. I don't wish to be ungallant, but she probably shaves off a few years. Not that it matters. As you've seen, she is beautiful and could easily pass for twenty-five."

"I presume she profited from Pearson's will?"

"As the residuary legatee, she was left comfortably off, but by no means filthy rich. In later years Pearson let his business slide. Hence the acrimony at the AGM. His stake was sold for a song shortly after his death. Perhaps she was disappointed. In any event, she wasted no time in tying the knot again."

"Tell us about de Villiers."

"He's a South African who came to Britain shortly before the Boer War. He saw the conflict coming and didn't have the stomach for it. By all accounts he's shy and self-conscious about his appearance. He was born with a cleft palate and endured several operations before it was corrected. By the time he came here, he was already a gentleman of leisure. In his early twenties he inherited a stake in the Kimberley diamond fields from his father, but business life never appealed to him. He sold out to Cecil Rhodes so that he could spend more time with his stamp collection. He is an obsessive philatelist."

Martha couldn't contain her astonishment. "He turned his back on diamonds for the sake of postage stamps?"

"Why not?" Rachel asked. "Think of them as miniature works of art and it makes more sense. The finest examples are worth a king's ransom."

"De Villiers has spent a fortune on prize specimens," Jacob said, "but he is also a canny investor who retains the best stockbrokers in the country. Despite the recent mayhem on the markets, he is five times richer today than when he first came to Britain."

"Has he been married before?"

"Yes, to an Englishwoman, but his wife died years ago and there were no children. They had a flat in London but spent most of their time in a mansion with two hundred acres in Shropshire. He was never one for the bright lights, and he always shunned publicity."

"What on earth possessed him to marry a woman like Kiki de Villiers?" Martha demanded.

"Can't you guess?" Rachel said drily.

"It was a whirlwind courtship," Jacob said. "De Villiers was sixty-seven. He doesn't like fuss, and the wedding was a small and private affair. They honeymooned in Bermuda before returning to the Cotswolds. Unfortunately, de Villiers suffered a stroke shortly after they arrived back in England. He'd had a couple of minor strokes previously, but this time he was severely incapacitated. His speech and ability to walk were badly affected, and although he's had the finest treatment money can buy, there's no chance of his making a meaningful recovery."

"So there is a pattern," Martha said. "She finds a rich man, more than twice her age. They marry and she waits for him to die. Because the husband has been in poor health for years, she doesn't have to resort to drastic measures to hasten the end."

"She needs to exercise patience," Rachel said. "And women like Mrs. de Villiers are not naturally patient."

Jacob nodded. "She spent next to no time with her husband after he fell ill. No bird of paradise wants to be caged up with an ageing invalid. I found out that she's also learned from her mistake with Pearson and made sure that she and old Edwin have a joint bank account. Supposedly so that she can supervise payment for his care. Of course, it enables her to enjoy the freedom she always craved. In fairness, the arrangement probably suits the poor old fellow as much as it does her. I can't picture the pair of them doing jigsaws together, or however young wives occupy themselves with their invalid husbands."

"So she struts around in the heart of London, while her husband moulders away in rural Shropshire?"

"You've put it in a nutshell."

Martha shifted in her chair. "You still haven't explained why you're interested in this woman."

"If I'm right, her real name is Louise Dabo, although she was usually known as Lulu Dabo."

"It's no crime to change your name," Rachel said quietly.

Martha glanced at her, but said nothing.

"No," Jacob agreed, "and it makes perfect sense if your life is in danger."

"What has she done?"

"Her mistake was to meet the wrong man."

Rachel shrugged. "Happens all the time."

"This man was very wrong. A ruthless, obsessive sadist who is wanted for murder. His name is Marcel Ambrose and for the past few years, everyone believed he was dead. Unfortunately for Kiki de Villiers, it turns out that he is alive and well and determined to find her. He believes she betrayed him, and he's out for revenge."

Chapter 11

"Can I tempt you to another Bosom Caresser?" Martha asked.

"How can I resist?" Jacob said.

As Trueman did the honours with the cocktail, Jacob toyed with a risqué joke, but one glance at Rachel made him think better of it.

"This story about Kiki de Villiers," she said with undisguised impatience. "How did you come to be involved?"

Jacob drew a breath. "The *Clarion* is a campaigning newspaper. Ever since our crusade against spiritualism came to an inglorious end up at Blackstone Fell, we've been casting around. Desperate for new battles to fight, new dragons to slay. In the end, Walter Gomersall decided it was time to go back to that old standby. White slave traffickers. Crime and corruption and the failure of the police to keep our God-fearing readers safe in their beds."

"Since you're the chief crime correspondent, the onus fell on you to dig out the stories?"

"Exactly. I reported on the murder of a man called Sobrino, one of the most notorious villains in Soho. He took one risk too many when he began an affair with a pretty young actress. She left her husband, a failed playwright who became insanely jealous. He shot Sobrino and then himself."

"I read about the case. Open-and-shut. Sobrino was no loss. Or have I missed something?"

"No, you're right. However, while I worked on the story, I came across an item in our files about Sobrino's past. My predecessor, Tom Betts, made notes for an article that was never published."

"What did the notes say?"

"Sobrino was rumoured to have killed one of his rivals, Marcel Ambrose. They were two Frenchmen, struggling for control of one of London's most lucrative rackets. There are hundreds of girls living in poverty on the Continent who will stop at nothing to cross the Channel and settle in England. They are convinced the streets really are paved with gold and they set their hearts on becoming British citizens. The likes of Sobrino or Ambrose encourage them, fill their heads with fantasies about the good life. The men are parasites, masquerading as protectors. They travel back and forth across the Channel, preying on the women they find. They offer to smuggle the poor creatures over here and find Englishmen willing to enter into marriages of convenience."

"Are many of these husbands for sale?" Martha asked.

"More than you'd guess. In their own way, the men are just as desperate as the strangers who become their wives. Out of work and finding it impossible to make ends meet. They are paid a few quid, while the women are charged a small fortune. Not that a flesh-and-blood husband is essential. Shortcuts are possible. Sometimes a woman is sold a marriage certificate."

"Forged?"

"Naturally. A woman who comes here has a simple goal. She longs to obtain a British passport so that she is no longer at risk of being deported as she makes her way in the promised land. Except that this isn't a passport to freedom. The husband, if there is one, makes himself scarce at the first opportunity. Before she can find her feet in a foreign country, she is set to work on the streets."

Rachel said, "The criminals put the fear of God in her, so she is too frightened to try to break away."

"Yes, men like Sobrino and Marcel Ambrose exploit these women ruthlessly. They think nothing of... Well, anyway, it's a lucrative trade and it was common knowledge that Sobrino wanted to rule the roost."

"Which meant getting rid of his rival."

"Ambrose rented a number of flats in the neighbourhood of Cambridge Circus. They were used for immoral purposes by the women who were under his control. One night, a fire broke out in one of the flats. The whole building had to be evacuated. The charred remains of a man were found inside the flat. The blaze was so intense that the features were unrecognisable."

Martha made a scornful noise. "A hackneyed ploy, isn't it? The hallmark of a second-rate murderer."

"Bear with me. This crime was cleverer than most. The corpse was dressed in Ambrose's clothes, or at least the remnants of them. Ambrose's teeth were perfect and so were the corpse's. The shoes were his. And Ambrose had posted a brief suicide note to a woman he knew. She was British, not French, and he was as close to her as anyone. The note said: *Goodbye Stilts. No money. No future. No point going on.* The note was typed on a Smith & Corona which was found in what was left of the flat and was signed in an illegible scrawl."

"Stilts?" Rachel asked.

"The woman's name was Annie Hitchen, but everyone knew

her by the nickname. They called her Stilts, because of her passion for high-heeled shoes."

Martha laughed. "So what was Ambrose's plan?"

"He was in the mire. Apart from being addicted to cocaine, he ran up heavy debts, to Sobrino among others. He'd sold several of his properties and there was talk of Sobrino threatening him. If he didn't cough up and then get out of England, he'd be cut into bits and fed to Sobrino's Alsatians."

"So the police fell for the suicide theory?"

"Give them some credit. According to the post-mortem, the deceased had received a blow to the head. It might have been an accident or even self-inflicted. But it was equally possible that he'd been knocked out and left in the flat to burn to death. An inquest recorded an open verdict. The private view at Scotland Yard was that Sobrino or one of his associates killed Ambrose. When Sobrino was questioned, he was cock-a-hoop. He loved taunting the police; he thought he was untouchable. Their difficulty was that he had a cast-iron alibi. On the night of the crime he was out of the country, spending his ill-gotten gains in the casino at Deauville."

Martha sniffed. "Isn't a cast-iron alibi suspicious in itself?"

"Admirably cynical." Jacob grinned. "We'll make a journalist of you yet."

"I haven't quite sunk that low."

He winced. "Tom Betts's contacts at the Yard told him they'd done their utmost to pin the crime on one of Sobrino's men. The problem was lack of evidence. Tom had a different theory. He wondered if Ambrose was still alive and had planned the whole charade."

"Why do that?"

"Sobrino was winning their long-running battle for territorial ascendancy. Ambrose's back was against the wall, but

Tom's investigations suggested that he salted away some of his money. It wasn't all squandered on the high life, as the police assumed. Ambrose knew the police would be suspicious of the convenient suicide of an unidentifiable corpse, but he reckoned that they were likely to blame Sobrino. It was good for Sobrino's ego as well as his reputation to be regarded as the man who had—one way or another—put paid to Marcel Ambrose. Especially since the police had no chance of pinning the crime on him. It left him free to do as he pleased. Until—so people were meant to think—one day he pushed a desperate man too far."

Jacob took another sip of his cocktail before putting the coupe down on a small oval table. "Tom talked to members of Ambrose's circle. Petty villains and prostitutes, mostly, who hung around a nightclub in Kingly Street called Chez Laurent. People in Soho are always tight-lipped when outsiders come along asking questions. Nobody is hated more than coppers' narks. But Tom had spent years cultivating his contacts and that helped when he went to the nightclub. Nominally, the place was owned by a man who called himself Jean Laurent. Most people thought he was French, but actually he was a petty criminal from Shoreditch called Johnny Laurence. He'd spent time in Marseille, and that's where he met Ambrose. Ambrose put up the money for Laurent to buy the club, and he called the tune. But Laurent insisted that Ambrose was dead and so did Stilts."

"Did Betts believe them?"

"He felt Stilts, at least, was telling the truth as far as she knew it. What frustrated him—and led him to suspect that there was more to the case than met the eye—was that he wasn't able to follow up a couple of leads. The club doorman was a small-time crook called Snelson who did a lot of Ambrose's legwork. Nobody had seen him since he'd had a bust-up with Ambrose, who accused him of fiddling from the petty cash. And then there was Lulu Dabo. Ambrose was besotted with her."

"Presumably Tom Betts interviewed her. Did she know that Ambrose was still alive?"

"Tom never found out. For the very good reason that Lulu had vanished as well."

Rachel stroked the rim of her coupe, as if in aid to thought. "Did Betts get a description of Snelson?"

Jacob grinned. "You're ahead of me."

"As usual," Trueman said.

"Tom discovered that Snelson was only a year or two older than Ambrose and was of much the same height and build. Tom's theory was that Ambrose lured Snelson to the flat, on the pretext of patching up their quarrel, then murdered him before setting fire to the place. After that, he'd made himself scarce. Tom was sure he'd skipped across the Channel and was lying low, waiting for Lulu to join him. He suspected that Ambrose's plan was to start up again on the Continent."

"Plausible," Rachel said.

"Unfortunately, he didn't have enough to go on to justify further expenditure of time and money."

"So the investigation petered out?"

"Yes. None of the material found its way into print. There wasn't enough evidence for him to sweet-talk the libel lawyers into giving him the green light."

"And that was where things rested until you came along?" Martha asked.

"Tom's idea that Ambrose had faked his own death seemed credible. What if the master criminal was still alive and kicking? Suppose he learned that Sobrino was dead? With his feared business rival out of the way, there was nothing to stop him from coming back to England. The police weren't looking for him;

they thought he was dead. Surely he'd find it tempting to take back control?"

Rachel leaned towards him, like a barrister conducting a cross-examination at the Old Bailey.

"What did you do?"

"Talked to my own contacts and dropped Tom's name whenever I got the chance. One of them, Sammy Postles, has an older brother called Joe who skivvies at Chez Laurent. I established that nobody had seen hide nor hair of Snelson since his disappearance, which bore out Tom Betts's thinking. When it came to Lulu Dabo, the waters were muddier."

"What do you mean?"

"Ambrose brought her to England six months before he was supposedly burned to a crisp. From the start he gave her special treatment. The other girls had rooms in squalid parts of central London to ply their trade. Lulu became Ambrose's mistress and was installed in a smart flat in Mayfair with her own maid. Pauline Mendy was imported from France to tend to her every need."

"No marriage of convenience for Lulu?"

"She didn't need one. Her parents died years ago, but rumour had it that her father was a fisherman from Great Yarmouth who died after his vessel capsized. Lulu's mother took her back to Paris and remarried a chancer called Dabo. But her real father was English."

"Meaning she was as entitled to a British passport as any of us."

"Correct, but Ambrose was as unscrupulous as every other *souteneur* in history. To begin with, he had her entertain a few wealthy gentlemen callers in Mayfair, though he allowed her to hang on to a healthy share of the proceeds. The trouble was that he became increasingly possessive. In truth, he wanted to keep her for himself. But Lulu was her own woman. The two of them quarrelled furiously. The maid let slip to Stilts that on one occasion they came to blows in the flat and Ambrose drew his knife. The maid intervened to try to protect her mistress and was slashed across the arm for her pains."

"When was this?"

"Days before Ambrose's supposed suicide."

"What about Louise Dabo? Did the police suspect her of having a hand in his death?"

"No. There was no evidence that she was in cahoots with Sobrino. The maid confirmed to them that her mistress hadn't left the flat on the night in question."

"If she was so devoted, she might have been lying."

"True," Jacob admitted. "Lulu didn't seem entirely heartbroken that Ambrose had killed himself and…"

"She could have been play-acting."

"Who knows? She told the police that Ambrose was on his uppers and was behind with the rent on the Mayfair flat. She said there was every chance she'd be evicted. From Scotland Yard's point of view, it fitted in with the theory that Sobrino was responsible for Ambrose's death."

"What exactly happened after that?"

"Within twenty-four hours, she disappeared from sight. So did the maid, Pauline. Nobody knew where they'd gone. Or if they did, they weren't willing to tell me."

"You talked to Stilts?"

"Yes. These days she's living in sin with a Communist poet. She gave nothing away. I felt sure she was frightened, but at first I wasn't sure what she was afraid of. She insisted that Ambrose was dead and she had no idea what happened to Lulu Dabo."

"Did you believe her?"

"I can't prove she was lying, but I wouldn't be surprised. Sammy Postles was equally evasive. So I went to Chez Laurent. Not that it calls itself a nightclub any longer."

Rachel nodded. "So many of these places run into trouble with the licensing laws."

"The police carried out a raid last year. Laurent was fined and threatened with closure. He turned it into a restaurant to reduce the risk of getting into bother for serving drinks after hours. The man is all smiles on the surface, but he's also a hard case. I didn't push my luck. If Ambrose was alive, he certainly wasn't going to tell me. My best bet was Joe Postles, brother of Sammy. His lips were sealed too, but I kept nagging away because he's not such a tough nut as the rest of them, and he does like to chat. He's childlike and unpredictable. I was sure he knew something."

"And did he?"

"It took time and a large chunk of the *Clarion's* expenses budget, but eventually I managed to prise something out of him. A blurred photograph taken at Chez Laurent shortly before Ambrose's supposed demise. The picture showed Marcel Ambrose with his arm around an attractive woman. Joe Postles told me that was Lulu Dabo. He was maddeningly cryptic; I think he was scared he'd already gone too far. All he said was: *Look to the lady.*"

"I don't suppose he realised he was quoting from *Macbeth*," Rachel murmured. "You have the picture?"

Jacob reached inside his jacket pocket. With a conjuror's flourish, he produced a leather wallet. He slid out a photograph and placed it on the table for Rachel and the Truemans to study.

The image was a close-up of two people, caught in profile. One was a swarthy, well-dressed man in his late thirties. His companion was a blonde-haired woman with a spit curl on her cheek.

"How could anyone tell if that was her?" Martha said after lengthy consideration. "There is a likeness to the photographs I've seen of Kiki de Villiers, but I'd never swear to it in a court of law."

"Her hair is a different colour and cut," Rachel said, "and the make-up is an effective disguise."

"See what you think of this," Jacob said smugly.

He produced another snapshot, this time a clipping from the *Clarion*. The caption read: *American golfer Jim Dobie sharing a joke with Mrs. Kiki de Villiers at Claridge's*. The camera had captured the handsome pair in profile as they sat on adjoining bar stools.

"Clever!" Martha cried. "Taken from almost the same angle. I suppose…yes, the bone structure is identical. But it's hardly proof that the two of them are one and the same. Far from it."

"Look closely at her eyes," Jacob said. "Very, very closely."

The two young women peered at the pictures. Rachel uttered a small cry.

"There's a faint mark—it might be caused by the poor quality of the photographs, but it's in exactly the same position in each case."

"Where?" Martha screwed up her own eyes to peer at the two images. "Oh…yes. So tiny that it's almost impossible to make out. In the left eye of each woman."

"Yes," Jacob said. "You can't tell from the photographs, but the pupil resembles a keyhole."

"So it isn't simply a smudge on the paper?"

"I did some research," Jacob said proudly. "That mark is a recognised medical condition, but it's far from common. A birth abnormality, which the medics call coloboma. Having seen Kiki de Villiers in the flesh, I can tell you that her left eye is affected in precisely that way."

"And Lulu Dabo?" Rachel asked.

"Stilts wouldn't tell me any more, but Sammy Postles was more helpful. It's clear that he found Lulu extremely attractive, but she was out of his league. Besides, he was too scared of

Ambrose to do anything more than admire her from a distance. He told me Lulu had a coloboma in her left eye. Not that he knew that term."

"It could be a coincidence," Martha said.

"But we distrust coincidences, don't we?" Rachel said.

"There will be other women with a similar mark on their left eye."

"Not many," Jacob said. "An optician told me that coloboma affects about one person in every ten thousand."

"Very well, I'm persuaded," Rachel said. "Excellent work, Jacob."

"So this means that Lulu didn't follow Marcel Ambrose to France," he said. "Instead she changed her appearance—apart from the coloboma—and reinvented herself as a social butterfly."

"Wasn't she taking a massive risk, given her previous association with Ambrose?" Martha asked.

"She's a born risk-taker. That's clear from everything I've heard about her."

"Like our friend Captain Malam," the maid said. "Wouldn't it be safer to lie low?"

"Not necessarily, if she believed Marcel Ambrose was dead or that she was safely out of reach because he was stuck in France. She had a new life under a new name. If Ambrose couldn't come back to haunt her, all she had to worry about was the chance that someone who knew her from the old days would recognise her. Maybe Stilts or one or other of the Postles brothers did. But even if someone threatened her with exposure, what's the worst that could happen?"

Rachel nodded. "Kiki de Villiers has never pretended to be an innocent. And she's certainly no shrinking violet. Who knows, disclosure of a racy past might simply burnish her reputation."

"What about Pauline?" Martha asked.

"I discovered that Mrs. de Villiers has a maid, with whom she seems to be on very close terms. The maid's name is Adeline. Not so very different from Pauline."

He allowed himself a theatrical pause. "Do you want to hear my theory?"

"We're agog," Rachel murmured.

Trueman could barely curb his impatience. "Get on with it."

"I reckon Ambrose's plan was that Lulu and Pauline would join him in France once it was safe to do so without attracting suspicion. But he was the sort who always keeps his cards close to his chest. So his apparent death came as a complete shock to his lover."

"You think he meant to break the news that he was alive and give her instructions about coming to France when the hue and cry had died down?" Rachel asked.

"Yes. But Lulu moved fast and didn't give him the chance. She was bored with being a kept woman. I think that when she entertained men at the flat in Mayfair, she came up with a strategy of her own. According to Stilts, her clients were all cut from the same cloth. They were old and rich, men with kinks who were willing to spend whatever it took to indulge them. My guess is that she saw an escape route. What if she married one of them?"

Rachel raised her eyebrows. "Exchanging one form of bondage for another?"

"She was just as adept as Ambrose when it came to confusing identities. As soon as he was out of her life, she used the money she'd saved to make sure he stayed out of her life. She became Yvette Charvet and cosied up to Pearson. I bet he was a former client who had taken a shine to her. Edwin de Villiers fitted the same template. Rich older men with serious health problems and no children or prospective heirs to complicate matters. With her protector out of the way, she was free to pursue them at her leisure. The old men were entranced by her. Just like Ambrose."

"I still say she's taken an enormous risk," Martha said. "Flaunting herself in public."

She looked meaningfully at Rachel as she spoke, Jacob noticed, though he couldn't guess what was in her mind.

"Look at it from her point of view. She's an extrovert blessed with good looks and a gift for charming people. Above all, men. Skulking in the shadows for the rest of her life would seem like penal servitude to someone like that. Sobrino had no quarrel with her, and while he was strutting around Soho, there was no danger of Ambrose forcing his way back into her life. Even if it turned out he was alive, after all. Lulu probably suspected that he was safely on the other side of the Channel."

"Sobrino's death changed everything," Martha said.

"Precisely. Even then, she must have hoped that if Ambrose was alive, he would stay in France."

"What makes you think he is back?"

"I covered Joe's palm with silver and finally he let something slip. Brother Sammy confirmed it this afternoon."

"What do you propose to do?" Rachel asked.

"After dinner, I'm heading for Chez Laurent. A long shot, but you never know. I might just bump into a dead man."

"If Ambrose is so fond of violence, you'd better take care."

"Don't worry. I'll watch my step."

Rachel finished her cocktail. "I'd like to come with you."

He stared at her. "Chez Laurent is no place—"

"For a lady? That's where you're wrong. From what I read in the newspapers, the restaurant is a favourite haunt of actresses and aristocratic ladies alike. It's the last word in chic. Are you suggesting that I wouldn't fit in?"

"Well, no, but…" He threw a look of appeal to Trueman.

"I don't like the sound of it," the big man said. "Why run such a risk?"

Rachel's eyes gleamed with excitement. "Because life without danger isn't worth living. We agreed that long ago, remember?"

Chapter 12

"First-rate brandy, Jarvis." Sir Morton Wragg raised the snifter to his nose. "Prune and walnut aroma, hints of cedar and spice."

A ruddy-faced, hefty man in his early fifties, he looked like a gentleman farmer. He did own a two-hundred-acre farmstead in Lancashire, but he also had a finger in countless different pies. A businessman first and last, his rare gift for making money had seen him continue to prosper despite the Slump. Having built his fortune in shipping, he'd devoted the twenties to diversifying his interests. Now he owned everything from companies that built aircraft and motor cars to a West End theatre and a luxurious private yacht. Currently his favourite plaything was the *Clarion*. Rivals mocked "Wragg's rag," but their derision was tainted by jealousy and possibly dread. Sir Morton was determined to make the *Clarion* the most popular and influential newspaper in Britain, and he was renowned for getting his own way.

As he allowed the Armagnac to caress his tongue, a silent waiter cleared the plates from the table with unobtrusive efficiency before making himself scarce.

"An admirable complement to a splendid dinner. My

congratulations." Wragg chortled. "Although perhaps I should congratulate the British taxpayer instead?"

He and Sir Hector Jarvis were facing each other, occupying high-backed chairs on either side of a long oak table large enough to accommodate a dozen people. Oil paintings of nineteenth-century prime ministers hung from the walls. A blazing log fire warmed the air. This private dining room was immediately beneath Sir Hector's office, but Wragg was blissfully unaware of the existence of the small department on the Top Corridor. As far as he was concerned, Sir Hector was simply a very senior civil servant, a prince among the pen-pushers.

Sir Hector patted his ample stomach. "I like to think the Great British public receive excellent value for their investment. If consulted, I'm confident they would agree the vital necessity of keeping their servants well fed and watered. Ready, willing, and able to perform their duties on behalf of King and country with diligence and determination."

Sir Hector and Wragg were acquaintances rather than friends. Both men were members of the Marylebone Cricket Club, with wives prominent in the Council for the Preservation of Rural England.

"Generous of you to allow an interloper from Fleet Street to partake of such excellent fare," Wragg said. "Especially after the *Clarion* has devoted so many column inches to denouncing the excesses of the privileged elite."

"Freedom of the press, old boy." Sir Hector was a picture of corpulent geniality. "Baldwin may describe you newspaper barons as an insolent plutocracy, but I take a more nuanced view."

"You do?"

"Absolutely, my dear Wragg. I firmly believe that you're much more responsible than people believe. Some of you, at any rate."

Wragg laughed. "The leader of the opposition's latest attack on our competitors delighted me. Beaverbrook and Rothermere must be spitting feathers." He mimicked the politician's sonorous tones. "'Power without responsibility, the prerogative of the harlot through the ages.' Damned amusing. Finest speech he's ever made."

"That line was actually written by Baldwin's cousin."

Wragg raised bushy eyebrows. "His cousin?"

"Rudyard Kipling."

"Ah, well. Connections count for a great deal in this world. The *Express* and *Mail* didn't report Baldwin's words, but we gave him pride of place on the front page. I insisted on writing our leader article myself."

"Recognised your turn of phrase, old boy. First-class piece of writing. You hit the nail on the head. These are dark days, as you rightly say. The fourth estate must be vigilant to protect the national interest. An immeasurably nobler calling than chasing circulation for the sake of it. Let alone attacking the authorities simply in order to further personal political ambitions."

"Rest assured, I'm not like the others. I'd rather sit on a bed of nails than on a bench in Parliament."

"Nicely put." Sir Hector clicked his tongue. "I was especially glad to read your stirring words given that the *Clarion* is sometimes accused of wallowing in filth."

"I say." Wragg recoiled as if he'd just been bitten by a pet spaniel. "Steady on, Jarvis."

"Forgive me," Sir Hector said comfortably. "You often say that you don't like people to beat about the bush, so I took you at your word. The fact is that mention of responsibility brings me to the reason I wanted to have a quiet chat with you."

"Oh, yes?" Wragg's tone had become terse. "When your note arrived at my office, I did wonder if there was an ulterior motive for such munificent hospitality at short notice."

"Bless my soul, you're far too sharp for me." Sir Hector wagged a plump finger. "Actually, there are two rather ticklish matters I need to raise."

"Two?"

"The first thing is that I hope to beg a favour of you."

"You can always ask," Wragg said.

Sir Hector polished his pince-nez. "You see, I've heard a whisper that your crime reporter has taken an interest in a certain lady."

Wragg stared. "What do you mean?"

"Oh, dear. I always prefer to remain discreet. I remember an old saying from my soldiering days. No names, no pack drill. Of course, old boy, I realise you didn't spend any time in the army, but I'm sure even a newspaper owner will agree that it's a wise precept."

Not many people realised that Sir Morton Wragg had managed to reach the age of fifty-three without ever serving in the forces. It wasn't something he cared to broadcast, although he seized every opportunity to ensure that the *Clarion* trumpeted its support for the defence of the realm.

Through gritted teeth he said, "You need to call a spade a spade. That's the trouble with you mandarins. If you don't explain what you're talking about, how can I be of assistance?"

"Very well, if you insist. The person in question is Mrs. de Villiers. Word has reached me that her background is being investigated. Your chap is enquiring into her past history. Talking to the people in her circle."

Sir Morton made a dismissive gesture with his hand. "These are editorial matters."

"I gather you take a close interest."

"I can't possibly comment."

"In confidence?"

"In confidence, you are correct."

"Still in confidence, is it possible that the *Clarion* may make certain allegations about the lady?"

"You can be sure," Wragg said stiffly, "that we employ the best lawyers in London. They are unquestionably the most expensive. Gomersall, my editor, is as smart as paint. He'll not publish anything that isn't checked and substantiated. We go to great lengths to avoid being hauled up before the courts. If necessary, our reporters will secure signed and witnessed affidavits from people they interview, testifying to the truth of what is said."

"Commendable precautions," Sir Hector murmured. "Pardon me, Wragg. I didn't mean to impugn the integrity of your correspondent's research. My point is simple. This story involving Mrs. de Villiers must not see the light of day."

Wragg gazed at him in stupefaction. His features were florid at the best of times. Now his complexion had turned the colour of an overripe beetroot.

"What in God's name do you mean? The blessed woman is always posing for photographers at some party or theatrical premiere. Don't tell me she's suddenly become a shrinking violet. She thrives on attention, loves to be talked about. Publicity is her oxygen, celebrity her lifeblood."

Sir Hector considered Wragg through his pince-nez. "What the lady wants is neither here nor there. The fact remains that the investigation must stop. The story needs to be—what's that term you fellows use?—spiked."

He spat out the final word as if it were poison. Wragg swallowed the rest of his brandy before replying.

"You're asking the impossible."

"Hmmm. Perhaps I haven't been sufficiently clear. It is contrary to the national interest for the story to be published. Ergo, as a self-proclaimed guardian of the national interest, the *Clarion* cannot print it."

"Ridiculous. How can anything we write about that woman possibly be contrary to the national interest?"

"I am sure you'll appreciate," Sir Hector said wistfully, "I am not at liberty to divulge any details. Not even to you, old boy."

"You mean that I'm supposed simply to take your word for it?"

"Yes," Sir Hector said, "if you put it in those terms, old boy, that is exactly what I mean."

"Out of the question. Dammit, man, you must realise it can't be done. Even if I were to accept what you are saying to me…"

"I trust you will," Sir Hector said amiably, "as one gentleman to another."

"Even then," Wragg continued, "there is such a thing as editorial independence. Gomersall wouldn't tolerate being overruled on such a matter. He has his pride. He'd resign first."

"Plenty more editors in the sea. Or in the Street of Shame, to use that vulgar term. As proprietor, you have the power. The ultimate right of veto."

"In theory, yes, but only in extreme circumstances. You simply can't expect me to insist that a story is dropped on your say-so. It's not as if the War Office has issued a D-notice." He puffed out his red cheeks. "Sorry, Jarvis. I enjoyed our chinwag over dinner, but I can't accede to your request."

"A D-notice isn't appropriate in this case." Sir Hector removed the pince-nez. His expression was mournful. "Even if it were, such things are purely advisory, as you well know. The reality is that the powers-that-be have to rely on the goodwill and good sense of the press."

"Why on earth would the powers-that-be have the faintest interest in an empty-headed clothes horse like Kiki de Villiers?" Wragg grunted. "Met her once at a charity banquet. A good-looking temptress, I'll grant you. Men cluster round her like moths to a flame. Frankly, if you're bothered about some junior minister who has fallen for her charms, that's his lookout. The same goes if he's in the cabinet. Even if it's that hapless old fool Ramsay MacDonald himself. Anyway, his stock is so low that a bit of saucy gossip would do his reputation a power of good. Whatever the truth, however you slice it, there's no possible justification for censorship."

Sir Hector drank some brandy. "I was afraid you might feel like that. That is your final word?"

Wragg folded his beefy arms. "It is."

Sir Hector heaved his bulky frame out of his chair and plodded towards an antique brass trolley at the far side of the room. A buff envelope nestled in between a decanter and a whisky bottle. He picked it up and dropped it on the dining table, under Wragg's nose.

"I mentioned there were a couple of things I wanted to speak to you about."

"I hope the second isn't as outlandish as the first."

"I'm afraid the question of press freedom raises its ugly head again," Sir Hector said. "This time, it concerns one of your competitors, but not the *Mail* or the *Express* or the *Mirror*. I wanted to forewarn you about a piece that will run in the *Witness* tomorrow."

Wragg wrinkled his nose, as if his host had just uttered an obscenity. "The gutter press, you mean."

"Their standards are lower than the *Clarion*'s," Sir Hector agreed. "I was anxious to give you advance notice of the story, given your personal involvement. Felt it was only fair."

"What in heaven's name do you mean?"

"Better for you to read the affidavit for yourself, old boy."

"Affidavit?"

"Actually, it's a fair copy. The original is locked in a safe. The *Clarion* isn't alone in preferring to seek the comfort of a sworn statement before committing sensational reports to black and white. Especially when memories are so short."

"I don't—"

Sir Hector interrupted. "The events described in the affidavit go back some time, but they retain…a certain interest to the prurient."

He took a foolscap sheet out of the envelope and passed it to his guest.

As Sir Morton Wragg studied the contents of the affidavit, the colour drained from his face. The hand holding the piece of paper trembled as he put it down on the table.

"Where did you find him?" His voice was hoarse, his demeanour uncomprehending.

Sir Hector clicked his tongue. "You will understand that I am not at liberty to disclose anything about the unfortunate young man who swore the affidavit. Actually, I see he was *very* young at the time of the encounters he describes. Doesn't he refer to an expensive present given to him on his seventeenth birthday?"

"It was a long time ago," Wragg said in a croak. "There was a war on."

"True." Sir Hector's voice hardened. "And of course, you were fortunate enough to be in London. You weren't stuck in the mud on a foreign field, risking your neck for King and country. The exemption you relied on was work of national importance, wasn't it? I have to say, it's a phrase I never cared for. Covers a multitude of sins, so to speak. Mind you, so many shocking and sinful things happen at times of tragedy."

He sat back in his chair, giving the words a chance to sink in, keeping his gaze fixed on his guest. "Of course, that's one of the reasons why we are so anxious to ensure that the country remains on an even keel."

There was a long pause. The newspaper proprietor gave a heavy sigh but words seemed to elude him.

"We are living through an unhappy chapter in our national story, old boy." Sir Hector's voice had lost its edge. He sounded melancholic. "Even the highest in the land risk losing everything. They receive scant sympathy from people suffering the ravages of poverty and unemployment. Fair enough, some may say. Yet to my mind, even their personal misfortunes strike me as matters for regret. However avoidable, however shameful the mistakes they made."

Wragg glared at the sheet of paper and took a deep breath.

"I don't suppose there is any point in telling you that this is a disgraceful tissue of lies, concocted by an unhinged and vengeful individual whom, against my better judgement, I did my utmost to help at considerable personal cost?"

The words hung in the air for fully half a minute before Sir Hector clicked his tongue again.

"None whatsoever, old boy."

"Very well." Wragg's voice was almost inaudible. "What do you want me to do?"

"I explained earlier," Sir Hector said equably. "I merely hope to persuade you that, in the matter of Mrs. de Villiers, the *Clarion* should adhere to its admirable tradition of exercising its immense power responsibly. As I said, it's a question of putting the national interest first."

There was another pause before Wragg said in a muffled voice, "Assume that the *Clarion* abandons its current investigation into Mrs. de Villiers and prints nothing about the lady other than the bland tittle-tattle that appears on every society page in the land."

"Yes?"

"What happens then to this farrago of disgusting nonsense?"

Sir Hector picked up the sheet and envelope and ambled across the room. Standing by the fireplace, he said, "Please don't upset yourself, old boy. I should make it clear that nobody at the *Witness* has read the affidavit. A messenger was due to take it to their offices at nine o'clock this evening. You will understand now why I was so anxious to discuss the question of freedom of the press."

There was another pause. Wragg bowed his head.

"On reflection, you are right. I may have spoken too hastily."

"Couldn't agree more."

"We are both Englishmen; we both love our country."

"Indeed."

"You're a man of your word, and so am I. On that basis, let me give you this personal assurance. The *Clarion* will print something untoward about Mrs. de Villiers over my dead body."

There was a pause.

Sir Hector said silkily, "I sincerely hope it won't come to that."

"Do we have an agreement?"

Sir Hector tossed the sheet of paper into the flames, watched it curl and burn.

"A civilised understanding between gentlemen, old boy? Between loyal subjects, two knights of the realm? Absolutely."

"If you allow me to make use of your telephone, I'll summon Gomersall to an urgent meeting." The newspaper owner exhaled. "As regards the original of the affidavit..."

A brisk shake of the head. "Perhaps in the fullness of time, an inventory of paperwork in safekeeping will be carried out. Documents of no possible value will be disposed of."

"How would you define 'the fullness of time'?"

Sir Hector smiled. "Civil servants are often accused by newspapermen of being overly fond of bureaucracy and detail. A fair criticism, arguably. Best not to worry too much about precise definitions, don't you think? We don't really need them, you and I. Not as men of honour."

———

"I must be dreaming." Walter Gomersall made an elaborate performance of rubbing his eyes. "For a moment, sir, I almost thought you were asking me to abandon our latest investigation."

"Sarcasm doesn't suit you," Sir Morton Wragg snapped. "The position is simple. Leave Mrs. de Villiers alone. Flint can find something else to write about."

They were meeting in his sumptuous office in Covent Garden. Wragg House was the nerve centre of his business empire. Like Sir Hector, he thought it best to conduct difficult conversations on ground of his own choosing.

Gomersall chewed a hangnail. "What is this all about? I have a right to know."

The men were both Lancastrians. Wragg's birthplace was in Aigburth, on the banks of the River Mersey, while Gomersall came from the county's industrial heartlands. They shared a healthy contempt for the softness of southern England and a robust belief in plain speaking. Occasionally they shouted at each other, but only in private. Gomersall was a hired hand, but he gave as good as he got. Not only did Wragg respect him for it, but he'd made Gomersall the highest paid editor on Fleet Street.

"I can't break a confidence," he said. "All you need to know is that it's a matter of the national interest."

Gomersall peered at his employer's rubicund face, but found no clues. "Curiouser and curiouser. What has the lady been up to? Don't tell me she's a fledgling Mata Hari?"

"I'm not at liberty to say."

"Sorry, sir," Gomersall growled, "but that isn't good enough."

"It will have to do."

"Young Flint has sweated blood over that story, and he has a habit of delivering the goods. Look at his scoop about the woman who cut off her own head. An unexpected dividend of the Kiki de Villiers investigation."

"Then at least his labours haven't been in vain."

"But sir..."

"My decision is final," Wragg's temper was fraying. "Break the news to Flint, will you? And make sure he obeys instructions. He's a loose cannon. Far too full of himself for a young whipper-snapper. You need to rein him in. I won't have him going off on a frolic of his own."

"The lad's raw, but he's a damn good reporter with a real nose for a story. If you ask me—"

"Are you deaf, man? The matter is settled. No ifs, no buts. Kill the story. I'm not asking you. I'm telling you."

Gomersall's face was now as crimson as his proprietor's. "Sir Morton, may I remind you that I am the editor of the *Clarion*? We agreed I would have editorial independence and control."

"There are limits," Wragg said. "And you're in danger of exceeding your authority."

"Then perhaps, sir," Gomersall said, "you wish to accept my resignation?"

"If it comes to that, by all means." Wragg stared back at his editor. "I told you, this is a matter of the national..."

"Interest, yes! But what exactly are we talking about?" Gomersall sprang up and jabbed a finger at his employer. "Do you really know or have you swallowed whatever some government lackey has fed you? The *Clarion* can't be beholden to mysterious vested interests. For all I know, you've been spun a line by the Bolsheviks."

"You won't need to resign if I dismiss you without notice for insubordination," Wragg bellowed. "Flint will get his marching orders too, if he's equally intransigent."

"I..."

"And don't think that the pair of you can flounce off and join the competition!"

Wragg heaved himself to his feet, breathing hard. Gomersall caught the whiff of brandy fumes. He opened his mouth to speak, but his employer hadn't finished.

"Or take the de Villiers story anywhere else. Don't think about kicking up a rumpus. If you do, I'll bloody well make sure that neither you nor Flint ever works in England again. And that's before the powers-that-be weigh in."

"What do you mean?"

"They are slow to anger, but take it from me, they are deadly serious. You'll be shining shoes and begging for spare farthings by the time they have finished with you. If you're lucky."

Walter Gomersall was no coward, but he entertained a healthy cynicism about becoming a martyr to a cause. Principles were all well and good, but they didn't pay the mortgage on his new house in Hampstead, let alone his sons' exorbitant school fees. As for pride, wasn't it a deadly sin? Never before had he seen Sir Morton Wragg in such a fury. Whatever pressure was being put on him must be crucifying. The man looked as if he were about to burst a blood vessel.

He took a deep breath.

"Perhaps I'm not seeing the full picture, Sir Morton."

"You're damned right you're not!"

"If I am to have a conversation with Flint, it would help to have some details."

"You're running a newspaper, not the bloody Oxford Union! Warn him off. If he knows what's good for him, he'll toe the line."

Gomersall bit his tongue.

"Understood?"

A long pause. Gomersall was a man of principle, but he didn't believe in cutting off his nose to spite his face. Whatever had got into old Wragg, there was no doubting his determination, or his ability to make good his threats. The time had come to accept the inevitable. At least for the time being.

"Understood, sir."

Chapter 13

The entrance to Chez Laurent was halfway down a poorly lit passageway which ran off Kingly Street. From the outside, the narrow building looked insignificant and devoid of character. The windows were heavily shuttered so that you couldn't see if the lights were on inside. A short flight of stone steps led up to the front door, but there was no canopy and no nameplate. If you didn't know the place existed, you would simply walk on by. And that was how it was supposed to be. Everyone who needed to do so knew where to find Chez Laurent.

"Ready?" Jacob asked.

"Absolutely." Rachel took his arm.

Trueman had dropped them off on Great Marlborough Street, opposite the archway and the Liberty Clock. During the short drive, he'd promised to remain close at hand. Just in case.

A smart commissionaire greeted them in the lobby. No need to show membership cards; the former nightclub was now a restaurant with a grill room for private dining, and a large ball-room. Rachel looked radiant, Jacob thought, as a cloakroom attendant took their coats. Just before they'd left Gaunt House, she'd popped upstairs and changed into an evening gown. The sheer black silk crepe, luxurious yet lightweight, hugged her body like a second skin. Catching his glance, she posed for him. Her smile was teasing.

"You approve?"

"Of your new dress?" He felt like a gawky schoolboy. "It's... amazing."

Until now he'd been so preoccupied with the scruffiness of his own suit that he'd paid little attention to the subtle design of Rachel's gown. The raised quilting seemed to trace the bones of her body.

"Tricks of the eye like this delight me," she said. "The designer is a favourite of mine. She shares my passion for the surreal and this dress is her latest experiment. Outlandish, even by her standards. She's such a perfectionist; she isn't satisfied with what she's done. She spoke about putting it to one side and doing more work on it some other time. But I wanted to wear it now. It appeals to my sense of the macabre."

"I've never seen anything like it."

"She stitched the outlines of human bones on the surface, then fed cotton through the lining to raise the fabric of the dress away from my skin. Or, to save your blushes, away from the black petticoat I'm wearing underneath. See how on the surface of the dress, the bones go through the thigh and connect with the ribcage, all the way up to the collarbone?" She paused before adding dreamily, "Tracing my body's skeleton."

He cleared his throat. "I won't ask how much it cost."

"No, don't. It'll be a nuisance if you faint when we have work to do. Money well spent, that's all you need to know."

"Yes," he breathed.

Passing through a pair of muslin glass doors, they found themselves on a mezzanine level which formed a wide balcony. There was an imposing Otis lift with brass doors and a

diamond-shaped window as well as thickly carpeted steps leading up to the upper floors and a spiral staircase which wound
down to the ballroom. Rachel moved to the black wrought-iron
railings and contemplated the large oval dance floor. The band
was playing "Body and Soul."

Jacob risked a quick glance at her slender figure as she
scanned her surroundings with an intensity that suggested she
was committing the layout to memory. How easy to become
intoxicated by the musky fragrance of Chanel, the cool touch
of her hand when it brushed against his. He bit his lip and told
himself not to get carried away. Rachel was out of bounds.

She indicated the spiral staircase. "Shall we?"

It was eleven o'clock and, by the standards of Chez Laurent,
the night was young, but already the ballroom was filling up. The
decor was a sumptuous mix of dusky rose, peach, and vintage
gold. Opposite the recess for the small orchestra was a huge frieze
in the manner of Toulouse-Lautrec depicting Montmartre at twi-
light. On either side of the oval dance floor were parallel rows of
small tables. Kaleidoscopic shafts of light projected down from
the ceiling, bathing dancers and musicians alike in ever-changing
colours, rich shades of orange, purple, red, and blue.

As if to celebrate Rachel's arrival, the band struck up with
"Remarkable Girl." She placed her gold mesh clutch bag on a
vacant table next to the ebony dance floor.

"Foxtrot?"

"Why not?"

Jacob enjoyed dancing, although his technique owed more
to enthusiasm than finesse. Holding Rachel in a gentle embrace,
he inhaled her perfume while improvising with his footwork.
Her eyes were half closed as she glided effortlessly around the
floor. Under the coloured lights, she was a vision of glamour, yet
as enigmatic as ever in her skeleton dress.

He dared not imagine what was going through her mind and could only hope she wasn't hating every moment. Perhaps she was afraid he'd tread on her toes. But then, she never seemed to be afraid of anything. To be so close to her was enough to make any man swoon.

The song came to an end. Rachel clapped and gave him a little bow.

"When did you learn to dance so well?" he asked.

"Trueman taught me on Gaunt. When the old judge was confined to bed and no longer able to tell anyone what they could or couldn't do."

"Trueman?"

"Wipe that look off your face. A heavyweight he may be, but he's surprisingly light on his feet."

"I'll take your word for it," Jacob said. "There's obviously more to him than meets the eye."

"There's more to everyone than meets the eye, Jacob. How many times do I have to say it? That's what makes human nature infinitely fascinating."

The band launched into "You're Driving Me Crazy." The composer might have had Rachel Savernake in mind, Jacob reflected. As they whirled around the floor, he spotted Laurent himself, a thickset man with sleek black hair and a toothbrush moustache. He was strolling around the tables, bestowing smiles on all and sundry. As Laurent saw him, he stiffened. The smile faded, but he gave no other sign of recognising Jacob before hurrying off up the spiral staircase.

"Are you all right?" Rachel murmured.

"Yes," he said. "Definitely."

"Only you have such a faraway look. Even though it's ages since you indulged in that Bosom Caresser."

He couldn't always tell when she was making fun of him,

although he had a gloomy suspicion that it was most of the time.

"I'm fine. Did you see the chap with the moustache?"

"Laurent?"

"You know him?"

"No, but he struts around as though he owns the place. Did you rub him up the wrong way when you questioned him? He didn't look overjoyed to see you."

"The interview was perfectly cordial. He was evasive and probably dishonest, but that's par for the course."

"I wonder what happened to wipe the smirk off his face."

"He probably thinks I'm here to stir up trouble and that I've brought you along as decorative camouflage."

"I've never been described as decorative camouflage before."

Wondering if he'd put his foot in it, he said hastily, "I'd best have a word with Joe Postles. What would you like to drink?"

"You might tempt me with a Dirty Martini."

"Your wish is my command." He tried to sound insouciant, but wasn't sure he'd succeeded. He consoled himself with the reflection that Rachel Savernake disconcerted not only him, but almost everyone else she met.

Two drinks waiters were threading through the crowd, but Jacob dodged their gaze and made for the bar. Joe Postles was at the far end of the counter with his back to Jacob, straining a cocktail with a deliberation so exaggerated it was almost comical. By nature he struck Jacob as childish, especially in his hero-worship of his brother, the former football star. Both the Postles drank too much; otherwise there was no obvious resemblance. Joe was a small, plump fellow in his late thirties with thinning curls and sad brown eyes. The squashed-up, juvenile features made him look like a dissolute cherub.

One of the waiters put a tray on the counter and said something to Joe. When the little man turned, he caught Jacob's eye. Jacob gave him a friendly nod, only to be rewarded with a look of panic. Joe looked over his shoulder before scuttling off through a door at the back of the bar, much to the waiter's bewilderment.

"Was it something I said?" Jacob said as the other barman poured his drinks.

The barman sniggered. "No offence, sir. If you know anything about Joe, you'll know he's a law to himself. Been like a cat on hot bricks all evening."

"What's up?"

A shake of the head. "I keep myself to myself, sir. Best way, in my experience. Was that everything?"

Jacob paid and took the drinks to their table. As the band launched into "You Never Did That Before," he told Rachel what had happened.

"Pity," he said. "Looks as though he's not in the mood to talk."

"Cheers." She raised her glass. "Why do you think that might be?"

"He's a funny cove. Unpredictable and occasionally volatile. According to Sammy, Laurent has sacked him more than once. If it wasn't for Sammy pleading on his behalf, he'd be walking the streets."

"There might be more to it than that." She tasted her drink. "Delicious."

"What do you mean?"

"The olive brine is *just* salty enough."

"No." For all her charm, Rachel could be infuriating. "I mean, why would Joe Postles scoot off at the sight of me?"

"You have this devastating effect on people. First Laurent, then Joe Postles." She allowed herself a rueful smile. "Sorry. I'm enjoying my night out too much. I meant that perhaps someone has given them a reason to be afraid of speaking to you again."

"Marcel Ambrose?"

"You did well to find out that he's returned from the dead. Now he's in England, he won't waste any time in going back to his old haunts and seeking to re-establish his business interests, will he?"

"You're right."

"For all we know, he's tucking into a steak dinner up in the grill room."

"I'm not so sure that…"

His voice trailed away as the lift doors opened on the other side of the ballroom. The gates inside rolled apart and a diminutive figure emerged. Joe Postles strode purposefully towards them.

"Do you know?" Rachel murmured. "I have a feeling we're just about to find out."

Jacob grinned as the barman reached their table. "Evening, Joe. For a moment there, I thought you were avoiding me."

Joe Postles wasn't smiling. Even in the fuggy, smoke-filled air of the ballroom, the reek of stale beer on him was unmistakable.

"There's someone wants to see you, Mr. Flint."

"Oh, yes, who's that?"

"Right now, if you don't mind."

"Fair enough. Send them over."

"Upstairs, Mr. Flint."

Jacob threw a wary glance at Rachel, like a pupil nervous of a teacher's disapproval. She was swaying slightly to the rhythm of the band's rendition of "Somebody Stole My Gal."

"Don't mind me, dearie," she said in tinkling falsetto with a hint of Cockney. "I'll just sit here like a wallflower till you important gents have finished your precious business."

She took a noisy slurp of her martini and made a shooing gesture.

Jacob got to his feet. "I'll only be five minutes."

"Oh, take your time, dearie," she said with a roguish titter. "No need to rush. You and me, we've got all night."

"Come on, Mr. Flint." Joe Postles was twitching with impatience. "Not everyone has got all night."

Jacob followed him. An attendant was holding the lift doors open for them. A huge man whose smart uniform was a couple of sizes too small for him, he looked as if he'd be more at home at the top of a beanstalk.

"Joe, what's this all about?" Jacob asked.

The little man shook his head. "I was just told to take you upstairs."

His taciturnity was out of character. Did he fear incurring Marcel Ambrose's wrath? At the time of Ambrose's supposed suicide, plenty of people in Soho must have breathed a sigh of relief. Yet the last time they'd spoken, Joe hadn't seemed to be unduly intimidated by the man's reputation. Not like Sammy. Something had changed.

The attendant stabbed a button with a massive forefinger. Their destination was the third floor. On his previous visit, Jacob had familiarised himself with the geography of Chez Laurent. The restaurant and kitchen were on the first floor and the private grill room and several offices on the second. On the third were storage rooms, and also Laurent's office. A place for conducting private business, well away from eavesdroppers and mischief-makers.

As the lift began to move, Jacob gave the attendant a cheerful nod. No response. Both his companions stared blankly at the evening's restaurant menu that was elegantly printed on a large card held in a slot on the wall of the lift. Jacob started to whistle "You're the Cream in My Coffee," but after a few moments he thought better of it.

They reached their destination. As the lift gates opened,

Joe Postles waved him out. "The guvnor's office, Mr. Flint. You know your way."

The little man shepherded him along a narrow, carpeted corridor before knocking at Laurent's door. To Jacob's surprise, the lift attendant followed them.

"*Entrez!*"

The crisp voice didn't belong to Laurent, and when Joe Postles pushed the door open, sitting behind the opulent walnut desk was a ghost. A man who was supposed to have been burned to death. His face was familiar to Jacob only from a blurred photograph dug out of the *Clarion's* archives. Marcel Ambrose hated having his picture taken; it suited him to do his dirty work in the shadows. He might not be dead, but there was something corpse-like about his sallow complexion and hooded, bloodshot eyes. He considered Jacob like a surgeon examining an unsatisfactory X-ray.

A bottle of Laphroaig single malt and a solitary tumbler stood on the desk. Lying close to them was a revolver. Ambrose picked up the gun, stroking the walnut handle and smiling as though it gave him sensual pleasure. Then he put it down again and poured himself a finger of golden whisky.

"Jacob Flint." He made it sound as if he were diagnosing a tumour.

"Monsieur Marcel Ambrose?" Jacob extended his hand, feigning the bonhomie of one golf club captain greeting another. "Nice to meet you. I'm glad to discover that the report of your death was exaggerated. Welcome back to these shores. It's... been a while."

Ambrose ignored the proffered hand and swallowed a mouthful of whisky. His gaze flicked towards Joe Postles.

"Leave us."

The lift attendant remained where he was, but the little man couldn't escape fast enough. As the door banged shut behind him, Jacob tried again.

"I really appreciate your seeing me."

"You've been asking questions." Ambrose's English was excellent, if heavily accented.

"You have to admit," Jacob said. "It's quite a story."

"What do you mean?"

"Everyone thought you'd killed yourself. Or that Sobrino had murdered you. Now here you are in the flesh. Large as life and twice as handsome."

There was a long pause.

"You think you are funny?"

Jacob breathed out. "No offence intended, Monsieur Ambrose. My editor at the *Clarion* wondered if you would like to give us an exclusive interview?"

The hooded eyes betrayed no flicker of emotion. "I do not care for people who invade my privacy."

"Sorry to disturb you, then," Jacob said. "I'd better not waste any more of your valuable time."

He edged backwards, but the lift attendant took a giant stride to move in front of the door and bar his path.

"I do not care for people who stir up trouble for me, either. Who is the tart you left downstairs?"

"Oh, just a girl I picked up this evening." Jacob risked a man-to-man wink. "Felt in need of a bit of company. All work and no play makes Jack a dull boy, you know?"

Ambrose frowned. "I don't think you are as stupid as you like to pretend. Apart from the prostitute, who else knows you are at Chez Laurent tonight?"

Jacob made a show of ticking people off his fingers. "A couple of colleagues. My editor, of course. And I may have mentioned it to…"

"Don't lie to me." Ambrose spat out the words.

The man was renowned for his hair-trigger temper. Perhaps the cocky approach hadn't been for the best, but Jacob wasn't sure what else he could have said. Show weakness to a man as ruthless as Ambrose and you'd live to regret it, but you'd probably not live for long. Time to try a little negotiation.

"What do you want, Monsieur Ambrose? I'm confident we can come to some mutually satisfactory arrangement."

The hooded eyes considered him. "I was wrong. You really are stupid. I didn't have you brought up here to make some kind of deal. Answer me this. You know Lulu Dabo?"

"Lulu Dabo?"

"Don't waste time playing games. Call her Kiki de Villiers if you wish."

"I met the lady for the first time the other night. A brief encounter at an art gallery. We were both invited to a private viewing."

"You talked to her about me?"

"I never got the chance to talk to her about anything. You heard what happened? A woman killed herself, the artist whose work was on display. The place was in uproar. It was absolute bedlam."

Ambrose lifted the gun from the desk and pointed it at Jacob. "Where is Lulu now?"

Jacob's mouth was dry. "I...I've no idea. Honestly, I simply don't know."

Ambrose banged the gun on the desk. "You're lying!"

"I swear to you, I'm telling the truth."

With a noise of contempt, Ambrose put the gun away in the drawer of his desk and finished his whisky.

"Ah, well. Perhaps you are."

Jacob breathed out. That was a close-run thing. With any luck, he'd get out of here in one piece.

Ambrose nodded to the lift attendant. "All right, Earlam. You know what to do."

The giant clamped Jacob's arm with a hand like a shovel. Jacob tried to wrench himself free of the man's grip but only succeeded in hurting his arm.

"What...what's this about?" It was almost a yelp. "You needn't have any fear about my..."

"I don't have any fear," Ambrose snapped. "Fear is for interfering troublemakers like you."

"I never meant to..."

"Shut your fucking mouth." Ambrose gestured to the attendant. "Deal with him."

Jacob tried to make a dash for it, but Earlam let a punch fly. Jacob dodged the full force of the blow but still took a glancing hit on the jaw. He staggered for a moment before a second punch felled him. As he sprawled on the floor, Ambrose opened the drawer again and removed something before stepping out from behind his desk.

Blinking away tears of pain, Jacob saw a thin rope in Ambrose's hand. For a terrifying instant, he thought the man was about to strangle him bare-handed. Instead, Ambrose bent down over his prostrate form. The whisky fumes were nauseating. He tied Jacob's wrists together with the ease of long practice.

"There's no need for this," Jacob blurted as the rope cut into his skin.

"Hold your tongue or I'll rip it out."

Earlam opened the door before grasping Jacob by the scruff of the neck. He dragged him along the corridor and Ambrose followed them out. At the end of the passageway was a small windowless door. It opened when the attendant pressed an unmarked button.

Jacob found himself looking into an unlit, waist-high service lift with a crude wooden tray for carrying goods up and down. A sort of glorified dumb waiter, operated by pulley and ropes.

Ambrose kicked Jacob in the stomach, making him retch.

"*Adieu.*"

Turning on his heel, he went back inside the office. The giant heaved Jacob into the lift. He might have been lugging a sack of potatoes. Jacob's brow cracked against the side of the narrow shaft. The impact made his head swim. Earlam was clumsy but strong. It was a tight squeeze, but he managed to bundle the whole of Jacob's body onto the goods tray.

"The floor won't bear my weight," Jacob gasped.

The attendant gave a shrug of his massive shoulders and closed the lift door.

Inside the shaft, it was pitch black. Jacob felt sick. His wrists were hurting and he felt a dizzying certainty that his life was about to end. He'd break his neck and spine if the rope gave way and he plummeted to the ground. Trewythian's warning had been spot on, even if it was a lucky guess. Survive the descent and someone at the bottom of the shaft would kill him. He'd either be clubbed to death or have his throat slit. They'd take his corpse away and dump it. Somewhere he would never be found.

The tray shuddered. He shut his eyes. The machinery jerked into life with an ominous creaking noise.

As the tray jolted downwards, he curled up into a foetal ball. His descent into hell had begun.

Chapter 14

The band struck up "Happy Days Are Here Again" as Rachel finished her Dirty Martini. She got to her feet and wove, bag in hand, past the dancers on her way to the lift.

The red light of the floor indicator showed that the lift was coming down. She stood against the wall and watched the door and gate open. Joe Postles stepped out and scanned the room.

Rachel slipped behind his back and into the lift carriage. When she gave a polite cough, Joe Postles spun round. There was no mistaking his anguish.

"Sorry, so sorry, miss," he stammered. "You can't go in the lift when the attendant isn't here."

She beckoned him forward and whispered, "Don't be shy, dearie."

He peered at her, as if trying to fathom why she was no longer talking in that funny little falsetto voice.

"It's not safe without the attendant, miss. House rules, miss."

"We'll be cosy together."

He glanced over his shoulder. Nobody was paying them any attention. "Come on, miss. If you'll just step out of the lift."

Rachel pressed a button and the inner gates began to close. Joe Postles threw himself forward and squeezed inside.

"Miss, you shouldn't!"

Rachel placed her left hand on his. "Where did you take Jacob?"

He shook his head. "You don't need to know that, miss. Listen, I'll give you a chance. Stop the lift and get out of here right now. Otherwise, they'll do away with you too."

"Little me?"

She smiled prettily before gripping his wrist and giving it a savage twist. Joe squealed and lost his balance.

Rachel stood over him as he lay sprawled across the floor of the lift. He looked up in mingled horror and amazement as she opened her handbag and pulled out a small Haenel Schmeisser waistcoat pistol.

"If I shoot you in the head at close quarters, even your brother won't be able to identify your remains."

"They beat up my brother because he talked to Flint," he whimpered. "They threatened him with..."

She trod on his hand with a stiletto heel. He whimpered in pain.

"Don't waste time. Where is Jacob? Quick sharp!"

"I took him up to the boss's room at the top." He was sobbing with terror. "Ambrose is going to do for him."

She pressed the button for the third floor.

"How and where?"

"There's a sort of dumb waiter. In the old days he used it to get rid of people. They get shook up on the way down. Earlam the lift man strangles them in the back yard and then buries the bodies in Epping Forest."

"Quickest way to the back yard?"

"Through the bar in the ballroom, then up the steps."

"Where is Earlam now?"

"Up at the top, waiting to come down in this lift."

They'd reached the mezzanine floor. Rachel pressed the stop button and as the lift came to a halt, she put the pistol back in her bag and ripped the dinner menu card from its slot.

The door opened. She stepped over Joe Postles and out of the lift. Down in the ballroom, the bandleader was all smiles, acknowledging the applause from the crowd. She kicked off her high heels and threw first one shoe and then the other at the lamps in the ceiling.

Her aim was true. There was a sound of breaking glass. First one of the coloured beams of light went out, then another. Taking a pace towards the balcony rail, she pulled a small box from her bag and struck a match.

"Help!" she screamed at the top of her voice as the flame caught the menu card. "Fire! Fire! Run for your lives!"

With a graceful movement, she tossed the burning menu over the railing and screamed again.

"Help! Help! Fire!"

Down in the ballroom, a woman echoed her scream. People started shouting and rushing about as Rachel raced down the spiral staircase. Even before she reached the ballroom, people had begun to rush up towards her in their desperation to escape. She squeezed past three of them but before she could get as far as the dance floor her route was completely blocked.

"Wrong way, wrong way! You need to get out!" a woman yelled at her. "Didn't you hear? The whole building is burning down!"

Rachel took no notice. Vaulting over the staircase handrail with athletic grace, she dropped onto the carpet a few feet below.

In the ballroom, pandemonium had broken out. The leader of the band kept calling for calm, but nobody took any notice.

The musicians had dropped their instruments and some were urging their colleagues to run for it. Most people had abandoned their tables, although a few were looking around frantically, trying to make sense of what was going on. A crowd was pushing and shoving its way to the staircase. A few optimists were waiting by the lift. No sign of the burning menu. Rachel supposed that someone had stamped out the flames.

Growing up on Gaunt, she'd run barefoot over rough and rocky ground for hour after hour, day after day, month after month. In stockinged feet she moved fast. As she crossed the ballroom, one of the bandsmen caught hold of her hand and tried to pull her back.

"They're saying the fire started in the bar!" he bellowed.

With a jerk of the wrist, she detached herself from her would-be saviour, leaving him to gape in wonder at her folly and ingratitude.

The drinks waiters had vanished and so had Joe Postles's fellow barman. When studying the ballroom and bar, she'd noticed that in addition to an internal door there was another marked *Emergency Exit*. Opening it, she found herself at the foot of the stone staircase Joe had told her about. Far above, the moon shone brightly.

She raced up the steps.

———

The tray carrying the huddled form of Jacob Flint bumped and banged its way down the shaft. His head was spinning. Every bone in his body seemed to rattle and ache. But the ropes didn't snap. As the tray hit the bottom, he was bruised and battered but still in one piece.

And still in the dark. He couldn't see anything. There wasn't even a pinprick of light.

Groggily, he reached out. His fingertips touched brick and then felt cold steel. This must be the hatch.

He pushed against the hard covering with all his strength. There was no give at all. His wrists were tied but he was able to move his hands around to see if there was a lock or some kind of bolt. Nothing.

So the shaft was accessible only from the outside. Was anyone there, ready and waiting? Or must he lie here in misery until Earlam made his way downstairs and dealt with him?

It wasn't in Jacob's nature to surrender to fate. If he had to die, he wanted it to be on his own terms. Suppose Earlam or another of Ambrose's thugs was about to finish him off. Better to go down fighting than meekly accept the inevitable. Taking a deep breath, he summoned his last reserves of strength.

Balling his fist, he banged on the steel cover. Would anyone outside even hear such a dull sound? He wasn't sure.

Gasping, he filled his lungs again. And then, before he could move a muscle, he heard a harsh scraping noise.

Someone was unfastening an external bolt.

Jacob uttered a silent prayer. Time to be thankful for small mercies. At least he wouldn't be left to starve to death in this claustrophobic hellhole.

What was his best bet? Should he rush his assailant or pretend to be unconscious and lull him into a sense of false security? He wasn't sure he was strong enough to scramble up off the tray and battle to save his life. Whatever he did would be fraught with risk.

A thought struck him like a blow to the solar plexus. What if there were two of them?

The steel covering shifted. The hatch was open. After being confined to the shaft, the moonlight was blinding. He felt woozy and nauseous but he knew he must force himself to remain silent and still.

"Jacob?"

Oh, God, a familiar voice! Trueman had come for him.

The relief was almost too much to bear. Jacob wept.

————

Rachel stood on the top step. The yard was surrounded by a high brick wall topped with barbed wire. Set in the wall was a steel gate that someone had left open. She saw shadows in the moonlight, one of them leaning on another. Trueman's bulk was unmistakable. The hunched figure with him must be Jacob. On the ground was a crumpled, motionless body.

"You said you'd only be five minutes," she said in a tone of cool reproach.

"Rachel?" Jacob's voice trembled. He swayed and would have fallen but for Trueman's grip on him.

"How bad is he?" Rachel asked.

"He's taken a hell of a hammering," Trueman said. "His wrists were tied; just as well I brought a knife. The Rolls is parked round the corner. We'd best get him home before this bastard's pals show up."

He pulled a torch from his overcoat pocket and shone the beam on the man's closed eyes. Blood leaked from a wound on the temple.

"Dead?" Rachel asked.

"Winded," Trueman said unsympathetically. "Found him crouched down by the hatch. Waiting for Jacob, I suppose. Lucky I brought my knobkerrie as well as the knife."

A fearsome club lay on the stony ground. As he picked it up, the man groaned.

"Not so lucky for him," she said.

"People were rushing up those steps a couple of minutes ago," Trueman said. "Two waiters and a barman, by the look of 'em, scared witless and running for their lives. They yelled about a fire. Anything to do with you?"

"You know I'm a bright spark."

He grunted. "Didn't want them mithering over Jacob or our friend with the bump on his head, so I said they'd been overcome by fumes and I'd lug them out the moment they came round. The blokes swallowed it and ran off down the alley."

"Let's go. We don't have much time."

Rachel took Jacob's arm and they propelled him out of the yard and through the gate. On the other side of the wall was a dog-legged alleyway. At the far end was a yellow lamp. Trueman pointed towards the dull glow.

"That way."

Rachel froze. "I can hear something. Get back."

She and Trueman dragged Jacob back into the yard. Now there was no mistaking it. Heavy feet were pounding towards them. They pressed themselves against the wall. The footsteps stopped outside the gate. They heard someone breathing hard.

A hefty man in a lift attendant's uniform took a long stride into the yard before stopping to stare at his colleague's body.

"Chalky! What happened?"

Trueman struck him with the knobkerrie and the man collapsed, hitting the ground with a jarring thud.

"Pick on someone your own size next time," Trueman said.

————

"He'll live," Hetty Trueman announced, applying a cold compress to the side of Jacob's head.

"Fleet Street breathes a sigh of relief and offers up a silent prayer," Martha said. "How would the *Clarion* manage without him? And it would be such a shame to waste all this fine cognac."

The kitchen of Gaunt House was serving as a makeshift

surgery. The housekeeper had put a first aid box out on the table and she and Jacob were sitting on adjacent stools as she tended to his wounds. Martha's contribution to his treatment had been to bring in a tulip glass containing a generous measure of reddish-brown medicine.

He winced as Hetty dabbed iodine on a cut on his cheek.

"You never learn, do you?" she scolded. "What is it they say about fools rushing in?"

"Take no notice of her," Martha said. "The whole aim was to confront Ambrose. Rachel gave you the nod, didn't she? She told me it was the quickest way to find out what was going on."

"And what is going on?" Hetty asked.

Jacob's brain was fogged, but at least his body was no longer aching in so many places and the waves of nausea he'd felt since being kicked in the stomach had begun to subside. The cognac was working its magic. He gave a throaty cough.

"Ambrose has taken up the reins of his vice business again. He wants to find Kiki de Villiers."

Martha leaned closer to him. "Perhaps he doesn't want to hurt her. He may delude himself into believing he can rekindle their affair."

"She's become rich and famous. What can he offer a woman who has everything?"

"Keep still," Hetty warned as she continued her ministrations. "There, how is that?"

"Much better, thanks," Jacob said. "You're a regular Florence Nightingale."

Hetty grunted. "There's not that much wrong with you, if you ask me. No sign of concussion and just a few bumps and bruises. Your knee might ache for a few days, but I'd say you got off lightly."

He managed a reproachful groan.

"So Ambrose is out for revenge?" Martha persisted.

"What else?" he muttered.

As Rachel strolled into the kitchen, Martha said, "The police need to know."

"You're right," Rachel said. "This is a case for Scotland Yard."

"I should talk to Inspector Oakes," Jacob said.

"Stay here tonight, Jacob," Martha said. "Get your strength up before you speak to the Yard."

Was there any other grand home in England, he wondered, where a housemaid could invite a guest to spend the night and her employer didn't bat an eyelid?

"Thanks." He yawned. "Must admit, I'm all in. Tomorrow, I'll get hold of Oakes."

"Call him after breakfast," Rachel said. "There's no time to waste."

"You agree that Kiki de Villiers is in danger?"

Rachel touched the graze on his cheek and he flinched. "Marcel Ambrose failed to kill you. He will take that as a mortal insult."

"So I'm at risk too?"

"Of course."

"And what about you, Rachel?" Hetty interrupted.

"Ambrose doesn't know who I am."

"Joe Postles will give him your description and tell him you had a gun," Hetty said. "He'll realise you're not some common or garden streetwalker."

"You're right, of course." Rachel sighed. "We left our coats in the cloakroom, and I dropped my handbag when I ran downstairs. I expect Ambrose will go looking for clues. Just as well I left a diary with a list of false names and addresses in the bag. He might just make a nuisance of himself with a bunch of London county councillors."

"You think of everything," Jacob murmured.

"If only." She sighed. "You lost your hat and coat, as well. I don't think it would be wise to try to retrieve it."

"Don't worry. The moths had nibbled them. I meant to go shopping for new ones."

She poked at a tear in the sleeve of his jacket. "And your suit is ruined. I feel responsible after encouraging you to go with Joe Postles."

"I'd have done the same regardless. Thank God you came along. Without you and Trueman…"

"Think nothing of it."

He bowed his head. "I need to warn Mrs. de Villiers. As long as Ambrose is a free man, she is in danger."

"You think she doesn't know Ambrose is back?"

"No idea, but I daren't take the risk. If anything happened to her, I'd never forgive myself."

"If you're planning to mix with the high and mighty," Rachel said coolly, "you can't go around looking like a tramp. You're a chief crime correspondent, not a cub reporter. The minute you've fixed an appointment with Oakes, you must get yourself properly kitted out. You need a new dinner suit, overcoat, and hat. And you may as well have a smarter suit for the office and a few decent shirts while you're at it. After breakfast, Trueman will drive you to Savile Row. I have an account with Anderson & Sheppard."

"So that's why he's the best-dressed chauffeur in London." Jacob glanced at Trueman. Despite the evening's exertions, he didn't have a hair out of place. "The only snag…"

"My treat," Rachel said. "You have a birthday coming up soon, don't you?"

"Well remembered," he said, taken aback.

"You were born on April Fools' Day. How could I forget? Consider this an early present."

"I don't…"

"I'll be mortally offended if you snub my generosity."

"Nobody in his right mind would offend you," he said.

Hetty was restive. "Ambrose has a score to settle with both of you now."

"I'll take my chances," Rachel said.

"But what are you going to _do_ about the man?"

"Scotland Yard can deal with him. My challenge remains the same. I want to solve Damaris Gethin's murder."

Chapter 15

Jacob rang Scotland Yard from Gaunt House the minute he finished breakfast. Limbs still aching from the punishment he'd suffered at Chez Laurent, he took care to avoid the art deco mirror above the telephone for fear of damaging his restored morale. Energy surged through him. Hetty's honey-sweetened porridge and two steaming mugs of dark Brazilian coffee—Trueman ground beans with the same vigour he applied to conjuring up cocktails—had worked their magic.

The woman on the Yard's switchboard rebuffed his opening gambits, but a mix of invention and bloody-minded persistence finally saw him put through to Inspector Philip Oakes. The police needed to know that Kiki de Villiers's life was in danger. There was no time to lose.

Over the past year or so, he'd striven to earn Oakes's trust. In a tricky case, they could give each other a helping hand. It suited both men to keep their occasional encounters confidential, and they usually met away from official premises. Jacob enjoyed Oakes's company and hoped that, for all the policeman's dislike of sensational journalism, the feeling was mutual.

This morning, however, the inspector was brusque. At first

he refused to listen, insisting that a meeting was out of the question.

"I don't have time to gossip with reporters."

"I know it's Saturday, but…"

"The day of the week doesn't matter. I'm too busy."

"But Inspector…"

"No more buts," Oakes said through gritted teeth. "I've just come out of a meeting with the assistant commissioner, and there will be hell to pay if I don't—"

"Please, I swear to you. This really is a matter of life and death."

A long pause. Jacob imagined the other man counting to ten.

"If you're wasting my time…"

"You know I wouldn't lie to you, Inspector."

A snort of derision. "You're a newspaperman."

"A woman's life is in jeopardy."

"Who is she?"

"Mrs. Kiki de Villiers."

Another pause.

"All right, be at the Yard at noon. I'll give you ten minutes. Not a second more."

Oakes banged down the phone before Jacob had a chance to utter another word.

"Success?"

Rachel came gliding barefoot into the hall. Her filmy silk kimono had a floral pattern in shades of orange, pink, and red. She'd washed her hair and her complexion was so fresh that she could pass for eighteen. The demure expression suggested a night's untroubled beauty sleep. Anyone would think she'd spent the previous evening playing solitaire or solving one of Ronald Knox's acrostics rather than causing mayhem in a night-club and rescuing him from certain death.

"Oakes is in a foul temper."

"Curious. He always strikes me as admirably calm. For a policeman."

"He needs to buck up his ideas," Jacob said waspishly. "He won't even see me until twelve."

"Lucky he agreed to see you at all."

Jacob frowned. "If he doesn't take the threat to Kiki de Villiers seriously..."

"Yes, yes, no need to harp on about it, Jacob. Now, off to Savile Row with you. Indulge your fashion sense." Was he being oversensitive in detecting a dash of irony in her words? "Spend as much as you like. After last night, you deserve a treat."

He began to thank her, only to be silenced with a negligent flip of the hand as Trueman emerged from the kitchen, immaculate in his chauffeur's uniform.

"Let's be having you," the big man said.

———

"I'll see if I have more luck in speaking to Mr. Spruce this morning," Martha said shortly after Jacob's departure. "His secretary said he'd be at his desk by nine."

Rachel nodded. "It would help if he corroborated my theory."

"You're going to call on Butterworth's solicitor?"

"Yes. Not that I expect to get much out of Benedict Rhodes-Denton. A good lawyer is always close-mouthed, and by all accounts he is a very good lawyer. Perhaps I'll pick up at least a clue about how an impoverished sapper could afford his services."

"And after that?"

"This afternoon I fancy a trip to the countryside."

"Romney Marsh?"

Rachel smiled. "You know me too well."

———

Jacob spent over an hour in Savile Row. Trueman watched with wry amusement as he was measured for a bespoke three-piece suit with alarming thoroughness by a sleek little tailor who smelled of hair oil. At Trueman's prompting, Jacob went on a spree. His purchases included an off-the-peg business suit, and shirts for every day of the week, together with a new dinner suit, a camel overcoat, a natty fedora, and two pairs of leather oxfords.

"So you're a friend of Miss Savernake?" the tailor said, totting up the cost with undisguised glee.

Jacob cleared his throat, but Trueman was too quick for him. "That's right."

His tone killed off any prospect of further intrusive enquiries and soon they were loading up the Rolls with the fruits of the shopping spree. Trueman drove Jacob back to his flat in silence. The chauffeur wasn't a man for small talk. When they reached Exmouth Market, he jumped out of the Rolls and held the passenger door open. For a fleeting instant, Jacob understood what it must be like to be rich and powerful. One look at Trueman's sardonic expression was enough to bring him back down to earth.

"Make sure you report back. Rachel wants to keep tabs on what the police do about Ambrose."

Jacob eyed him curiously. "Any idea what she makes of this business?"

A shrug of the massive shoulders. "She's a law unto herself. Always has been, always will be."

With that, he was gone. Jacob changed into his new business suit and consigned its predecessor to an unimpressed rag-and-bone man who happened to be passing by. He wondered whether to sport the fedora for his meeting with Oakes, but decided against it. His left knee throbbed with pain each time he put weight on it, so he drove in his new Riley 9 to Scotland Yard rather than walking.

When he arrived, he wondered for the umpteenth time how the police headquarters had earned its name when it wasn't in Scotland and wasn't even in a yard. On speaking to a minion behind a big desk, he found himself directed to a windowless cubbyhole in the basement. The waiting room might have doubled as a prison cell. The light was dim, and a stale smell hung in the air. A solitary wooden chair was coated in dust. An hour or two in here, he thought, and you'd probably confess to anything. He was brushing an inquisitive spider off his crisply creased new trousers when a young policeman came to conduct him to the inspector's office.

Oakes's greeting was terse. "Make it snappy."

Jacob glanced around the small room. There were no photographs, just a bookcase dominated by *Archbold: Criminal Pleading, Evidence and Practice* and Hans Gross's *Criminal Investigation*. Not so much as an Edgar Wallace for light relief. Oakes didn't offer his hand, and Jacob didn't wait for an invitation before taking a seat and firing his opening salvo.

"Marcel Ambrose isn't dead. He's alive and well and back in London."

"Do you intend to print a story to that effect?"

The detective's expression betrayed nothing. So they already knew. Jacob felt a stab of disappointment. He always loved to break news.

"I won't jump the gun, no need to worry about that. Arrest him first." Jacob rubbed his sore cheek. "Obviously, I'd be glad if you could let me know as soon as he's under lock and key."

The inspector peered across the desk, and Jacob felt

uncomfortably conscious of his painful cheeks. There wasn't much bruising, but the marks wouldn't escape Oakes's sharp eyes.

"These shenanigans in Kingly Street overnight. You didn't take part, by any chance?"

"You heard about that spot of bother? I suppose if you already have Ambrose under surveillance…"

"We keep ourselves informed; that's all you need to know. Spit it out. Were you at Chez Laurent last night?"

Provoked, Jacob said, "I went for a dance. With Rachel Savernake, as it happens."

"A dance?" The poker face flickered. For a moment Oakes sounded like Lady Bracknell, enquiring about a handbag. "With Miss Savernake?"

Jacob suspected that Oakes's admiration for Rachel was prompted by something more than mere professional curiosity and a desire to solve the mystery of what made her tick. For her part, she had a high opinion of the inspector. He was shrewd and diligent and exuded quiet charm. On top of that, Jacob grudgingly admitted to himself, the chap wasn't bad-looking. No wonder some of his colleagues in the CID longed to take him down a peg or two. It would do no harm to remind him that nobody was closer to Rachel than Jacob. Other than the Truemans, of course.

"She moves around the floor like Adele Astaire," he said in a dreamy tone.

Oakes glanced at his watch. "Cut to the chase."

"I believe Ambrose is well known to Mrs. Kiki de Villiers."

"Is that right?"

The inspector was by nature discreet, but Jacob had never known him to be quite so irritatingly inscrutable. Unable to suppress a touch of asperity, he said, "They were as thick as thieves before he vanished."

"Oh, yes?"

"In those days she called herself Lulu Dabo. Now she has a new life, and he bears her a grudge because she's much better off without him. He's trying to track her down and given half a chance, he'll kill her. She needs protection. To be guarded around the clock until Ambrose is behind bars."

"Thank you for the advice."

Jacob stared. He found himself involuntarily clenching his fists. "Listen, the woman's life is in danger."

"So you tell me."

"Ambrose is violent and ruthless. In his mind, this woman betrayed him, and now he'll stop at nothing to get his revenge."

The detective folded his arms. He seemed determined not to be impressed. Provoked, Jacob found himself saying more than he'd intended.

"Yesterday evening, he almost succeeded in having me murdered."

Oakes's eyebrows arched. "Really? Funny thing is, I've never seen you looking so debonair."

"Never mind that. Once his thug had done his worst, I looked like something the cat had dragged in."

"That's a new suit, isn't it? You must give me the name of your tailor."

"Look, I'll tell you exactly what happened."

"Be quick about it. I've got an urgent inquiry on my hands."

Jacob gave him a rapid if selective precis of the previous night's excitements at Chez Laurent.

"So you see," he concluded, "Ambrose doesn't want anyone else sniffing around after Kiki de Villiers. He has his own plans for her; I'd stake my life on it."

"You may be right." Still no trace of emotion. "By the sound of things, you can thank your lucky stars that Miss Savernake came to your rescue. I'll bear in mind what you say, but right now I have other priorities."

"What do you mean?" Jacob was outraged. "Ambrose is a hardened criminal who murdered someone in order to fake his own death. Now he's about to kill his former mistress."

"Did Sammy Postles tip you off to that effect?"

Oakes fired the question out of the blue. Jacob found himself groping for an answer.

"Come on, Inspector, you know I can't reveal my sources."

"Don't worry about Sammy lodging a complaint."

Something in the detective's sour tone made Jacob's stomach churn.

"What do you mean?"

"His corpse was hauled out of the Regent's Canal early this morning." Oakes paused. "The hands and ankles were roped together. Someone had gone to town on him with a razor. He was probably still alive when they chucked what was left of him into the water."

Jacob closed his eyes. He felt sick.

"Ambrose murdered him," he said at length. "Retribution. Sammy paid with his life for talking to me."

Oakes stood up. "Lousy thing to have on your conscience. Now, if you'll excuse me, I have work to do."

Chapter 16

"I seldom see prospective clients on a Saturday morning," Benedict Rhodes-Denton said, leaning back in his leather-upholstered chair. "Let alone at such short notice. For the daughter of the late Judge Savernake, though, I felt that I should make an exception."

"I'm much obliged," Rachel said pleasantly as she scanned her surroundings. One wall was devoted to shelves of calfskin-bound legal tomes. On others there were framed legal certificates and photographs of an array of racing cars. "You knew the judge?"

"Not personally. I was a very junior solicitor at the time he retired from the bench. Remarkable man, by all accounts." A well-fed man with multiple chins, he looked at her with unvarnished curiosity. "Sad business, when ill health strikes someone down like that."

"His mind failed," Rachel said curtly.

"Very direct," the solicitor said in an approving tone. "Yes, that was my understanding."

"Forgive me, but I prefer not to speak about the judge."

"As you wish, Miss Savernake. What can I do for you?"

"It's a matter of some delicacy," she said. "I have come here on behalf of a dear friend."

"Really?" He wrinkled his brow.

"Yes, I was recommended to you by an acquaintance. Another friend—or perhaps a friend of a friend would be closer to the mark. His name is Butterworth."

Rhodes-Denton stared at her. "Not Edward Butterworth?"

Rachel smiled. "I know him as Ned, but, yes, that's his full name."

"I don't understand," he said coldly, with no trace of his previous geniality.

"Ned advised me that you were a man to be counted on. Never mind the cost, he said, your services are worth every penny."

The solicitor frowned. "I'm afraid there must be some mistake, Miss Savernake."

"I don't think so," she said smoothly. "Ned recommended you in the most glowing terms. I know he didn't actually dip into his own pocket for the fees, but he's certainly pleased with the outcome."

The chins jutted forward. "I'm not aware that you have any connection with the company concerned."

"The company?"

"Perhaps you could tell me why you have come to see me."

"Ned said you might be able to help. You see, I am friendly with a gentleman who has got himself into a little difficulty with the police."

"May I have his name?"

"Oh, dear." Rachel pretended to be flustered. "I don't actually have his permission to disclose it. You see, Ned told me..."

"I'm sorry, Miss Savernake." Rhodes-Denton began to lever himself out of his chair. "I am unable to accept instructions from intermediaries acting for individuals who don't give their name."

"A moment ago you implied that Ned's fees were underwritten by a company that..."

The solicitor got to his feet. "I must say I find your references to Mr. Butterworth rather curious. With your...ahem, pedigree, you must be aware that I cannot possibly discuss my clients or indeed their financial arrangements. And by the way, that should not be taken as confirmation that I act for Mr. Butterworth or anyone else. I'm afraid that if this visit is some kind of fishing expedition, then you will be disappointed."

Rachel pouted. "Really! I don't know what you mean."

Rhodes-Denton's solitary arm waved towards the door. "Good day to you, Miss Savernake."

———

After dropping Jacob in Exmouth Market, Trueman found a safe place to park the Rolls before walking to Farringdon. He hoped to arm himself with some local intelligence about Sapper Butterworth. The pub nearest to the man's home was the logical starting point.

Trueman was fond of a pint and from time to time he left the women in Gaunt House to their own devices while he sampled the local hostelries. He wasn't gregarious by nature, and his size and build made strangers wary of him, but he didn't mind listening to other people's conversations. It had occurred to him that, in his own taciturn way, he was almost as nosey as Rachel.

He reached Cowcross Street and soon found The Castle. He'd never roamed this far in order to quench his thirst, but he was aware of the tavern's curious claim to fame. The Castle was the only pub in London with a pawnbroker's licence. Sure enough, he spotted the sign of three golden balls hanging above the door.

Two toothless old men were sipping stout in a dusty alcove. Otherwise he was the first customer of the day. Ordering a pint of best bitter, he invited the landlord to have one himself. Mine host, who sported a patch over his left eye and had a formidable beer belly, beamed his gratitude as they clinked tankards.

"Your very good health, mister."

"Good health, eh?" Trueman became mournful. "Chance 'ud be a fine thing. Thirteen years since I was in France, and…ah, well, never mind. No point in maundering on about it."

"It's a free country," the landlord said. "Even if they never gave us a land fit for heroes."

"You can say that again." Trueman downed some ale. "Between you and me, I woke up at three this morning, covered in sweat and suffering from the heebie-jeebies. Even after all these years, I keep thinking I'm about to cop a packet."

The landlord gave a sympathetic grunt.

"Ah, well," Trueman said. "There's plenty worse off than me."

"And me."

The landlord leaned forward and lifted his eye patch for a split second. The socket was empty.

"Passchendaele," he said.

"Bad luck. Rotten show, that."

"Least said, soonest mended, eh?"

"You never said a truer word."

The door swung open and a tall, heavily built man lumbered up to the bar. His arm was in a sling and there was bruising on his face and jaw. Trueman's expression didn't flicker, but inwardly he exulted.

"Care for a pint?" he asked before the newcomer could utter a word.

The man gave him a sour look. "All right."

"The usual, Ned?" the landlord asked.

Trueman managed to stifle a nod of self-satisfaction. So this was indeed Sapper Butterworth. My lucky day, he thought.

The man's suit and shoes had seen better days. There was a faraway look in his eyes, as if mentally he was somewhere else. He'd fallen on hard times, Trueman thought, but not so hard that he couldn't afford a good lawyer when he found himself in a troublesome situation.

"Name's Butterworth," the man said grudgingly.

"Cliff Trueman. Pleased to meet you."

He put out his hand and Butterworth shook it with no sign of enthusiasm before starting to sup his beer. He drank steadily, pausing only to wipe the froth from his mouth.

"Looks like you've been in the wars," Trueman said, gesturing at the sling.

Butterworth grunted. The landlord shot Trueman a warning glance.

"Actually, we was talking about the war when you came in," Trueman said. "I was in the Borderers."

The sapper put down his tankard. "I never talk about the war."

"Bad business, wasn't it?" Trueman said. "I still have the shakes, I don't mind admitting. Shell shakes, I call 'em."

No answer. Trueman waited for a minute before saying, "Tried everything to get over it, I have, but nothing seems to work."

Butterworth drained his glass and said, "I keep myself to myself. All right?"

He sounded better-educated than Trueman had expected. A scholarship boy from a grammar school, perhaps, one who had fallen on hard times.

"I was only making conversation," Trueman said in an injured tone.

The other man caught his wrist and said, "Well, don't bother on my account. Leave me be, all right?"

The landlord said anxiously, "Eh, Ned, we don't want any trouble."

"Trouble? I've had a bellyful of it." He gave Trueman's wrist a slight twist.

"This gent was only trying to be friendly."

Butterworth gave a sardonic laugh. "He can sod off, that's what he can do."

Trueman yanked his wrist from the other man's grip. "No need to be like that, mister."

Butterworth banged his tankard down on the bar and marched out without another word. Trueman looked sorrowfully at the landlord.

"Ned doesn't like to talk about the war."

"So I gather. Why's that?"

"He was blown up. Shell shock, just like you, but a very bad case. Left him with a shocking temper. The slightest thing can set him off like a firework."

"Is that right?"

"Yes, you don't want to get on the wrong side of Ned Butterworth. Say something out of turn and he'll knock seven bells out of you, mark my words." The landlord gave a sage nod of his head. "One of these days, he'll go too far."

———

"Butterworth is unstable," Trueman said after re-joining Rachel and his sister in Gaunt House. "A loose cannon."

"Getting into an argument in a pub is one thing," Rachel said. "Blowing up another man's car is rather different. Do you really think he is capable of premeditated murder?"

"Yes." Trueman rarely prevaricated. "If he had a grudge

against Malam, if he thought the man had ruined his life, I can see him plotting a cold-blooded revenge."

"So unless the police can rule him out," Martha said, "he must be the prime suspect for the bombing."

Rachel nodded. "You say he was shabbily dressed. All the signs are that he is close to destitute."

"The landlord told me that he loaned Butterworth some money only last week, so he could pay the rent," Trueman said.

"Benedict Rhodes-Denton is a first-rate lawyer, shrewd enough to see straight through me when I tried to bluff him into breaching a confidence. Ned Butterworth could never afford his services."

"Did they come across each other during the war?"

"Rhodes-Denton lost his arm before the war, so I doubt it. And if someone else stumped up the fees, who was it? And why were they so generous? He mentioned a company, but I couldn't wheedle a name out of him."

"A company?"

"Companies can be useful vehicles for concealment. If you don't want to know who is footing a bill, the answer is to make the payment through a business you control."

"Do you have anyone in mind?"

"Rhodes-Denton loves motor cars, despite the fact they cost him an arm. Photographs of Bugattis and suchlike adorn his walls. Chances are, he's pally with Captain Malam. Who happens to have his finger in any number of corporate pies."

"Malam?"

Rachel sighed. "We're finding more questions than answers. Why would Malam fund the defence of a man whose name he gave to the police? The man he believes tried to blow him to high heaven?"

———

On leaving Inspector Oakes's office, Jacob tottered to the nearest lavatory. He got there moments before disgorging the porridge he'd guzzled at breakfast. He stumbled out of the building and into the open air. There was an empty bench on Victoria Embankment. He slumped down onto it and put his head in his hands.

A strong wind was blowing in from the river. Jacob shivered.

Only now was the cold reality sinking in. Less than forty-eight hours earlier he'd witnessed a woman decapitating herself. The next evening he had himself come within a hair's breadth of a grisly end. Only fools rushed into a murderer's lair in the way he'd waltzed into Chez Laurent. If not for Rachel, by now he'd be dead and buried. Food for the maggots and worms.

His lurid imagination had become a curse. Hands shaking, he couldn't help picturing the scene in some remote patch of woodland. What if he hadn't been quite dead when they shoved him underground and piled a hundredweight of soil on top of him? In his mind, he could smell the wet earth as it squeezed down on his heart and lungs, crushing out the last gasps of life.

Tears trickled down his cheeks. Yes, he was still in one piece, but guilt weighed on him like a mortuary slab. Sammy Postles's death was his fault. Although Ambrose had given the order, there was no escaping the shameful truth. If Jacob hadn't bribed Sammy to talk, the man would still be alive and drinking. His thoughts roamed, raw and wild. Imagine being trussed up like a chicken, as the thug's razor got to work. Imagine the gag on your mouth, stifling your screams. Imagine the clammy helplessness as well as the agony you suffered each time Ambrose's man slashed your flesh, cutting you to ribbons before throwing your torn remains into the dank depths of the canal. Imagine...

Bile rose in his throat.

Enough! He must stop this self-flagellation, take a firm grip of himself. The downward spiral of despair was almost as dangerous as that lift shaft at Chez Laurent.

Grinding his teeth, he forced open his eyes, blinking away the salty dampness. Numbed by the shocking news of Sammy's death, he didn't feel so much as a pinch of embarrassment when passers-by gave him a wary glance before averting their gaze and hurrying on. His windswept hair and blotchy features must make a startling contrast to the brand new suit and shoes. He probably looked like a cross between a tailor's dummy and a cry baby.

How to atone for the mistakes he'd made, the cavalier method of investigation that had nearly cost his own life before leading to another man's death? There was only one answer. He must do everything in his power to protect Kiki de Villiers. Never mind that he hardly knew the woman. She'd become his responsibility. Whether she knew it or not, she was about to become Ambrose's next victim.

The type of man Ambrose was, he was likely to take personal charge of her murder so that he could wallow in the pleasure of destroying her. Jacob couldn't allow that to happen. Not now that Sammy had been cut up and thrown into the water. They hadn't even bothered to sink his remains. If the body had been found so quickly, it was because Ambrose wanted that to happen. He was making a statement. He was back in London and determined to destroy anyone he deemed a traitor.

The conversation with Oakes had been a gut-wrenching anticlimax. What was wrong with the inspector? Jacob couldn't make sense of his attitude, but the truth was plain. He dared not rely on Scotland Yard moving fast enough to protect Kiki de Villiers. It was up to him to warn her of the threat she faced and help her to dodge Ambrose. Could he find her a secure hiding place until the man was no longer a threat?

His stomach made a noise to remind him it was empty. Struggling to his feet, he blundered along the road almost blindly until he found himself outside a tiny café. Chewing a slice of unbuttered toast and sipping from a glass of water, he fought to recover his composure. You could never change the past, you could only learn from it. Tormenting himself about the savagery of Sammy's murder wouldn't bring him back. All that mattered now was to make sure that Mrs. de Villiers didn't suffer an equally vile fate.

She had a penthouse in Cheyne Walk. He ought to get over to the *Clarion's* office and write a piece about the murder of Sammy Postles, but that would have to wait. His first priority was to see Kiki de Villiers. From the recesses of his memory, he dragged out the name of her apartment block. Du Plooy Mansions. He flung a handful of coins onto the wooden table and hastened out into the street.

A spring returned to his step as he headed for his car. He hated being at the mercy of events. At last he was *doing* something. He was trying to save a woman's life.

———

Du Plooy Mansions proved to be six storeys of beige brick, rounded corners and long, horizontal windows; the name came from its Dutch architect, a pupil of Lutyens who had set up on his own after developing a taste for the avant-garde. A week's tenancy probably cost more than Jacob paid in rent for a year. The block was the last word in luxury. There was a garden on the roof, a swimming pool on the ground floor, and a gymnasium in the basement. The chandelier in the entrance lobby wouldn't have looked out of place in the Palace of Versailles. Behind a polished mahogany desk sat a grizzled concierge whose build and demeanour suggested a cross between a retired policeman and a bulldog.

The man was writing on an envelope with the exaggerated care of someone more accustomed to wielding a truncheon than a fountain pen. As Jacob limped towards him, he placed the envelope, face down, in a wire basket on the desk. The squeak of Jacob's shoes on the marble floor prompted him to look up and glare at the cause of the disturbance. Blimey, Jacob thought, what if I hadn't put on my smart new suit?

"Yes, sir?"

His accent was Scottish, his tone forbidding.

"My name is Jacob Flint. I'm here to see Mrs. de Villiers."

"You don't have an appointment."

Not a question, but a blunt statement of fact. How does he know? Jacob wondered. And what happened to the *sir*?

"We met at the Hades Gallery, the evening before last," he said, aiming for insouciance. "Both of us were guests. Charming lady, delightful company. We had a jolly conversation, and she invited me to drop in any time."

A decisive shake of the head.

"I don't believe you."

Jacob hadn't expected such unvarnished hostility. Attack was the best form of defence.

"You don't happen to be her social secretary, by any chance?" he demanded. "I can assure you that…"

"Listen to me, laddie." The concierge lumbered to his feet. "I don't know what your game is, but you can sling your hook."

Given that the fellow was six feet three and powerfully built, Jacob hastily revised his tactics. Discretion the better part of valour and all that.

"Please, hear me out. It's vital that I speak to Kiki…Mrs. de Villiers. A matter of life and death."

The concierge sat down again and folded his beefy arms.

"Kiki, you say?" The question dripped with sarcasm. "Close friends with her, are you, laddie?"

"I don't mean to be forward," Jacob said meekly. "Or impertinent. Kiki's well-being is my sole concern."

He gestured to the telephone beside the wire basket. "If you don't believe me, please can you call her? I'm sure she'll see me once she hears what I've got to say."

"The lady isn't in," the man said. "As you would know, if you and she were on such intimate terms."

"When will she be back?"

"I don't know, laddie. And if I did, I wouldn't tell you."

Jacob reached for his wallet and pulled out a five-pound note. "Is she still in London?"

The concierge glared at the banknote. Jacob produced another.

"I desperately need to talk to her. Her life is in danger."

"You're a newspaperman," the concierge said flatly.

Despite himself, Jacob couldn't help being impressed. "How on earth did you know?"

"We often get your sort in here, laddie. Pestering the residents. Most of all Mrs. de Villiers. Just to get a paragraph of tittle-tattle in your precious rag. You all think money talks. It's the only language you understand."

"Touché," Jacob said lightly. "Seriously, though. Can you at least get a message to her?"

"A message?"

He took a breath. In for a penny, in for a pound. "Tell her that Marcel Ambrose is trying to find her. She needs to keep out of sight until the police catch up with him."

The concierge was unmoved. "You'd best be off, laddie."

Jacob leaned over the desk, putting his hand on the wire basket.

"Will you pass on what I said?"

"I won't tell you again."

Jacob tugged the wire basket so that it clattered to the floor. The envelope slipped out.

"Now look what you've made me do! I'm all fingers and thumbs!" he cried as he bent to pick up basket and envelope. In an instant, both were back on the desk. "Sorry about that."

The concierge stood up again and growled, "You will have something to be sorry about, laddie, if you don't get out of here this instant."

"All right, all right. I see you don't care what happens to the lady. On your head be it. I'm on my way."

Heedless of his sore knee, Jacob scooted out of the lobby. At the door he turned to give the man a cheeky wave. Impossible not to feel a surge of triumph. He'd guessed right. A few moments earlier it had struck him that, if Kiki de Villiers had left her flat for an indefinite period, she might have asked the concierge to redirect her correspondence.

And so he had. The envelope came from Harrods and presumably contained a bill, but that was neither here nor there. In his careful, sloping hand, the concierge had crossed out the details of Du Plooy Mansions and written in his crabbed hand a quite different address:

Sepulchre House,
Sepulchre Street,
Rye,
Sussex.

Chapter 17

"Sammy Postles is dead," Martha said at the other end of the telephone.

"Oakes told me," Jacob said shortly.

"We heard the news on the wireless a few minutes ago."

"You did?" For a moment, stupidly, he was taken aback. "Ah, because he was once a famous footballer, that makes it a story. Otherwise he'd just be one more sad drunk who fell foul of a villain with a blade."

"Don't torment yourself about Sammy Postles," Martha said. "It sounds as if he'd have come to grief before long anyway."

"Maybe, but the fact remains..."

"Hang on, I suppose you want a word with Rachel?"

"Please."

"Be quick. We're about to go out for the afternoon."

He knew better than to ask where they were going. If they wanted him to know, they'd tell him.

"Jacob." Rachel's cool tones flowed down the line. "I gather that Ambrose has taken out his fury on your wretched informer."

"One of his brutes cut Sammy Postles to pieces and threw him into the Regent's Canal."

"Is that so? The BBC spared us the gory minutiae. As soon as Ambrose discovered you escaped, I suppose he had Sammy Postles put to death. *Pour encourager les autres*."

Jacob swore.

"No need to be coarse, Jacob. Or bitter. Men like Sammy Postles live on the dangerous edge of things."

"Ambrose is a brutal swine," Jacob said thickly. "I'd like to see him swing for what he did to Sammy."

"Don't let your emotions get the better of you." A steely note entered her voice. "Sammy Postles wasn't his first victim, not by a long chalk. If he's to be the last, you'll need all your wits about you."

A pause. "I suppose you're right."

"Yes," Rachel said. "By the way, Trueman tells me your shopping excursion was a success."

Disconcerted by the change of tack, he stammered, "I...well, I spent much more than I ever intended."

"Thank goodness for that. Decent clothes cost money. I hear your new look puts Douglas Fairbanks to shame. I can't wait to see you waltzing in here like something out of *The Mark of Zorro*."

"You wanted to know what Oakes made of the threat to Kiki de Villiers," he said briskly. "The short answer is, not much. I might as well have complained about the theft of a milk bottle."

"Interesting."

"Disastrous, don't you mean? Ambrose is planning to kill her even as we speak. Maybe he's already set the wheels in motion." Jacob's voice rose as his frustration bubbled to the surface. "Oakes should be ashamed of himself. Isn't it bad enough for Sammy to be butchered like an animal? What are the police for, if not to protect innocent people?"

"Why do you think Oakes responded in the way he did?"

"He's swamped with work. That's his excuse."

She sighed. "Use your head, Jacob. He's a good detective and, for what it's worth, I'm sure his heart is in the right place."

"You wouldn't think so from the way he brushed me off."

"You say he'd just come back from a meeting with his superior and he was in a bad mood. Obviously he knows Ambrose is alive and already he's got a shrewd suspicion what that means for Kiki de Villiers."

"Ye-es."

"So there are two possible interpretations, aren't there?"

"Go on."

"For a start, Scotland Yard may be about to pounce on Marcel Ambrose and throw him behind bars."

Jacob exhaled. "It would be good to think so."

"Yes."

Something in her voice made him tighten his grip on the receiver. "You said there is another possibility?"

"That's right."

"Which is?"

"Surely it's as plain as a pikestaff. Whatever a pikestaff is."

"Tell me."

"Oakes has been warned off."

———

Major Whitlow believed in thorough preparation. He worked in a business where taking risks came with the territory, but he preferred to leave little or nothing to chance. He was poring over closely typed notes on a foolscap sheet when someone rapped twice on his door. A third rap followed after a ten-second pause. The major put down the sheet. He'd given an order that he wasn't to be disturbed, but this was the visitor he'd been waiting for.

"Come in."

The man who entered the room moved noiselessly across the floor. In his late thirties, he had thinning hair and rimless spectacles. Clean-shaven and tidy in a blue serge suit, he might have been a brush salesman or a bank clerk. A nondescript fellow, the sort you'd rarely notice in a crowd. An unremarkable appearance was part of his stock-in-trade. The surname on his birth certificate was Duncalf, but different people knew him by a dozen different aliases.

"You made good time from the wilds of Scotland," the major said. "Take a pew."

Duncalf sat down. "You said it was urgent, sir."

"Salmon fishing on Speyside, eh?"

"That's right, sir. Always wanted to catch a March springer."

"Any joy?"

"Yes, sir."

Major Whitlow cleared his throat to indicate that the pleasantries were now concluded. He slid the sheet into a buff folder and pushed it across the desk.

"All the information you require should be there. If you need anything in addition, speak to me personally. Day or night. No other messages until the deed is done."

"Very good, sir."

The major pinched the end of his nose. "There is one thing I should point out."

He nodded towards the folder. Duncalf lifted the flap and removed the contents. In addition to half a dozen sheets of notes there were half a dozen photographs and other documents, together with a wad of banknotes secured by a rubber band. Two of the pictures showed the face and profile respectively of Kiki de Villiers in black and white. The third was a full-length shot of her, posing for the camera in a restaurant; it was in colour, and her red tresses were dazzling.

"So the subject is a woman," Duncalf said softly.

"Yes," the major said. "Does that concern you?"

Duncalf was expressionless. "Not at all, sir. Duty is duty."

"Good. I knew I could count on you." The major paused. "There is another subject. A housemaid."

Duncalf turned up a photograph of a woman with short hair and a demure expression.

"I see," he said in a neutral tone.

"Less than ideal, I know," the major said. "There is an outside possibility that the maid will not be present at the scene, but you must expect her to be there. She is devoted to her mistress. They have been through a good deal together and are exceptionally close. Unhealthily so, perhaps."

Duncalf took off his glasses before reading the first card. There was, the major knew, nothing whatsoever wrong with the man's vision.

"Her home is in Sussex?"

"This is a pied-à-terre that she's very secretive about. I've highlighted the best route from London on the Ordnance Survey map and sketched a rough street plan showing your destination. There's also a photograph of the house. Her bolthole is at the end of a quiet cul-de-sac. That is where she will be this evening."

Duncalf's eyebrows lifted. "You want the deed to be done so quickly?"

"Time is of the essence." The major gave a mirthless smile. "Only in exceptional circumstances would I presume to interrupt you during a fishing trip."

Duncalf didn't return the smile.

The major waited, as if half expecting an objection, but Duncalf bent his head and scanned the information from the file, rapidly absorbing the essentials. The fellow was the son of a merchant seaman and had never had the benefit of a public school education, but Whitlow had a high opinion of his native intelligence. Duncalf would, he felt sure, have prospered in any number of conventional careers had his instincts not led him down a less orthodox path. Perhaps it wasn't so surprising that he had a passion for angling. The sport shared some of its appeal with his chosen vocation.

At length Duncalf laid the paperwork down on the desk. "You'll appreciate, sir, that I would prefer more time to prepare. Especially with two subjects, rather than one."

"Indeed. Alas, time is a luxury that we don't have." He gestured to the banknotes. "Hence the bonus payment. That is the first half. You will receive the balance when the deed is done."

Duncalf picked up the money and stuffed it into the inside pocket of his jacket. "I'm obliged, sir."

"You'll understand that I'm not authorised to discuss the background to this assignment," Whitlow said. "However, you can take it from me that by accomplishing it, you will be doing your country a great service."

Duncalf contemplated the colour photograph of Kiki de Villiers. A faint smile hovered on his lips.

"I'm a patriot, sir. It's a privilege to be entrusted with the responsibility."

Whitlow gave a nod. To his surprise, he found himself suppressing a momentary spurt of distaste. Duncalf had served under his command during the war, and he entertained not the slightest reservation about the man's loyalty or expertise. He was as nerveless as he was discreet. Yet those invaluable qualities were not enough to explain why Duncalf had reached the pinnacle of his peculiar trade.

The simple truth was that the man loved his work. He took pleasure in killing people.

———

Jacob slipped into Clarion House by the back entrance and took the rear stairs up to his office. The *Clarion* had a sister paper, the *Sunday Clarion*, and today was a busy working day for many members of its staff, but he didn't want to be disturbed while he roughed out the story of Sammy Postles's murder. He still had to decide what to do about Kiki de Villiers.

The article didn't take long to write. He knew enough about Sammy's footballing career to tap out the requisite number of words with ease. Football sold newspapers, just as murder did. He indulged himself by ending with a flourish of optimism on the part of an unnamed senior police officer who was entirely imaginary but said what he thought Inspector Oakes *should* have said. Scotland Yard was hot in pursuit of a vital lead and arrests were expected to be made within the next thirty-six hours.

Chewing his pencil, he changed the deadline to twenty-four hours. Suppose Ambrose read the piece; he was too smart to quake in his boots, but there was just an outside chance he'd be needled into some kind of indiscretion that would help him on his way to an appointment with the hangman.

On his way out, he sauntered through the main reception area, only for the young woman behind the desk to hail him.

"Mr. Flint! Mr. Flint! Oh, there you are!"

The anxiety in her voice, the nervousness with which she beckoned him over, made him fear the worst. Gloria was a recent arrival at Clarion House, but he'd already detected a tendency towards melodrama and an unhealthy zest for breaking bad news. One thing was for certain. She didn't simply want to pass the time of day. What was it now? Surely not another obstacle to his attempts to save Kiki de Villiers' life?

"What can I do for you, Gloria?"

"Mr. Gomersall needs to see you. Toot sweet, he said."

He took a breath. Why hadn't he left the building by the same route he'd entered?

"When was that?"

"An hour ago. He's been searching for you high and low." She lowered his voice. "His secretary told me that he's been in a terrible temper ever since last night."

"What happened last night?"

"He was summoned to an urgent meeting with Sir Morton Wragg."

"Sir Morton Wragg?"

"You know, the man who owns the *Clarion*!"

"Yes," he said gloomily. "I know."

"I told him I hadn't a clue where you were, or even whether you'd be in the office today. He had me ring your flat and everything. And now you've turned up here!"

"Ah, well, can't be that important," he said faintly. "I expect it will keep until Monday."

Gloria's lower lip trembled. Anyone would think he'd blasphemed in church.

"I'm afraid it won't, Mr. Flint. Honestly, I've never seen him in such a state."

Jacob's heart sank. He respected Gomersall, but the *Clarion's* editor wasn't a cheery soul even at the best of times.

"He's angry?"

"Furious, I'd say, the way he rampaged around. He knocked over the potted fern and didn't even seem to notice. As for his language...well, really. Heaven only knows who has managed to upset him." She made a belated attempt to offer solace. "Not you, I'm sure."

"I wish I shared your confidence."

"Get away with you, Mr. Flint," she smirked. "All the same, I really would make sure you speak to him. Before he blows a gasket."

———

"I don't understand," Jacob said in bewilderment.

"It's quite straightforward, lad," Walter Gomersall said. "Nothing to lose sleep over."

Never mind sleep, Jacob thought he must be dreaming. Their conversation had proved as surreal as anything Damaris Gethin ever created. As he'd knocked on the door of the editor's inner sanctum, he'd steeled himself for a fusillade of criticism. Possibly even the sack. Although he had no idea what he'd done wrong—something to do with the chaotic events at Chez Laurent?—that wasn't the point.

He remembered the *Clarion*'s literary editor extolling a novel by some dead author—German? Czech?—about a man who was arrested for an unspecified crime he hadn't committed and spent the rest of the book trying to find out what he was accused of. It sounded depressing, which probably explained why nobody had bothered to translate it into English. Surely such a misfortune could never happen in Fleet Street?

Nor had it. There was no sign of Gomersall's alleged temper. Everything was sweetness and light. The editor's greeting was astonishingly fulsome, taking the form of a broad smile, a firm handshake, and an invitation to join him in a glass of Harvey's Bristol Cream. This genial host was unrecognisable from the gasket-blowing tyrant of Gloria's lurid description.

The conversational preliminaries finally eased to a conclusion as Gomersall handed Jacob a second glass of sherry. He cleared his throat, and Jacob expected a question about progress on the de Villiers investigation. Instead the editor said he wanted

Jacob to handle an exciting new idea, a series of features articles about famous historic crimes. A sort of *Newgate Calendar de nos jours* for busy readers with short attention spans. When Jacob asked how much time he should take off from his current activities, he was told to forget them and concentrate all his energies on this latest commission. The advertising wallahs reckoned it would put ten thousand a week on the circulation.

"Surely we'd do far better with the de Villiers story, sir. It's dynamite. Absolute dynamite."

Gomersall's smile faded. "One problem with dynamite, lad. It can blow up in your face."

"But only the other day you were saying…"

"Things have changed. The lawyers are panic-stricken. They've given the story the thumbs-down."

"Because of the risk of a libel suit?" Jacob ran a despairing hand through his unruly hair. "That's never stopped us before. A person can only sue for defamation if they have a decent reputation to defend. Marcel Ambrose is a homicidal gangster; Kiki de Villiers a prostitute who married well."

"You're talking about people with deep pockets, lad."

"We've never been afraid to take on the rich and powerful. It's not as if Sir Morton Wragg—"

"Leave Sir Morton out of it." Gomersall's expression hardened. "I'm the editor of the *Clarion*. This is my decision. Mine alone."

Jacob put down his sherry glass. Realising he'd touched a nerve, he looked into his employer's eyes. For the first time he could recall, Gomersall blinked first.

"Of course," he said, "my thinking is informed by commercial realities and the best legal advice. But I believe this decision is in our readers' interests."

"Surely our readers want to know about the criminals roaming the streets of London right now. Not those who trooped off to the gallows donkey's years ago."

Gomersall lifted his head. "We've spent a lot of time and money investigating contemporary crime. Now's the right moment to adjust our strategic priorities; that's all there is to it."

"Strategic priorities? We're on the brink of a breakthrough." How much should he say about the threat to Kiki de Villiers? "We can't give up now. Honestly, I believe this is a matter of life and death."

"Look, Jacob." This must be serious, Jacob thought. When did he last call me by my Christian name? "We've campaigned long and hard against corruption in Soho. I'm proud of that, but the truth is, the vice stuff is old hat. Most of the night-clubs in town have closed their doors for good. Those that survive are struggling because their customers are tight for cash. If the Slump gets any worse, soon there'll be no dens of iniquity left."

Jacob's jaw was set. "Marcel Ambrose is definitely back in town."

"Do the police know?"

"Yes."

"Then leave them to do their job."

Jacob closed his eyes. "Sammy Postles was one of my best snouts. Last night Ambrose had Sammy cut up and drowned. Punishment for talking to me. Sammy's remains were fished out of the Regent's Canal this morning. I just wrote up the story."

Gomersall was quiet for a few moments. "Sorry to hear that."

"Not as sorry as I am."

In normal circumstances, not even Jacob would have dared to speak to Gomersall like that. Had he gone too far? He realised that, if he had, he didn't care. Some things simply must be said.

"Look here, Jacob." Gomersall didn't sound angry. What

was going on? "It's hard, I know, but sometimes we just have to…move on. I've not lost my nerve, whatever you may think, but I have a business to run. We can't waste any more precious resources on Ambrose and de Villiers. In case you're wondering, the board is right behind me. Sir Morton too. Marcel Ambrose is yesterday's news."

"What about the stuff you want me to write? Positively prehistoric."

"We can learn from history," Gomersall said portentously. "Crime is a constant, even in the most civilised society. I want you to explore the fascinating stories—"

"Kiki de Villiers's life is in jeopardy."

"The police will take care of her. Leave her be. The woman has a sick, elderly husband. For all we know, he hasn't got much time left. She's already suffered one bereavement. If she wants to seek a little pleasure, an escape from the humdrum, so be it. It's not our business to act as moral censors."

"Only the other day we ran a front-page—"

"The other day?" Gomersall put his thumbs in his waist-coat pockets and loomed over Jacob like a prosecution barris-ter, about to urge the jury to condemn the accused. "I'm telling you, this campaign is dead. I simply wanted to tip you the wink before everyone else. Didn't want to take you by surprise in an open meeting. That way it would look like a slap on the wrist."

For the second time in a matter of hours, Jacob put his head in his hands.

"Look." Gomersall became avuncular again. "You did a first-rate job on the Hades Club business. Sir Morton was impressed. I heard it from his own lips. Play your cards right and you'll become his blue-eyed boy. We couldn't ask for a better return on the investment of time."

"And that's what matters," Jacob said heavily.

"You're a crime correspondent, not some idiot on a soapbox at Hyde Park Corner."

"That's your final word?"

"Yes. Leave it there. Regarding Mrs. de Villiers—forget you ever heard her name. As far as the *Clarion* is concerned, she no longer exists."

Chapter 18

"My sincere condolences." Laurent spoke in a hushed voice. His eyelids were lowered as he leaned back in his leather chair. "I'm truly sorry."

Joe Postles twitched. His face was drained of colour. "Sorry won't bring my brother back."

"No."

They were in Laurent's office. The club manager lifted a crystal decanter and poured two generous measures of cognac into a pair of tumblers. His big brown eyes were misty with sentiment.

"Here's to Sammy. He was a good man, Joe."

The little man rubbed his wrist before lifting his glass. Rachel had cracked a bone and it hadn't stopped hurting.

"The best."

"We all like a tipple now and then," Laurent savoured the tang. He'd abandoned any pretence at a French accent. "With Sammy, it was different. He needed the stuff, couldn't manage without it. The drink made him desperate for money. Trouble was, it loosened his tongue."

Joe wiped his mouth and said in a muffled voice, "He couldn't help it!"

"We all make choices, Joe."

"Easy for you to say. You weren't asked to go to the morgue and look at…"

"Nobody should have to do that," Laurent interrupted. "Not for their little brother. It's not fair. But then, life isn't fair, Joe. We all know that."

"Sammy was a fine-looking boy," Joe muttered. "But they made such a mess of him with the razor…" He choked back a sob.

Laurent gazed at the ceiling. Anything to avoid the little man's distress. "None of us wants any unpleasantness."

"It was murder, plain and simple!" Joe burst out. "There wasn't no need to kill him! If only Ambrose would've warned Sammy, he'd have been sure to—"

"Look, Joe, you've got to be reasonable. That isn't how these things work. You've been around a long time, you know better than me. Nobody likes a copper's nark."

"Sammy never blabbed to the police, not ever!"

"He talked to that kid who scribbles for the newspaper, didn't he?"

Joe scowled but said nothing. Laurent finished his brandy. "Stool pigeon, see?"

"Sammy was no stool pigeon."

"Come on, Joe, there's no getting away from what he did."

"Whatever you say, Ambrose didn't have to…"

"Look, Joe. That's enough. You know I liked Sammy, everyone did. But he couldn't keep his trap shut, that's what did for him." Laurent leaned back in his chair. "Put yourself in the guvnor's shoes."

"That piece of shit!"

"Hey!" Laurent said sharply. "Show some respect. Remember who pays your wages. And your ma's rent. If the guvnor doesn't crack down on a stool pigeon, people will start taking liberties. Sure as night follows day."

"But…"

Laurent banged his fist on the desk. "Listen to me. It was bad enough that the journo got away and Bob Earlam took a hell of a beating. The guvnor couldn't simply smack Sammy's legs and tell him not to be a naughty boy. People would say he's gone soft in his old age, those years out of England have been the ruin of him. He had to make an example of Sammy. If not, who knows where we would all have been? You've got to have discipline."

Joe was sullen. "He didn't need to slash him to ribbons."

"Look, Joe, I said I'm sorry. It wasn't personal. Monsieur Ambrose told me to give you this."

Opening a drawer in the desk, he pulled out a packet.

"It's for your ma. Two hundred quid. So that Sammy can have a good send-off; it's the least he deserves."

"Blood money," Joe said. "Stick it up your arse."

"No need to be coarse, Joe. This ain't for you, but your ma, like I said. A personal gesture from the guvnor. Make sure she gets the cash. And the message."

There was a long pause. Finally Joe reached across and took the packet. Laurent gave a nod of approval.

"That's better. Sensible."

Joe made a scornful noise. Laurent frowned.

"That'll do, Joe. You need to mind your *p*'s and *q*'s, my friend. Now Monsieur Ambrose is back, he's watching all of us like a hawk. And he's not best pleased with you. Thinks you might have told Sammy not to act so stupid."

"It wasn't my fault!"

"He's worried you might have blabbed too. I stuck up for you, put my neck on the block. Told him you've changed, that these days you keep your lips buttoned. So don't let me down. You need to make him trust you again. And don't even think about stepping out of line. That's the way people get knocked over." Joe stood up. "Hey, where do you think you're going?"

"Taking the cash home, like you said."

"Ah, fair enough. There's just one more thing."

The little man turned at the door and gave him a dirty look. "What?"

"Ambrose has a job for you. He needs a driver."

"You know what he can do."

"Don't be silly, Joe. Remember who calls the tune." He paused, but Joe said nothing. "Monsieur Ambrose, that's who. Bob Earlam is still in hospital. Seems they may need to operate. One thing's for sure, he won't be driving anyone anywhere for a while. So you need to do the guvnor a favour."

Joe frowned. "A favour?"

"Yeah, it's a chance for you to show willing. Prove where your loyalty lies."

"What is he after?"

"You're to drive him to Rye."

"Rye?"

"East side of Sussex. On the coast."

"Oh, yeah, near Camber Sands? Me and Sammy went there years ago with our ma."

"That's the place. Lovely spot in summer." Laurent opened his desk drawer and took out a slip of paper. "Take a gander at this."

Joe peered at the words scribbled in capital letters. SEPULCHRE HOUSE, SEPULCHRE STREET, RYE.

"Can you remember that, Joe?"

"Nothing wrong with my memory," the little man said sullenly. "So what's a sep—sepulchre, then?"

Laurent thought for a moment. "Kind of resting place."

He tore the piece of paper into tiny fragments. "Now don't you forget where you're taking the guvnor."

"He's only just got back to London. Why does he want to go to the seaside? I don't get it."

"You don't need to get it."

"I'm busy."

"Don't mess me about, Joe. I'm a patient man, I've known you a long time, but there are limits, right? Fact of the matter is, Sammy broke the cardinal rule. He let the guvnor down. You don't want to make the same mistake, do you?" Laurent waited. "I mean, do you?"

"No," Joe said sullenly.

"There you are, then. Now, get off home. Give your ma the cash and get yourself a bit of shut-eye. You've got a fair old drive, to Rye and back. You don't want to fall asleep at the wheel."

"He wants to go there today?"

"Tonight," Laurent said. "He's paying a call on an old friend. You need to sit tight till he's done, then bring him straight back here. Set off at seven, aim to be back here before midnight. Put the guvnor's car away in the garage and then forget you ever went out. Him and me were playing cards all evening. Right?"

"What's this all about?"

"You don't need to know."

Joe Postles breathed out. "Come on, if I don't have a clue what's going on, I might put my foot in it. Without meaning to."

Laurent deliberated. "This goes no further, understand?"

"Uh-huh."

"I'm serious. It's just between me and you. Remember what happened to Sammy."

"I won't forget that," the little man mumbled. "All right. Cross my heart and hope to die."

"That's more like it." Laurent lowered his voice. "Lulu Dabo lives in Rye. The guvnor wants to pay her a surprise visit. Talk about old times, know what I mean?"

There was a long silence.

"So it's just like before?" Joe asked.

"How do you mean?"

"Remember what happened to that blonde in Charlotte Street? Took up with some copper when she thought no one was watching? Ambrose shot her in the head."

"You've got a long memory," Laurent said.

Joe nodded.

Laurent took another sip of brandy. "Memories ain't healthy. Some things are best forgotten, take it from me."

"So Ambrose is going to kill Lulu?"

"I didn't say that. He's going to look her up, that's all."

"And put a bullet through her brain?"

"Take my advice," Laurent said. "Don't ask no more questions. Actually, don't think; that's not healthy either. Just drive him where he wants to go. After last night, he's like a cat on hot bricks. So do whatever he asks. No argy-bargy. Please, Joe, it's the only way. One death in the family is enough. Ain't it?"

———

Five minutes after leaving Chez Laurent, Joe Postles stepped into a telephone kiosk and dialled the office of the *Clarion*.

"Jacob Flint?" the girl on the switchboard repeated. "Who shall I say is calling?"

"Joe Postles. He'll talk to me."

"Hold the line... Putting you through now."

"Mr. Flint?"

There was a pause. "I wasn't expecting to hear from you, Joe. Not after last night."

"Yeah, sorry about that, Mr. Flint. You know how things are."

Jacob took a breath. "Bad news about Sammy."

"You heard what happened?"

"Yeah, Ambrose killed him."

A brief silence. "I've got something for you."

"Fire away."

"This woman you're looking into."

"Kiki de Villiers, yes."

"Or Lulu Dabo."

"What about her?"

"I know where she is today, if you're interested."

"I'm interested, all right. Shall we meet?"

"No time for that, Mr. Flint."

"Can you give me the details over the telephone?"

"It's a place in Sussex. Town called Rye."

"Not Sepulchre House, by any chance? In Sepulchre Street."

"You're ahead of me, Mr. Flint."

"Does Ambrose have her address?"

"Yeah, he does. And you know what that means."

"I do, Joe. Thanks for calling."

A nervous cough. "No hard feelings after last night, eh?"

"No hard feelings. And I'm truly sorry about your brother."

"Me too," Joe Postles said.

———

In his room on the first floor of the Hardwick Hotel, Duncalf sat on the edge of his bed. He wore gloves and was studying the contents of the folder from Major Whitlow. The buzz of a fly distracted him. He looked up and saw it scuttling along the cornice. The sound it made was as irritating as a toothache. He needed peace and quiet when he was preparing to go to work, and he couldn't tolerate any kind of interference.

Much of his life was spent in hotels. On arriving in London, he had taken a room with a view over Russell Square. As usual, he'd chosen one of the less imposing hotels on the square; although money was no object, fripperies like the winter gardens and Turkish baths to be found at the Imperial held no appeal for him. Nor did fine cuisine.

His choice was entirely practical. The Hardwick was large enough to function in an efficient fashion, modest enough not to attract clients it needed to fuss over. For Duncalf, small guest houses run by inquisitive landladies were only a last resort. He'd learned that lesson the hard way early in his career. One night, a blowsy woman who had flirted with him from the moment he booked bed and breakfast at her grubby establishment had burst into his bedroom wearing a wholly inadequate nightgown. At that very moment, he was loading his trusty Webley Mark VI revolver. Disposing of the woman and making sure that nobody connected him with her disappearance had caused an inordinate amount of trouble. All because he'd chosen a cheap billet and then omitted to lock his door. Mistakes never to be repeated.

The fly buzzed its way across the carpet towards him. He watched and waited, still as a statue, until it came within reach. In a swift and silent movement, he raised his foot and crushed the insect. After scraping the remains from the sole of his shoe, he tipped them into the wastepaper bin.

The small act of violence calmed him. Over the years, one or two people had presumed he was nerveless, but that wasn't quite right. Unless the adrenaline flowed, you never achieved the best results. This task represented a challenge. The circumstances were far from ideal. He prided himself on careful preparation and regretted Major Whitlow's insistence that the deed be done within a matter of hours. But you had to expect the unexpected, to be ready to adapt your plans at a moment's notice. Inflexibility and reliance on lazy assumptions were hall-marks of a third-rate assassin, the sort who came to grief after two or three kills.

A seasoned professional had to trust instinct. You could never anticipate everything, although taking pains over the preliminaries helped to minimise the risk of being confounded by a peculiar turn of events. All the same, doing a job in a rush increased the danger. Major Whitlow knew that as well as anyone. Duncalf had no idea what had forced the major's hand—or should that be claw?—and he didn't care. He'd never suffered from the curse of curiosity or been plagued by a roaming imagination. The secret of success lay in being single-minded and not fretting about what might have been. You had to play with the hand you were dealt.

He picked up the folder again and pored over its contents. He'd skimmed through them twice already, to fix the outline of the plan in his mind, but now he needed to memorise the key details. He had impressive powers of recall, matched by an abil-ity to move on and forget. These qualities had stood him in good stead ever since he was eight years old. He'd finally returned to the dingy hovel from which he'd run away after a fierce row with his widowed mother to find her hanging from the ceiling and his younger brother drowned in the bath. A scrawled, semi-literate note explained that not only had bailiffs taken all the family's possessions but the landlord was about to evict them. After that, the young Duncalf had wanted nothing more to do with the rest of the world. He yearned for the earth to swallow him up so that he disappeared for ever. These days, he exulted inwardly at his sheer invisibility. Moving unnoticed through crowded streets was strangely thrilling. It gave him a sense of power.

The photographs revealed that Mrs. Kiki de Villiers was attractive, but he wasn't interested in her looks, let alone in speculating about whatever peccadilloes had caused her to become a marked woman. All that mattered was her mass of red hair. It made her an easy target. According to his brief, she had a flat in central London, while her husband lived out in the country. Yet there was every confidence that she would be in Rye tonight. One of the major's tried and tested stratagems was to have a subordinate set up some bogus assignation, tying the target to a particular location at a particular time. Possibly he'd done the same in this case. Duncalf wasn't interested. The background arrangements didn't concern him. He did his own job and expected other people to do theirs.

Unfolding the map, he studied the route to the south coast. Timings were bound to be approximate, but he didn't have much of a margin for error. Cover of darkness was invariably helpful in his line of work, and his instructions were to reach his destination after sunset, but without delaying his arrival beyond a further half hour. He made mental calculations, allowing for the unfamiliarity of the roads, the possibility of hold-ups, and the need to adjust his speed in the dark.

Next he turned to the street plan of Rye. It would be unwise to park his car in Sepulchre Street, but he needed it to be within easy reach, in case of an emergency. The major had flagged a couple of convenient locations. Duncalf would make a final decision when he was on the spot.

He subjected the neatly sketched floor plan of Sepulchre House to a minute examination. According to the brief, he was likely to find Mrs. de Villiers in her sitting room at the front of the house, but that couldn't be taken for granted. Her devoted maid represented a serious complication. Apparently, the relationship between mistress and servant was so intimate that they might be spending the evening in each other's company.

His orders were to shoot both women. This was fortunate.

Stabbing or some other method would have made his task more difficult. The modus operandi was a crucial part of the major's planning. A gun must be the intended scapegoat's weapon of choice.

How much simpler the assignment would have been if his employers had lured the maid away from the scene of the crime. There must be compelling reasons why she could not be permitted to survive. Presumably because of what she knew.

Duncalf sighed. Why did people never learn? Ignorance really was bliss. It was a cardinal mistake to know too much.

Chapter 19

Romney Marsh brooded under vast ashen skies. Threads of mist gave the lowlands an otherworldly atmosphere. Trueman drove the Austin Seven with a sure touch, concentrating with his habitual intensity. He'd not uttered a word since they'd left London behind, long before undulating countryside gave way to flat ground, much of it below sea level. The Phantom would have been tricky to manoeuvre through the narrow, twisting lanes and ditches, but the smaller car made good progress through the labyrinth.

Rachel's nose was stuck in a gazetteer. Martha, sitting by her side, knew she was committing its contents to memory. It reminded her of when they were growing up on Gaunt and Rachel had combed through the books in the judge's astonishing library. Martha often teased her about it, but Rachel always gave the same retort.

"I want to know *everything.*"

To this day, she hungered for knowledge. Sometimes her craving came at a cost. Right now she was missing the chance to absorb the forlorn beauty of this corner of southeast England, a stark yet compelling patchwork of snaking watercourses and reed beds.

At this time of year the mood of the Marshlands was uncompromising. Wind had bent the few trees and everywhere seemed empty and barren. Even the sheep seemed to be in sombre mood. This was a bleak and isolated corner of England. And yet. There was something tantalising about the sparse landscape that Martha found weirdly seductive. Almost mystical.

"So this is the Fifth Continent," she said, determined to break the silence. "Reclaimed from the sea, with drainage channels criss-crossing the fields."

Rachel looked up from her book. "Those waterways are known as sewers. Pleasingly sinister, don't you think?"

"They look innocent enough to me."

"The Marsh has a dark history. Once upon a time, the Black Death ravaged the population. For centuries, people were struck down by marsh fever. They paid a price for trying to subjugate nature. Preventing the waves from taking back what used to be theirs."

"Things change. This is green pasture, not some poisonous swamp. The fields are lush. Sheep graze whichever way you look."

"They outnumber human beings by a hundred to one. Their wool is so thick and luxurious that in olden times it was worth its weight in gold. Flemish wool traders paid a fortune to have fleeces smuggled over. There were lots of medieval churches on the Marsh and their vaults were used to store wool, brandy, and tobacco. The snag was this: the smell of the baccy was so strong that anyone with a good nose could sniff out its hiding place."

"Weren't they afraid of committing blasphemy? Treating the house of God as a warehouse for contraband?"

"The Marshmen were always a law unto themselves. In medieval times, their godlessness provoked the authorities. Clerics slept with their parishioners and one adulterous couple was whipped five times around the marketplaces of Romney and Hythe. Later on, the Lords of the Levels kept order. Flooding was a constant threat. So were the French. Coastal defences saved the land from being drowned by the sea, and the Royal Military Canal was built to deter Napoleon from invading. There was a saying: *Serve God, honour the King, but first maintain the Wall."*

"Here endeth the first lesson," Martha murmured.

Rachel shut the book and stowed it away in her handbag. "Sorry, I got carried away."

"This place really is cut-off. We haven't passed another car for a good ten minutes."

"Evan Tucker likes it. A world away from the city bustle."

"Such a lonely spot." Martha considered. "Perhaps that's why he started throwing parties and chummed up with Roddy Malam's sister-in-law."

"Perhaps."

The car slowed as they approached a fingerpost marked *Dykesbridge*. Trueman turned down a narrow track.

"Almost there," he said.

"You've made excellent time," Rachel said.

Martha scanned the bare, featureless fields. "Looks like we've arrived in the middle of nowhere."

"Dykesbridge is a lost village. Its main claim to fame was a mention in the Domesday Book. The old Saxon church fell into decay and disappeared centuries ago. All that remains is a handful of farm buildings, most of which have been abandoned— and that fingerpost. Together with two other properties. The homes of Evan Tucker and Nurse Wardle."

"Why would anyone build out here?"

Rachel shrugged. "There's a place on the coast called

Littlestone a few miles away. Fifty years ago an entrepreneur tried to develop it as a resort to rival Hythe or Broadstairs. His company bought a few inland plots on the cheap, to provide fancy homes for folk who dreamed of living close to nature. But he ran out of capital and only two were built."

"Look over yonder," Trueman said, steering round yet another bend.

Tall chimneys loomed ahead of them. They belonged to a sturdy Victorian country house. The roof had red tiles and the sides were angled to resemble the wings of a butterfly.

"So this is The Risings," Martha said. "Hard to imagine as a setting for wild parties. It's as quiet as the grave."

"All the better for people who want to let their hair down," Rachel said. "There are no neighbours to complain. Drop me outside the gate, Cliff."

"Sure you don't want us to come with you?" Martha asked.

"No need. You both have work to do."

Martha was conscious of her friend's body stiffening by her side.

"You're excited," she said.

"Why wouldn't I be?" Rachel gave her a wicked smile. "I'm about to confess a terrible secret."

———

Duncalf checked his watch. Time to collect his delivery. Putting on his cloth cap and mackintosh, he locked the door behind him and hurried down a corridor to the back stairs. Nobody was about. Once outside, he found himself in an alleyway running along the side of the hotel. He walked to the far end of the passage and saw a middle-aged woman in a brown coat walking sedately down the street towards him. She was carrying a brown parcel tied up with string.

He ducked back into the alley and leaned against the wall of the hotel. A dustbin stood at the end of the alleyway. On reaching it, the woman paused and cleared her throat noisily.

Without looking at Duncalf, she said, "Warm for the time of year, isn't it?"

"Quite unseasonal," Duncalf agreed.

Satisfied with his response, the woman lifted the dustbin lid and dropped the parcel inside. She walked on without a backward glance.

Duncalf counted to five before delving into the dustbin. There was no one in sight. Yanking out the parcel, he tucked it under his arm and retraced his steps back up to his room. Again he didn't pass anybody inside the hotel. All very satisfactory. Locking himself in, he opened the parcel.

Inside was a bundle, loosely wrapped in newspaper and containing several items. The first was a mortice key for the door of the house in Sepulchre Street. There was no chain, he'd been told. The subject must assume she was safe there. The major would have sent someone to the property, posing as an official from the rating authorities or suchlike, to conduct a reconnaissance and take an impression of the key.

There was also a Lebel revolver, a Modèle 1892 with a walnut grip and half a dozen cartridges. Duncalf had a good working knowledge of hand weapons, and he was aware that the Lebel had been a standard-issue sidearm for officers in the French military during the Great War. To this day it remained popular with members of the gendarmerie. Duncalf preferred the Webley for stopping a man in his tracks. He would only use the Lebel in single-action mode, since the trigger pull for double-action firing was stiff and unreliable. However, there was always rhyme and reason to the major's planning. The scapegoat must favour the Lebel. Perhaps he was a Frenchman.

Duncalf put the key in his trouser pocket. After a final skim of the information in the major's folder, he lit a match and started to burn its contents, item by item. Finally the folder itself was set alight. This was a painstaking process, but he knew better than to cut corners and leave telltale fragments of information for someone to decipher. In the end he was left with a pile of ash, which he poured into a large bag, taking care to spill nothing.

He opened the window to let the smoke escape and tidied the room thoroughly. Although his intention was to come back tonight after completing his mission in Rye, he was well aware of the fate of the best-laid plans. He must ensure that if he could not return for any reason, no trace of his presence here could be discovered.

After shutting the window he put his things in a grubby and inconspicuous holdall, with the bag of ash at the top. Then he loaded the gun and secreted it in a capacious, specially designed pouch inside his mackintosh. Turning to leave, he caught sight of himself in the mirror. For once he allowed himself the indulgence of a contented smile.

Three weeks earlier, he'd reached the age of thirty-nine. If he'd devoted himself to becoming an athlete or a boxer or an oarsman, by now he'd be past his peak. In this career, however, he was approaching his prime. Tonight's assignment presented formidable obstacles, but he savoured the prospect of surmounting every hurdle.

In his own particular way, he was a sportsman. Actually, on second thoughts, warrior was nearer the mark. And he was raring to enter the field of battle.

———

The Risings stood at the end of a short drive with ground elder poking up through the gravel. To one side were semi-derelict outbuildings and a brick garage large enough to house several vehicles. As Rachel approached the house, the front door swung open. The sound of raised voices came from inside. A moment later, a woman stumbled out. Rachel recognised her at once. Phoebe Wardle was wearing the same maroon overcoat that she'd had on when she left the Hades Gallery.

Evan Tucker followed her outside. When he spoke, it might have been a child wailing. "I can't believe you'd do this!"

Suddenly he caught sight of Rachel. She fixed on her brightest smile and greeted him with a cheery wave.

"Mr. Tucker!" she called. "I promised to pay you a visit!"

Phoebe Wardle gave Tucker a decisive nod of farewell and set off down the drive. Rachel changed course so as to intercept her. After a moment's vacillation Tucker moved towards them.

"Nurse Wardle, isn't it?" Rachel thrust out her hand. "My name is Rachel Savernake. Captain Malam is a friend of mine. Perhaps he's mentioned my name?"

With evident reluctance, the other woman shook hands. She seemed haggard and weary.

"Rachel Savernake?" Nurse Wardle frowned, as if delving into her memory.

"We didn't get the chance to speak, but I saw you the other night at the Hades Gallery. What a terrible business."

"Yes, dreadful." The other woman was torn, Rachel thought. Desperate to escape, yet definitely keen to make sense of a wholly unexpected encounter. "You were a friend of Damaris Gethin?"

"An admirer. I collect art, you see. That's why she invited me. And then I bumped into Roddy—and saw you, in conversation with Mr. Tucker here."

Evan Tucker gave a little cough and adjusted his spectacles. "Miss Savernake is an accomplished pianist. She even writes music."

"A rival, Evan, or a protégée?" Phoebe Wardle seemed amused, despite herself. "How sweet."

"I called on Mr. Tucker in Denmark Street," Rachel said. "I'm delighted to meet you. Captain Malam mentioned your name to me."

"Did he?"

Phoebe Wardle was good at masking her feelings; it was part of a nurse's stock-in-trade. But Rachel had no doubt that she was puzzled.

"I was sorry to hear you lost your husband. Roddy—the captain—says you've been awfully brave."

"Oh, really?"

"Absolutely. The way you keep the clinic going, for instance. Can't be easy in these straitened times."

"No." Phoebe Wardle took a breath. "As it happens, I've closed it down. My late husband wanted me to carry on his work, and I've done my utmost to honour his wishes, but the time has come to admit defeat."

Rachel looked down at the ground. "That is very…disappointing news. Was this a sudden decision?"

"Not at all." The nurse seemed to gain confidence, as if glad to get something off her chest. "My patients are younger women who suffer from serious nervous complaints. Some cases can be very harrowing. Rest and recuperation in a quiet backwater like Dykesbridge is the best remedy. Because I've had to manage with next to no help since Giles died, I can only take on patients one at a time. Even that has proved extremely taxing."

"We all understand that, my dear," Evan Tucker said. "But as I keep saying, you're being very hasty. To throw up such a valuable practice on a whim…"

"It's not a whim," she said firmly. "My mind is made up. I need to take a break. What suits my patients is no good for me. I have to get away from this desolate place. Frankly, it's like living at the end of the world."

She gestured at their surroundings, the vast, sombre sky and the flat grazing land stretching out as far as the eye could see. There was a nip in the air and the first drops of rain were beginning to fall.

"What will you do for money?" Evan Tucker demanded.

"I'll manage."

"Where will you go, even if you do find someone to buy your home?"

Phoebe Wardle spread her arms. "In the long run, who knows? For the time being, I just want to escape to somewhere warm where there's life and laughter. Away from the cold and the wet and the stench of antiseptic."

"It seems so rash. So sudden. When we talked the other night, you never gave me an inkling..."

"Damaris Gethin's death gave me the shove I needed." The nurse trembled. "A life snuffed out in an instant. All three of us witnessed it. When the guillotine fell... I'll never forget it."

"Nor I," Tucker said in a low voice.

"A shocking reminder of our mortality. Life is short; I must make a break. Giles only left a pittance, but I've saved a few pounds, and I'm ready to spend them. What happens after that, who knows?"

Tucker exhaled. "I pray that you'll reconsider."

"I'm sorry, Evan. You won't change my mind."

"But..."

"That's my final word." She nodded at Rachel. "Goodbye, Miss Savernake. I don't expect we'll meet again."

Chapter 20

"This must be the clinic," Trueman said.

They'd reached the only other building in the neighbourhood that wasn't part of a farm. Phoebe Wardle's home was
called Orgarswick, after another of the Marsh's lost villages.
There was no name on the stone gatepost or anything to indicate the presence of a clinic.

"Discretion assured," Martha said as she got out. "I'll have a
look-see and join you outside the pub later. If I'm not there in an
hour, come and rescue me."

Trueman started up the Austin again. He'd familiarised
himself with an ordnance survey map of this part of the Marsh
before setting out, and he knew exactly where he was going.
The lane looped around the farmland and the ditches before re-
joining the road they had left earlier. He rounded a bend and a
scattering of cottages and other buildings came into view.

He came to a halt in front of a small public house. A notice
above the door stated that the licensee was one Job Mipps.
Trueman reversed into a yard at the side of the tavern. Beside
an old wooden garage was a board bearing the legend: *Taxis,
Undertaker, Prop. J. Mipps.*

"Pays to be versatile," he muttered to himself.

A pub sign with faded paint was swinging in the breeze. Trueman could make out a man holding a lantern as others unloaded contraband from a rowing boat at dead of night. The pub was called The Owlers.

"Owling" was an old slang term for smuggling wool. The owlers were nocturnal desperadoes who risked their necks to cheat the revenue men. They communicated with each other by way of melancholy sounds inspired by the hooting of owls. The ditches and the dykes of the misty Marsh made perfect hiding places when customs officers came hunting after them.

The pub's door was firmly closed, but a light burned inside the saloon bar. Although it was illegal to serve drinks after three o'clock in the afternoon, Trueman doubted the owlers' descendants would scruple at breaking the licensing laws in order to enjoy a little liquid refreshment on a dour Saturday afternoon.

He looked around, using his knobkerrie as a walking stick. There was nobody outside the pub, but when he peered through a grimy window, he saw three or four people congregated by the bar. Moving away, he picked up a pebble and lobbed it against the window. Leaning on the knobkerrie, he waited for the door to open.

A portly, red-faced man came out and stood in front of the open door, folding his arms with a stern proprietorial air as he looked for whoever had disturbed the peace. Mr. Mipps, Trueman presumed.

He gave a cheerful wave. "Any chance I can wet my whistle?"

"We're closed. Don't you know what time it is?"

Trueman put his hand in his pocket and produced several coins. There was enough cash in his palm to buy half a dozen rounds.

"I don't mind paying over the odds."

The man told him where he could go with his money.

Trueman took a long stride towards him. "I only want a drink and a bit of a natter."

Solidly built as the landlord was, Trueman dwarfed him.

"I'm not much of a one for book reading," he said conversationally, "but *Doctor Syn* is a hell of a yarn. This is smuggling country, ain't it?"

As Mipps stared at him, Trueman began to recite:

> *Here's to the feet wot have walked the plank—*
> *Yo-ho for the dead man's throttle!*
> *And here's to the corpses afloat in the tank*
> *And the dead man's teeth in the bottle.*

As if provoked by the verse, a thickset, weather-beaten individual in his forties blundered out of the pub.

"All right, Job?"

The landlord jerked a thumb at Trueman. "This 'un's after a drink."

The newcomer belched. "Funny feller, hey?"

"I don't want no trouble," Trueman said.

The other man spat noisily on the ground. "You'd better piss off, then."

Trueman still had on his leather driving gauntlets. His huge right hand reached out and grasped the thickset man by the shoulder. Tightening his grip, he provoked a yelp of pain. He lifted the man an inch off the ground and shook him hard before letting him down ungently, so that he stumbled backwards and ended up in a heap on the ground.

"Hey!" the landlord said. "No call for that."

Trueman picked up his knobkerrie. "No hard feelings, gents, but I did ask nicely. Any chance of that drink?"

Pausing only to deposit the bag of ash in a dustbin a hundred yards from his hotel, Duncalf walked briskly through light drizzle. His destination was a back street near Smithfield Market, where his car was stored. On reaching London, he'd filled up with petrol and given the vehicle a thorough check before leaving it in a lock-up garage. This he rented from a man called Hobson, who managed an abattoir. Hobson was an old army acquaintance, someone else who presumably hadn't had his fill of slaughter during his time in the trenches.

Duncalf had a practical turn of mind. He liked tinkering with motor engines and enjoyed driving. Cars were an exception to his rule about remaining unobtrusive at all times. The need for speed and efficiency when in a tight corner trumped everything else. He reckoned it was an unnecessary risk to hire cars from people who might ask awkward questions, so he always used his own. The nature of his profession made it necessary to change models every few months. He regarded it as a perk of the job. At the turn of the year he'd purchased an MG Sporting Six with a top speed of 85 mph. On the trip down from the north of Scotland he'd cruised along at a mile a minute. A return trip to Rye would be child's play.

As he approached the street where the garage was located, he was jerked from his thoughts by someone shouting his name.

"Oi! Duncalf!"

He froze. Instinctively, his right hand slipped inside his mackintosh and took hold of the revolver. The voice hailing him had a strident edge.

Hobson.

Duncalf turned to see the man weaving unsteadily towards him. He'd just tottered out of a spit and sawdust pub and was much the worse for wear. It didn't help that his foot had been blown off by a grenade in the war. Duncalf swore under his breath even as he released his grip on the Lebel. This was a rotten stroke of luck. Hobson got up very early to work in the market and by this time of day he was usually propping up a bar.

"Penny for 'em!" The words were slurred. "Taking the jalopy out for a spin? Up to no good, I'll be bound!"

"Been away for a few days' fishing," Duncalf said, feigning good cheer. "Back on the road tomorrow. It's all go!"

"How's...how's business?"

Hobson was under the impression that Duncalf worked as a salesman, specialising in motor parts for trade customers. As he lurched forward, Duncalf was assailed by the stench of beer fumes.

Duncalf took a step back. "So-so. You know how it is."

"We...we must have a noggin together one of these days."

"Surely."

Hobson looked as though he meant to keep maundering on, but Duncalf gave a decisive nod of farewell and strode away. Thankfully the fellow made no attempt to follow him. When Duncalf reached the street corner, he looked back and saw Hobson had slipped on the wet cobbles and ended up in a heap on the floor. Any minute now he'd probably be sick.

A depressing encounter. Duncalf suppressed a sigh as he headed for the lock-up. Hobson threatened to become a nuisance; in his younger days, the man had been admirably taciturn, but alcoholics could never be trusted not to talk out of turn. That spelled danger. It would be a chore to find another suitable lock-up, but Duncalf would rather do that than risk finding his privacy compromised and be forced to kill the man. Further evidence, not that he needed it, that it didn't pay to get close to anyone. Thankfully, he never found himself yearning for company. On the contrary, a solitary existence suited him down to the ground.

———

Marcel Ambrose's car was garaged in a mews approached through an entrance under a building in Regent Street. At ten to five, Joe Postles arrived there. He'd knocked back a stiff whisky to steady his nerves after the terrible events of the past few hours, but he was sure it wouldn't affect his driving. He settled himself in the driver's seat and inhaled the smell of the leather upholstery. Laurent had moved fast to buy a Lancia Lambda for Ambrose as soon as he learned the man was about to set foot back in Britain. This was the latest version of his favourite automobile and Joe supposed today would be the first time he'd had much of a ride in it.

Joe had put on the jacket and peaked cap that Ambrose liked his chauffeurs to wear. The man wasn't so different from a toff who belonged to the landed gentry. He had his standards and woe betide any servants who didn't keep up to scratch. He'd only been back in the country for a matter of days, yet it was almost like old times. Thanks to Laurent's energetic efforts, Ambrose had picked up where he'd left off.

Would things have been different if Laurent had taken a stand and tried to freeze him out? In Ambrose's absence Laurent had ruled the roost at the club, and most of the time he'd kept on the right side of the law. Sobrino had insisted on a cut of the takings, but he had other fish to fry and didn't cause them much bother. Joe was no angel, but the status quo suited him. Ambrose's return changed everything.

At first Joe had wondered how Laurent would take to playing second fiddle again, but the truth was, the man didn't have the bottle to take Ambrose on. He'd resumed his position as

Ambrose's sidekick without skipping a beat. Did he secretly prefer it that way, or did he itch to become a gangster and simply lack the guts? Whatever the truth, it was a crying shame. If Ambrose had stayed in France, Sammy would still be alive.

Gritting his teeth, Joe drove the car round to Kingly Street and waited. At five o'clock precisely, Marcel Ambrose emerged from an unmarked door which afforded a private access to Chez Laurent. He wore a double-breasted overcoat with a seal fur collar and a homburg. The bulk of the coat didn't quite disguise the bump of his holster and gun.

Joe jumped out and held open the rear door. Ambrose gave the Lambda an affectionate pat on the bonnet and climbed into the back of the car. Joe took his place behind the wheel.

"Sorry about your brother, Joe."

Joe took a breath. "Thank you, sir."

"You know how it is."

"Yes, sir."

"Your ma got the money?"

"Yes, sir. Thank you, sir."

Ambrose grunted. Having dealt with the niceties to his satisfaction, he leaned back in his seat and closed his eyes. By the time they crossed the Thames, his snores were rumbling through the car's interior, almost a match for the noise of the engine.

———

"I'm sorry to make a nuisance of myself," Rachel said.

"Not at all," Evan Tucker said absently, watching his neighbour stride out of sight. "We were simply having a little disagreement, nothing more to it than that."

Rachel's expression became mischievous. "A tiff?"

"I told you before," he said quickly. "Phoebe and I are neighbours and friends. Nothing more, if that's what you're hinting."

"I apologise," she said meekly. "You're obviously dismayed that Nurse Wardle wants to give up her practice."

"I'm thinking of her," he retorted. "Roddy Malam is a very dear friend of mine, and I was fond of poor Giles too. Since his death, I've tried to help Phoebe to… Well, things aren't easy for a young widow in this day and age."

"Generous of you."

"One does what one can. I'm afraid she's making a big mistake."

He took off his glasses to wipe away the drops of rain.

"Oh, dear, the weather is turning, isn't it?" Rachel looked hopefully towards the house.

"Yes, yes." He seemed flustered. "I suppose you'd better come in before we both get drenched."

"How kind."

They entered a hall with a quarry tile floor. It was draughty and dark. Shepherding her into a large sitting room, Tucker urged her to take a seat in an armchair with floral upholstery. A venerable Bechstein piano stood at the back of the room. There was a bookcase as well as a large sideboard with photographs and knick-knacks on top. On the wall hung a painting of two slender, fair-haired young men in shorts, staring out to sea. Rachel recognised the brushwork of Henry Scott Tuke.

"I'm afraid I can't offer much in the way of hospitality. A friend is coming to visit, and I need to make the place look more respectable. I used to have a married couple living in, but they left a fortnight ago. Until I can find more servants, I have to make do with a woman who comes in twice a week from Dymchurch."

"Goodness, how tiresome for you."

"Never mind," he said bravely. "May I offer you a cup of tea?"

"Thank you, I'd love a drink. Perhaps I could explain why

I've landed on your doorstep before I get back on my way. Not that I want to be a bother if you're expecting company."

"It's no bother," he said. "I must admit that I'm intrigued by your visit."

The moment he left the room, Rachel began to snoop around. First she looked inside the sideboard, but it was full of crockery and table linen and she found nothing of interest there or among Tucker's books about music. She lingered over the photographs. One showed Roderick Malam in his white flannels, leaning on his cricket bat in front of the pavilion at The Oval. He'd inscribed it with a flourish: *To Evan—Semper Fidelis*. She had to admit that the captain cut a dashing figure. His friendship with Tucker seemed one-sided, but was that the reality?

There were half a dozen publicity portraits autographed by well-known musicians. She was admiring one of them when Tucker returned, carrying a tray of tea things.

"Noël Coward," she said. "Signed to *a dear neighbour and friend.*"

Tucker gave a dismissive wave of the hand. "Noël has a place at Aldington, a few miles from here. We first met when he rented a cottage at Dymchurch. In the old days, we saw quite a lot of each other. It's different now he's always gallivanting."

"I suppose he's very busy," Rachel murmured, picking up another photograph. "And here is Leslie Sarony. Very popular, isn't he?"

"If you like that sort of thing," Tucker said. "Perhaps that's the mistake I've made. I've had too much self-respect. If I had more sense, I'd copy Sarony and write novelty songs. Nonsense like 'Jollity Farm.'"

Rachel began to croon. "Don't be cruel to a vegetabuel..."

Tucker groaned. "Utterly dreadful. Why do people lap up such puerile drivel? No, I simply couldn't lower myself."

"You're a true artist," Rachel told him.

"Thank you." He poured the tea. "May I ask what brings you out here? I mean, I'm charmed to see you again, but it's a long way to come for a casual social call."

Rachel bowed her head. "You can see right through me."

He shook his head. "I'm not sure I can."

She heaved a sigh. "This is very painful for me, but I made a promise to myself. I mustn't keep pretending that everything's all right. I swore that I'd be frank with you. There's something about you that makes me feel I can trust you with my secrets."

There was a strange, eager light in his eyes.

"Please feel free."

Rachel swallowed and dabbed at an imaginary tear. "I'm afraid that I have been very, very foolish."

Chapter 21

Orgarswick House was a sizeable place, constructed in the shape of a letter Y. Martha rang the doorbell three times, but there was no reply. She looked through the ground-floor windows but saw nobody. As far as she could tell, the whole place was deserted. No patients, no servants, and no Nurse Wardle. She began to scout around outside. The grounds amounted to two or three acres, but they didn't seem to have much of a story to tell.

There was a small garage with a hole in its roof and a tumbledown garden shed with a broken window. Martha peeked inside each ruin in turn but failed to find anything of interest. The wind was gaining strength, blowing rain into her face, but having spent her formative years in the tumultuous climate of an island out in the Irish Sea, she barely noticed.

Phoebe Wardle and her late husband had neglected the garden. Behind a bushy, unkempt hawthorn screen ran a tiny stream and a grassy path which wove through bindweed, dock leaves, and stinging nettles. The boundary of the grounds was marked by a rickety post-and-wire fence. The stream ran into a ditch on the other side. As Martha made her way round, she caught her foot on a thin, jutting slab of concrete. Out of curiosity she levered it up, only to discover that she'd stumbled on the lid of a foul-smelling cesspit.

Martha grimaced. The delights of remote rural living were matched by the drawbacks. She was following the curve of the path back towards the house, when she heard a woman's strident voice.

"Hey! What the hell are you doing?"

She looked around for a moment, but saw no one. Then she glanced up and made out a dim figure at a first-floor window. The woman was wearing a headscarf, as if she'd just come in. She'd opened the window to make herself heard.

"Nurse Wardle?" Martha called.

"This is private property." The woman seemed to be shaking with anger. "You're trespassing!"

"I came here to see you."

"Who are you?"

"I'm a trained nurse, and I'm looking for a job."

Martha uttered the lie with so much conviction that she surprised even herself. Rachel's influence, she thought.

"The clinic is closed." A pause. "For good. I've seen my last patient."

"Oh, no!" Martha was crestfallen. "I was counting on you."

"You've no business here."

Martha wiped her face with her hand and made a noise resembling a stifled sob. When she opened her mouth again, the words came out in a rush. "Oh, I knew it would be no use! But I'm desperate, you see. Things are so hard these days. A friend told me about your clinic."

"Who told you?"

"My friend heard about it from a gentleman. His name is Captain Malam."

"Stuff and nonsense!"

"Please!" Martha wailed. "Won't you—"

"Get off my property or I'll call the police."

Martha bowed her head. The threat was empty, but she couldn't think of a way to inveigle her way into the house. Time to sound the retreat.

"I'm sorry," she said in a muffled voice. "It's my mistake."

"I'll say! Now get back to wherever you came from. And never let me see you here again."

———

As Rachel dabbed her damp cheeks with a lacy handkerchief, Evan Tucker made soothing noises.

"Are you absolutely sure?" he said at length.

She looked straight at him. "There isn't a shred of doubt. My God, I wish there was!"

He'd let his tea go cold as he listened to her tale of woe. Now he took another quick sip before speaking again.

"We only met the other day; we're virtually strangers. Why have you confided in me?"

"Because there is no one else," she said earnestly. "Nobody who would understand. Nobody who could...help."

In the long silence that followed, Rachel kept her head bowed, as if trying to count the threads in the Persian rug stretched out between them.

"What makes you think I can help, my dear?"

"You're a kind man," she said. "I can tell that. My instinct never fails. At least..."

His voice sharpened. "It's not just a matter of kindness, is it?"

"No." She blew her nose. "Actually, Roddy—Captain Malam—said something to me once. I don't think he meant to let it slip. He implied you had the right connections and were able to help someone who was...in a predicament."

"Did he now?"

Rachel nodded.

"I think I follow you, Miss Savernake."

"Do call me Rachel."

"Thank you, Rachel. I understand what you need. But you must take my word for it, these matters are never straightforward to deal with. Nor cheap."

"Money is no object!" she cried. "My mind is made up. I know what I want to do, and I'm determined to go ahead. Whatever the cost."

"That does resolve one common difficulty." He sighed. "However, I'm afraid there is more to it than you realise."

"There is?"

"That little scene you interrupted when you turned up a few minutes ago."

"Your quarrel with Nurse Wardle?"

"Phoebe happens to be the expert in these matters. She is the one who administers the treatment."

Rachel put her hand to her mouth. "Goodness!"

"Didn't Roddy mention that? There's no need for concern, I assure you. Phoebe may not be a qualified doctor, but she is a first-class nurse. She possesses all the expertise you could possibly require in such a delicate situation. Her husband taught her well."

"You mean that Giles Malam…"

"Giles had almost as much charm as his famous brother. Always a sympathetic bedside manner, especially with female patients. As he developed an interest in treating their nervous disorders, he came across an increasing number of women who faced a very particular difficulty. As a result he began to… diversify."

"I suppose they were all wealthy women," Rachel said in a small voice.

"Giles was determined to offer his patients the best possible treatment, plus the time and care necessary to allow for complete recovery. No expense spared. The operations carry a high degree of risk. Naturally, his fees were high. Bear in mind that his career and his professional reputation were at stake. So-called civilised society is heartless. It does not look kindly on professionals who give succour to women in that kind of distress. If anyone ever found out what he was doing, the scandal would have destroyed him."

There was a long pause.

"And when he died, his widow carried on where he left off?"

"Phoebe kept up the good work," Evan Tucker said. "And now she's throwing it all away."

"Dear me," Rachel said, putting her head in her hands. "What hope is there for me now?"

————

Jacob parked his car on Rosebery Avenue and plodded across towards Exmouth Market. Rain was falling and his dismal mood matched the weather. At the Hades, he'd watched helplessly as a woman killed herself. Last night a man had been tortured and drowned for daring to talk to him. Now he was expected—no, instructed—to stand idly by while a brutal criminal slaughtered another woman, simply because she'd had the spirit to escape from his clutches and find a better life.

He was afraid for Mrs. de Villiers. Ambrose was vengeful and cruel; Jacob hated to think what fate the man might have in store for her. The manner of Sammy's death had been shocking enough. Oakes had given him no confidence that the police would move fast enough to save her life. Why didn't they see the urgency? Equally depressing was the conversation with Gomersall. For all his foibles and moods, the *Clarion*'s editor was no ogre. By the standards of Fleet Street, he ranked as a man of principle. So why wouldn't he lift a finger to stop Ambrose committing yet another heinous murder?

Jacob wrestled with the riddle of official indifference. Was it simply a question of snobbishness? Once upon a time the woman had been a prostitute. Didn't the police deem her life worth preserving? Surely that wasn't in Oakes's nature. Yes, he was an establishment man, but he regarded organised crime as a cancer and criminals like Ambrose as tumours that needed to be surgically removed from society for the good of London's health. Besides, why would Gomersall turn his nose up at a front-page story?

Was Rachel right? It seemed inconceivable that men as formidable in their different ways as Oakes and Gomersall could be persuaded to go against their instincts and turn a blind eye to the fate of Kiki de Villiers. Jacob couldn't believe that Ambrose had corrupted them or somehow put the fear of God into them. Something else was going on. But what?

Helplessness enveloped him like a straitjacket. He didn't have a clue about his next move.

On the corner of Exmouth Market stood a red telephone kiosk. The answer presented itself. He'd ring Rachel Savernake.

As he dialled the number of Gaunt House, a still, small voice in his head murmured that he was making a mistake. He was developing a habit of leaning on Rachel, of turning to her for guidance when he should be making up his own mind. Shouldn't he have more self-respect; shouldn't he learn to stand on his own two feet?

"Gaunt House."

The voice belonged to Hetty Trueman, not Martha.

"This is Jacob. May I speak to Rachel, please?"

"She's out."

It was on the tip of his tongue to ask where, but Hetty was very different from Martha, whose quick wits and mischievous humour delighted him. Hetty's guiding principle was to tell people what she thought they needed to know. In other words, as little as possible.

"When will she be back?"

"No idea."

Hetty wasn't a cheery conversationalist at the best of times. In the early days of their acquaintance, Jacob had regarded her as a sourpuss. Her fierce, unswerving devotion to Rachel was beyond question, but she seemed suspicious of his fascination with her. Over time he'd detected hints of a generous heart buried deep beneath the carapace, and he'd learned that she worried constantly about Rachel. Given that Rachel's lack of fear often verged on recklessness, he could understand. Yet he believed something more lay behind Hetty's anxiety, some shared secret from their past. He couldn't begin to guess what it was. Neither the Truemans nor Rachel herself showed the slightest inclination to explain.

"It's about Kiki de Villiers."

"Oh, yes?"

"Not only is Oakes refusing to move a muscle to protect her from Ambrose, but my editor has taken me off the job. No ifs, no buts. The whole story has been spiked."

"So you want Rachel's help?"

Stung, Jacob retorted, "I thought she'd like to know the latest."

"I'll tell her when she gets in." Down the line came a noisy sigh. "You're so headstrong, Jacob. Don't do anything stupid."

"Thanks for your wise counsel," he snapped.

He stomped out of the kiosk and headed for his flat. The conversation left a bitter taste in his mouth. It was in Hetty's nature to be blunt, but even if she meant well, her habit of treating him as an impulsive, unreliable child felt like a slap on the face. True, Rachel had helped him out of one or two scrapes, but he was a grown man, the youngest chief crime correspondent on Fleet Street. Much as he loved collaborating with Rachel Savernake, he didn't depend on her.

He shook the raindrops from his coat and put on the kettle. If strong-minded men as senior in their respective organisations as Oakes and Gomersall were being discouraged or prevented from getting too close to Mrs. de Villiers at the very moment when her life was under threat, powerful forces were at work. The stakes must be extremely high. And that meant there was a story to be told.

The back of his neck prickled. It was as if he was blundering through a maze, but had finally caught a glimpse of the hidden centre. Perhaps Marcel Ambrose wasn't the only person keenly interested in Kiki de Villiers. Perhaps someone else was looking for her, someone with exceptional reach and influence.

Was that why she'd left London? If so, how many people knew her present whereabouts?

Pouring tea into a chipped cup, he wondered whether he could find a telephone number for the woman at her home in Rye and speak to her. He could warn her about Ambrose and at the same time pump her for further information, try to find out exactly what was going on.

No, that was leaving too much to chance. Even assuming he traced her number, there was no guarantee she would even come to the telephone or even that he could convey the extent of the threat to her life. What if she dismissed him as a crank, or even suspected he was one of Ambrose's minions, trying to force her out into the open?

The only solution was to speak to her face to face.

Swallowing a mouthful of strong, restorative tea, he realised he didn't need Rachel's wisdom after all.

No more wasting time, no more wishing and hoping, no waiting for others to act. It was up to him to do what was necessary.

Decision made, he put down his cup and sprang to his feet.

Time to go to Sepulchre Street.

Chapter 22

Duncalf wasn't a fanciful man. To get distracted by imagination could be dangerous. Even so, as he drove to Rye, his thoughts drifted to salmon fishing and what it had in common with his work on behalf of Major Whitlow. Anticipation, that was what it boiled down to.

On Speyside, each morning he'd taken pleasure in pulling on his waders, setting up his rod, and tying on the fly of his choice. Exercising patience and restraint, cast after cast, waiting for the one that mattered. And then the exhilaration of feeling that delicate tug, the effort of mastering the temptation to lift until the line went tight. You needed to be fully briefed in advance, yet prepared to change tactics if circumstances so dictated. The secret was to adopt a methodical approach and to get into the right frame of mind from the start. When all was said and done, preparing to kill a fellow human being was not so very different.

The heavens had opened, but the MG handled beautifully on the wet road surfaces. Beyond London, the traffic was light. In the absence of delays he had a good run all the way to Rye, reaching the town's medieval gateway ten minutes earlier than expected. A gale driving in from the Channel whipped the rain against his windscreen, but he didn't care. Dreadful weather suited his purpose. Even on a Saturday evening, local people wouldn't linger on the streets without good cause.

A hundred and fifty yards from Sepulchre Street, he found a small patch of open ground next to a butcher's. With no moon and an absence of lamplight, this was the perfect place to park the MG.

———

As Joe Postles drove through Sussex, he recalled handing his mother the wad of cash. She'd screeched with rage and thrown it back in his face. For as long as he could remember, she'd worshipped Sammy almost as much as she'd despised him. Her brain had been fading for years, and the news of Sammy's death had tipped her into a demented fury. She'd screamed obscenities and clawed at his face with brittle fingernails until he pushed her down onto the threadbare sofa. She lay there sobbing and moaning that she wished he was dead and she was dead. Anything if it would bring her perfect boy back to life.

"Ma…" he began.

"Shut up," she hissed. "I hate you!"

In years gone by, Joe had always been able to get her to snap out of her wild tempers, but he'd lost the knack. Things had gone too far. She'd never be right in the head again.

Ambrose was still snoring. Of course, none of them had had much sleep overnight. Joe felt exhausted; it required all his concentration to keep his eyes on the road.

That afternoon, his nerves stretched to breaking point, a shocking impulse had driven him to do something terrible. As his mother's frenzy subsided, he'd bent down over her skinny body and pressed a cushion down over her face. She'd fought only for a few moments before giving up. She'd meant it, he thought, when she'd said she wished she was dead.

And now she was.

He'd carried her body to her room and laid it out respectfully on the bed. Time was ticking by and he was due to drive Ambrose to the coast. He wouldn't call a doctor, let alone the police. The authorities would come round soon enough.

———

Standing in the shadows beside his car, Duncalf turned up his coat collar against the wind and rain and adjusted his hat so that it came down over his eyes. A tug at his leather driving gauntlets made sure they were comfortable. He'd had the pair specially made by a glovemaker in Yeovil so he could keep a firm grip on the tools of his trade and go about his business without leaving a single fingerprint. After the long drive, the muscles in his shoulders and back felt tight, but he stretched his arms and composed himself. However many assignments he carried out, at this point he always felt keyed up. That was as it should be. No complacency, no carelessness.

Now for it.

He scrutinised his surroundings but saw nothing to disrupt his plans. No doubt things got rowdier the closer you got to the quayside, but Mrs. de Villiers had chosen a discreet refuge. Taking brisk strides, he stuck to the far side of the road, so that he could keep going if anyone happened to be lurking in Sepulchre Street. As he neared his destination, he slowed and glanced around before crossing over. Still not a soul to be seen. Nobody who could testify to his presence in the town.

An old gas lamp stood by the entrance of Sepulchre Street, with another couple further down. There were shadowy patches, but his eyesight was keen. The street was empty. At the far end, the bulk of Sepulchre House loomed. A shrewd choice of crime scene on Major Whitlow's part. A block of flats in central London would present all manner of difficulties, not least the potential number of witnesses.

Duncalf took care not to splash through the puddles, keeping all his wits about him in case a cat yowled or a courting couple slunk out of a doorway. The heavy damask curtains of Sepulchre House were drawn, but a chink of light shone through a gap at one of the lower windows. In his mind he'd fixed a mental image of the plan of the ground floor. Yes, that was the sitting room. He pictured Mrs. Kiki de Villiers taking her ease inside in the warm.

She didn't know it, he thought, but she was waiting to die.

————

Before setting off for Rye, Jacob had a quick wash and shave and put on his fedora, oxfords, and camel overcoat. He'd even acquired a pair of driving gloves. The shopping spree had come at the right time. By looking presentable, he had a better hope of convincing a rich, glamorous woman to take him seriously when he broke the news that her life was in jeopardy.

He chose to drive to Sepulchre Street rather than taking the train. When you didn't have a clue what to expect, a car would be useful—for instance, if he persuaded Kiki de Villiers to accompany him and go into hiding. His thinking was vague, but that was inevitable. He couldn't rule out the possibility that she already knew about Ambrose but was determined to stay put in Sepulchre House. All he could be sure of was that he'd much rather do something than nothing.

One snag was that he'd never been to Rye and knew next to nothing about the place. However, it wasn't in his nature to allow little details like that to get in the way. Stopping off at a stationer's in Farringdon Road, he managed to find a map and a guide to the Cinque Ports. The latter included the layout of each town and he discovered that Sepulchre Street was a dead end. According to the guide, it was popularly known as Graveyard Lane. Charming. The house should be easy enough to find.

Despite the rain and unfamiliar roads, he made rapid progress. As the Riley 9 bowled along, he continued to try to make sense of the attitude of Oakes and Gomersall. Who could have warned them off? And why?

Jacob conjured up half a dozen theories ranging from the eccentric to the wild. Had Ambrose kidnapped Mrs. Gomersall or one of the children and threatened to kill the captive if the police and the *Clarion* didn't abandon their investigations?

No, it was no good. He was making bricks without straw. No point in further speculation until he'd discovered what Kiki de Villiers had to say. He needed to win her trust and persuade her to confide in him.

His stomach rumbled. Pangs of hunger nagged at him, but he owed it to Mrs. de Villiers to reach her as soon as possible. If he failed to save her by a matter of minutes simply because he'd felt the urge to guzzle a sandwich, he'd never forgive himself.

Only as he was approaching Rye Foreign did an unpleasant thought belatedly occur to him.

What if Ambrose had beaten him to it? What if he'd not only discovered the secret bolthole but had arrived in Sepulchre Street already?

———

A signpost told Joe Postles that he was five miles from Rye. The snoring behind him had become muted. Little stirrings from the back of the car suggested that Ambrose was coming round.

Joe tightened his grip on the steering wheel. The Lancia's

headlights picked out the road ahead, but the rain and darkness meant he couldn't see far. It was the same with his life, he told himself. What was going to happen?

It dawned on him that he knew the answer. Actually, he'd known it in his heart from the moment Laurent ordered him to take Marcel Ambrose on a journey meant to culminate in murder.

Over the years there had been too many deaths and the past twenty-four hours had shown there would never be any let-up for as long as Ambrose was around. Sammy was gone, and their mother too. Her blood was on Ambrose's hands as far as Joe was concerned.

And now Lulu Dabo was to become the man's latest victim. Joe supposed that Ambrose would torment her with the knowledge that she was about to die before shooting her in the head. The thrill of extracting a brutal revenge wouldn't keep him satisfied for long. There would always be someone else who crossed him, one more troublemaker who had to die.

Joe put his foot down. The Lancia responded with a surge of power, roaring over the wet road surface. The needle on the dial flickered. Fifty-five. Fifty-seven.

Behind him, Ambrose stirred.

Joe didn't glance over his shoulder but kept his eyes fixed on the road as he continued to accelerate.

Sixty. Sixty-two.

"Everything all right?" a groggy voice asked.

Sixty-four.

"Yes, sir," Joe said. "Everything is fine."

Sixty-five.

Ambrose liked to wear some sort of fancy French cologne. Joe smelled it as the man put his head forward.

"It's teeming down outside."

"Cats and dogs, sir. Not a nice night."

"Watch how you drive."

Sixty-six.

Joe swerved round a bend. It was a miracle that the car stayed on the road.

"Hey, what are you up to? Slow down, for God's sake!"

Joe said nothing.

Ambrose raised his voice. "Didn't you hear me?"

When Joe didn't answer, he heard a movement in the back of the car. He guessed his employer was taking his gun out of the holster.

"Listen to me!"

Joe wasn't scared. What good would shooting him do? The car would career off the road and burst into flames. Both of them would die. What did it matter if they broke their necks before their bodies were incinerated?

"Slow down, I said!"

No doubting the panic in the bastard's voice now. He began to rant, pouring out the obscenities.

Joe eased his foot off the accelerator.

"That's better." Ambrose's relief was pathetic. "No need to be reckless. What…what's got into you?"

"You shouldn't have done it," Joe said.

"Done what?" A nervous question. He must have an inkling that this wasn't going to end well.

"You should never have killed Sammy."

"I…look, he was a stool pigeon, he…"

"He was my brother."

Joe trod on the accelerator and the Lancia flew along. A hundred yards ahead, a pool of water had formed in the middle of the road, close to a sharp double bend. Twenty feet beyond the point where the road zig-zagged stood a tall tree, maybe an oak.

"Slow down, you fool!"

The man's terrified, Joe thought. He smiled to himself.

"Do you want to kill us both?"

Ambrose was screaming now.

So Joe screamed back.

"Yes!"

As they raced towards the bend, he kept his eyes open and his foot down. The car skidded off the road and smashed into the tree.

The last sound Joe heard was an ear-splitting crash, the last emotion he felt was a shuddering thrill of triumphant self-sacrifice.

This is for Sammy.

Chapter 23

Duncalf strode across the street to Sepulchre House and removed the mortice key from his pocket. The scapegoat for Kiki de Villiers's murder must be someone she knew, given the major's instruction that there was no need to force an entry into the house. If, however, time permitted after the deed was done, Duncalf was at liberty to smash a window from the outside to make it look as though there had been a break-in. Presumably the man on whom the crime was to be pinned was a disgruntled lover, someone she might let into her home or just as easily refuse to admit. Or possibly someone who might over-elaborate by pretending to have broken in. The major had a good brain and a taste for complication. Duncalf's personal instinct was to keep things simple.

A last look over his shoulders. Sepulchre Street was as silent as the grave. How appropriate, Duncalf thought.

This was what he lived for. Excitement pulsed through him like an electric charge, but his hand kept steady as he slid the key into the lock of the front door. Not only did the key fit, but it turned smoothly and without making a sound. He exhaled in relief as he nudged the door open and returned the key to his pocket. So often duplicates were clumsily made by tradesmen who took no pride in their work.

The hallway stretching before him was broad and long. Paintings hung on each wall, large abstract works of modern art. The sort of fancy rubbish delighted in by folk with money to burn. Farther down the hall, a wide staircase wound up to the floors above. There were a couple of doors on each side of the passageway, with another at the end, leading to the kitchen and scullery. With satisfaction he noted the thick pile of the exotically patterned carpet. Ideal for deadening the sound of footsteps.

He crossed the threshold. This was always a crucial moment, a milestone in an assassin's journey. He'd penetrated the target's home, yet she still didn't have the faintest clue about his existence, let alone what he intended to do. The door of the sitting room was ajar. As he moved forward, his nostrils were assailed by a powerful scent: rich, fruity, and floral. Duncalf almost gagged. Had she bathed in the stuff? Some men would find the aroma intoxicating. Not him. What made his flesh tingle was the prospect of what he was about to do.

He strained his ears. After a few moments of silence, suddenly there was a burst of music, the opening bars of a sentimental song. She had set a record to play on her gramophone.

An American woman began to warble.

"Please don't talk about me when I'm gone."

Duncalf stifled the urge to laugh out loud. Extraordinary. Anyone would think his victim had a premonition that she was about to die.

Time to decide. When he pushed the door open, he could either shoot from outside the room or take a pace forward before firing. His preference was to exploit the element of surprise. The fact that both his prospective victims might be in the room made it wise not to give either of them any chance to react. Double killings could get messy.

He whipped the Lebel out of his mackintosh. His spine throbbed with anticipation. This was true power, the power of life and death. The supreme moment, when he experienced utter euphoria. So rare, so precious. Nothing else could touch it.

Gun in hand, he put his knee against the door and shoved it open.

The woman was sitting in a high-backed armchair with her back turned to him. The mass of red hair was unmistakable. She'd let it down for the evening and the long tresses tumbled over the shoulders of her gown, their reflection shimmering in a small oval mirror above the gramophone. In a split second he took in the fact that nobody else was present. The music drowned out the soft movement of the door. Duncalf made up his mind. She was well within range, a sitting duck; there was no need to go in.

As he took aim, the thrill of conquest rippled through his body. Shivering with ecstasy, he shot her in the back of the head.

———

Slowing down as he approached Rye, Jacob wondered if he'd let his heart rule his head. Oakes and Gomersall had warned him off. So, to all intents and purposes, had Hetty Trueman. Was he making a terrible mistake?

He took a deep breath. In for a penny, in for a pound. Admittedly this philosophy sometimes landed him in a hole, but he'd come too far to give up now. He drove into the town, peering through the darkness at every street sign. It didn't take long for him to locate Sepulchre Street, but he drove straight past and did not stop until he found a deserted side street a few hundred yards away. He parked in front of a disused building that had once housed a chandlery.

During the drive his damaged knee had stiffened, and he tested it gingerly after getting out of the car. The legacy of his visit to Chez Laurent was a slight limp, but it could have been so much worse. His spirits rose. At last he was doing something. The fedora, purchased as a gesture to fashion, served as a useful disguise. Pulling the brim down over his forehead, he set off for Sepulchre Street.

———

"Please don't talk about me when I'm gone."

As the singer reached her final refrain, Duncalf mounted the stairs, gun in hand. He'd kicked open each of the remaining doors on the ground floor in turn, searching for the housemaid, but there was no sign of her. He'd heard no response from the woman to his shot. No scream, no cry of surprise, no frantic scurrying for safety, nothing. Even the most resilient and disciplined soul would have reacted in some way to his sudden and violent intrusion into the tranquillity of Sepulchre House.

In his own mind he was convinced that the maid wasn't on the premises, but he had to make sure. It didn't take long to fling open the bedrooms and look around or go up to the spacious attic, full of lumber, at the top of the building. The woman was nowhere in the house.

Hurrying back downstairs, he squinted into the sitting room. The body lay crumpled in the armchair and there was a lot of blood and mess, but no obvious indication that anyone else had been present that evening. On the contrary, a single half-empty glass of sherry stood on an occasional table beside the chair.

The back door was locked and none of the windows were open. In his professional opinion it was beyond belief that the maid had escaped since he had entered Sepulchre House. A wraith might have done it, but not a woman of flesh and blood.

Had the major been misinformed, or had Mrs. de Villiers simply given her maid an evening off? Duncalf supposed that a last minute whim of that sort was the likeliest explanation. Women were unreliable. Impossible to predict.

It didn't matter, he told himself. A single kill is always easier and more satisfying. In his experience, a second murder always left something to be desired. Its execution never gave him the same climactic thrill.

The immediate question was whether to improvise and stage a break-in. He decided against it. Although he'd accomplished his principal mission, he felt no sense of triumph. The physical joy of achievement had already dissipated. The absence of the maid was unsettling. Timings were unpredictable and the scapegoat might turn up at any moment.

Better not gild the lily. He should get out of here, carry out his final task in Rye, and then race back to London. Major Whitlow expected him to report in person before midnight.

Easing the gun back into its pouch, he put his head round the front door. The rain had stopped and the quiet of Sepulchre Street was undisturbed. He could be reasonably confident that nobody had heard the shot.

When he shut the door behind him, he didn't lock up. This was as per his instructions. The major didn't want to prevent the scapegoat from gaining access. What happened when he went inside was anyone's guess. Again, the detail was immaterial so far as Duncalf was concerned. He'd done his job to the best of his ability. The housemaid's absence nagged at him like a flesh wound, but it couldn't be helped. He wasn't to blame.

———

Luck was on Jacob's side. This part of the old town was quiet, with little traffic and few pedestrians braving the elements.

He reached the final street corner. As he turned into Sepulchre Street, he glimpsed a figure on the opposite pavement, a man in a cloth cap and mackintosh. He was so inconspicuous as to seem like a will o' the wisp.

Jacob's heart skipped a beat but he carried on walking, keeping to the inside of the pavement. He let out a soft sigh of relief as the man moved away. He bore no obvious resemblance to Marcel Ambrose. In theory, Ambrose might have delegated the murder to one of his acolytes, but that didn't fit in with what Jacob knew about the man. Snuffing the life out of Kiki de Villiers was likely to be an experience Ambrose insisted on reserving for himself.

————

Duncalf walked down Sepulchre Street, as casual as if taking an evening stroll. At the end, he saw another man come round the corner and walk down the opposite pavement. He had a slight limp. Where else could he be heading for but the house? The stranger glanced in his direction, but Duncalf didn't break stride until he'd got out of sight.

Fifty yards on, he paused and counted to twenty before retracing his steps. When he poked his head round the street corner, the stranger had vanished. Excellent. The fellow had arrived earlier than anticipated, but he'd entered Sepulchre House according to plan.

Close to an abandoned warehouse was a gap in the cobbles, the site of an old broken drain which gave off a whiff of sewage. Duncalf took out the Lebel and dropped it into the cavity. The hole was small and shallow, and if you looked with any care, you'd see the revolver's handle.

It wasn't Duncalf's concern, but he presumed the gun would help to condemn the man he'd passed in Sepulchre Street. He'd worn a smart overcoat and a wide-brimmed fedora which prevented Duncalf from seeing his face. That didn't matter. Nor did his name. Duncalf knew the man's destiny.

He would be tried and convicted for the murder of Mrs. de Villiers. And then he would hang.

Chapter 24

Victorian gas lamps illuminated short stretches of Sepulchre Street. The rest remained in shadow. A spooky place, Jacob thought. No wonder they called it Graveyard Lane. A voice in his head demanded to know where the other man had come from. There were no other dwellings or occupied buildings, just a large and imposing house at the end.

He reached the front door. It had shiny brass trimmings and a nameplate.

Sepulchre House.

Light filtered out through a chink in the curtains on the ground floor. So Mrs. de Villiers was at home. Quite a relief. He cleared his throat and considered ringing the bell, but gave the door an experimental shove. It swung inwards. She'd left the main entrance unlocked and he couldn't see a key.

Curious.

And worrying.

In his mind, he heard the sombre tones of Hetty Trueman.

Don't do anything stupid.

Time to cut and run? If he fled, would he miss the scoop of a lifetime? And if he abandoned Kiki de Villiers to her fate, could he ever look himself in the eye again?

Taking a deep breath, he moved inside. A lamp in the hallway illuminated framed examples of surrealist art on the walls. Jacob spotted an elegant signature in the bottom right-hand corner of one of the abstracts.

Damaris Gethin.

Well, well. Perhaps it wasn't surprising, given that Kiki de Villiers had been an invited guest at the Hades Gallery. What exactly was the connection between the two women? Artist and collector, was it as simple as that?

Someone had left ajar the first door to his left. From inside came the bright glow of an electric light. He wrinkled his nose as he recognised the distinctive feminine fragrance wafting from the room. Narcisse Noir, yes. Mrs. de Villiers was wearing her favourite perfume. And tonight she certainly hadn't stinted on it.

The silence made his flesh creep. Was she fast asleep? What about that devoted housemaid of hers? What was she up to? Was she even on the premises?

He inched across the hall carpet until he was in a position to put his head around the door and look into the room.

His legs buckled beneath him as he took in the sight of the dead woman's body. She was slumped at an unnatural angle in the high-backed chair. There was a mess of blood and horrid bits and pieces. Although he could see the red tresses, part of her head seemed to have been blown away by a gunshot.

Jacob covered his mouth, an instinctive gesture. He'd been sick once already today and it was just as well that his stomach was empty.

Too late, he was too late. Despite his best efforts, Ambrose had beaten him to it.

———

Duncalf's itinerary included one more stop in Rye. As instructed, he drove to Mermaid Street and found an old black-and-white hostelry, the Mermaid Inn.

A handful of people were milling around outside, apparently local revellers engaged in a raucous sing-song of some kind. He pulled up and switched off the MG's engine. Next he flashed the headlamps twice in rapid succession before sounding his horn three times. Major Whitlow hadn't explained whether the person standing by to receive this message was inside the Mermaid or some other nearby property. They might be one of the revellers on the street. Nor did Duncalf know whether they were a member of the local police or a more secretive organisation. He was merely obeying orders.

Without more ado, he set off for the capital. The rain had ceased and the wind had dropped, so the journey presented few problems. Nevertheless, he was plagued by a blinding headache and a sense of dissatisfaction that felt suffocating. In the aftermath of a kill, when he had nothing much to look forward to, his spirits often dipped, but this was different. For him, work involved a constant quest for perfection, and tonight he'd failed to tie up an important loose end. The housemaid, what had happened to her?

He told himself not to worry, there was bound to be a simple and innocent explanation, but he'd been in this game for a long time and had a nose for trouble.

Something had gone wrong; he knew it in his bones.

—

One glimpse of the grisly tableau in the sitting room was enough to convince Jacob that checking for a pulse would be a waste of time. In truth, he couldn't bring himself to do it. The spatters of blood over the dead woman's red hair and the fruity, overripe smell of her perfume made him feel queasy.

In the hall, those random splotches of dark colour on Damaris Gethin's formless yet macabre works of art were dizzying. Sepulchre House was enveloped in a miasma of rotting decadence. It threatened to suffocate him.

Was the housemaid dead too? Or hiding upstairs, terrified in case the gunman had come back to finish her off? He dared not prowl around in the hope of finding out. His priority was to summon the police, but even if there was a telephone in Sepulchre House, he worried about destroying crucial fingerprint evidence. Better to use a public telephone kiosk instead.

What would Oakes make of this tragedy, and the brutal realisation that he'd let Mrs. de Villiers down? The savage and undeniable truth was that if she'd been alerted in time, she would still be alive.

An idea hit him out of the blue. The shock was like being coshed on the back of the head.

Suppose the police didn't want to save her. Absurd, surely—or was it? How else could he make sense of Oakes's inexplicably laissez-faire attitude that morning? The inspector never let the grass grow under his feet. Dark forces were at work, and when people behaved strangely out of character, you had no choice but to think the unthinkable.

Fear paralysed him. Put a foot wrong now, and he'd court disaster. Hetty's warning echoed in his brain. He dared not do anything stupid. But what seemed sensible now might look like a suicidal error of judgement in the cold light of day.

A picture sprang into his mind, of the man sauntering away from Sepulchre Street. Perhaps he had a sinister purpose. But it wasn't Ambrose, and he certainly hadn't been fleeing in a mad panic. Perhaps the fellow had a perfectly respectable reason to be out and about in Rye on a Saturday night. Yet if he was a blameless local resident…was the murderer still lurking here, at the scene of his crime?

Jacob's throat felt scratchy. Edging backwards, he listened hard. Nothing but silence. Yet he dared not jump to the conclusion that he was alone. Time to escape this hellhole. Holding his breath, he moved to the front door and looked outside.

Nobody was in the street. Such a lonely place, this Graveyard Lane. Jacob breathed in the damp night air and stepped out of the house. He felt unsteady on his feet. A new terror seized him by the throat. Suppose he keeled over in a dead faint and was discovered outside the home of a murdered woman?

With every passing moment, his plight became more serious. Even if he survived the next few minutes, he'd walked into a disaster. Yes, he'd arrived here with the best of intentions—but who would believe that? It was asking too much to expect sympathy. He'd blundered in, despite Scotland Yard telling him not to get involved. When Gomersall found that his own orders had been disobeyed, he'd spit feathers. More than likely, this would end with the sack.

Stumbling along the wet pavement, Jacob tripped and lost his footing. He banged his knee hard on the ground and yelped in agony. For a moment, the shock paralysed him as he waited for an unknown enemy to leap from the shadows and blow out his brains.

Nothing happened and he struggled to his feet. He'd caught his toe on the edge of a hole in the ground. Bending down to look at it, he caught a whiff of sewage. A gas lamp cast enough light for him to see the revolver lying within the cavity.

He had literally stumbled upon the murder weapon.

Jacob gnawed his lower lip so fiercely that it began to bleed. The killer had abandoned his gun after doing his deadly work and made little effort at concealment. The most casual search in the vicinity of the murder scene would reveal it. How careless.

Or was it? Suppose the disposal of the gun was a deliberate

ploy, part of a crafty scheme to cover up the truth of Kiki de Villiers's death. What if the culprit was trying to implicate some other individual?

Hang on a minute.

What if that person was Jacob himself?

Twenty-four hours ago, Marcel Ambrose had ordered his death, only to be thwarted by Rachel Savernake. Taking an instant revenge on Sammy Postles wouldn't be enough to satisfy the wounded *amour propre* of a ruthless gangster. How tempting to kill two birds with one stone by shooting Kiki de Villiers and making Jacob the scapegoat.

Jacob groaned. With any luck, this theory had as many holes as a colander. Most of his theories did, according to Rachel, but for the moment he was in no fit state to analyse the situation. His thoughts swam, thrashing around like drowning passengers from a sunken ship. Hungry, bewildered, and terrified, he simply didn't know what to do.

If he called the police, they'd treat him as the prime suspect. He was good at talking his way out of tight corners, but he didn't know what other tricks Ambrose might have up his sleeve to pin the murder on him. He'd met the victim in person after investigating her for weeks. He couldn't deny that he'd also been in the presence of her corpse within minutes of the fatal shot. Although he hadn't touched the gun, the killer had surely wiped off any fingerprints. The police wouldn't care that he lacked a motive for murder. At the very least he'd face a harrowing interrogation. There was every chance he'd spend the rest of the night in a prison cell.

The urge to ring Rachel Savernake and beg her for help was almost irresistible. Nobody else kept such a cool head in a crisis or had such a flair for unravelling the most devilishly tangled knots. If anyone could rescue him from calamity, it was Rachel.

He dug his nails into his palm. No, no, no. It was too humil-iating. He couldn't demean himself by treating Rachel as some kind of crutch. Besides, she was a woman, not a miracle worker. He was a grown man, supposedly an expert in crime, and he needed to show some self-respect. He'd got himself into this mess and it was up to him to fight his way out of it.

Hauling himself upright, he hobbled to the street corner. His aching knee was the one that he'd hurt at Chez Laurent and the pain made him cringe at every step. Thank goodness he hadn't parked far away. He limped along for another fifty yards.

The roar of a car engine ripped through the darkness. A bell clanged, an ominous cacophony. He ducked back under a shop canopy and watched a police car racing by. On its way to Sepulchre Street, without a doubt.

Smothered in misery, he watched as the car sped around the corner and disappeared into the dead-end street.

The killer had beaten him to it and raised the hue and cry. Jacob could imagine no other explanation.

There could be no question about the purpose of the deadly scheme. He was being framed for the murder of Kiki de Villiers.

Chapter 25

"I got nothing out of the Wardle woman," Martha said.

Her expression was disconsolate. She and her brother were with Rachel in a roadhouse halfway back to London, pooling the information garnered in Dykesbridge over an evening snack. As they ate, Rachel had recounted her visit to The Risings and then listened to Martha's careful account in pensive silence.

"Who knows?" Rachel said. "We may have learned more than you think."

She turned to Trueman. "Any joy at The Owlers?"

He put down his knife and fork. "Joy is pushing it. The pub is a godforsaken dump. At least the beer is cheap, and this time I didn't get into a fight."

"People were willing to talk to you?"

"Took a bit of gentle persuasion," he said with the glimmer of a smile. "Not sure I found out much. Dykesbridge is only a twenty-minute walk away, but it might as well be another world. It's a lost village—and good riddance, as far as the locals are concerned. Tucker and Wardle have never made much effort to mix with them."

"I hope that doesn't discourage people from gossiping about them."

"Far from it."

"Excellent. What do they say?"

"There was plenty of excitable talk about goings-on at The Risings. Rumours of wild orgies and Lord knows what, but no hard facts. Everyone is dismayed because Tucker hasn't hosted a party for ages."

Martha laughed. "Folk love to have something to chatter about. Give them a chance to moan about the immorality of the idle rich and they're in seventh heaven."

"How about his servants, Cliff?" Rachel asked.

"Mostly people from the fishing quarter of Dymchurch. One by one, they have drifted away over the past twelve months. Tucker is short of the readies. He doesn't pay wages on time, runs up debts with local tradesmen. Word gets around. As a result, he's struggling to find full-time staff. A woman called Collyer goes in every Monday to do a bit of housework, but that's about the size of it. People are desperate for work, but they need paying."

"No wonder The Risings looks neglected. You asked about Tucker's famous friends?"

"Noël Coward's name cropped up. He lives on a knoll above the Marsh. The pair of them used to be on good terms, but these days Coward keeps his distance. He regards Tucker as a bore."

Rachel nodded. "Coward is funny, stylish, flamboyant. Everything that Tucker isn't."

"As for the individuals we're interested in, the one name that came up was Malam's. Tucker brags about their friendship, but nobody can make out what Malam sees in him. A famous daredevil and a washed-up composer."

"Perhaps Malam deserves credit for refusing to drop Tucker," Martha suggested.

"The real question is why he keeps so close to him," Rachel said. "Whatever Roddy Malam's virtues may be, they don't include selflessness or fidelity."

Trueman leaned back in his chair. "Let's call a spade a spade. Do you think they are lovers?"

"I've wondered," Rachel said. "There's a clue to Tucker's nature in his artistic tastes. He collects the work of Henry Scott Tuke, who was never happier than when he was painting naked boys. Roddy Malam, on the other hand..."

"I've heard about what these public schoolboys get up to when lights go out in the dorm," Trueman said darkly.

"Let's not be prejudiced; it's the enemy of clear thinking. There's more to Malam's friendship with Tucker than meets the eye. Did you hear anything about Phoebe Wardle?"

"Her husband drank himself to death, and people regard her as stand-offish. She keeps herself to herself, but we knew that already. Fact is, people give Orgarswick House a wide berth."

"Why?"

"Word got around that Giles Malam turned it into a sort of posh asylum for very rich women. Now it's become so exclusive that Wardle only takes on one patient at a time."

"She's played her cards well. People fear mental disturbance. So she can ply her trade without unwanted interruptions."

"You're quite sure about what she gets up to?" Martha asked.

Rachel nodded. "We may not have absolute proof, but the circumstantial evidence is persuasive. Evan Tucker is on the lookout for women who are rich and pregnant and desperate to be rid of the child. He introduces them to Phoebe Wardle and they become patients at her abortion clinic."

———

Duncalf wasted no time in getting back to London. The only delay came a few miles outside Rye, shortly before Peasmarsh. Someone had skidded off the road at a sharp bend. By the look of it, his car had burst into flames. There wasn't much left of the vehicle and probably even less of whoever had been inside it. Firemen had extinguished the blaze and the police were supervising operations. The road space was restricted and a uniformed constable was marshalling the traffic. Not that there were many cars or lorries around at this time of night.

He kept his eyes fixed on the road and moderated his speed. The crash was a warning and he'd better take heed. No sense in taking unnecessary risks in treacherous conditions. An accident was the last thing he needed.

An obscure sense of disappointment nagged at him like an arthritic twinge. It was illogical, given that he'd accomplished his principal mission, but he suspected that Major Whitlow would be dissatisfied. Duncalf feared no one, it wasn't in his nature, but something about the major always made him uneasy. Each of them was ruthless, but what motivated them was very different. The major didn't seem to derive pleasure from exercising power over who lived and who died. No, the man was driven by a passionate belief in doing the right thing. Duncalf had come across plenty of top brass who talked about duty but he'd never met anyone whose life was ruled so absolutely by a commitment to King and country. In his opinion, the major was that rare beast, a genuine patriot.

———

Jacob sat in his car, rubbing his sore knee and wondering what to do. If he rang the police, he'd face a barrage of tricky questions. Fleeing from Sepulchre House was eminently logical, but an unimaginative bobby might regard it as the furtive behaviour of a man with a guilty conscience. If he'd broken the news about the murder, at least he'd occupy the moral high ground. An unscrupulous, quick-thinking enemy had denied him that luxury. He faced the prospect of a long and miserable night in a police cell. On an empty stomach, swamped by a desolate sense that his personal failure had cost a woman her life.

What was the alternative? To race back home and lick his wounds before making a rational plan with the benefit of a square meal and a good night's sleep. Tomorrow he might consult Rachel, but their conversation must be on equal terms. He couldn't quite bring himself to plead for her assistance.

He had a desperate urge to get going, but for once caution restrained him. Was it too risky? If he failed to raise the alarm after stumbling over a woman's corpse and went back home to bed instead, he'd have plenty of explaining to do.

Assuming, of course, that he admitted having visited Sepulchre House. He'd told no one that he intended to visit Kiki de Villiers, and as far as he knew, nobody had noticed him on the way to Rye or during his short time in the town. If he sat tight, nobody would be any the wiser. He wouldn't even be telling the lie direct. The only witness to his presence in the town was the man he'd spotted in Sepulchre Street.

Suppose that fellow happened to be the killer. It was inconceivable that he would come forward. Even if he did, how could he prove that he'd seen Jacob? The new fedora was a godsend. Nobody other than Trueman and the tailor had seen him wearing it, and the wide brim meant he'd been impossible to recognise. Jacob was tempted to pat himself on the back for his choice of headgear. A criminal's clumsy attempt to incriminate him would be self-defeating.

There was another angle. Jacob was a journalist to his

bootstraps and one thing stared him in the face. A first-hand account of the terrible scene in Sepulchre House would sell newspapers by the lorryload.

His vivid imagination conjured up the headline.

The Scented Room of Death.

Nothing was more likely to sway Gomersall than putting thousands on the *Clarion's* circulation, but Jacob would take care not to frame the report as an eyewitness story. His recall of the horrific scene he'd witnessed in Sepulchre House would give his story a tang of authenticity even as he made it crystal clear that he'd never set foot in Rye.

Through the mist of misery, he began to discern a path to safety. Common sense told him to rush back home now, before anyone spotted him. And live to fight another day.

———

"I wonder what Roddy Malam is up to this evening," Rachel said as the car moved through the London streets.

"Gone into hiding?" Martha suggested. "Making sure the bomber doesn't get a second chance to blow him up?"

"Whatever else you can say about the captain, he doesn't lack courage. Or perhaps the right word is recklessness. It's getting late, but I'd like to pay him a quick call."

"Right," Trueman said. "Maida Vale, isn't it?"

Twenty minutes later they reached the luxurious block where Malam had a first-floor flat. While Trueman and Martha waited outside, Rachel rang at his door.

The bell was answered by Malam's elderly valet, a little man called Ware, who had pebble glasses and a hearing aid. He was devoted to his master, who often joked that his valet's poor sight and deafness were invaluable assets for any gentleman's gentleman. Hear no evil, see no evil.

"Hello again, Ware. We met once when I called on the captain, remember?"

"Ah, yes, Miss…" He screwed up his wizened face, a sign that he was racking his brains. "Sorry, madam, my memory isn't what it was."

"Never mind. Is the captain at home? So sorry to call unexpectedly and rather late, but I wanted to have a quick word."

"Sorry, madam," Ware said again. "He's…gone away."

Rachel pointed to a trunk in the hall. It was festooned with large luggage labels bearing the captain's name.

"He hasn't taken his trunk."

"Sorry…"

"Yes, yes, I'm sorry too. He shouldn't ask you to lie for him."

Ware's rheumy eyes blinked. "Madam!"

Rachel heard a woman giggling somewhere in the recesses of the flat.

"Ah." She raised her voice. "The captain has a visitor?"

Ware looked as though he might burst into tears. Before he could say sorry again, a door banged and Malam appeared in the hallway. Clad in a purple dressing gown, he was barefoot and his hair was rumpled.

"Rachel?"

"Sorry to interrupt, Roddy, but I'm glad to see you've found a way of taking your mind off exploding cars."

He considered her for a moment. "In situations like this, the chap is supposed to say *I can explain*. But I won't waste your time."

Rachel pointed to the trunk just behind him. "That looks big enough to hold a body."

"You have a wonderfully suspicious mind."

"With some justification, I think you'll agree."

He gave a shark's grin and stood back to allow her a better

view of the trunk. "Be my guest. Rummage around among my underpants to your heart's content."

"Thank you, but no. Just one question."

"Fire away."

"Did you arrange for Butterworth's legal fees to be paid?"

He raised his eyebrows. "You're remarkably astute, Rachel. The answer is yes."

"Why do that if you thought he'd tried to kill you?"

"You wouldn't understand."

"Try me."

He looked her in the eye. "We were in the same regiment. Comrades in arms."

The unseen woman giggled again. Ware gave a nervous cough.

"And now," Malam said, "if you'll excuse me?"

She gave him a wintry smile. "So we won't be going to Monte Carlo together after all."

"My loss," he said. "Show Miss Savernake out, will you, Ware?"

He gave a little bow of farewell and then turned on his heel and padded back to the bedroom.

———

Hardly any lights were burning in Whitehall as Duncalf entered Major Whitlow's office, but his superior was making notes on an official document with the painstaking care of a monk making textual emendations to an illuminated manuscript.

Did the man never sleep? It struck Duncalf how little, over the years, he'd learned about the major. Even before his hand was blown off in the war, he'd been an enigma, a man alone.

Neither of them wasted time with small talk before Duncalf gave his report. He spoke in a clipped tone, neither embellishing nor omitting salient details. The major's expression was as unyielding as the north face of Ben Nevis. Duncalf detected no clue to his thinking, other than a sporadic tap-tap-tap of the steel claw on the edge of his desk. Not an encouraging sign.

"The journey to and from Rye," the major said. "Smooth, was it? No mishaps?"

Duncalf frowned. Not a question he'd expected. He sniffed, like an animal scenting danger.

"None, sir." The steel claw tapped with increased vigour. "Other than a slight hold-up on the way back. Some idiot had spun off the road outside Rye, but I was only delayed a minute or so."

The major sighed. "The car was a Lancia Lambda. The occupants were incinerated."

Duncalf shifted in his chair. "Oh, yes, sir?"

"Charred remains are always problematic. Always got to be on the *qui vive* for jiggery-pokery when bodies are unidentifiable."

The worm of doubt began to nibble at Duncalf's intestines.

"Yes, sir."

"That said, all the evidence points in the same direction." The major lifted his claw and pointed straight at Duncalf. "The dead men are Marcel Ambrose and his driver. I don't suppose you know Ambrose's name?"

"Afraid not, sir."

"No reason why you should." The major paused. "I may as well be frank. Ambrose is a French vice merchant. He operated in Soho for a number of years and was...close to Mrs. de Villiers. Because he was at loggerheads with another gangster, he found it politic to fake his own death and leave the country. His rival is now dead and Ambrose recently returned to Britain. We had reason to believe that he was making for Sepulchre Street. He had a grudge against Mrs. de Villiers, and we presumed that he wanted to kill her, but she is a formidable woman. We couldn't rule out the possibility that she might charm him into sparing her life, perhaps by offering to rekindle their relationship. Hence the urgency of your assignment."

So Ambrose was the scapegoat, and he'd lost his life en route to Rye. Duncalf's thoughts whirled.

"If he faked his death once..."

The major nodded. "He might repeat the trick and give himself an alibi for the killing of Mrs. de Villiers, yes indeed. But his gun was found in the wreck of the Lancia. According to our information, Ambrose had some fancy dental work done in France a year ago, so the teeth of the corpse in the passenger seat need to be checked. Our working assumption, however, is that Ambrose is dead. So is his driver. A man, by the way, who had good cause to hate his employer."

"You think the chauffeur ran the car off the road deliberately? Suicide combined with murder?"

The steel claw gave a loud rap. "So it seems. Not that it matters. What is certain, subject to confirmation from the dentists, is that Ambrose is dead."

"In other words, the man I saw approaching Sepulchre Street wasn't...expected to be there?"

"Correct. In that street, as you have seen, there is only one building currently occupied. You're sure the fellow was making for Sepulchre House?"

Duncalf considered. "He walked towards the house. I kept moving, so I can't guarantee he entered the building."

"I appreciate that," the major said tightly. "But realistically?"

"Realistically, I'm confident. There is no other explanation for anyone going down Sepulchre Street. As you know, it's a dead end. Pulling the brim of his fedora right down over his face was a simple and effective way to conceal his identity, but the very fact he did so speaks volumes."

"I agree." The major was pensive. "Any distinguishing features?"

"Smart camel coat. Well-polished oxfords. I'd say he was youngish, twenties or thirties, but he didn't move freely. It was as if he'd hurt his leg, giving him a slight limp."

"Which leg?"

"The left."

"Very well. A few crumbs are better than nothing. When you left Sepulchre House, you closed the door behind you?"

"As per my instructions, sir." Duncalf was conscious of the major's piercing scrutiny. "I'd swear to it."

"You see, when the police arrived at the house, the door wasn't quite shut."

"That is the proof, then. The man I saw went inside."

The major nodded. "I need hardly tell you that he'd made himself scarce by the time the police arrived. I'm assured that the response to your signal was immediate, so he can only have spent a few minutes in the house."

"I suppose he took one look at the corpse and made good his escape. Is it possible he was a burglar?"

"Did he look like a burglar?"

Duncalf shook his head. "Hard to say on the evidence of a quick glance, but I reckon that overcoat cost a pretty penny. Smart shoes, fancy hat…"

The major snorted. "That settles it, unless burglary in Sussex is a job for Beau Brummels."

"Is it possible that the man was in cahoots with Ambrose?"

"At present, we can rule nothing out, but it seems unlikely."

"So we can presume he was personally acquainted with the lady and intended to call on her."

"That seems logical. Unless the housemaid had a friend who is a natty dresser."

A dangerous glint lit the major's cold eyes. That worm of doubt deep within Duncalf gnawed and wriggled.

"The housemaid, yes. As I mentioned, there was no trace of her in the building."

"You're sure of that?" the major said softly.

Duncalf swallowed. "I searched the house as thoroughly as possible in the time available."

"You didn't overlook anything?"

The worm became a greedy monster, guzzling Duncalf's innards. "To the best of my knowledge..."

"You see," the major said, lifting his claw so that its tip was an inch from the assassin's forehead, "tonight's assignment did not go according to plan."

"Are you suggesting that the maid was present in Sepulchre House without my knowledge, sir?"

"Not exactly that."

Duncalf stared at him, holding his breath, conscious of the monster devouring him.

The major smashed the desk with his claw. In the silence of the top-floor room, the noise sounded like a thunderclap.

"You didn't kill Kiki de Villiers. The woman you shot in the back of the head was her housemaid, Pauline Mendy."

Chapter 26

Duncalf didn't believe in God. Yet as he struggled to regain his customary composure, he thanked providence that the major never wasted time in crying over spilt milk. Whatever anger he felt about Duncalf's failure to examine his victim's corpse to confirm her identity, the priority was what to do next.

"The police have a dead body on their hands. A wealthy woman's maid has been murdered. Even if we wanted to keep her death quiet, it wouldn't be possible. We need to adapt to circumstances."

Duncalf ground his teeth. "Is there any clue to why the maid was masquerading as her mistress?"

"Lord only knows what goes on inside a woman's head. The maid was devoted to Mrs. de Villiers. They had...been through a good deal together."

"Which is why I was asked to kill both of them," Duncalf said, thinking aloud.

"It was...an unhealthily close relationship." The major's shrug didn't disguise his contempt. "Whether that explains why the maid was wearing a red wig and dressed like Mrs. de Villiers, I have no idea."

"She'd soaked herself in perfume," Duncalf muttered.

"Yes, the same brand her mistress favoured. There's no doubt she idolised her. The psychiatrists would have a field day, poring over her motives. I don't give a damn about what went on inside her head or what the two women got up to when they were alone together. All I want is to sort out this mess."

"You want me to find Mrs. de Villiers…?"

"And finish the job?" the major said wryly. "No, that ship has sailed. Ironically, the problem which gave rise to the need to dispose of her has been addressed by the lady herself . The question now is how to resolve the question of the maid's murder."

"Does anyone care?" Duncalf asked. "I mean, a servant…"

The claw crashed down again. "I care, dammit! And you'll care too, if you know what's good for you."

Major Whitlow took a breath. It was the first time Duncalf had ever seen him swayed by raw emotion.

"You see," the major said in a quieter voice, "relations between my department and Scotland Yard are in a wretched state because of this business. The police hate us interfering—as they see it—with their operations. They'd love nothing better than to show that we're not to be trusted. The stakes couldn't be higher. If they can pin the blame for this debacle on us, then I'll be out on my ear and probably lose my pension into the bargain. More importantly, the safety of this country will be imperilled."

"I understand, sir."

"Thankfully, there is one obvious suspect for the Sepulchre Street murder."

"The man in the fedora?"

"Precisely." The claw rapped the desk. "He poses a danger to the public and we must get the word out. Time is of the essence. Call the police station in Rye. As a good citizen, you must give them a description of the man you saw. You'll be too embarrassed to give your name. But alerting the authorities isn't enough. We need the information in the public domain. The fourth estate needs to take up the hunt."

Duncalf tugged at his left earlobe, a habit acquired in childhood during moments of stress.

"You're not expecting me to talk to the newspapers?"

"A brief anonymous telephone message giving the suspect's description, nothing more. Despite this evening's unfortunate developments, you're not expendable." He allowed himself a bleak smile before adding, "Yet."

"What if they catch up with this fellow and he turns out to have a perfectly good explanation for being in Sepulchre Street?"

The claw made a dismissive gesture. "Immaterial. Once he is found, he'll be taken in for questioning. As you have gathered, certain members of my staff have been seconded to the police. Once our bird is safely in a cage, he won't fly away again."

"Ah." Duncalf leaned back in his chair. Finally he was beginning to relax. "A death in custody."

"Quite," the major said. "If I'm not mistaken, he'll hang himself with the laces of his smart shoes. Tormented by guilt, you see. Killing that poor benighted servant will prove too much for his conscience to bear."

———

Jacob arrived at Clarion House at nine in the morning. After driving back from Rye in a daze and collapsing into bed, he'd slept in fits and starts. Awaking from a nightmare in which he sped from a murder scene only for a corpse dripping with blood to rear up right in front of his car, he'd abandoned hope of further rest. A vivid bruise disfigured his knee, but after a night's rest it wasn't hurting so much. A quick bath and breakfast gave a much-needed boost to his battered morale.

Glancing at his reflection in the bathroom mirror caused him to wince, but it could have been worse. The bags under his eyes and furrows in his forehead might be blamed on working too hard. As far as the outside world was concerned, he'd spent yesterday evening at home, getting his thrills vicariously from a dog-eared Richard Hannay adventure.

He toyed with the idea of rushing over to Gaunt House, so that he could tell Rachel about his experiences in Rye. What would she make of it all? No, it wasn't a good idea. Come what may, he had to be his own man.

The best course was to pop into the office. He wasn't expected there, but the nature of crime reporting required him to be ready and willing to work around the clock, so no one would bat an eyelid at his presence. He was itching to find out what information—if any—the police had released about the murder of Kiki de Villiers. Gomersall's refusal to allow him to persist with his original investigation now looked like a blessing in disguise.

Not many people were taking the air in Fleet Street, but the news mill didn't stop grinding on the Sabbath, and Clarion House was far from empty. As he walked through the reception hall, Gomersall emerged from the lift.

"Ah, Flint," the editor said. "Just the man!"

Words to make even the most buoyant heart sink. Jacob contrived a feeble smile.

"Morning, sir. You wanted to see me?"

"That's right, lad. A word in your ear." A beefy finger beckoned. "Come to my room."

Following his master down the corridor like an obedient puppy, Jacob wondered what was in the wind. When they reached the office, Gomersall bestowed a paternal smile, invited him to take a seat, and rang through to his secretary for two cups of tea.

"Glad to see you this morning. Didn't expect you'd turn in on a Sunday morning. Not that I was surprised, mind; you're a diligent lad."

Perched on the edge of his chair, Jacob managed a nervous smile. If there was one thing more alarming than the editor's wrath, it was his bonhomie.

"Sorry if I was a bit hard on you yesterday."

An apology! Jacob was tempted to pinch himself, to check whether he was still asleep and dreaming. Gomersall wasn't a man for regrets. He subscribed to the maxim of the late Master of Balliol: never apologise, never explain.

"That's all right, sir."

Gomersall cleared his throat. "Fact of the matter is, there's been a development."

"A development?" Jacob said in a scratchy voice.

"Yes, last night was pretty eventful down in Sussex."

"Really?" Now was the time to start establishing his alibi. Conjuring up a rueful grin, he said, "Things were deadly dull in Exmouth Market, I can tell you."

"A murder was committed in Rye."

Jacob engineered his features into an expression that he hoped was bright and enquiring. "Who was killed?"

"A woman was shot in the sitting room of the house where she lived in the centre of the town. She was in an armchair, listening to music. The police found a record on the gramophone. The murderer shot her from behind. Blew half her head away."

Jacob's gorge rose. He could see it now. And taste that sickly perfume on his tongue. He dared not trust himself to speak.

"I won't beat about the bush, lad. The house belonged to Mrs. de Villiers. Yet another of her country retreats. How the other half lives, eh?"

Jacob examined his fingernails.

"Thank God she wasn't in the building at the time." Gomersall coughed, as if realising that his remark wasn't in the best of taste. "The victim was her housemaid."

A long silence followed. To Jacob, it seemed to last an hour, but a minute would have been closer to the mark. If Gomersall had smashed an upper cut into his solar plexus, he'd not have felt so stunned. He was incapable of speech.

Kiki de Villiers was alive. Horror at the sight of the corpse had prevented him from testing his natural assumption that the body he'd discovered belonged to the owner of Sepulchre House. But those vivid red tresses—who else could it have been? He wasn't aware that the maid resembled her mistress. Something strange was going on. About to ask a question, he choked it back. It would be far too easy to give himself away.

Gomersall patted his stomach, as if in self-congratulation. It wasn't often that his irrepressible chief crime reporter was struck dumb.

"The police keep their cards close to their chest, lad. They don't admit to knowing her ladyship's whereabouts. By all accounts, she's not in Rye. Their spokesman claims they are following up several promising leads. I've got my own ideas. If you ask me, the killing was a case of mistaken identity."

Jacob twitched under Gomersall's scrutiny. At all costs, he mustn't raise any suspicion that he'd disobeyed his order of the previous afternoon. Better say something, however anodyne.

"I suppose Marcel Ambrose…"

"Is the obvious suspect?" Gomersall shook his head. "In theory, you're right, lad. In practice, you couldn't be more wrong. That shady devil is definitely in the clear."

"Another fake alibi?" Jacob piled on the scorn.

"Alibis don't come any more convincing than this one."

Gomersall's tone of unvarnished irony made Jacob's stomach tie itself in a knot.

"Sorry, sir. I don't understand."

"He died in an accident. His fancy new car veered off the road a few miles north of Rye."

Jacob's eyes opened very wide. "Ambrose has been killed?"

"Along with his chauffeur. The bodies were burned to a crisp, but the police are confident about their identities." A long pause.

"They were confident Ambrose was dead before."

"This is different. Apparently Ambrose ordered one of his minions to drive him to Rye. The brother of that footballer who was fished out of the canal. Name of Joe Postles."

Jacob flinched. One blow after another. On his way back home last night, he'd passed the site of the crash. Even in his dazed state, he'd felt a pang of sadness for anyone who had been inside the car when it turned into a roaring ball of flame. He'd never dreamed that he knew the occupants.

Poor little Joe. For all the man's faults, Jacob had a soft spot for him. And now, if Gomersall was to be believed, both brothers were dead. Thank God he was sitting down; otherwise, he'd have staggered like a punch-drunk boxer who has braved one bout too many.

Gomersall misinterpreted his reaction. "I suppose you're thinking that it's no coincidence."

Jacob made an indeterminate noise.

"Between you, me, and the gatepost, I don't mind admitting you're right. Ambrose was obviously intent on confronting Mrs. de Villiers. Given his record of violence, who knows? Odds are that he'd have killed her. But someone else did his dirty work for him."

"Is it...is it possible that Ambrose shot the woman and then his car crashed on the way back to London?"

"Good question, but I'm told the answer is no. The car spun off the road as it was heading *towards* Rye."

From what Jacob had seen in the dark last night, this was probably true. In which case, who had murdered the housemaid?

Gomersall read his expression. Just as well he couldn't read everything in Jacob's mind. "It's a puzzle, and no mistake. Now the Sunday paper has been put to bed, I thought of asking Will Morgans to look into it…"

"No," Jacob snapped. "Let me handle the story."

Morgans had recently moved from the *Daily Herald* to report on crime for the *Sunday Clarion*. A devout atheist and class-conscious socialist, he had a gleeful specialism in misbehaving clerics and the murkier antics of the landed gentry. He and Jacob worked separately for the most part, which suited them both, although Gomersall occasionally insisted on collaboration if he thought it would save money.

"All right, lad, no need to bite my head off. I was about to say that, bearing in mind our conversation yesterday, I don't mind if you take the lead. See if you can track down the gunman. Shouldn't be too difficult."

"You think not?"

Gomersall frowned. "Not for any investigative reporter worth his salt. The police say the killer is a threat to public safety and they've issued a description. A witness saw him fleeing from the scene of the crime."

Jacob couldn't hide his amazement. "How can they be sure he's the guilty man?"

"The witness saw him tossing a gun away over his shoulder. No effort at concealment, he was obviously in a panic. An amateur in crime, that much is clear. The police picked up the weapon right away."

Was the witness the man Jacob had seen, the passer-by in cap and mackintosh?

"For all I know," Gomersall said, "the killer is a maniac, some kind of sex-crazed pervert."

Jacob gaped. "Really?"

"Yes, I expect he lusted after the maid and seized the moment when the lady of the house left Rye. Chances are, he had murder in mind from the start. Otherwise, why carry a gun? If he meant to kill Mrs. de Villiers, perhaps his temper flared when he was thwarted. The possibilities are endless. But I mustn't write the story for you, must I?"

"No, sir." Jacob swallowed.

"All that matters is that he's caught without delay."

"What…what does this suspect look like?"

"In his twenties or thirties. Sounds like a fancy pants."

"Is that so?" Jacob's scalp prickled.

"Believe it or not, he went out to murder a woman, wearing a wide-brimmed fedora and a smart camel overcoat and oxfords. I suppose he wanted to impress the maid."

"A fedora?" Jacob said faintly.

Gomersall slapped his thigh as he remembered a final point of detail. "Another thing. He had a slight limp. Left leg."

Jacob's left knee throbbed provocatively. His editor bared large fangs in a ferocious grin.

"There you are, lad, the bobbies have handed the story to you on a plate. You won't have much trouble tracking down such a distinctive murderer, will you?"

Chapter 27

Sunday lunch in the dining room at Gaunt House. Hetty had excelled herself with a lavish helping of roast pork accompanied by apple sauce and crackling. Jacob savoured the aroma before spearing a slice of meat with his fork and smearing it in a cider gravy seasoned with sage and bay leaves. The food tasted delicious, and for a few fleeting seconds he forgot that he was the most wanted man in London.

One look at the housekeeper's sombre expression reminded him that he was a murder suspect. At this very moment the police were hunting him, along with half of Fleet Street.

Hetty opened her mouth and, remembering their telephone conversation the previous afternoon, he expected her to say, "I told you so," but she simply asked if he liked the gravy, an experiment with a new recipe. His mouth was full but he nodded vigorously.

But he felt a jolt of dismay. If Hetty was being kind to him, things really must be serious.

That alarming conversation with Gomersall had left him flailing around, unable to decide what to do for the best. Should he confess all and risk dismissal or worse? Or was it smarter to brazen things out and wait for the hue and cry to die down?

He felt like a miserable sinner in need of a father confessor, but absolution wouldn't suffice. He was in a deep hole and needed help in digging himself out of it. When in doubt, swallow your pride. He'd come here to seek Rachel's wise counsel.

On arrival, he'd spilled out a garbled version of the previous evening's events before a restorative glass of sherry improved his coherence and he gratefully accepted an invitation to stay for lunch. Hetty was a generous cook, and there was plenty of food to go round, especially once Rachel whispered something to Trueman and sent him out on an errand.

As he helped to take the dirty plates into the kitchen, he asked, "What do you think I should do?"

"They say Benedict Rhodes-Denton is a hotshot lawyer," Martha whispered in his ear. "With any luck, he'll make sure you don't swing for your crime."

Rachel said briskly, "First things first. You need a new set of clothes. A cheap trilby, shoes, and a suit from Petticoat Lane market. Thankfully, it's open on Sundays, so I asked Trueman to pop over there before the market closes. After your trip to Savile Row, he's got an idea of your measurements."

Jacob blinked. "Thanks, it's very good of you."

She waved his gratitude away. "The least I could do in return after listening to such a bizarre story. I must be honest with you, Jacob. You never cease to amaze me."

He doubted this was a compliment, but had the sense to keep his mouth shut.

Rachel loaded some cutlery into a basket and placed it inside her new dishwasher. This was a strange and gimmicky contraption, in Jacob's opinion, powered by an electric motor and made by a German company called Miele. Rachel must be their best customer in London. Gadgets of all types fascinated her and Gaunt House was full of them. But given that most of her crockery was too fine and fragile to be entrusted to the machine, Jacob couldn't see how it would catch on.

"I need to talk to Inspector Oakes," she said.

"If his superiors have muzzled him, he won't be able to help."

"Since you spoke to him, Ambrose has died, Mrs. de Villiers's housemaid had her head blown off, and the lady herself has vanished. The tectonic plates have shifted. If Oakes is the man I think he is, he won't allow himself to be bullied into inaction."

"What if his idea of action involves locking up a mysterious stranger with a gammy leg and a fedora?" Jacob rubbed his knee by way of emphasis. "I've got a strong preference for any plan that keeps me out of jail."

Rachel switched on the dishwasher, which rumbled furiously as the propeller began to swirl water around the tub. Jacob stared at the machine. He half expected to hear the sound of crockery being smashed to smithereens.

"One thing at a time," she said. "You're always in a rush. The first rule of strategy is to gather information."

"Did Machiavelli say that?" he asked grumpily. "Or was it Sun Tzu?"

"Rachel Savernake," Martha said.

Jacob sighed. "I can't imagine who killed the maid, or why. All I know is that it wasn't me."

"Think about the context. The police were persuaded to postpone any attempt to protect Kiki de Villiers from an urgent threat posed by Ambrose. Your editor was prevailed upon to stop you from investigating her. The way was left clear for her to be murdered."

"Except that she wasn't murdered."

"True. It's possible that the maid was the assassin's intended target all along, although I find that hard to believe. What is certain is that whoever was responsible—the killer or whoever instructed him—has a remarkable amount of power and influence. To cause both Scotland Yard and the *Clarion* to turn a blind eye to murder—and that's what it adds up to—requires an astonishing reach."

"A criminal gang? Rivals to Ambrose and his henchmen?"

"I was thinking of a different kind of gang. Not so much criminal as people who consider themselves above the law."

"Members of Parliament?"

Rachel smiled. "Not quite, but you're getting warmer. I'd hazard a guess that the truth may lie somewhere in Whitehall."

"What do you mean?"

"Remember our old friend Major Whitlow?"

Jacob clenched his fists involuntarily. "Whitlow? He's no pal of mine but I certainly won't forget him in a hurry. I thought we'd seen the last of that fellow."

"His survival skills are formidable. Inspector Oakes told me that after the debacle at Mortmain Hall, he was shifted to another highly secret government office. Something about this business in Rye reminds me of him. A formidable combination of menace and extreme ruthlessness. Who else, other than Whitlow and his crowd, could intimidate the Yard as well as your employers?"

Was that a note of admiration in her voice? Jacob had seen Rachel act ruthlessly herself when the need arose.

"So I can't help wondering if the woman's murder bears his fingerprints," she said. "Or should I say, the mark of his claw?"

Trueman returned with an assortment of cheap clothes which he presented to Jacob with a dour grin.

"Too good to last, eh? Leastways when you wear this lot, you won't stand out in a crowd. Go into any pub or football ground, and nobody will give you a second glance. Not if they're hunting for a crazed killer who shares a tailor with the Prince of Wales."

Jacob managed a weak smile and adjourned with the others to wash the meal down with coffee in the drawing room. As he made himself comfortable in the luxurious armchair, he thought it was a supremely conventional English scene: the well-to-do family and friends relaxing after a sumptuous Sunday lunch. Hetty was knitting a muffler, while her husband studied the latest issue of *The Autocar* and Martha leafed through the *News of the World*.

Jacob said in a low voice to Rachel, "Can I ask you about Captain Malam?"

"Feel free."

"To be honest, I never understood your relationship with him."

"It's quite simple. He was only a name in the newspapers until we bumped into each other one day at the Royal Academy. Once he realised who I was, he became desperate to further the acquaintance. Unfortunately, my bank balance was more attractive to him than my womanly charms."

Jacob tutted. "Incredible."

She stirred cream into her drink. "Please don't try to be gallant, Jacob. It doesn't suit you."

He looked down at the carpet. "Sorry."

"When I made enquiries, I discovered that Malam was quite hard up."

"Surely he has money to burn?"

"You're a journalist; you should know better than to believe what you read in the papers. Especially when it concerns people in the public eye. Roddy is a spendthrift. Racing cars don't come cheap and playing cricket pays no bills—he takes the field as a gentleman and amateur, of course, not a professional. What's more, although he claims to have a shrewd financial brain, he's drawn to bad investments like a bee to honey. He doesn't come from the landed gentry. So how does he finance his extravagance?"

"I'm all ears."

"He's as patient as an angler, fishing for wealthy admirers. Men and women alike rise to the lure. That is, a veneer of sophistication, chiselled good looks, and man-of-action charm. That's why he frequents galleries, even though he knows no more about art than you do. He goes there to hook rich collectors."

"Hence his stake in the Hades Gallery?"

"Precisely—and when he ran short of funds, he bailed out at a loss. Typical. His modus operandi is simple. Once someone takes his bait, he persuades them to invest in some dubious business venture. He pockets an outrageous commission and usually ends up shedding crocodile tears when the whole pack of cards falls apart."

"Did he try to tempt you to speculate?"

"In some gold mine in East Africa, yes. Almost certainly it doesn't exist and even if it does, it probably contains as much gold as a coal cellar in Croydon. I prevaricated and eventually he gave up. I suppose he set out to land a more gullible catch."

"So you were the one who got away?"

She smiled. "My taste in crime is exotic. I crave mystery. Common or garden swindles leave me cold."

"But?"

"I always knew that Malam lacked a moral compass. Now I wonder if I underestimated the lengths he'd go to in order to get what he wants."

"Any news about who planted the bomb in his car?" She shook her head. "Or about what drove Damaris Gethin to kill herself?"

"That mystery we did solve." Rachel lifted her cup. The rich aroma of the coffee filled the room. "Or so I believe. The challenge is—what to do next?"

"Blimey, that was quick. Come on, don't leave me in suspense. How on earth did you make sense of it?"

"I asked myself what could possibly drive a successful woman with a long life ahead of her to make such a terrible decision. She made it very clear to me that she regarded herself as a victim of murder."

"Her motive must have been very powerful."

Rachel nodded. "She wasn't simply taking a quick way out when diagnosed with terminal illness and facing the prospect of a long and painful decline. She was specific—I was to do justice on her behalf by discovering the person or people she held responsible for her death. What horror could she have experienced?"

"Hard to imagine."

"At first I wondered if she'd been a victim of some form of shocking sexual assault."

Jacob blinked. "You did?"

"If so, Captain Malam was the likeliest suspect. I knew he'd had a fling with her. As far as I was aware, she'd not been involved with anyone else since that affair ended. On the contrary, she shut herself away from the world for more than a year. I wondered why. Was it possible he'd forced himself on her?"

"And?"

She shook her head. "Malam has plenty of vices, but he doesn't strike me as a likely rapist."

"How can you be sure? I mean, in some respects you've led a sheltered life…"

She turned on him, her voice icy. "Do you really think so? You don't know everything about my years on Gaunt, not by a long chalk, but you should have learned enough to realise that is far from the truth."

Jacob was ashen-faced and contrite. "Sorry, Rachel. That was a stupid thing to say."

"Yes." Her tone softened slightly. "It's true that one can never say never where dark impulses are concerned. An apparently pleasant individual may lose all self-control and behave like a beast in the wild. But Roddy Malam is vain and manipulative, rather than obsessed with exploiting his crude physical strength. If he couldn't persuade a woman to join him in bed of her own free will, he'd regard it as a personal failure."

"So he's the sort who prefers volunteers to conscripts?"

"I asked myself what was known about Damaris Gethin during the time she cut herself off from the outside world. It was clear she'd sunk into a deep depression, but what caused it?"

"If she pined for Malam after they broke up..."

"Damaris was made of strong stuff. Men meant nothing to her in comparison to her artistic vocation. Yes, she had affairs over the years but her one true passion was her work. She was obsessed with art as performance. The act of *creation*. Yet she'd produced nothing for a long time. I couldn't find out much, but it was clear that towards the end of her relationship with Roddy Malam, she'd suffered headaches and nausea and that her moods had been hopelessly unpredictable."

"The artistic temperament?"

Rachel sighed. "Those symptoms can have several different causes."

"Such as?"

"Pregnancy."

He stared at her. "What are you suggesting?"

"If she'd miscarried, that might explain her mood of despair. Such an experience is deeply painful and can overwhelm a woman. Society tells her it's nothing out of the ordinary and she needs to get over it, but that's easier said than done. The sense of loss is appalling; it can feel too much to bear."

"How do you know?" he blurted out.

From her chair on the other side of the room, Hetty put aside her knitting and said quietly, "I had a miscarriage."

He stared at her.

"Four, as a matter of fact. Did you never wonder why Cliff and I don't have children?"

There was a brief silence. Jacob wished the floor would open and swallow him up.

"I'm so sorry. I had no idea."

"You weren't to know. I don't care to speak about it, some things are too...difficult. But Rachel understands the ordeal I went through."

"If Damaris had miscarried," Rachel said calmly, "that was unlikely to explain why she accused someone of murder. So what were the other possibilities? It occurred to me that she might have had an abortion."

"But that's a crime!"

Rachel let out a moan of exasperation. "For goodness sake, Jacob, don't be so naïve. Whatever you may think about the legal and moral rights and wrongs, you should understand one thing. Women will always demand to have control over their own bodies. Especially when their lives have been turned upside down. If a woman wants rid of an unborn baby, she will usually be in a wretched state of conflicting emotions."

Jacob kept quiet.

"When I considered the guests who attended Damaris Gethin's exhibition at the Hades," Rachel said, "I asked myself if it was significant that they included a trained nurse."

"Malam's sister-in-law," he said.

"Ah, light is dawning." Rachel's eyes glittered. "Do you recall telling me what she said? That she'd once done Damaris a good turn."

"She could have meant anything."

"Agreed. Realistically, though, a good turn from a nurse would often involve her medical know-how. Given that Phoebe

Wardle lives out in Romney Marsh, I found it hard to picture the two of them spending much time in each other's company, let alone becoming friends. They had little in common."

"Go on."

"Stray bits of information began to come together and form a pattern in my mind. Captain Malam is charming and well-connected, very much a ladies' man. Yet he's often in need of cash to meet his considerable expenses. Evan Tucker used to host glamorous parties, but he ran short of money too once his songs fell out of fashion. He lived close to the clinic set up by Malam's brother, and run after his death by Phoebe Wardle. I knew that Giles Malam's medical career had suffered a major setback when a young woman patient died during an operation. The clinic catered to female patients, and in recent years they were only admitted one at a time."

"My God," Jacob said, "I see what you're driving at."

"Martha spoke to an eminent surgeon who knew Giles Malam's father. He said the scandal broke the old man's heart. There was a rumour that Malam had carried out an illegal abortion in return for a handsome fee, but it went badly wrong. Malam senior managed to get everything hushed up, but the price Giles paid was to give up on surgery and ply his trade as a doctor a long way from London."

"Romney Marsh."

"Yes. Unfortunately, he remained chronically short of money. After his father's death, he went back to his bad old ways. Illegal abortion is a trade that thrives in the back streets of every town in our supposedly green and pleasant land. But it's a deadly business, often conducted in appallingly unsanitary conditions by women whose methods are crude and dangerous. The brutal truth is that a lot of their patients die. Others are permanently damaged. Inevitably, there is an opportunity for the unscrupulous to target women who are wealthy and can afford to pay whatever it takes in order to terminate their pregnancies safely and discreetly."

"Ah, I see."

"Unfortunately, Giles Malam wasn't a skilled doctor. He drank too much and his practice was in an impoverished part of the country. I wondered if he'd seen the chance to make money out of the misery of others."

"He'd have been struck off the medical register if the authorities found out. And that's only the half of it. He'd finish up in prison."

"Like his brother, he was a born risk-taker."

"Giles Malam died before Damaris Gethin..."

"Yes, but he set up the lucrative trade that his widow continued. My suspicion is that there was a conspiracy between the two Malams, the nurse, and Evan Tucker—who hero-worships the captain. I saw how it could work, how everyone had a part to play in the scheme."

"Namely?"

"Roddy Malam's social connections were a vital asset. So was his gift of the gab. If he or Evan Tucker learned on the grapevine that a rich woman was pregnant and unhappy about it, she'd be invited to a party at The Risings in Romney Marsh. There she would be introduced to the Malams..."

"And a deal would be done?"

"Including the opportunity to spend as long as she needed in recuperation at Orgarswick."

"Orgarswick?"

"Nurse Wardle's clinic. Yesterday, while you were on the trail of Kiki de Villiers, we paid Evan Tucker and Phoebe Wardle a visit, out in the wilds of Romney Marsh."

"You did?"

"The back of beyond," Martha said.

"Compared to the island of Gaunt," Rachel said, "the Marsh is positively suburban. However, it's ideal for hiding away from the prying eyes and loose tongues of London society. The price of staying at Orgarswick is bound to be extortionate. Enough to give each of the conspirators a fat profit. However, these patients were women for whom money was no object."

"You think that's what happened to Damaris Gethin? She got pregnant, and then went to Orgarswick to..."

"I suspect there is more to it than that," Rachel interrupted. "What if she were torn about whether to keep the baby? Especially if she felt that, at her age, it was her last chance to have a child?"

"Why did she bear a grudge?" Jacob asked. "Your theory means that she accused Malam, Tucker, and Wardle of murdering her. If she was happy to undergo the operation and pay a large amount of money to stay at the clinic, why blame them after the event?"

"You're taking far too much for granted. I'm sure *happy* is the wrong word."

"All right, all right," he said, "but Nurse Wardle said she'd done Damaris a good turn. To be stigmatised as a murderer would horrify her."

"No doubt," Rachel said drily. "If you're saying there was something special about this particular transaction, I'm sure you're right."

"What do you mean?"

"What if Damaris's baby was Roddy Malam's."

Flabbergasted, he said, "That really is quite a jump."

"Asking *what if?* is my favourite pastime. Any experienced journalist will tell you, most of the best stories come from intuitive leaps." Her words cut like razors. "If Oakes were here, he'd be honest enough to admit that imagination plays a part in professional detective work. I simply follow an idea until I find something that proves that I'm wrong."

Jacob put up his hands in mock surrender.

"For all I know," she continued, "the child was conceived during one of Evan Tucker's sybaritic parties. The captain was bored with Damaris and had no desire whatsoever to be the father of her offspring. Given the collapse of their relationship, she probably had mixed feelings about bringing his baby into the world. I expect he prevailed on her to submit to Phoebe Wardle's tender mercies, with Tucker egging them on. We can surmise why he wrote off his stake in the Hades. It was his financial contribution to solving the mess he'd created."

Jacob absorbed all this.

"Afterwards, Damaris regretted what she'd done?"

"Bitterly, I would guess. I can't know the precise details of what happened, let alone what went through her mind, but the psychological scars must have run very deep. And probably she endured continuing ill health."

"More speculation?"

"Speculation," Rachel said patiently, "is my stock-in-trade. But remember this. I hate to say it, but for a woman to suffer lasting physical damage after undergoing a botched abortion is hardly uncommon."

"Phoebe Wardle is a trained nurse."

"That doesn't make her Florence Nightingale," Rachel said tartly. "For all we know, she lacked the skills required to deal with complications. Or perhaps there was another factor..."

"Such as?"

She ignored the question. "Whatever the truth, there's no doubt that Damaris Gethin was driven to end her life in the most shocking fashion. She held a number of individuals responsible.

So she invited them to her exhibition and brought me along, in the hope I might avenge her death."

Jacob finished his coffee in silence. "You've given me plenty of food for thought."

"Good for your digestion. And it will take your mind off the hunt for the stranger in Sepulchre Street."

"Oh God." He felt a sudden stab of despair. "I still don't know what to do."

She clapped him on the back. "Courage, Jacob! Remember that attack is the best form of defence."

He eyed her nervously. "What do you have in mind?"

"We need to talk to Inspector Oakes."

"You'd better leave me out of it. There's a bounty on my head, remember."

"Don't flatter yourself. I've not heard of any reward on offer for the person who brings you to justice."

"But seriously..."

"I'm perfectly serious."

He looked straight at her. With a sinking heart, he realised she meant what she said.

"You're forgetting your Chesterton, Jacob. Can you recall his wise words? He asked where is the best place to hide a leaf? In a forest, of course."

"Sorry, my head's spinning. I'm not with you."

"Where is the best place to hide a wanted man? In a conversation with the smartest officer from Scotland Yard."

As Jacob closed his eyes, Rachel gave a mischievous smile before adding, "Preferably after church. Lest we forget, this is the Sabbath."

Chapter 28

"How did you manage to persuade him?" Jacob asked half an hour later.

While Martha had told him about the trip to Romney Marsh, Rachel had telephoned Inspector Oakes at home. She'd come back with the news that he was willing to meet Jacob and her that evening.

Rachel laughed. "Oh, Jacob, I do worry that if I give away all the tricks of my trade, you'll start to find me wearisome."

"Never," he said softly.

"Besides, I'd miss your expression of tetchy bewilderment. I hate to sound patronising, but nudging you off balance is addictive. A guilty pleasure."

"I can't win with you, can I?" he said.

"Nobody can," Martha said.

"I'll take pity on you," Rachel said. "Oakes did sound reluctant to see me urgently, I must admit."

Martha was unimpressed. "I thought he was quick on the uptake. And I'm sure he's taken a shine to you."

"He made some feeble excuse about working all the hours under the sun and needing to catch up with his domestic chores.

I'm keeping the inducement of a meal cooked by Hetty up my sleeve, so I was forced to drop Major Whitlow's name into the conversation."

"You can't possibly be sure that Whitlow has any skin in this game," Jacob protested.

"Just as Oakes can't be confident that it was Whitlow's masters who pulled strings to prevent him from investigating Kiki de Villiers. But I bet he has his suspicions, and before this evening's over, we'll find out for sure."

"By then I may be under lock and key," Jacob grumbled.

Rachel laughed. "Don't worry. Philip Oakes's isn't the only private number I've managed to get hold of. If the inspector hauls you off in chains, I'll be on the phone to Rhodes-Denton in a jiffy. So long as you behave yourself this evening. In other words, let me do the talking. You just put on your Petticoat Lane outfit and concentrate on *not* limping."

————

Rachel hummed a few bars of "The King of Love My Shepherd Is."

"A pleasant service, Inspector. Balm for the soul."

"If you say so, Miss Savernake," Oakes replied.

They were leaving St. George's Church in Bloomsbury after evensong. As they emerged from the grand Corinthian portico, Rachel craned her neck to gaze upwards.

"See the pyramid at the top of the tower?" she said. "Nicholas Hawksmoor took his inspiration from Pliny's description of the Mausoleum at Halicarnassus. One of the seven wonders of the ancient world."

"Your breadth of knowledge never ceases to amaze me," Oakes said.

"I like finding things out. It keeps me out of mischief."

Oakes gave her an old-fashioned look.

"Well, sometimes it does, at any rate. Put my nosiness down to a misspent youth. I always want to *know*."

They were joined by Martha, Trueman, and Jacob, who was desperately trying not to limp. To distract the detective, Rachel gestured towards the building.

"Hawksmoor's churches are so wonderfully baroque. All those dark corners and wild flights of fancy. This portico is his version of the Temple of Bacchus at Baalbeck. Even though he never visited the sites, he was able to bring his fantasies about them to life through his work. No wonder people called him the devil's architect."

"I didn't have you down as an expert in old buildings, Miss Savernake," he said. "Nor as a churchgoer, to be frank."

Rachel looked contrite. "Here's my confession, Inspector. I find sinning more fun than repentance."

"So many of my customers do."

"I'll do my best to escape your clutches for a while longer," she said.

"Just as you dodged Marcel Ambrose at Chez Laurent the other night?"

She laughed. "Ambrose must be the least-mourned man in England. Did I hear that you suspect his driver crashed their car deliberately?"

"You're remarkably well informed." Oakes gave Jacob a sour look. "I see you're keeping in close touch with Fleet Street."

"You sound exhausted, Inspector. I'm not surprised, with so much on your plate. Thank goodness that, now Ambrose is dead, you should be able to close a lot of your files. Laurent is slippery, but you should find enough to put him and his henchmen behind bars. Richly deserved after they tried to hurt poor Jacob. Luckily, he was smart enough to get out of the place with no damage done."

Jacob felt an overwhelming desire to massage his sore knee but somehow mastered it.

Oakes frowned. "It's possible that certain arrests are imminent. You'll understand that I can't make any official comment."

"Commendably discreet," she said. "Any luck with tracing the person responsible for that murder in Rye?"

"We have a team of men hunting the suspect. From the witness's description, the killer shouldn't be hard to spot. He won't be able to dodge us for long."

"Especially not with the press breathing down his neck. You and your chums at the *Clarion* are pulling out all the stops to find him, aren't you, Jacob?"

Jacob gritted his teeth. "Our every reader is a potential detective. You watch: they'll latch on to him quicker than the Yard."

Oakes allowed himself a smile. He was beginning to unbend, just as Jacob felt the urge to mop sweat off his brow. It was too soon for him to relax. Any slip could be fatal.

"Shooting a defenceless woman in cold blood." Rachel tutted. "Appalling."

Martha couldn't resist giving Jacob a sly glance as she chipped in. "Hanging's too good for him."

"Any idea of the murderer's motive, Inspector?" Rachel asked.

"We can't yet be sure whether the woman who died was the intended victim or not," Oakes said. "However, the odds are that his intended target was Mrs. de Villiers, not her maid."

"A bad mistake to make."

"Not quite as stupid as you might think. This information isn't in the public domain as yet, but between you and me, the deceased was in the habit of dressing up to look like Mrs. de Villiers. Her mistress was amused, flattered perhaps. She even gave the woman a red wig to complete the illusion."

Rachel said calmly, "Goodness me. That really is taking devotion to extremes."

The inspector cleared his throat. "She idolised Mrs. de Villiers."

"And what does the lady have to say for herself?"

Oakes glanced around. Jacob tried to make himself look inconspicuous.

"She's mortified, of course. In floods of tears, by all accounts. Blames herself for leaving the maid on her own in the house last night."

"Where did she go?"

"To call on an acquaintance."

Rachel smiled sweetly. "Dare I ask the gentleman's name?"

Oakes deliberated. Jacob could imagine his inner conflict. The inspector knew he ought to keep quiet, but he was angry about the way his superiors had treated him, and he knew there was nobody more discreet than Rachel Savernake. And more than likely, he wanted to find out what she was up to. You scratch my back...

"This was a lady," the detective said quietly. "Name of Phoebe Wardle."

———

"I hate to make a nuisance of myself," Oakes said for the third time, as he clambered out of the Rolls outside Gaunt House.

"Please, think nothing of it," Rachel said. "It's my pleasure to offer you a little hospitality. After your recent travails, you deserve a break from the bachelor life. Hetty will rustle up something to eat and Trueman will mix us a cocktail while we reminisce about old times."

"A cosy chat about dark deeds at Mortmain Hall?" he said wryly. "Or confronting killers up at Blackstone Fell?"

Rachel laughed. "On second thoughts, let's not get nostalgic. Frankly, there's enough happening now to keep us fully occupied. Why on earth was Mrs. de Villiers calling on Phoebe Wardle? I didn't realise they were such great pals. Besides, Nurse Wardle lives out in the wilderness of Romney Marsh."

"The Marsh isn't far from Rye," Oakes said as Trueman opened the front door for them. "Although the town is in Sussex, it lies on the county border with Kent. People call it the gateway to the Marsh. Twenty minutes in a fast car and you're there."

"I suppose the lady has a fast car," Rachel said thoughtfully.

"Very fast."

"So why did she go there?"

Oakes cleared his throat. "This goes no further."

"Of course."

The detective threw a glance at Jacob, who was concentrating on looking like a man who'd never limped in his life and certainly wouldn't be seen dead wearing a fedora.

"Jacob knows that what is said in Gaunt House remains within the four walls," Rachel said as she stepped over the threshold. "And he definitely knows better than to betray a confidence."

Oakes turned to Jacob. "The Postles brothers talked to you, and look what happened to them."

Jacob flushed. "That wasn't my..."

The detective allowed himself a wintry smile. "No, I know. At least Joe did the world a favour by ridding us of Marcel Ambrose."

They went inside. Trueman went off to tell his wife about the additional guest and as soon as they'd settled in the drawing room, Rachel turned to Oakes.

"Back to my question. What took Mrs. de Villiers to Romney Marsh?"

The detective considered. "She came into Scotland Yard

earlier today to speak to one of my colleagues. She'd heard the news of her housemaid's murder on the wireless."

"Very public-spirited," Rachel said. "What did she say?"

"Her story is that she renewed acquaintance with Nurse Wardle at the Hades Gallery on the night of Damaris Gethin's death. You were there; you may have seen them talking together."

"As far as I could see, they kept a safe distance from each other. Not that I kept them under observation all evening."

"The Wardle woman mentioned that she was going to shut her clinic—Orgarswick, it's called—and move abroad. Mrs. de Villiers says she had a bright idea. She wondered if the clinic might be adapted into a home for her invalid husband. At present he's stuck up in Shropshire and she'd like them to be closer, so it's easier for her to keep an eye on him."

"How caring." Jacob couldn't conceal his scepticism.

Rachel ignored him. "What do you know about the clinic, Inspector?"

"Nothing. Why do you ask?"

"I suspect Damaris Gethin had an illegal abortion there."

Oakes's eyes opened very wide. "What makes you say that?"

"There are several pointers, but nothing that would stand up in a court of law. So may I ask this? I know you're not investigating the death of Damaris Gethin personally. It's clear she killed herself. But the case is newsworthy and given your standing at the Yard, I'm sure you've been kept informed. Do the results of her post-mortem support my theory?"

They waited while the detective made a silent calculation.

"It's extraordinary," he said slowly, "but you've stumbled on to something."

Martha grinned; her faith in Rachel was absolute.

"I'm not sure about *stumbled*," Rachel said. "The medical evidence?"

"I don't need to go into sordid details," Oakes said hurriedly. "The report that passed across my desk indicated that an illegal abortion had been performed. The signs of tearing and scarring established that beyond doubt."

"The operation was recent?"

"Within the past eighteen months, they thought. Whoever was responsible made a mess of things. The pathologist said Damaris Gethin was lucky to have survived. The recuperation process must have been long and painful. Perhaps that explains why she took her own life."

"Nothing was seen of Damaris in public for a long time. Now we know why."

"I can arrange for inquiries to be made at the clinic."

"Too late, Inspector. As you say, Nurse Wardle has shut up shop. I presume that all trace of any nefarious activities has been destroyed. For all I know, the botched operation on Damaris Gethin prompted her decision to cut and run. Her clients were wealthy. If one of them died or suffered serious complications, questions would be asked."

"You suspect Mrs. de Villiers was also a patient of hers?"

"There's no reason to think so. If the gossip columns are any guide, she's hardly been out of sight for a moment in recent times. As far as I'm aware, there's never been any suggestion of her being under the weather, so to speak, even for a very short time. No doubt the two women met through Captain Malam. He happens to be Nurse Wardle's brother-in-law."

Oakes was thoughtful. "Malam? Yes, that makes sense."

"I'm glad you think so. You described Mrs. de Villiers's account of events as a story. Do I take it that you're sceptical?"

"Mrs. de Villiers is a rich woman with influential friends. I need to be careful about what I say, especially since she isn't a suspect in the murder of the housemaid."

"But?"

"But you're right. I don't believe she's being entirely candid with us. She claims that she had a careful look round the property and accepted the nurse's suggestion that she spend the night there. She wanted to sleep on her decision, but in the end she wasn't ready to make an offer. While she was at Orgarswick, she heard on the wireless about what happened at Sepulchre Street."

"And so she made it her business to drive straight from Romney Marsh to give assistance to Scotland Yard?"

"That's right. She also wanted to make sure it was in order for her to spend tonight at the house in Rye. If she puts it off any longer, she says she'll probably never pluck up the courage to go back to the place. The crime scene investigations have concluded, so she was given the go-ahead."

Rachel said, "All entirely plausible."

"So far as it goes, yes, but I'm not sure she's told us the whole truth. Not that it matters to us officially."

"What do you think is the whole truth?"

"I'm betting that she arranged a rendezvous with an admirer. And I can't help wondering if she persuaded this nurse to provide her with an alibi."

"An alibi for what?"

"For meeting someone she didn't want anyone to know about."

"Who?"

"I can only hazard a guess."

"Make an intuitive leap, you mean." Jacob aimed a satiric grin at Rachel.

"If you say so." Oakes ran a hand through his hair. "I'll never be able to prove it, but my money is on Captain Roderick Malam."

Chapter 29

With a flourish worthy of a magician revealing the lady he was about to cut in half, Trueman produced a tray of cocktails.

"Port glasses, frosted with sugar and decorated with slices of lemon peel," Rachel said. "Do tell, what are you treating us to this evening?"

"A dash of orange juice, with French and Italian vermouth plus Plymouth gin." He allowed himself a rare grin. "They call it One Exciting Night."

She lifted her glass. "An excellent choice. Your very good health, everyone. There's one thing I don't understand, Inspector."

The detective savoured his cocktail. "Only one, Miss Savernake?"

They were like duellists, Jacob thought, two people whose respect for each other masked their fundamental differences. Martha was right, Oakes had taken a shine to Rachel. Yet Jacob didn't believe the detective would ever get anywhere with her on a personal level. In her own special way, she was untouchable.

"Mrs. de Villiers is a married woman, but she's never been discreet about her liaisons with other men. I've no wish to pass judgement, but some would call her brazen. So why would she suddenly become so coy about what people might think? Who cares who she sleeps with?"

"A good question."

Rachel radiated charm. "Dare I hope for a good answer?"

Oakes nibbled at a hangnail. "Unfortunately, we've reached murky waters. I'm out of my depth."

"Let's not beat about the bush, Inspector." Jacob always marvelled at Rachel's shapeshifting ability. One minute, the delightful hostess; the next, a figure of quiet menace. "What you mean is that your superiors are preventing you from doing your duty."

The detective bristled. "Remember, I hold the office of constable. I'm a public servant and accountable as such. I swore an oath to uphold the rule of law. You're a free agent, Miss Savernake, but I am not."

"If higher authorities are less scrupulous about the rule of law, you're placed in an invidious position."

"So I would be," he said cagily, "if that were the case."

The charm vanished. "Come on, Inspector. This isn't the time or place for pomposity or evasion. Jacob made valiant efforts to persuade you of the dangers Mrs. de Villiers faced. You failed to offer her protection from a murderer. I'm sure it wasn't inertia, and I'm sure it was against your better judgement too. The only possible conclusion is that you were forbidden to save her."

Oakes's knuckles were white. "We can't simply jump when a journalist tells us to jump. There are checks to be made, procedures to be followed. It takes time."

Inexorably, Rachel continued. "Within a matter of hours, murder was done at Sepulchre House. Her bolthole, supposedly a place of safety. Very few people even knew of its existence. But the police did. A woman died, and you did nothing to save her. So much for the rule of law, Inspector."

"There was a short delay, yes. The reason I was given was…"

"Cock-and-bull," Rachel interrupted. "Kiki de Villiers escaped by the merest chance. If you're right, by slipping off to an assignation with a former lover. Perhaps in some hotel where they believed nobody would recognise them?"

"I suppose so," he said heavily.

"You haven't checked?"

"It's outside my remit, and it's not relevant. Don't forget, Mrs. de Villiers is an innocent party in all this. She isn't suspected of a crime."

"Yet someone wants her dead. Why is that, do you think?"

"Listen, we're working night and day to find the maid's killer. No stone will be left unturned. We'll speak to every tailor in the south-east. The man in the fedora…"

"Is a man of straw," Rachel interrupted.

"What do you mean?" he snapped.

She folded her arms. "Have you asked yourself who this mysterious eyewitness might be? Why the description he gave is so curiously specific? You can bet he doesn't limp or wear a fedora. I'm afraid you haven't launched a manhunt, Inspector, but a wild goose chase."

Jacob risked an enthusiastic nod of agreement, provoking a sidelong glare from Rachel.

Oakes groaned. "It's the best lead we have."

"Surely the question we should ask is—*why*? Why did someone want Kiki de Villiers dead? A very powerful someone, mind. Someone who could prevail not only over honest and diligent officers at Scotland Yard but also Jacob's strong-minded masters at the *Clarion*. There can only be one answer, don't you agree?"

The policeman swallowed the rest of his cocktail. Jacob thought that Oakes's mind must be whirling. Was he torn between his sense of duty and the urge to confide the truth?

"Well, Inspector?"

"I don't have any evidence," Oakes said.

"Understood, but you're a very good detective. What's your hunch?"

There was a long pause.

"There's a certain department in Whitehall. Its sole function is to safeguard...a small and...um, closely knit group of people who are central to our national life."

Rachel digested this. "Closely knit?"

"Very." He seemed uncomfortable.

"Like a family, perhaps?"

Oakes coloured. "I heard a whisper that our old friend Major Whitlow was transferred to that office after what happened at Mortmain Hall. He is now personally responsible for ensuring the protection and well-being of...a particular member of that group of individuals I mentioned."

Rachel nodded.

"This individual has striking qualities and a winning personality. He's widely admired. For many British people, he represents the modern face of this country. Its future too. Others would like to see him stripped of any influence or power, because of weaknesses in his character. They say he lacks moral fibre."

"How awful." Rachel took a sip of her drink. "A ladies' man, then?"

"Indeed. And he has managed to entangle himself with Mrs. Kiki de Villiers."

"Good God," Jacob said, unable to restrain himself any longer.

Oakes said unhappily, "I've been told in strictest confidence that he is besotted with her."

"A married woman with a lurid past." Rachel ticked the points off on her long fingers. "A former prostitute. The mistress of a gangster with a homicidal streak."

"Yes."

Rachel gave a wry smile. "Oh, dear."

"He risks precipitating a constitutional crisis on a scale Britain hasn't experienced for more than a century. Not since the Glorious Revolution, and that was largely bloodless. Given our current economic miseries, we mightn't be so lucky this time. Millions of people are unhappy and desperate. Who knows where an acrimonious fracture in the leadership of this country could lead? Do we finish up saluting a Mussolini of our own? The likes of Oswald Mosley are waiting eagerly in the wings, you can depend on it."

"So Major Whitlow devised a neat solution. Remove the lady, and you remove the problem."

"Until the next time the gentleman in question does something stupid, at any rate."

"Yes, the major is a skilled tactician, but not a long-term strategist." Rachel considered. "However, I struggle to picture him employing such an easily recognisable assassin."

"The fedora was an effective disguise."

"Even so, it smells like a red herring." She sighed. "So Mrs. de Villiers's life remains at risk?"

Oakes shook his head. "At least there's good news on that front."

"Really?"

"I'm led to believe that she has broken the news to her famous lover that the affair is over. He is heartbroken, but she is adamant. All his pleas have been in vain."

Rachel said coolly, "Britain's survival is assured for the time being, then. A narrow escape. Was this prompted by the murder of her maid?"

"No, she spoke to her Very Important Admirer shortly after Damaris Gethin killed herself."

Jacob frowned. "Has she really decided to sacrifice her happiness for the good of the country?"

Oakes was scornful. "You must be joking. She'd simply found someone else."

"Why do you think it is Captain Malam?"

"Two reasons. First, when she ended the affair, she indicated that it was because a lover from her past had rekindled the relationship. Second, when my colleague interviewed her about her whereabouts last night, she let Malam's name slip. She tried to cover it up, but there was no earthly reason why she should have made that mistake if he wasn't involved."

"Strange. I'd have expected her to be a first-class liar."

"Oh, my colleague found her convincing. But when I got the story from him, I had my doubts."

"I realised there was someone else in the captain's life." She explained about her visit to Malam's flat the previous evening. "I didn't realise it might be Kiki de Villiers."

"She's a notoriously desirable woman."

"True. On the other hand, Captain Malam doesn't usually care to rekindle old flames. Once the spark is gone, it's gone, that is how he puts it."

"A man can change his mind."

"Happens all the time, doesn't it? However, I got the impression that it was almost a point of honour with him, never to go back. A question of pride, self-esteem, even. Even when he suggested that in my case things were different, I wasn't convinced."

Oakes coughed. "I don't mean to be undiplomatic…"

"But?"

"But even if it wasn't his habit to…um, revive past relationships, he might have made an exception for Mrs. de Villiers."

"She is certainly a remarkable woman," Rachel said drily.

Jacob was growing impatient. He'd been itching to put

his motto in and now he could contain himself no longer. "Regardless of that, what about the bomb in Malam's car? What if Major Whitlow's crowd planted it?"

Oakes made a derisive noise. "Why would they do that?"

"Just a thought," Jacob said sulkily.

"Whitlow has enough on his plate, if you ask me. As for the bomb, Malam's financial jiggery-pokery has earned him plenty of enemies. That fellow Butterworth remains the obvious suspect, but unless we turn up evidence to link him with the explosion, he'll keep hiding behind his smart lawyer."

"I'm still curious about the fact Benedict Rhodes-Denton represented him," Rachel said dreamily.

Oakes shrugged. "None of my business."

"You say that, Inspector," she said, "but something tells me that when we answer that question, we'll have a better understanding of what's really going on."

"Oh, really? Would that be your feminine intuition, by any chance?"

Her expression tightened. "Please, Inspector. I realise you're tired, but there's no need to condescend to me."

He looked injured. "I've been very frank with you. I could be sacked on the spot."

"Don't think I'm not grateful." She finished her cocktail. "I'm also relieved that the country isn't going to succumb to mob rule just yet. However, there's still a great deal we don't know."

"There's always a lot we don't know," Oakes said. "For a start, where to find that man in the fedora."

Chapter 30

"Where does all this leave me?" Jacob said twenty minutes later.

"Deprived of your fedora for the foreseeable future, by the sound of things," Rachel said. "Forget the smart clothes. Go back to looking like you never owned an iron or a clothes brush."

"That's rather harsh," he complained.

She gave him a look, while Martha stifled laughter. Trueman had taken Oakes home, and Hetty, a devout believer in "early to bed and early to rise," had already said good night.

"I'm a marked man," he said gloomily.

"Stay here for the night, if it feels safer than going back to Exmouth Market," Martha said. "I'll make up the bed."

"Thanks, I'll take you up on that." He yawned. "The excitement's catching up with me."

"Before you start snoring," Rachel said, "I'd like the address of the woman you interviewed, Annie Hitchen."

"Hitchen?" he said.

"Her nickname was Stilts, so you told me."

"Oh, yes. You want to talk to her?"

"It's a long shot, but I wonder if she can cast any light on the relationship between Mrs. de Villiers and Captain Malam."

"You think the inspector is right about that pair?"

Rachel gave him a brief summary of her visit to Malam's flat the previous night, adding, "He's cooking something up, I'm sure of it."

"Why do you say that?"

"I've spent time in his company; I know what makes him tick. Charming and good company in a self-adoring way, but congenitally untrustworthy. His way of life is expensive, and these are hard economic times. There's no doubt he's dug himself into a financial hole and is desperate to climb out of it."

"Don't forget he's a victim, no less than Kiki de Villiers. What about the bomb that blew up his car?"

"One of his cars."

"Even so."

"The bomb is one of the reasons why I think he's up to no good."

"What do you mean?"

"Suppose Butterworth is innocent of the crime."

He yawned again. "Seems unlikely."

"Humour me."

"All right. If Butterworth didn't plant the bomb, who did?"

"Think about the timing. Malam was almost blown to kingdom come—but not quite."

"Must be difficult to arrange these things precisely."

"What if the timing was extremely precise?"

"Do you mean that the bomb was exploded simply as a warning?"

"There is another possibility."

He frowned. "Break it to me gently."

"Malam himself."

Jacob stared at her. "You're not serious? I thought he funded Butterworth's legal costs out of a sense of noblesse oblige, because he felt sorry for a fellow Royal Engineer. Why would he plant a bomb, make Butterworth the scapegoat, and then underwrite the man's fees?"

"Crazy, I agree. But leaving aside Butterworth, who else could be responsible?"

"Malam misled plenty of people about investments, you said so yourself."

"How many of his victims were capable of planting a bomb?" Rachel shook her head. "Roddy Malam had the necessary expertise."

"It doesn't make sense. Why go through such an elaborate charade?"

"A very good question." Rachel was pensive. "I wish I knew the answer."

———

"Sleep well?" Rachel asked as Jacob joined her at the breakfast table.

"Like a top."

Jacob helped himself to kedgeree and orange juice. How on earth did Rachel and Martha keep so slim when Hetty was such a wonderful cook? If he lived at Gaunt House, he'd soon become a regular Billy Bunter.

"Coffee?"

This morning Rachel was the perfect hostess. Her robe was made of black hand-embroidered silk and had a floral fringe. She never seemed to wear the same thing twice. Her wardrobe must be the size of an aircraft hangar.

"Wonderful, thanks."

He'd recovered his good humour. His natural optimism never took long to reassert itself, and he felt stirrings of hope that the Yard would tire of hunting the man with the fedora.

"Good. I'd like you to do some digging for me today."

"Your wish is my command."

"Splendid, that's exactly the right attitude. I want you to go to Maida Vale and make enquiries about a missing car."

———

Stilts lived in sin. As Jacob explained to Rachel, in practice this meant a flat in Islington, shared with her lover. He was a Communist poet called Joel Bradbury, who didn't believe in marriage or wage slavery, let alone inherited wealth. His father, an actuary and a robust pillar of the Conservative party, had cut him off without a penny. Joel had been forced to sacrifice his principles and accept a modest legacy from a maiden aunt so as to be able to write his verse without needing to squander his talents languishing in servitude behind a desk in an office.

Rachel was ushered into a poky kitchen. There was a lingering aroma of fried bread and burned toast.

"I don't like to disturb Joel when he's working," Stilts explained as she put the kettle on.

She was a well-built brunette with a welcoming smile. Evidently, she was still very much in love. Bradbury must be utterly different from the pimps, petty criminals, and paying customers around whom she'd lived for most of her life. Through a gap in the door, Rachel could see the great man seated at his desk in the next room. He was skinny with a high forehead and was probably ten years Stilts's junior. His eyes were closed, and Rachel couldn't tell if he was seeking inspiration or simply having a nap.

"Heaven forbid," she said brightly. "It's very good of you to talk to me, Miss Hitchen. I won't take up much of your time."

"I can't believe what has happened," Stilts said in a rush. "Poor Pauline! That's how I always think of her, even though she called herself Adeline. How terrible! It's a miracle that vile beast Ambrose didn't murder Lulu—Mrs. de Villiers, I mean—as well. Thank goodness he was killed himself just afterwards. Makes you believe in divine retribution, don't you think? What does your friend Mr. Flint have to say about it? Reporters always know much more than they print in their papers, don't they?"

Rachel had anticipated that Stilts would be agog for information about the murder in Sepulchre Street and also that she'd assume Ambrose was responsible. She was under the impression that Rachel was Jacob's errand girl, a secretary with dreams of journalistic glory.

"The police have talked to Mrs. de Villiers, and she is safe and well."

"Thank heaven for small mercies. But it's heartbreaking about Pauline. I was very close to her in the days when we were…seeing a lot of each other."

"In Soho?"

"Well, yes. Not that I like to talk about the old days. I've turned over a new leaf since I met Joel. He's a genius, you know, if people did but see it. So very brainy and deep. He'll make his name one day, you mark my words. Though, as he says, first we need to clear out the people holding him back. The whole rotten establishment needs to be brought down."

"That day may come sooner than you think," Rachel said. "Now, tell me about Adeline and Lulu."

Stilts became misty-eyed. "Pauline stuck with Lulu through thick and thin, could never do too much for her. Personally, I thought Lulu took advantage, but I suppose that's only natural. You get what you can in this life, don't you?"

"You stayed in touch after Ambrose was supposed to have died?"

"The two of them disappeared together. Vanished without a

trace. I had no idea what they were up to, but Pauline got in touch with me. She said Ambrose had faked his own death and gone back to France. You know what? They were meant to follow him, but Lulu saw it as the perfect chance for them to escape his clutches."

"Understandable," Rachel murmured.

"Oh, yes, Lulu was always very smart. And tough. A survivor." She paused to pour the tea. "Obviously she still is. Give her a sniff of an opportunity, and she'll grab it before you can say Jack Robinson."

"Did you keep in touch with Lulu?"

"Oh, no. Once Ambrose was out of the way, she was hellbent on making a complete break from the past. She forbade Pauline from speaking to anyone—even me, and I was closer to her than anyone except Lulu herself. Pauline hated to disobey, but she did keep in touch. We spoke quite often, usually when Lulu was off gallivanting."

"So you were aware of Lulu's marriages?"

"And how rich her husbands were. And how many boyfriends she had. Oh, she has an eye for the main chance, but who can blame her? I was glad enough to make a fresh start after I met Joel."

"Pauline didn't have a bad word to say about her?"

"She worshipped the ground that woman walked on. Knowing Lulu, I was sure she'd get sick of being fawned over, but I suppose she felt flattered. She even encouraged her. So Pauline thought she mattered more to Lulu than any man."

"But Lulu cared more for the gentlemen?"

"For herself, more like. As for Pauline, she was obsessed with Lulu. You know what? She even told me in confidence that she wore Lulu's cast-offs and made herself up to look like her." Stilts put a hand to her mouth. "Is that why Ambrose shot her? Did he mistake her for Lulu?"

"More than likely." Rachel drank some tea. "Tell me about Captain Malam. What did your friend make of him?"

"No man was good enough for Lulu as far as Pauline was concerned. Malam was one of Lulu's fancy men, but their fling didn't last long."

"A little bird told me they got back together again recently."

"If they did, it's the first I've heard about it. Lulu dumped Malam when she found someone even richer and more famous."

"Who was that?"

Stilts frowned. "Pauline refused to tell me. She was very coy. I wondered if she was afraid Joel would be angry if he ever got wind of it. Not that I ever discussed Pauline with him. He always hates any reminder of…what I got up to in the old days."

"What else do you know about Lulu's relationship with Captain Malam?"

"Nothing, really. I'd have said he was a real catch, but you know what? That's Lulu for you. The instant a better bet came into view, she dumped him."

Stilts leaned closer and lowered her voice in conspiratorial fashion. "Between you, me, and the gatepost, Pauline gave me the impression that Lulu was counting the days until her old man died. I bet she still is. You know what I think?"

"Do tell."

"The prime minister is a wealthy widower. Just her type! If you ask me, Kiki will become the next Mrs. Ramsay MacDonald!"

———

The telephone in Gaunt House began to ring as Rachel was taking off her hat and coat.

"Rachel?"

"Hello, Jacob, found the man in the fedora yet?"

"Very funny."

"Actually, your timing is excellent. I've just arrived home after an entertaining visit to Stilts's. She's convinced that Mrs. de Villiers's secret lover is the prime minister."

"What?"

"You never know; perhaps she's onto something. Maybe Major Whitlow's fears were entirely unfounded after all. Marriage to a glamorous socialite may be MacDonald's only hope of repairing his reputation. Not that it matters to anyone if the secret services were wrong about the identity of Kiki's lover. Except the poor housemaid they shot by mistake."

"Don't forget the poor devil in the fedora."

She laughed. "He'll soon be forgotten by everyone."

"I pray that you're right. Incidentally, there was no sign of that car you were asking about. Does that help?"

"It doesn't prove anything, but thanks for checking. As for the murder in Sepulchre Street, I'm sure that Mrs. de Villiers was the gunman's intended target."

"She likes dangerous liaisons," Jacob said grimly.

"What makes you say that?"

"I wanted you to be the first to know. I've just been talking to Scotland Yard. Captain Malam's body was discovered this morning, out at Romney Marsh. Someone has battered him to death."

Chapter 31

"Dead in a ditch," Rachel shook her head as she absorbed Jacob's news. "In Dykesbridge."

"Very alliterative. Have you ever considered taking up journalism?" Jacob paused. "Malam must have gone back to Romney Marsh yesterday."

"Who discovered the body?"

"A farm worker, name of Cobtree. He was taking a shortcut across the fields early this morning when he saw a flock of gulls taking a close interest in something by a hedge. They roused his curiosity, so he went over to see for himself. The corpse was lying face down in the ditch. There had been an attempt to cover it with pieces of turf and bracken, but small animals hadn't wasted any time in picking away at the camouflage."

"An unsophisticated method of concealment," Rachel said. "If you wanted to hide a body so that it couldn't be found, why not bury it? Or find a deeper ditch? There's no shortage of them on the Marsh."

"Perhaps Malam was killed on the spur of the moment and everything was done in a rush."

"Perhaps."

"At first Cobtree thought the corpse belonged to a tramp, but the clothes were too smart. He turned the body over—not that he should have touched it, of course—and found himself staring into the face of someone even he recognised. The legendary sportsman and man-about-town Captain Roderick Malam."

"What was the murder weapon?"

"A piece of steel was lying in the ditch, close to the body and smeared with blood."

"A piece of steel? Be more specific."

"Apparently it's known as a fork, and it's a component of a motorbike."

"Suggestive."

"Very."

"I suppose the police are hunting for Butterworth?"

"Makes a change from chasing after innocent fellows in fedoras," he said with feeling. "As it happens, they've already collared him."

"Very quick work," Rachel said thoughtfully.

"It wasn't so difficult. He had an accident on his Flying Squirrel last night."

"Oh, really?"

"He'd drunk several pints and was in a foul temper. Came off the road five miles north of Dykesbridge."

A pause. "Well, well."

"Guess where he'd been drinking?" Jacob couldn't hide his jubilation. It wasn't often that he had Rachel at a loss for words. "The Owlers!"

"Goodness, it's a small world."

"Isn't it just!"

"Was he badly hurt in the crash?"

"Cracked his kneecap and smashed his pelvis. He'll never walk properly again. But they reckon he'll live. So he was lucky."

"Until he hobbles to the gallows."

"There is that," Jacob conceded.

"What took Sapper Butterworth to Romney Marsh?"

Jacob sighed. "He must think the police are stupid. Believe it or not, he's relying on the same story that got him off the hook last time."

"Another tumble down the stairs?"

"Not that story. The phone message from a tailor wanting to place an order for garters and braces. Another urgent request."

"Did the tailor explain what went wrong last time?"

"According to Butterworth, this was someone from the office ringing on the tailor's behalf. He was told he'd be given a full explanation and apology as soon as he showed up. Not to mention a lucrative order to make a long journey on a Sunday worth his while."

"So he agreed?"

"Says he was desperate for a few quid."

"And surprise, surprise, the tailor was nowhere to be found?"

"They were supposed to meet at The Owlers at opening time, but of course the man never showed up. Butterworth spent the next hour drowning his sorrows before setting off back to London, distinctly the worse for wear."

"So this time he has both motive and opportunity. And his enemy is dead."

"Yes, the poor sap. Or poor sapper, if you like. I can't see he has any choice but to plead guilty. He'll need a damn good lawyer to save him from the gallows. The pity of it is, this time there's no fairy godmother to pay a small fortune for the services of Benedict Rhodes-Denton."

————

"Penny for them," Martha said.

Rachel was sitting at the piano, tinkling her way through

Evan Tucker's repertoire. Having played "How Many Days of Sadness" and "Don't Count the Days," she'd embarked on "Forever My Love."

"I'm wondering about Evan Tucker."

"What about him?"

"How will he cope, now that Malam is dead?" Rachel asked.

"I'm not sure what you mean."

"He was in love with the man."

Martha shook her head. "Malam may not have realised. He prided himself on being a man's man, didn't he?"

"Oh, he knew very well what he meant to Tucker. He didn't shun him. On the contrary, he gave him some encouragement."

"You're not implying he was...interested?"

Rachel finished on a discordant note and pulled down the piano lid. "I spent enough time in Roddy Malam's company to be under no illusion about his egotism. He didn't have a faithful bone in his body; he was steadfast only in his selfishness. And his preference was definitely for women. Even so, it's perfectly possible that he exploited Tucker's devotion."

"How?"

Rachel didn't answer directly. "I said before, the captain was up to something. The big trunk in the hall of his flat is significant."

"You don't really believe there were human remains inside?"

Rachel flashed a smile. "No, but it's confirmation that he was planning to be away for some time."

"You already knew he was going to Monte Carlo."

"So he told me. I wonder if he was planning a much longer trip. Perhaps he didn't intend to go to Monte. Or to come back to Britain."

"What makes you think that?"

"He had good reason to get away from it all. His financial

jiggery-pokery was coming unstuck. He was short of money and, amidst the current economic misery, I imagine his creditors were circling like vultures. Butterworth hated him and he certainly wasn't the only one." Rachel looked at Martha. "Does all that remind you of anybody?"

The housemaid considered. "Marcel Ambrose, I suppose. He was in much the same boat when he faked his own death. Desperate to escape England."

"Exactly."

"The resemblance ends there, doesn't it? Unless Jacob has been fed a load of codswallop, the corpse in the ditch wasn't disfigured. Even a farm worker in Kent who has nothing to do with high society was able to recognise Malam. There can't be any doubt about the body's identity in this case."

"You're right," Rachel said slowly.

"But?"

"What if Evan Tucker got wind of Malam's plans?"

Martha considered. "He'd be upset. Emotional."

"To say the very least. Suppose he couldn't bear the prospect of losing the man he worshipped? Suppose they quarrelled?"

There was a short silence.

"Where does Butterworth come into it, then?"

"Good question," Rachel said. "To find out, we'd better go back to Romney Marsh."

———

"Thanks for coming here at short notice," Rachel said as Jacob took a seat in the drawing room.

"Glad to be of service."

Jacob was in chirpy mood. The murder of a national hero was guaranteed to knock all that nonsense about Sepulchre Street off the front pages. Far more newsworthy than the death of an obscure housemaid in Sussex. With any luck, his visit to Rye would soon seem no more dreadful than a bad dream.

"What's the latest?" Rachel asked.

"Oakes gave me a few moments of his time on the phone. The police in Kent wasted no time calling in Scotland Yard. Malam's fame means there will be a lot of scrutiny. The connection between his death and the bomb in the Bentley is just one of the strands of inquiry."

"So the inspector has taken on the case?"

"He's heading for the Marsh this afternoon."

"And what does he make of it all?"

"He thinks Butterworth is as guilty as sin."

"Presumably Rhodes-Denton hasn't come riding to the rescue?"

"Not this time. Chances are, Ned Butterworth will finish up being defended by a dock brief. Ironic, isn't it? If Malam hadn't stumped up for the fellow's legal fees out of a sense of regimental solidarity, he'd still be alive today."

"I agree that Malam paid the lawyer. Through a company. I've always been baffled by what he did. It doesn't chime in with what I know of his character."

"He and Butterworth were comrades in arms."

"The old pals' act, yes, I understand. But Malam was strapped for cash. And he was many things, but hardly selfless. Why make such a grand gesture?"

"A streak of generosity? A pang of conscience after leading Butterworth to the financial abyss?"

"The psychology of it doesn't make sense."

"A lot of things don't." He sighed. "It's a funny old world."

Rachel drummed her fingers on the table. "A simple philosophy, Jacob, but not remotely helpful."

"What do you expect me to say?" he demanded. "You knew

the captain better than I did. I wasn't among his flock of admirers. Not like Kiki de Villiers. Or Evan Tucker, come to that."

Rachel thought for a few moments. "You're right, Jacob. How about a trip to Dykesbridge?"

"Why not?" He gave her a rueful grin. "It can't be as terrifying as Sepulchre Street."

Chapter 32

As the Austin sped towards Romney Marsh, Rachel was lost in thought. Earlier in the journey she'd thumbed through her gazetteer, but now she'd put it aside and her eyes were closed. Jacob had seen her like this before. He knew her imagination was roaming as she tried to make sense of everything that had happened since that terrible night at the Hades Gallery.

Martha was by his side. Her perfume was a subtle blend of peach and bergamot. She was unique, he reflected, the only housemaid in Britain who regularly indulged her taste for Chanel. An enthusiastic traveller, she was gazing out at the countryside, drinking in the sights even on a grey, miserable day. For once she wasn't in a chatty mood, and he resisted the temptation to try to strike up a conversation. He was acutely aware that if he disturbed Rachel's concentration, she was capable of telling Trueman to stop the car and deposit their unruly passenger by the wayside. His knee had almost stopped aching, but he didn't fancy a long walk back to Exmouth Market.

Since their very first encounter, Rachel had fascinated him to the point of obsession. He told himself it was nothing to do with her looks or her money, although on those rare occasions when she flashed a radiant smile, he felt like one of those lovers in an Evan Tucker song. Heart skipping a beat and all that.

Evan Tucker. What part did he play in this rigmarole? The ditch where Malam's body had been found skirted the boundary of The Risings and passed close to Orgarswick. Inspector Oakes hadn't mentioned Tucker. Was it possible that he'd seen Butterworth in the vicinity? Interviewing him was a top priority. So was trying to ascertain whether Kiki de Villiers could cast any light on Malam's final movements. Oakes reckoned that she'd been with Malam the night before last, and Rachel's visit to the flat in Maida Vale seemed to confirm his suspicion.

Whatever the precise truth, this was a hell of a story and he was in on the ground floor. His knowledge of the protagonists gave him a massive advantage over his rivals from the *Witness* and elsewhere. He must make the most of it before Romney Marsh was swamped by reporters scouring every ditch and cranny for a fresh angle.

"Not far to go now," Martha murmured.

Jacob stared out at the Marsh. A vast, lonely landscape beneath sepia clouds. Spring was almost here, but a fierce wind was blowing. It had shaped the trees, bending them to its will. Even the sheep seemed melancholy. His skin prickled. In a place so far off the beaten track, sinister crimes might never come to light.

"I checked the maps," Trueman said. "There's a rutted farm trail leading off the lane on the far side of Tucker's house. We passed it on Sunday afternoon. I bet the police will have set up down there."

They were the first words he'd uttered since they'd left London. He'd kept his eyes on the road, pushing the car as hard as he could. Even as they flew along the country byways, Jacob never felt in danger. Trueman was skilled and confident; fast as he drove, he never took unnecessary risks.

"First stop, The Risings," Rachel said.

A few minutes later, they turned into the short drive of Tucker's home. A bicycle leaned against the front wall and a uniformed police constable was talking to an elderly woman in a hat and coat that had seen better days.

Trueman pulled up and Rachel sprang out of the car, with Jacob on her heels.

"Good afternoon," she said. "We're looking for Mr. Evan Tucker."

"He's not here!" the woman said.

"Friend of Mr. Tucker, are you?" the policeman said. "Can I have your name, ma'am?"

"I'm Rachel Savernake. Has Inspector Oakes arrived from Scotland Yard?"

"Another pal of yours, is he?" His tone was jocular and disbelieving.

"As it happens, Philip Oakes and I dined together yesterday evening," she said coolly. "After church."

The policeman looked as if he'd swallowed something that didn't agree with him. As he struggled to digest her reply, Rachel addressed the woman.

"You're Mrs. Collyer, aren't you?"

The woman gaped as if being addressed by a magician or mind reader. An impressive trick, Jacob thought. Trueman had picked up the cleaning lady's name at The Owlers, and Rachel had filed it away in her memory. One of her gifts was that she understood the value of teamwork.

"Why, yes, ma'am. However did you know...?"

"Any idea where Mr. Tucker might be?"

"There's not a trace of him anywhere."

"He didn't leave a note for you?"

"No, it's awfully peculiar."

"Why?"

"Usually I see him here on a Monday morning, before he sets off for London. If he's not at home, he'll leave an envelope with my money in and any instructions about what he wants doing."

"But not today?"

"No, not a penny piece for my trouble!"

"And he's not laid up in bed or lying at the bottom of the steps to the cellar?"

"Goodness me, no! I've given the whole place a quick once-over. I'm very thorough, you know."

"I'm sure. Has he disappeared like this before?"

"Never! I come in one day a week, to do the rough. I'm the last one left after the other servants packed their bags. Not that I get much thanks…"

"Has his bed been slept in?"

"Actually, no, it hasn't. Why do you ask?"

"Is it common for him not to sleep here on a Sunday evening?"

"Not at all. I can't remember the last time it happened."

As he listened to these exchanges, Jacob was conscious of excitement rising within him, bubbling up to the surface. He simply couldn't contain himself any longer.

"So Tucker has done a bunk. Maybe Butterworth isn't the only suspect!"

Ignoring him, Rachel strolled over to the garage. She took a quick look through a small side window before re-joining the little group at the front of the house. The policeman couldn't take his eyes off her. It was as if she'd mesmerized him. Jacob felt a spurt of sympathy. Rachel did have that effect on people.

"Tell me, PC…"

"Leather, ma'am."

"Well, then, PC Leather. Two vehicles are in the garage. I recognise the Aston Martin. Captain Malam owned several cars and that was one of them. He must have driven here in it after his Bentley was bombed the other day. Did you find his trunk inside?"

"Yes, ma'am."

"Packed and ready for a journey he never made." She shook her head. "Then do I presume that the Crossley standing next to it belongs to Mr. Tucker?"

Mrs. Collyer piped up. "You're right, miss. His pride and joy, that car is."

"Wherever he's gone, then, he hasn't driven there."

"That's true, ma'am," PC Leather said. "Mind you, there's a very good train service in these parts. The stations at Appledore and Hamstreet aren't that far away."

"A very stiff walk from here."

"Yes, ma'am, but once you're there you can get to pretty much anywhere you want." He spoke with a touch of parochial pride.

"How convenient."

Mrs. Collyer sniffed. "And some folk say this is the back of beyond!"

A car engine roared and they all turned their heads. Philip Oakes's status as the coming man at Scotland Yard was reflected in the fact that he was being driven towards the house in a smart new Daimler. He jumped out and exchanged salutes with PC Leather.

"Afternoon, Miss Savernake. What brings you here?"

Chronic nosiness, Jacob was tempted to say, but he kept his lip buttoned.

"I hope it's not too much of an imposition when you're so busy, Inspector." Her manner was demure, which Jacob always found worrying. "Dare I ask a favour? Would you accompany me to the scene of the crime?"

Oakes shook his head. "The chief constable is due here in half an hour. I'm afraid he'll expect me to..."

"Please, Inspector, I know you're a busy man. This isn't a frivolous request. We may find something new, something important."

He cast a glance over his shoulder at the police constable, who was now exchanging a word with Oakes's sergeant. "The local men have examined the spot where the body was found."

"Twenty minutes of your time is all I ask."

"I don't..."

"Have I ever let you down?"

He groaned. "Very well. Against my better judgement, I'll say yes. Twenty minutes, mind. Not a second more."

"Thank you, Inspector. You're right, there's no time to waste."

Chapter 33

Oakes led Rachel and Jacob through the grounds of The Risings until they squeezed through the insubstantial fence marking the boundary of Tucker's property. A strip of land separated the fence from a narrow channel of mud-brown water that formed a natural division between the fields. Barely two feet deep, the ditch was clogged with reeds.

"You've interviewed Nurse Wardle?" Rachel asked.

"I sent a message ahead, asking the men on the spot to make sure that neither she nor Tucker left the area before I spoke to them. Unfortunately, Tucker had already made himself scarce. Whether there's a criminal reason for his departure, it's too early to say. By the look of things, he may have left his home yesterday."

"And Nurse Wardle?"

"I saw her at Orgarswick. She was co-operative, but I didn't get much out of her. She maintains she was desperate to get away from the Marsh even before she heard of her brother-in-law's violent death. From what you've told me about her...activities, I presume she was telling the truth."

"You didn't question her about what has been going on at the clinic?"

He looked Rachel in the eye. "No, I didn't. There are more urgent priorities. A man has been murdered."

"Can she cast any light on what happened to Captain Malam?"

He shook his head. "She claimed she was astonished to hear he'd turned up in the neighbourhood. He'd not been in contact with her, so she could only presume that he'd come to visit Tucker. Logical enough, I suppose."

"Where is she now?"

"While I was speaking to her, a taxi was waiting to take her to the station. She told me she's been planning to leave the country."

"Did you ask her to stay in England?"

"No need. She told me candidly that she didn't care much for Malam, but even though they were never close, his death has come as a great shock. So she has booked into a small hotel in London for the next few nights and expects to stay there until after the funeral."

In the stiff wind, Jacob felt cold and impatient. "You don't think she's hoping to inherit? With his brother dead, Malam didn't have any close family."

"Inherit what, exactly?" Rachel sounded dismissive.

"Just a thought," he said moodily. "Was the body found here?"

"No," Oakes said. "A few hundred yards away. Halfway between The Risings and Nurse Wardle's clinic. There's a rough track that leads from the lane. They used it to shift Malam's remains into the ambulance. This way."

They tramped along beside the watercourse. Finally they reached the farm track. A ruined brick building stood nearby. Small and square, it had windows open to the elements.

"What's this?" Jacob asked.

"They call them lookers' huts," Rachel replied. "Ever since the Black Death laid waste to the Marsh, absentee landowners have paid lookers to keep an eye on their flocks. Sheep are docile; they don't jump ditches, and the lookers used to work for more than one master, covering a huge amount of ground. These old huts were built for them to use, especially when the time came for lambing and shearing."

"You're a mine of information, Miss Savernake."

Oakes's admiring tone grated with Jacob, who said grumpily, "She reads a lot of books."

"I assume the hut has been examined, Inspector?" Rachel said.

"Of course. No obvious clues there."

The hut had an ancient wooden door, almost off its hinges. She went inside and looked around before emerging with a shake of the head.

"As you say, there's nothing. So Captain Malam's body was found in the ditch at this point?"

"That's right. The farm worker came up the track from the lane. When the local constable got here, he soon discovered what seems to be the murder weapon."

"Strange, don't you think?" She pointed across the field towards a larger drainage ditch, running in a straight line as far as the eye could see. "Why dump Malam's body here, in such a shallow grave, with very little attempt at concealment? The sewer over there appears to be wider and deeper. More suitable as a last resting place for a body you don't want to be discovered in a hurry."

"If the murderer was in a hurry..." Oakes began.

"If someone had the time to bring Malam's body here, why not take it a little farther?"

"Spoiling the ship for a ha'porth of tar," Jacob said sagely.

Rachel winced. "Please spare us your homespun wisdom, Jacob. You're not writing for the *Clarion* now."

"All right, how about this idea? Suppose the murder was committed right here. Butterworth might have agreed to meet Malam at the hut and bludgeoned him to death when he turned up? After that, perhaps he panicked and ran for it."

"Not a bad theory," Rachel said. "However, it begs a number of questions. For instance, why would Malam venture out to such a lonely place to meet a sworn enemy?"

"Especially if darkness was falling," Oakes said.

"Don't dismiss an idea simply because it seems unlikely," Jacob retorted. "We all know that it's often difficult to account for a murderer's actions."

"You have a point," the detective said. "Especially in the case of a man like Butterworth. He's suffered from shell shock for years. His memory's faulty and his behaviour is scarcely rational."

Rachel shook her head. "Shell shock and amnesia are misunderstood. Usually by people who have never experienced them. It's easy for them to become simple explanations for things we don't understand."

Jacob turned to her. "Do you think Tucker is involved in Malam's death?"

"We know there's a connection between them. And Malam parked his car at The Risings. The obvious assumption is that he came straight from his London flat to meet Tucker."

"Why?" Oakes asked. "And anyway, does it matter?"

"The answer to your second question, Inspector, is yes. And the reason is that finding the right answer to your first question will unlock the whole mystery."

"Too deep for me," Jacob grumbled.

"There's something else. It won't have escaped your notice

as we were walking here that there are curious impressions on the ground."

She bent down and indicated marks where the grass had been flattened. The indentations could barely be seen by the naked eye. Jacob hadn't actually spotted them until now.

Oakes nodded. "I saw that scuffing. You can make out some of the marks, even though someone seems to have tried to trample the ground to hide them. What's more, it rained heavily during the night. But they are still just about visible. Looks to me as though something has been dragged along by someone wearing gumboots."

"That something being the body?" Jacob said.

"First-rate deduction," Rachel said. "However, two types of marks are just about visible, aren't they? Those made by boots and some others. Looks like something has been used to transport the body."

"Whatever it is," Oakes said, "we haven't found any other evidence of it."

Jacob shrugged. "Obviously the murderer took it away with him."

"Where was it taken?" Rachel demanded. "And why?"

"Very good questions," he admitted.

"That's what people say when they can't be bothered to work out the answers. Think, Jacob!"

Oakes cleared his throat. "Fairly straightforward, isn't it? Butterworth wouldn't want to be lumbered with anything as he made good his escape. Maybe he dropped it in one of these drainage ditches. I'll order a search to be carried out. Pity we don't know what exactly we're looking for, but..."

"We are looking for a sled," Rachel said.

"A sled?" he echoed. "Sorry to be dense, Miss Savernake, but you'll have to explain."

"Are you familiar with the skeleton, Inspector?"

He stared at her.

"It's a winter sport, very fashionable these days. Captain Malam was good at it. In the days when he was trying to impress me with his feats of derring-do, he let slip that he'd won medals for it."

"And the sled is called a skeleton?"

"Yes, you lie on it and ride down a frozen track." She indicated the impressions on the ground. "Runners, you see?"

Oakes nodded.

"I couldn't help thinking that if one made a few adjustments to a sled—adding a rope and so on—it would be a splendid means of transporting a corpse."

"Good grief," Jacob said.

Rachel wasn't wearing a hat and the wind was whipping up her hair. She pushed a few strands out of her eyes as she contemplated the ditch which had become a makeshift grave.

"Ironic, don't you think, if the captain's own skeleton was used to dispose of his remains?"

———

For a few moments they stood in silence. The wind had gathered strength and rain was in the air. The only living creatures in sight were the sheep, and they'd been roused from their torpor to go in search of shelter. Jacob leaned against the wall of the lookers' hut.

"I don't suppose we could reconstruct the crime?" he said hopefully.

"Would you really like me to hit you over the head and shove you into a ditch?" Rachel asked. "No, you suppose correctly."

"What next, then?"

"Orgarswick is close by."

She pointed. They could see the roof of the clinic, even

though the bulk of the building was obscured by thickets of hawthorn.

"I really ought to be getting back." Oakes took a step towards the rutted farm track. "There's a lot to do, and your twenty minutes is up. The chief constable will be expecting me to pull rabbits out of my hat."

"Please indulge me just a little longer, Inspector. I've come up with an idea which I'd like to test. You won't find it a waste of time." She smiled. "I may even find you a rabbit."

He heaved a sigh. "You're dangerously persuasive, Miss Savernake. All right."

As they headed towards Orgarswick, Jacob said, "You believe Tucker is up to his neck in all this, don't you?"

"Yes," Rachel said.

"You think he's hiding behind Butterworth?" Oakes demanded. "Using him as a blind for purposes of his own?"

"What if it was Tucker who paid Butterworth's legal fees, not Malam?" Jacob said.

"Why would he do that?" Rachel asked.

"Why would Malam blow up his own car?" Jacob said. "None of it makes sense."

"I disagree. There's a pattern here. Look carefully enough, and we'll find it."

"You're not hoping to take advantage of Nurse Wardle's absence to search her house?" Jacob said.

"What would I hope to find? She is an intelligent woman and she'll have removed any evidence of criminal behaviour. Besides, if I was contemplating an illegal trespass, would I have invited Inspector Oakes along as a witness?"

"What, then?"

"Martha came here on Saturday. She gave me a good description of everything she did."

"And?"

"One little thing she mentioned made me sit up and take note." Rachel gave a thin smile. "Patience, Jacob. I promise, you won't have much longer to wait."

They'd reached the edge of the grounds of Orgarswick. Inspector Oakes stopped by the fence.

"You're enjoying this, aren't you?"

Rachel smiled. "It's the thrill of the chase. I yearn for it like an addict craves the needle."

"What exactly are we chasing?" Jacob asked.

"If you kept your eyes on the path as I've been doing, you'd have an idea," Oakes said. "Someone has tried to scuff up the earth and conceal them, but you can still pick out some of the marks made by the sled. Or whatever it is."

Jacob looked down and peered at the ground beneath his feet. "Oh, I see what you mean."

Oakes said to Rachel, "You expected to find this, didn't you?"

"I thought the murderer was likely to have brought the sled here, yes."

The fence was no deterrent. She eased through it and beckoned the two men to follow.

"We're very close now."

She led them a short distance along a grassy path before coming to a halt.

"Here."

Her slim forefinger pointed to the ground. Barely visible beneath the bracken was a thin slab of concrete.

"What is it?" Jacob asked.

"A cesspit," Rachel said. "Martha stumbled over it. The thought occurred to me that an underground tank on private property would make a wonderful place to conceal a body. Far superior to a shallow ditch. The lid can't be heavy, Inspector. Perhaps you'd be kind enough to lift it up."

Oakes looked at her, searching her expression for a clue to what was in her mind. He soon gave up.

"All right."

He bent down and grasped the edge of the concrete lid with both hands. It was easy to prise up, but he wasn't prepared for the stench that wafted out from below ground. He swore vividly.

"Can you see anything?" Rachel asked.

Oakes took a breath before bending down again. There was a long pause. When he spoke, his voice was hoarse.

"There is something. Looks like it might be a sled."

"Good. Anything else of interest?"

The inspector craned his neck. "My God, yes."

They waited. Jacob held his breath.

"It's the body of a man."

Rachel looked over his shoulder. "As I thought. Severely disfigured, but…"

"Who is he?" Oakes interrupted.

Rachel hummed a snatch of a tune.

Oakes stared. *"Don't say I didn't tell you so?"*

"Well recognised. Yes, this is the songsmith who fell on hard times. Evan Tucker."

Chapter 34

Dusk was gathering as they watched an elderly Alvis with a choleric engine jolting up the drive of Orgarswick.

"Here comes the chief constable," Oakes muttered.

"You sound like an errant schoolboy," Rachel said. "Awaiting a headmaster who is about to administer six of the best."

"I hear the major splutters even more than his car," Oakes said. "One murder in his bailiwick is bad enough. Two may give the old boy apoplexy."

In the short time since the discovery of Tucker's corpse, the lost hamlet of Dykesbridge had become a hive swarming with activity. Oakes had summoned all available police resources; meanwhile a doctor and ambulance had arrived. So had the Austin; anyone would think Trueman and Martha had turned up by prior appointment.

Perhaps they had, Jacob reflected. Had Rachel foreseen the grisly discovery in the cesspit? He wouldn't put it past her.

"We need to get on," she said as the Alvis juddered to a halt. "I don't suppose I dare distract you any longer?"

The inspector shook his head. "There is urgent work for me here, Miss Savernake. Believe me, I'm grateful for your help."

The chief constable lumbered towards them. Familiar with the local climate, he was so well wrapped up in his coat, muffler, and trilby that it was hard to discern anything but an enormous handlebar moustache and bushy eyebrows.

"Oakes, is it?"

Rachel, evidently invisible as far as the chief constable was concerned, strolled towards her car as the men shook hands. After deliberating whether he might eavesdrop on the official conversation, Jacob caught her up.

"Going back to London?" he asked.

"Not yet. First I want to satisfy myself that my ideas about this case are correct. We can give you a lift to the nearest station if you need to get back to Fleet Street."

"Plenty of time for tomorrow's edition. Can I tag along with you instead?"

Negligently, she said, "If you really want to."

"Where are you heading?"

"If I tell you, do you promise not to ask any more questions?"

"I'll be a regular Trappist. Word of honour. Cross my heart and hope to die!"

Trueman raised his eyes to the heavens.

Rachel said pleasantly, "Be careful what you wish for, Jacob."

"Honestly, you can trust me. After these last few days, I reckon I'm ready for anything."

"Excellent attitude. It will stand you in good stead."

"Thanks very much. So what's the destination?"

"Rye," she said.

His jaw dropped. "You're not going to...?"

"Yes," she said. "Sepulchre Street."

Jacob felt a clammy sense of apprehension as they reached the rugged stone gateway to Rye. Memories of Saturday night came flooding back. The dark streets, the mysterious stranger who turned the tables on him by framing him for the murder of a defenceless woman. An image rose in his mind of her blood-soaked corpse. He fought to banish it. That way madness lies, he told himself.

Trueman drove smoothly. No hesitations, no second thoughts. Had Rachel planned this trip even before they left Gaunt House? What was in her mind? He was almost sick with curiosity, but he dared not risk her wrath by quizzing her. It would be pointless, anyway. She'd never tell him more than she wanted him to know.

Another corner turned. Suddenly he knew precisely where he was. A cul-de-sac he'd never forget.

"Journey's end," Rachel said. "Didn't you say that the locals call this street Graveyard Lane? Many a true word, don't you think?"

The Austin slowed to a crawl along Sepulchre Street. Jacob couldn't suppress a low groan.

Trueman glanced over his shoulder. "I'll park in front of the garage."

"You read my mind." Rachel turned to Jacob. "Revisiting the scene of the crime, eh? Don't worry, nobody will recognise you. Not without the smart suit and fedora."

He mustered a weak smile. "To think that at the Hades Gallery, I was desperate to question Mrs. de Villiers. Tonight I'll be happy to leave you to ask whatever you want."

"It's very simple," Rachel said. "She can confirm the truth about the murders of Roderick Malam and Evan Tucker."

Trueman got out and opened the door for her. They exchanged a few words in a whisper, but Jacob didn't risk trying to eavesdrop.

"You're staying in the car?" he asked Martha.

"I'll wait for you and Rachel."

Rachel beckoned, and he followed her to the front door. The damask curtains were drawn at every window, but through the chinks light shone from several rooms. Typical of Kiki de Villiers, he supposed. Sharing a bank account with a millionaire husband obviously encouraged profligacy.

Rachel rang the doorbell. They waited, but nothing happened.

"What next?" Jacob asked.

For answer, Rachel pressed her thumb on the bell and kept it there.

On the first floor, a curtain twitched.

Jacob made a disgusted noise. "Ridiculously early to have gone to bed."

"She was downstairs when I rang and hurried upstairs to take a surreptitious peek at her unexpected visitor."

"You think? I suppose she's afraid. Ambrose's acolytes may still be hunting her."

"She's afraid, all right."

Rachel rang the bell again. Within seconds, the door opened.

Kiki de Villiers stood just inside the hall. Tonight she seemed to Jacob more glamorous than ever. The clinging gown, geranium-rouged cheeks, flowing red locks, and seductive scent of Narcisse Noir, all of them left him feeling weak at the knees. The legendary sapphire eyes—coloboma and all—considered Rachel. Whatever was going through the woman's head as a result of this sudden intrusion into her evening, she gave no sign of being concerned.

Her nonchalance must be an illusion, Jacob thought, yet he was almost convinced. But then, she'd spent years playing a part. For the customers Ambrose sent her way. For the rich old men she'd charmed into marriage. For the gossip columnists who dogged her footsteps. She was a finer actress than most who trod the boards.

"Yes?"

"My name is Rachel Savernake. We haven't met…"

"I know who you are," she said disdainfully. "Roddy Malam spoke of you."

"He wasn't too unkind, I hope?"

"He told me you're a meddler. That's why he grew wary of you. You poke your nose into other people's business."

Rachel put her hands up. "Guilty as charged."

"There's nothing here for you." Kiki glanced at Jacob. "Or your pet newshound."

"I disagree. May we come in?"

"Certainly not."

Kiki tried to shut the door, but Rachel had put her foot in the way.

"I need to talk to you. Perhaps Captain Malam didn't mention all my peccadilloes. One is that I don't take no for an answer."

"This is outrageous! I must ask you to go."

Rachel shook her head.

"Leave at once or I'll call the police!"

"Be my guest, Mrs. de Villiers. We can have a cosy chat with them. Discussing, among other things, the identity of the woman who spent Saturday night with Captain Malam."

A defiant stare. "So you know I was with him?"

"I didn't accuse you of anything."

She put her hands on her hips. "If you think the police are interested in what happens between consenting adults, you're as deluded as your lackey from Grub Street."

"You misunderstand me. Deliberately, I'm sure. You don't seem heartbroken by Malam's death. Entirely reasonable—neither am I. What interests me is the reason why he was murdered. As well as his part in the killing of Evan Tucker."

Kiki de Villiers's face went blank. "Tucker is dead?"

"You didn't know?"

"What…happened?"

"His body was found in the cesspit at Orgarswick. Together with Malam's skeleton sled."

There was a long pause.

"I don't know what you expect to gain by coming here," Kiki de Villiers said.

"Let us in, and I shall explain."

"Don't be absurd. You can't hope to worm your way into a private home like this."

"We can talk about Roddy Malam's plot to fake his own death."

Jacob scratched his head. What was Rachel talking about? The strange thing was that Kiki de Villiers seemed to understand. Her lovely features betrayed no sign of confusion. It was as if they were talking in code.

Rachel leaned forward, poking her nose over the threshold. In this mood, she was inexorable. "Or if you prefer, I am happy to call the police myself. And you can explain yourself to them at the station."

"What do you want?"

"The truth."

There was another silence.

"Very well. Come in."

———

Experiencing a surreal sense of déjà vu, Jacob followed Rachel into the hall. Two huge suitcases stood in an alcove. On the left, the door to the room where he'd found the body was shut. He dug his nails into his palm, urging himself not to relive those terrible moments.

"The scene of my poor Adeline's murder," Kiki said,

noticing his expression. "The door is locked; we will not go in. Of course there has been no opportunity to finish...cleaning up."

She ushered them into a large room at the back of the house. Two walls were lined with books from floor to ceiling. A single window looked out onto the garden. An exotic Persian rug made a striking contrast with dark parquet tiles. A small grandmother clock ticked noisily and there was a desk with a chair as well as an opulent leather sofa. Kiki indicated that they should take a seat.

Jacob found himself next to Rachel, trying to make himself seem as inconspicuous as possible. He hadn't a clue what she would say or do. The only thing he was certain of was that he daren't disrupt her plans.

"The library," Kiki said. "Not that I've read any of the books. They came with the house."

She spoke in crisp, clipped tones. Tonight she seemed less exotic than on their first encounter at the Hades. Not so much a bird of paradise as a watchful raptor. She even sounded different. Less theatrical, more sophisticated. More English.

Jacob recalled that her father was a fisherman from Great Yarmouth. Did it amuse her, pretending to be a rich and empty-headed French socialite? Was her public manner a form of play-acting, of pandering to prejudice and preconceived ideas? Or was she just amusing herself with a little mimicry?

Sitting down on the chair by the desk, she said, "Forgive me for not offering the two of you a drink. I'm not much of a hostess and, after what you've said already, you'd probably be scared to touch anything I gave you."

Rachel laughed. "Yes, let's dispense with formalities and get down to business."

Kiki peered at her, like a scholar trying to decipher a message in hieroglyphs. "Roddy told me you're a strange one. His sixth sense told him you were keeping secrets of your own, but he never got close to finding out what they were. Meanwhile you roam through the dark recesses of other people's lives."

"Self-indulgent of me."

"My guess is, you're not really a hypocrite. Solving puzzles that come your way is a pleasing way of escaping from the mysteries of your own past."

"You're quite a psychologist."

"Oh, it's simply a fellow feeling. Given my own past, I can make a stab at understanding what goes through your head."

Rachel nodded. This was, Jacob thought, like watching a contest between two gladiators who entertained a degree of respect for each other. He fervently hoped they didn't intend to fight to the death.

"When I first met Captain Malam," Rachel said, "I was intrigued. He enjoyed the trappings of wealth, but was obviously strapped for cash. He hadn't inherited a fortune and his expenditure far exceeded his apparent sources of income. Soon it became clear that he supplemented his finances by using his reputation to leech off naïve investors. He introduced them to a variety of get-rich-quick schemes and took a hefty commission. It was rather like buying a ticket in a sweepstake. Occasionally, these ventures paid off. More often they failed miserably. Those who were naïve enough to put all their eggs in one of his baskets suffered the most."

Kiki shrugged. "This is the nature of business. The capitalist system. Don't tell me you're a devotee of Stalin?"

"No, he reminds me of Malam."

"Really?"

"Both men seduce those who are easily impressed and use them for their own ends. I discovered that the captain was a common or garden confidence trickster. When he found I wasn't as gullible as he hoped, he went in search of easier prey."

"Sure you didn't have a lovers' tiff?"

Rachel took no notice. "When we met again, it was obvious that he was still up to his old tricks, but I sensed a new agenda. The bomb that blew up his car puzzled me. Such a drastic step for anyone to take."

"I hear it was a miracle that nobody was killed."

"It didn't seem quite so miraculous once it occurred to me that the bomb was a stunt."

Kiki screwed up her face in incredulity. "Are you trying to suggest that Butterworth didn't want to kill Roddy Malam?"

"If he did, why would Malam fund his legal fees?"

"An act of generosity for a fellow soldier who had fallen on hard times." Kiki gave her a sly glance. "You wouldn't understand."

"On the contrary, I had a good idea of Malam's personality. He was looking for a convenient scapegoat, someone he could manipulate."

"Into blowing up his car?" Kiki scoffed.

"Butterworth was a cat's paw. He had a violent temper and a grudge against Malam. Shell shock affected his memory and he was desperate for cash. How easy for Malam to trick him into an appointment with a prospective customer who didn't exist."

"Far-fetched."

"Not at all. Malam's scheme was a variation on a theme you're familiar with. The supposed death of Marcel Ambrose, which actually involved the sacrifice of an unwitting victim."

"You're talking nonsense."

"There was only one psychologically credible reason why Malam would pay a lawyer to get Butterworth—a man who supposedly wanted him dead—off the hook with the police.

Because he saw the cost as an investment. The aim was to establish an apparent pattern of behaviour on Butterworth's part. If another attempt was made on Malam's life—successful on this occasion—and Butterworth was on the spot for a second time, the case for the prosecution would be overwhelming. Especially if no sharp-witted lawyer rushed to the rescue this time."

"What you are saying is childish. Roderick Malam wasn't stupid. He wouldn't try to arrange his own death."

"Please don't embarrass yourself," Rachel said brusquely. "There's no point in pretending you don't understand."

Jacob cleared his throat. Surely it was about time he said something?

"Are you suggesting that Captain Malam planned to fake his own death?"

"Bravo!" Rachel mimed applause. "Exactly that."

"When Ambrose did that, he killed someone else to supply charred remains to be found after the fire."

"Yes, and Malam's plot involved finding a victim of his own."

Jacob stared at her.

"Evan Tucker?"

"Yes." Rachel's tone was icy. "Malam set out to kill two birds with one stone."

————

There was a pause while Jacob digested this. The ticking of the clock seemed louder, the aroma of Narcisse Noir more suffocating than before. Kiki de Villiers leaned back in her chair and expelled a long sigh.

"Fanciful in the extreme."

"Roderick Malam was worried about Butterworth," Rachel said. "The man had already assaulted him. A bruised face didn't matter, but what was he capable of? And then there was Evan Tucker."

"They were friends."

"Tucker hero-worshipped Malam, but his affection wasn't returned. He was becoming a serious nuisance. The two of them had collaborated for some time, introducing rich young women in need of abortions to Malam's brother and his wife. A lucrative business. But tensions were rising. Tucker's parties no longer attracted London's bright young things. There were fewer bright young things around anyway. And almost certainly, fewer paying patients."

Kiki de Villiers's face was stripped of expression. Jacob held his breath as Rachel continued to talk.

"Tucker's run of success as a composer was over. He'd lost his touch. Such as it was. Like Malam, he was short of money. Given that he was a nasty piece of work, I suspect he also dabbled in blackmail. He may even have tried to prise some money out of Damaris Gethin, although he'd have had no joy with her. Others were probably easier targets. So it wouldn't have been a huge leap for him to put pressure on Malam."

"Blackmail him, you mean?" Jacob stared. "But they were friends."

"Not in a conventional way. When Malam ceased to find Tucker useful, he became a bore and a burden. I imagine that for his part, Tucker dreamed of sharing his life with Malam. Taking him away from all the shallow women he dabbled with."

Kiki de Villiers said coldly, "Like me?"

"And me."

"Whatever else you are, Miss Savernake, I wouldn't accuse you of shallowness."

"May I return the compliment? Damaris Gethin was another complex and formidable woman. It was just unfortunate that she made the mistake of getting pregnant and then sinking into a pit of depression after having an abortion. In Tucker's eyes, though, in our different ways we were all distractions. My impression is that he was becoming increasingly difficult and demanding. He was worried that Nurse Wardle was losing interest in the clinic, and he was afraid that Malam would move out of his orbit. Probably he tried to force Malam to show him more affection. After all, he knew enough about the captain to destroy his reputation. If he blew the gaff on what was happening at Orgarswick, they'd both end up behind bars."

Jacob said, "You think Malam decided to kill Tucker and disfigure the body so it would somehow be mistaken for his own? And people would suppose Tucker had done a bunk?"

Kiki snorted. "Fantasy."

"Not at all," Rachel said. "Although the two men didn't resemble each other in obvious ways, they were of much the same height and build. Their hair and eyes were also rather similar."

"Evan Tucker had a beard and glasses."

"A beard could be shaved off post-mortem. Tucker's spectacles could be destroyed. Nobody tests the eyesight of a dead man."

"Roddy was fitter and stronger than Tucker."

"Corpses don't do physical jerks."

Jacob resisted the urge to mention cadaveric spasm. He still couldn't quite see where all this was leading.

"If you maintain Butterworth was innocent," Kiki said, "who can possibly have killed Roddy Malam?"

"Isn't it obvious?"

"Are you accusing me of battering Roddy Malam to death?"

Rachel shook her head. "Not you."

"Then who?"

"Phoebe Wardle."

Chapter 35

Disgust was written all over Kiki de Villiers's lovely face. "You surely can't expect me to believe such a bizarre accusation."

"This is the truth and you know it." Jacob had seldom seen Rachel speak with such intensity. She was utterly relentless. "Phoebe Wardle conspired with Malam to kill Tucker, only to betray him."

Kiki shook her head. "She and Roddy were chalk and cheese. They didn't even care for each other. The idea they planned a murder together is fantastical."

"They'd known each other a long time, ever since she married his brother. Captain Malam was a womaniser, and Phoebe Wardle's good looks must have been a temptation. However, her personality is cold."

"Reserved," Kiki said.

Rachel shrugged. "Malam mentioned to me that Giles used to complain about her frigidity. The captain is the kind of man who relishes such a challenge, but she kept him at arm's length. Besides, she was his sister-in-law. So he kept his distance while his brother was alive. Widowhood made her fair game."

"Tasteless supposition."

"Detectives purr over physical evidence. The significant

bloodstain, the suggestive footprint. I find psychological clues more illuminating. Each individual behaves in a distinctive way. Even when someone goes against type, perhaps to put others off the scent, they often give themselves away."

"How eloquent, Miss Savernake. In the cause of justifying wild guesswork."

"Phoebe Wardle's lack of interest fuelled Malam's desire. He was like a big game hunter, chasing another trophy. In the end she pretended to give in."

"What do you mean?"

"She fooled him into believing that his feelings were reciprocated."

"Now you really are indulging in make-believe."

Jacob was bewildered. Unable to restrain himself, he said, "On Saturday night, at Captain Malam's flat…"

"A woman was present when I visited," Rachel interrupted. "That's right, Mrs. de Villiers. Inspector Oakes of the Yard suspects you were in his bedroom."

Kiki smirked. "A lady never tells."

"That's the impression you hoped to create, isn't it? When in fact, Malam spent the night with Phoebe Wardle. She was the one I heard giggling. Of course, she was trying to create the illusion that you were there."

"Ridiculous. And why would I care about Malam's lovers anyway?"

"Because," Rachel said, "you are infatuated with Phoebe Wardle."

———

For a long time, no one spoke. The only sound was the ticking of the clock. Jacob realised he was holding his breath. He itched to ask a dozen questions, but he dared not open his mouth.

Kiki de Villiers's face gave away nothing. Jacob was sure she was making calculations, although he couldn't guess how they added up. Her features hardened into an ugly glare. Even her perfume seemed to have turned sour.

"That is a vile slander. If you repeat it outside this room, I shall sue."

"Feel free to summon your lawyers," Rachel said lazily. "Let me give them something else to fume about."

The women eyed each other. Kiki blinked first.

Rachel allowed herself a bleak smile. "You and Phoebe Wardle conspired together. Roddy Malam's plot to kill Evan Tucker and leave the wretched Butterworth to take the blame was turned inside out. The reality was that you took advantage of his scheming. He became your puppet. Your aim was to rid yourselves of him, along with the dismal baggage of your past lives."

The other woman took a breath. The famous sapphire eyes glinted with anger.

"Malam told me that your father went mad. Insanity must run in the family."

"Don't mistake me for Judge Savernake."

Kiki gave a little clap. "Ah, so I've touched a nerve."

"The three of you had something in common," Rachel said. "You were all desperate to escape. Malam was fleeing his creditors, as well as a disturbed man who wished him harm, and a homosexual who posed a serious threat to his reputation. Phoebe Wardle had tired of her sickening trade at the clinic. And you wanted to be free of Marcel Ambrose forever. Not to mention ridding yourself of Adeline."

A noise of derision. "Adeline? Truly, you are deranged. She adored me."

"And you found that flattering. But as Malam discovered

with Tucker, dog-like devotion can become a bore. And what if the devotee wants to keep the beloved all to herself?"

Kiki shook her head.

"You lent Adeline clothes and encouraged her to masquerade as you. I expect the wig was a gift from you. Whether you always intended to use her fondness for taking your place as a means to destroy her, who knows? When Ambrose came back to Britain and set about tracking you down, you saw a chance to dispose of her and at the same time cheat Ambrose of his prize."

"Ludicrous."

"On the contrary. As soon as you discovered that Ambrose had returned, you made yourself scarce. The story that you wanted to look at the clinic with a view to moving your invalid husband there was a transparent invention. Knowing Ambrose as you did, you realised he'd move fast. Dashing off to Romney Marsh kept you out of harm's way. What you didn't realise was that Ambrose wasn't alone in wanting you dead."

Kiki gritted her teeth. "I read in the newspaper about this man in the fedora. I've no idea who he is."

Rachel patted Jacob on the shoulder. "Permit me to introduce the elusive Pimpernel. Not looking quite as natty as when he last came to this house."

"What?" Kiki stared at Jacob. "I don't understand."

"You're stealing Jacob's favourite refrain," Rachel said. "In a nutshell, your affair with a Very Important Person ruffled feathers in Whitehall. He didn't realise that you didn't seriously contemplate a long-term relationship with him. Neither did the authorities. They decided you posed a threat to the nation. So they decided to remove you."

Kiki clutched at her throat. "You're telling me that Adeline wasn't shot by one of Ambrose's minions?"

"No. Ambrose intended to do the deed himself, but he made the mistake of engaging a chauffeur who hated him."

"I heard about the car crash."

"It was no accident. The driver had lost the will to live. So he ended it all and took Ambrose with him. Jacob came here under his own steam, with the purest of motives. He wanted to warn you that your life was at risk."

There was another pause.

"Yet now," Kiki said heavily, "you dare to come to my home and accuse me of conspiracy to murder?"

Rachel folded her arms. "Ironic, isn't it? Now that I've satisfied your curiosity, you might return the compliment. Was your affair with He-Who-Cannot-Be-Named a mere charade? An amusing dalliance to pass the time while you laid plans for a new life with Phoebe Wardle?"

"What makes you think that I…?"

"A widowed nurse who is short of money can't afford gowns by Lanvin. The money might have come from Malam, but I wondered about you. Men had misused you. In the past you'd had a…close bond with Adeline. Phoebe Wardle is attractive. I asked myself if you might have formed an attachment."

Kiki closed her eyes for an instant. Jacob presumed that she would refuse to answer.

To his amazement, she said, "All right. The time for pretending is over."

"Yes."

"I knew from the start that the romance with…You-Know-Who was doomed. When a man from…such a family…falls in love with a woman like me, it can only ever end in disaster. For her, of course. He will walk away unscathed. Naturally, I was dazzled. And so, I might say, was he. I told him I was incapable of having children, because of things that happened to me when I was younger. He said he didn't care. If I were still impressionable, I might have been convinced."

It was, Jacob thought, as if she were talking to herself.

"You should read his letters to me," she continued. "However, there was no future in it. I'd spent too long as a plaything for men. Occasionally it was exciting. Often it was lucrative. But I came to realise I needed...something utterly different."

"A life with Phoebe Wardle?"

Kiki looked her in the eye. "You're an interesting woman. Don't worry, I won't pry into your own private fancies. Let me just say that in her own, much nobler, way, Phoebe had spent her life serving others. She saved countless women from misery."

"What she did was against the law," Jacob said.

Kiki rounded on him. "The law is cruel and wrong and made by men."

"She played Russian roulette with the lives of her patients."

"What does a boy like you know?" She spat out the question. "I don't pretend that every operation was perfect. Phoebe did her best in the circumstances."

"For Damaris Gethin," Rachel said, "her best wasn't good enough."

"Damaris was an emotional cripple. You could see it in that wretched art of hers. In every tormented brushstroke. She was damaged goods long before she went to Orgarswick."

"After what happened there, she no longer wanted to live."

"She wanted justice," Jacob said.

Kiki shook her head. "Damaris Gethin made her choice. And that was what Phoebe offered her patients. A chance to escape calamity."

"Would giving birth have been so terrible?" Jacob asked.

"How would you know? What right have you to judge?"

Jacob frowned. He didn't quite know how he'd managed it, but he felt he'd surrendered the high ground.

Kiki turned to Rachel. "Did you realise that Roddy Malam was the father of Damaris's unborn child?"

"It seemed a logical inference."

"How cold you are!"

"Logic is neither cold nor hot. It's simply an attempt to introduce a touch of order into a random universe."

Kiki made a scoffing noise. "Anyway, Roddy talked Damaris into solving her problem. He had absolutely no interest in becoming a father. The money she forked out was a consideration, of course. For him and for Evan Tucker."

"And Phoebe Wardle."

"She went into nursing to help others. When she met Giles Malam, her life changed direction. Roddy introduced her to me at one of Tucker's parties. At first I didn't warm to her. She was very buttoned-up, very British, you might say. Severe, hard to get to know. But I sensed she yearned for something more from life. I began to realise I was thinking about her more and more. A strange attraction, unlike anything I'd known before."

"How romantic."

"Sneer if you wish, Miss Savernake. You did say you wanted the truth."

"The truth is that you crave things you're not supposed to have. Like your royal lover."

Kiki gave a shrug. "Eventually, Phoebe thawed. Having a place in Rye was useful. Easy for me to sneak across to Romney Marsh."

"Orgarswick was where you hatched your plan, wasn't it? To escape from Malam and Tucker and Ambrose and Adeline." Rachel paused. "To use Roddy Malam as a weapon."

Kiki arched her eyebrows, but said nothing.

Rachel continued. "Phoebe Wardle only needed to unbend a fraction for him to become putty in her strong hands. Killing Tucker and faking his own death was her suggestion but your idea, inspired by Ambrose's chicanery. Malam was too arrogant to see that his own death was the final link in the chain. Once he'd done your dirty work for you."

Jacob could almost see Kiki's mind working. Finally, she spoke.

"Neat, don't you think?"

Rachel nodded. "Let me tell you what I believe happened. Malam supplied Phoebe with the telephone number of Butterworth's lodgings. She fooled the poor devil into coming to Romney Marsh while Malam called at The Risings under a pretext. He killed Tucker with a fork from the same type of motorcycle as Butterworth's. Next he dragged the body on the sled as far as the lookers' hut. Phoebe had arranged to meet him there. The idea was that Tucker's face would be horribly disfigured so that his body could be passed off as Malam's. Malam made a start on that wretched task. Phoebe was meant to shave Tucker's beard and strip the corpse before dressing it again in old clothes of Malam's."

Kiki pursed her lips, as if judging a student's dissertation.

"How did she kill Malam?" Rachel asked. "With the razor or the fork?"

"The razor, actually. She made as if to embrace him and then slit his throat. She said she'd never forget the look on his face as he realised what was happening."

Rachel said coolly, "I can imagine."

"Don't waste any sympathy on Roddy Malam."

"I don't."

"He was happy to kill Tucker and see Butterworth hang for the crime. Selfish to the bone."

"So were you all. Malam's body went in the ditch, the filthy grave he'd intended for Tucker. Phoebe dragged Tucker's corpse on the sled to Orgarswick. There she shoved body and sled into the cesspit. It can't have been easy, but I imagine she's always had plenty of strength."

"Yes."

"The pair of you were determined to get out of Britain and start a new life together. Money would be the least of your problems. I presume you've already drained your husband's bank account?"

Kiki smiled. "He still has his stamp collection."

"Phoebe has already made it plain that she intends to leave the country. You will tell all and sundry that your distress about the deaths of Adeline and Malam means you can't bear to stay here a moment longer. You've done your best to muddy the waters by hinting to the police that you spent Saturday night with Malam, when really it was Phoebe."

"How can you be sure?"

"There is a little circumstantial evidence. Jacob made enquiries in Maida Vale. Your Peugeot is distinctive but nobody saw it anywhere near the captain's flat. Regardless of that, I'm sure you drove to Orgarswick that day. Whether you gave Phoebe a lift to London or whether she took the train doesn't matter. You spent the night in Romney Marsh and as soon as you heard on the wireless about the murder here, you headed straight for Scotland Yard. After that, you came here."

Jacob opened his mouth but before he could say anything, Rachel continued. "For the second time, your plans were disrupted by chance. First, it was Ambrose, then the farm worker who decided to cut across the fields. Malam's body was meant to be found, but not so soon. No doubt Phoebe telephoned you with the bad news and you agreed to improvise."

Kiki yawned. "You've been busy, Miss Savernake. But it's

time to ask the only question that matters. Where is all this leading? Don't tell me you want me to give an exclusive interview to your tame hack before handing myself in to the police?"

Jacob sat up hopefully.

"Is it such a bad idea?" Rachel said.

"You're joking, I hope." Kiki's laughter sounded hollow. "Look at things from my point of view. The choice is simple. I can give myself up and sit patiently in a cell waiting for my appointment with the hangman. Or I can go abroad with Phoebe and create a new identity for myself. I've had plenty of practice at that. What would you do in my shoes?"

"I'm afraid it isn't quite so straightforward. Jacob and I know what the pair of you have done."

A touch of unease scraped Jacob's spine, like a cold, hard fingernail. It was one thing to witness the revelation of an ingenious criminal plot, quite another to stand between a ruthless killer and freedom.

Kiki said, "I could ask you to promise to keep quiet for a few days, until we were safely out of the authorities' reach."

"Even if we agreed, how could you rely on us keeping our word?"

Jacob wanted to gabble some improvised words of reassurance, but a glance from Rachel silenced him.

"No," Kiki said. "You're right. I can't leave it to chance."

"Why not consult your partner in crime?" Rachel suggested.

Kiki glared at her. "How do you suggest I do that?"

"Surely she's listening at the door?"

For a moment Kiki seemed thunderstruck. Then she gave a harsh laugh. "Guessing again?"

Rachel shook her head. "Where else would she be? She took a taxi from Orgarswick to the station and caught the train to Rye. I noticed her name on the label of one of those suitcases in the hall."

There was a pause. "Observant of you."

Rachel raised her voice. "You may as well come in."

Jacob's eyes shifted to the door. Only now did he realise that Kiki had left it ajar. It swung open and Phoebe Wardle entered. He was shocked by her haggard appearance. Her face was devoid of colour, and her shoulders were stooped. Was it fanciful to think she was weighed down by guilt? Her grim trade must have accustomed her to pain and suffering, but he supposed nothing prepared you for killing someone in cold blood.

"Why did you interfere in our lives?" Phoebe Wardle's voice was hoarse. "What gives you the right?"

Rachel picked up her handbag and got to her feet. For a moment Jacob was nonplussed. Were they about to leave? Did she intend to give the two women a chance to flee across the Channel?

"Damaris Gethin felt driven to take her own life. In her own mind, she was murdered. She asked me to solve the crime and to see justice was done."

"She'd lost her mind."

"Perhaps."

"You're not entitled to play God."

Rachel looked her in the eye. "Do you believe you were entitled to kill?"

Jacob heard a click. They'd taken their eyes off Kiki. When he looked back in her direction, he saw she'd taken a small gun out of the desk drawer.

She pointed it straight at Rachel's heart.

———

The silence lasted no more than a few seconds, but to Jacob it felt like an eternity. His tongue was dry. Even if he'd wanted to speak, he could barely have managed a croak.

And the clock kept ticking.

"A Haenel Schmeisser pocket pistol, I see," Rachel said. "Snap! I have one myself. Yours was a present from Marcel Ambrose, I suppose."

Kiki inclined her head.

"Did he mention that even at close range, it is notoriously inaccurate? Shoot at me and there's every chance you'll hit poor Jacob here." A pause. "Or even your ailing lover."

"Ailing?" Kiki said through gritted teeth.

Phoebe Wardle moved forward.

Rachel said to her, "At the Hades, I noticed that you lost your balance. Of course, that can happen to anyone. Outside in the street, your hands were trembling. Understandable, after such a shock. At Orgarswick, when you shouted at Martha, you shook with anger. Reasonable enough. However, I wondered. Was something else going on? Might you be suffering from some ailment of the nervous system?"

Phoebe Wardle glared at her. "You think you're very clever, don't you?"

"Parkinson's disease, perhaps, or something of the sort? In a severe case, the symptoms are demoralising. With your medical training, I imagine you fear the worst."

"Excellent treatments are available in Europe," Kiki snapped. "There's a specialist in...the country we're heading for. He's invented a revolutionary new machine that involves stretching the spinal cord. By this time next week, Phoebe will be on the road to recovery."

Rachel sighed. "But will it work?"

"How dare you!" Kiki gestured with the gun. "You should be on your knees, you and your boyfriend, begging for your lives."

Jacob shifted on the settee. "Actually, I'm sure we can come to a reasonable—"

"Be quiet and leave this to me." Rachel turned to the women. "Listen. The facts are simple and you may as well face them. Killing us achieves nothing. It will only infuriate my chauffeur, who is waiting outside. Malam may have mentioned him to you. They loathed each other on sight. Trueman is armed and believe me, he is dangerous. Never mind running off to some clinic in the Alps or wherever it may be. Your brains will be spilling over the cobbles before you reach the other end of Sepulchre Street."

Kiki was breathing heavily. Phoebe Wardle stifled a sob.

"Your luck has run out," Rachel said. "I understand why you both acted as you did, but the game is up."

"It's not a game," Phoebe said.

Rachel shrugged. "Isn't life itself a game?"

"Malam and Tucker were worthless creatures," Kiki said. "Can you really blame us? Is the world a poorer place without them?"

"What about Adeline? She was killed for falling in love. What about Butterworth? Not to mention Damaris Gethin, driven to such a terrible end?" Rachel turned to Phoebe. "Did a tremor in your hands account for the mess you made of her operation?"

The nurse closed her eyes. "I won't make excuses."

Kiki made an impatient movement.

"Give the gun to me, Mrs. de Villiers," Rachel said calmly.

"I'd rather take my chances."

Kiki raised the pistol. Jacob held his breath.

The window of the library smashed. In the quiet room, the noise sounded like a grenade blast.

Rachel slipped her hand into her handbag, and then flung the bag at Kiki in the same quick movement. Diving at Jacob, she pulled them both down to the floor.

Kiki's gun went off, and they heard a scream of agony.

Jacob turned his head. The shot had hit Phoebe Wardle. She

was gasping and clutching her midriff. Blood oozed over her hand as she staggered and fell to the floor.

Kiki gave a strangled cry of horror.

Trueman's head and shoulders poked through the curtain masking the broken window. Jacob saw his knobkerrie in one huge paw, a revolver in the other.

Kiki blundered across the room to her lover's side. Jacob realised that Rachel had a gun in her right hand. She'd removed it before hurling the bag at the other woman. As they lay huddled on the rug, her left arm circled his waist. Her touch was firm. Even in such a sinister tableau, he found it strangely comforting.

Kiki bent down and kissed the moaning woman.

"Put the gun down," Rachel hissed. "Lift it, and Trueman will blow your head off."

For answer, Kiki turned the revolver to her face.

"I'll save him the trouble," she said.

"No!" Jacob yelled.

But with a sad smile, she pulled the trigger.

Chapter 36

"The case is closed," Sir Hector said, with a cheerful click of the tongue.

On the other side of the desk, Major Whitlow glowered. "We still haven't—"

"The case is closed," Sir Hector repeated, more loudly. "I have discussed matters with the Great and the Good. Not to mention at the highest level within Scotland Yard."

"And the man in the fedora?"

"A chimera. We forget him. If he ever existed." Sir Hector's eyes narrowed. "It isn't inconceivable that your chap invented him, to cover for his own failure to deal with the target as per instructions?"

Whitlow ground his teeth. He looked as though he wanted to score the desk with his claw.

"Understood?"

"Understood, sir."

Sir Hector leaned back in his chair. He was in an avuncular mood.

"Splendid. One needs to take the broad view in these matters, Whitlow."

"Yes, sir. I was merely wondering…" The major's voice trailed away.

"Go on."

"I read Flint's story in the *Clarion*. It's a farrago. Utter tosh."

Sir Hector beamed. "Decent journalism by the standards of that rag, I thought. More interesting for what he didn't report, of course, than what he invented."

"Flint could never have tracked the de Villiers woman down without outside help. This business has Miss Savernake's fingerprints all over it. And Oakes is pretty much complicit."

"You sound bitter, Whitlow."

"She has no business to meddle, sir."

"You mustn't bear a grudge, man. Lord knows what makes the woman tick, but she's damned intelligent. One of these fine days, we might want her to meddle in something on our behalf."

Whitlow didn't quite manage to stifle a groan.

"Chin up! The inquests will be taken care of and Flint's imagination has served up a tale to keep the great British public happy. As far as they are concerned, Tucker killed Malam and then himself. Mrs. de Villiers and Nurse Wardle died as a result of a grief-stricken suicide pact. Nonsense, certainly, but damned neat nonsense. Remember what Mark Twain said?"

"No, sir."

"Never let the truth get in the way of a good story." Sir Hector clicked his tongue appreciatively. "Not bad for an American, eh?"

"Indeed, sir."

"As for our Very Important Person, let's hope he's learned a salutary lesson, eh? Apparently the de Villiers woman kept a cache of letters from him. Highly compromising, needless to say. She probably regarded them as some form of insurance, but if she'd got away to the Continent, I wager she'd have been tempted to indulge in a little blackmail. Now they've been found in her belongings, and every page burned to ash, we can all sleep easier in our beds. I'm sure His…our Very Important Person will have learned his lesson."

"You think so, sir?" Whitlow said heavily.

"Absolutely. We can only pray that he soon finds consolation with a plucky English virgin who takes her pleasure from opening flower shows and bearing rosy-cheeked children to inherit… Well…anyone would do, as long as she's not some other suspect foreigner with a taste for bedroom gymnastics, eh?"

"We can but hope, sir."

"That's the ticket. Optimism. It's what makes this country great. Along with our genius for pragmatism and compromise."

"Yes, sir."

Sir Hector patted his stomach reflectively.

"You know, Whitlow, I don't usually care to count my chickens, but I'd say all's well that ends well."

———

In the drawing room of Gaunt House, Rachel was playing the piano. Jacob laughed as she began to sing the chorus.

"I've danced with a man, who's danced with a girl, who's danced with the Prince of Wales."

"Not one of your own compositions this time," he said.

"No, Herbert Farjeon wrote that one and the Prince gave his approval. People say he's a good sport."

Jacob was about to make a ribald remark, but Martha interrupted.

"I liked your article in the paper, Jacob."

"Thanks." He frowned. "A shame I had to make so much of it up."

"Truth is stranger than fiction," Rachel said. "And more troubling."

"You think Damaris Gethin would be content that justice was done?" Jacob asked.

Rachel shrugged. "Who knows?"

"I still don't see why my report couldn't..."

"It's not simply a matter of keeping Scotland Yard and Major Whitlow's masters quiet," Rachel said. "What would be gained by telling the real story?"

"People prefer lies," Martha said.

"But..." Jacob began.

"Think of all the women who were patients at Orgarswick," Rachel said. "Haven't they gone through enough? They don't deserve to have your less scrupulous rivals sniffing round in the hope of uncovering juicy scandals. Let them keep their secrets."

Jacob found himself wondering what secrets Rachel and the Truemans kept. Was it better not to know?

She began to play a tune of her own, and his thoughts turned back to Sepulchre Street. Or Graveyard Lane, as they called it. The place where so many hopes and dreams were buried forever. Among all the horrors, all the revelations, one memory stood out. The recollection of Rachel's arm snaking around his waist, her warm grip of reassurance.

He'd never forget it.

Trueman offered him a drink. "See what you reckon to this."

Rachel brought her tune to an end and came over to join the others.

"A Bloodhound cocktail, Cliff?" Rachel sniffed. "Pleasingly tart. Gin and vermouth, garnished with strawberries. Definitely appropriate."

"We need a toast," Martha said.

"Shall we drink to crime?" Jacob asked.

Rachel shook her head as she raised her glass.

"To living dangerously."

CLUEFINDER

Cluefinders were popular during the "Golden Age of Murder" between the two world wars. British and American detective novelists alike delighted in demonstrating that they had "played fair" with their readers by highlighting at the end of the book some of the hints and indications in the text about what was really going on. The Rachel Savernake books reinvent Golden Age tropes in various ways and, when writing *Mortmain Hall* and *The Puzzle of Blackstone Lodge*, I had a lot of fun reviving the Cluefinder. Readers tell me how much they enjoy Cluefinders, so even though *The House on Graveyard Lane* is as much a thriller as a detective story, I've continued to play the game.

INDICATIONS THAT DAMARIS MAY HAVE BEEN PREGNANT DURING HER RELATIONSHIP WITH MALAM

Page 17: *raging headaches and erratic behaviour*

Page 37: *having headaches and being overcome with nausea*

Page 38: *I used to tell her she needed to buck up. Don't mourn what might have been.*

Page 39: *"And Damaris Gethin felt the same? She never wanted to settle down? Or have a child?"*

For a few moments, Malam looked troubled. He seemed to be weighing things up.

Page 63: *"You mustn't pay too much attention to my moods. I'm not like Damaris Gethin, I promise."*

"You certainly aren't," he said fervently.

"No neuroses," Rachel insisted. "No headaches, no bouts of nausea."

Page 63: *Malam gave a rather nervous smile. "Of course not."*

Page 81: *"As time passed, the swings of her mood became more extreme."*

"Was she in poor health?"

"Not to my knowledge," he said quickly.

TUCKER'S SEXUAL ORIENTATION AND INTEREST IN MALAM

Page 13: *"He swoons over the paintings of the late Henry Scott Tuke."*

Page 18: *As the bearded man caught Malam's eye, he gave a shy smile and beckoned him over.*

AN INDICATION THAT PHOEBE WAS RESPONSIBLE FOR DAMARIS'S ABORTION

Page 31: *"I did her a good turn once,"*

THE STATE OF PHOEBE WARDLE'S HEALTH

Page 18: *The woman turned away from the captain, only to lose her footing.*

Page 31: *almost tripping over*

Page 32: *her hands were trembling*

Page 33: *"Shaking with the shock of it."*

Page 213: *The nurse trembled.*

Page 225: *The woman seemed to be shaking with anger.*

MALAM'S POOR BUSINESS JUDGEMENT AND HIS BEHAVIOUR AFTER DAMARIS'S ABORTION

Page 40: *"Because she stopped working, there were no exhibitions. In the end, I asked Damaris to take the lease off my hands. Free, gratis, and for nothing."*

"Generous of you."

He shrugged. "She'd been unwell and I wanted to do her a good turn."

PHOEBE WARDLE'S UNEXPLAINED AFFLUENCE

Page 41: *"Evan Tucker's companion was rather chic. I adored her blue gown. Designed by Lanvin, if I'm any judge."*

GILES MALAM'S DUBIOUS MEDICAL PRACTICES

Page 41: *"He made a hash of an operation and a woman died."*

TUCKER'S RESEMBLANCE TO MALAM

Page 74: *He was roughly the same height and build as Captain Malam*

Page 75: *Behind the spectacles, pale blue eyes blinked.*
(compare page 64: Malam's pale blue eyes gazed into hers.)

*TUCKER'S GUILT OVER DAMARIS'S MISFORTUNES

Page 78: *"Such a pity that she has been...professionally inactive of late. Do you happen to know why?"*

A flush came to his cheeks. "Not in the mood, I suppose."

TUCKER'S ASSOCIATION WITH MALAM IN THE ABORTION RACKET

Page 80: *"I'll make sure to take advantage of the captain's wisdom and experience."*

"Very sensible. He's a good friend to have. Well-connected."
He paused. *"Always willing to help someone out if they get into a ticklish situation."*

TUCKER'S AWARENESS OF DAMARIS'S PREGNANCY

Page 81: *"As time passed, the swings of her mood became more extreme."*
"Was she in poor health?"
"Not to my knowledge," he said quickly.

RACHEL'S HINT THAT DAMARIS IS PREGNANT AND MAY BE SEEKING AN ABORTION

Page 83–84: *"I'm a creature of impulse."*
"Nothing wrong with that."
"Once or twice lately, it has got me into…rather a lot of trouble."
He moved closer to her and she could smell the gin on his breath. *"You know what they say. A trouble shared…"*

KIKI'S CONSPIRACY WITH A FEMALE LOVER

Page 96: *"Don't you see, chérie?"*
(compare page 15: *"Roderick, chéri!…"* when addressing a male admirer)

KIKI'S PLOT AGAINST MALAM

Page 304: *"First, when she ended the affair, she indicated that it was because a lover from her past had rekindled the relationship. Second, when my colleague interviewed her about her whereabouts last night, she let Malam's name slip."*

KIKI'S MOTIVE FOR WANTING ADELINE/PAULINE OUT OF THE WAY

Page 311: *"Knowing Lulu, I was sure she'd get sick of being fawned over, but I suppose she felt flattered. She even encouraged her. So Pauline thought she mattered more to Lulu than any man."*

AUTHOR'S NOTE

This is a work of fiction, with invented characters and incidents, but I try to give even the most dramatic elements a touch of believability, and I'm grateful to everyone who has helped me with my research and the writing of the story. In the recent past, when taking part in the Rye Arts Festival, I've seized the opportunity to explore that fascinating town and Romney Marsh. I'm grateful to John Case, the festival director, for reading the manuscript and supplying me with a great deal of background information about Rye. John introduced me to Pat Argar, who also commented on the story and provided helpful information about Romney Marsh. The old maps and photographs that John and Pat sent to me helped me to imagine what the area was like more than ninety years ago.

Nigel Moss, an expert in Golden Age fiction, gave detailed comments on the manuscript, while Richard Barnett again advised on vintage cars. Father David of St. George's Church, Bloomsbury, responded generously to my request for information. Simon Dinsdale, a retired detective superintendent and lecturing colleague, kindly introduced me to his niece, a doctor, who supplied information about abortions in the 1930s, a sensitive subject about which I was especially anxious to ensure accuracy. I borrowed the titles of Evan Tucker's songs from the less well-known hits in the catalogue of an immeasurably superior songwriting team, Burt Bacharach and Hal David. The lines quoted by Trueman come from Russell Thorndike's *Doctor Syn*.

As I've done so many times in the past, I want to acknowledge the support and encouragement of my family—Helena (who drew the Major's map), Jonathan, and Catherine—as well as that of my agent, James Wills, and my publishers, who do such a great job with the Rachel Savernake series. And finally, my thanks go to all those readers throughout the world whose enthusiasm for the books is invaluable and highly motivating.

—Martin Edwards
www.martinedwardsbooks.com

Chapter 1

"Seeing isn't always believing."

Nell Fagan was talking to herself. She stood on a wide ledge of rock, a natural platform jutting out from Blackstone Fell. Under a low autumn sun, this remote corner of the Pennines masqueraded as a green and pleasant land. Beech leaves gleamed golden in the ravine below. A river rushed from the gorge past the village which shared its name with the Fell. Mellow light bathed the grey stone of manor house, rectory, church, and graveyard. Beyond the church, a tall round tower cast long shadows.

Her mind whirled. Could she believe the evidence of her own eyes, or was her vivid imagination playing a cruel trick? She'd hoped the peace and quiet up here would help to straighten out her thoughts, but she lacked Rachel Savernake's cool head. If only she had someone to confide in, to help her make sense of the apparently impossible; but she'd misjudged her approach to Rachel and made an enemy of her. In any case Rachel was in London, and so was Peggy, her oldest and closest friend. Nell was on her own, two hundred miles from home. The Smoke and the Slump belonged to a different world.

Nobody in Blackstone Fell knew who she was or how she

earned a living. Far less that murder had brought her here. She'd adopted a false name and was pretending to be an ardent photographer. It gave her a good excuse to poke around, snapping pictures of people and places at every opportunity.

Last night she'd walked down to the lower village to wet her whistle at The New Jerusalem. The public bar was a stronghold of taciturn masculinity, but she'd made her way in a man's world, and the old curmudgeons weren't going to intimidate her. Even if she was no diplomat, nobody could accuse her of lacking courage or self-belief. Announcing herself as the new tenant of Blackstone Lodge, she insisted on standing everyone a round of drinks.

She was bursting with curiosity about her new home, she explained. What was this story about its strange past? Why had nobody ever lived there until now? Had people really disappeared without trace? Should she be afraid? The regulars responded with shrugs and vague mutterings and turned their attention back to the dartboard. If an outsider was stupid enough to rent a place with such wretched history, that was her lookout.

The rector's wife was right, Nell thought. Judith Royle maintained that the villagers gave nothing away to strangers. Certainly not to an ungainly Londoner who reeked of tobacco and gin and could talk the hind legs off a donkey. When she wondered aloud about what went on inside Blackstone Sanatorium, nobody paid any attention. If the R101 had crashed on Blackstone Moor the other day, rather than a French field, they'd barely have spared the airship a glance before getting back to their dominoes and shove ha'penny.

She felt an unexpected chill. The sunshine was deceptive, like Blackstone Fell. A gust of wind rattled the tripod on which her camera perched precariously. It was a Vest Pocket Kodak in a vivid shade known as Redbreast. To be on the safe side, she unscrewed the camera from the tripod.

A sudden cacophony shattered the silence, deafening enough to make her bones rattle. She glanced up. A huge lump of rock was thundering down the jagged slope, heading straight for her. Throwing herself backwards, she lost her balance. She collapsed in a heap and the camera slipped from her hand. The boulder missed her head by inches and smashed the tripod to smithereens.

———

The shock dazed her. Her ears were ringing and her ankle hurt. She'd grazed her cheek and bruised her elbow. The taste of blood was on her lips. Heart pounding, she wondered if she'd be buried in an avalanche. She dared not move an inch.

Craning her neck, she stared at the rocky outcrop above her head. Not a soul to be seen. Birds sang in the distance. The breeze ruffled her hair. Nothing else happened.

As the minutes passed, her confidence rose. Gingerly, she shifted her leg. The movement made her wince, but she'd not broken a bone. She was still in one piece.

"Better to be born lucky than rich," she told herself.

Was the falling boulder a chance event, an act of God? The face of the crag was unstable, loosened by recent storms. When she'd mentioned coming to the Fell to take photographs, the rector's wife had warned of the risks and urged her to keep away. Nell took no notice. Over the years, more than one villain had tried to cause her harm. For an investigative journalist, jeopardy came with the job.

Struggling to her feet, she dusted herself down. The pain in her ankle was easing. Shame about the tripod, but thank goodness her camera was undamaged, even if its red sheen was scarred. At least she'd not lost her precious photographs.

A long soak in her tub would set her right. The descent from the ledge wasn't challenging, and she put her best foot forward, only to halt in mid-stride. Placing weight on the damaged leg brought tears to her eyes.

For a good five minutes, she massaged her ankle. Her scuffed satchel had escaped the boulder. She groped inside for her flask and swallowed a mouthful of brandy.

That was better. Fortifying.

She closed her eyes and tried to persuade herself that she was a victim of freakish misfortune. The fall of the boulder was pure bad luck.

In her head she heard Peggy's brisk voice, reproaching her long ago for a childish fib.

"You're not so good at lying as you think. I can see straight through you."

Stern words. Peggy had become her governess when she was five years old and she never stood for any nonsense, but she didn't mean to be unkind.

Nell couldn't say the same for Rachel Savernake. There was a menacing edge to Rachel's cool disdain. Nell itched to find out more about her. Why was she so fascinated by crime? Nell knew in her bones that a story lurked behind that lovely, enigmatic facade, begging to be told. Unfortunately, Rachel guarded her privacy with a ruthless zeal. Their one and only meeting had ended in disaster. She'd felt the lash of Rachel's scorn as the young woman echoed Peggy's old rebuke.

"Did you really imagine that I'd fall for such a tissue of lies? You're only deceiving yourself."

Nell breathed out. Any journalist worth her salt played games with the truth, but this was no time for wishful thinking. Peggy and Rachel were right. She must be honest, if only with herself. The boulder hadn't crashed down of its own accord.

Someone wanted her dead.

She expelled a long, low sigh. No hope of catching her assailant. This side of the Fell was steep; the climb above the ledge was best left to mountain goats. Out of sight, a gentler ascent from the lower village wound up the far side of the crag to the summit. Yesterday, Nell had lumbered up that way, intent on getting her bearings. At the top, in the teeth of a fierce north wind, she'd steadied herself against a cairn. The boulder was poised on the edge. To shift it wouldn't require great strength. Now that lump of rock had almost killed her.

This ledge was visible to anyone standing close to the cairn. Perhaps someone had climbed Blackstone Fell with murder in mind, or perhaps they merely wanted to spy on her. Nell imagined an enemy catching sight of her as she bent over the bright red camera. Kodak's advertising boasted of its gloriously colourful appearance and urged girl graduates, brides, and debutantes to take up photography. A would-be assassin had found Nell an irresistible target and come close to committing the perfect crime. When her body was found, everyone would presume she'd suffered a tragic misfortune and that the boulder had tumbled of its own accord.

Already, the culprit might be anywhere. Crossing Blackstone Moor or strolling along the riverbank back to the upper village, with no one any the wiser.

Nell took another gulp from the flask.

The brandy burned her throat, a sensation she adored. Alcohol fuelled her self-belief. Squaring her shoulders, she breathed out. Now she knew what she was up against. The attempt on her life proved she was on the right track. Blackstone Fell was home to a killer. Perhaps more than one.

A couple of Woodbines and a dog-eared copy of *The Amateur Photographer* had slipped out of the satchel. She retrieved them and put the camera in its case. If she'd made a false move, she

wasn't alone. Her arrival in Blackstone Fell had panicked someone into attempted murder. But she'd lived to tell the tale.

———

A muddy path forked close to the base of Blackstone Fell. One
route zigzagged down to the river. The other led to the mouth
of a cave before looping back to re-join the main track at the
riverbank, close to the stepping stones at Blackstone Leap.

Nell strode in the opposite direction, away from the ravine.
She followed the path along a shelf of land which jutted out
above the water and then descended towards the clapper
bridge. On the other side of the bridge was a pebbled lane that
meandered through the upper village. The river flowed down
the sloping land towards the lower village, known as Blackstone
Foot. The main path followed the course of the river, while a
track branched off and wound back up the incline to meet the
lane close to the churchyard. Whoever pushed the boulder had
a choice of routes from any part of the village to the far side of
the Fell and back again.

Halfway across the bridge, she heard a rifle shot.

She froze. There was nowhere to hide. And nobody in sight.
She didn't dare to breathe.

A second shot rang out a few moments later. A distant squeal-
ing filled the air.

Looking up, she saw a flurry of birds flying off towards the
Tower.

She waited.

Nothing. The tension seeped out of her. She realised where
the shooting came from. Yesterday afternoon, the rector's wife
had invited her to tea. Judith Royle had mentioned that her husband owned an old rifle, and enjoyed taking pot shots at birds in
the rectory orchard or the open countryside.

That must be it. The Reverend Quintus Royle was a man of God. He didn't want to kill her, just a harmless bird or two.

Nell exhaled. Her prejudices about rural England were confirmed. She'd always regarded Wordsworth and Thomas Hardy as overrated. As for the season of mists and mellow fruitfulness...

"Welcome to Blackstone Fell," she muttered to herself. "I'd sooner take my chances in Soho."

———

Nell headed down the lane. On her right was an empty stone cottage. The land agent had offered her a tenancy, but she'd chosen to rent the tower gatehouse. The cost was a pittance, thanks to Blackstone Lodge's dark history.

Imposing wrought-iron gates on the left marked the entrance to the manor house, home to Professor Sambrook and his two adult children, Denzil and Daphne. At the turn of the century, the professor was renowned as Britain's leading alienist, a rival to Freud, Adler, and Jung. Shortly after building Blackstone Sanatorium to treat his patients and conduct research, his wife had been killed in a car accident. For the past twenty-five years he'd shunned the outside world.

Nell was itching to discover what went on inside Blackstone Sanatorium. She had a prejudice against psychiatry—witchcraft for the intellectual classes—but she'd come here to follow up a curious lead. Was something sinister going on behind those high stone walls out on the windswept moor?

Now something else had happened, something that—

A dark blue car roared out of a gateway, swinging past her nose and into the lane. The shock made her stagger and the driver gave a belated fanfare on his horn.

"Hey!" she bellowed. "You could have killed me!"

He screeched to a halt. The car had shot out from the grounds of a house opposite Blackstone Manor. Its sleek appearance and acceleration were worthy of Le Mans. Turning in his seat, the driver pulled off his goggles and waved at Nell.

"Awfully sorry!" he called. "She really is a fast lady. Keeps taking me by surprise."

"Me too," Nell growled.

"A thousand apologies." The man's grin was undeniably engaging. "We met yesterday afternoon when I called at the rectory. Mrs. Royle introduced us."

"Of course I remember, Dr. Carrodus."

As she approached the car, she was conscious of his scrutiny. "That's quite a limp. Surely I didn't wing you? I'd never forgive myself. I'm supposed to heal people, not hurt them."

"Don't worry, you're not to blame."

"You've not been hopping over Blackstone Leap? Those stepping stones are lethal."

"Tripped as I was making my way down the Fell." The untruth rolled off her tongue with the ease of long practice. "Wrecked my tripod, but I'm still in one piece."

If Carrodus had missed her with the boulder and then failed to run her over, he seemed remarkably sanguine about her survival. He was a bachelor on the right side of thirty whose good humour and faint Welsh lilt contributed to his charm. He lacked the professional gravitas of an elderly physician, but Nell was willing to bet he had an admirable bedside manner. The rector's wife certainly seemed taken with him.

"With any luck, you've nothing to worry about. Tweaked muscle rather than a sprain. Apply a cold compress and for heaven's sake, rest up. As for that graze on your cheek, give it a good wash and a touch of iodine, and you'll be right as rain. I'd offer to take a look-see in the surgery, but I'm late for my weekly clinic at the sanatorium and after that I've got a long drive."

"Thank you, Doctor, but I'm a quick healer. I'll be running around in no time." She assumed a serious expression. "Not like those poor souls cooped up in the sanatorium."

"Don't you worry; they are in the best possible hands. Professor Sambrook is a leader in his field."

"So I hear."

"Brilliant mind, but his academic papers go over my head. Frankly, I'm flattered that he allows a humble village GP to darken his doors." He guffawed. "Between you and me, I feel like a Jung pretender."

He was so delighted with his pun that Nell felt obliged to laugh. "I wonder…"

"Sorry, must dash!" He waved. "And watch your step in future. Cheerio!"

His eyes vanished behind the goggles, and he sped off in a cloud of fumes.

———

Watch your step.

Many a true word, Nell thought. Rounding a bend, she spotted Major Huckerby in his shirt sleeves. He was up on a ladder, trimming the holly hedge that separated his garden from the rectory. They'd chatted earlier, as she wandered around on a reconnaissance of the village, taking photographs at every opportunity. He was a widower and she diagnosed loneliness; his pleasantries had an undertow of melancholy. Perhaps she was reading too much into a single conversation. Peggy always said she let herself get carried away too often for her own good.

The major waved his shears in greeting.

"You're hobbling," he called.

"Nothing serious."

"Young Carrodus didn't send you flying with that flashy new Lagonda of his?"

She smiled. "Turned my ankle on the Fell. My own stupid fault."

Major Huckerby's dark hair was liberally flecked with grey. Twenty years the doctor's senior, he remained a fine figure of a man despite an incipient paunch. Nell had a romantic vision of him striding across a parade ground, immaculate in military uniform, medals gleaming in the sunlight.

"Glad to hear it. Carrodus is a decent cove, but the way he tears around the country is a damned menace. Anyone would think his name was Henry Segrave."

"And look what happened to poor Sir Henry," Nell said. "Such a shocking waste. There was simply no need to kill himself. Why on earth do people throw away their lives for no good reason?"

The major's brow furrowed. He lifted the shears as if to shoo her away before resuming his onslaught on the hedge. As she limped past the lychgate of St Agnes Church, Nell wondered if somehow she'd offended him.

Blackstone Tower reared up ahead of her, above an avenue of ancient black poplars. Even on a lovely afternoon, it seemed to brood over the village, menacing and malign. The man who owned the Tower had a demeanour to match. Nell had encountered him that morning. Powerfully built with thinning grey hair and a grizzled beard, he'd strode down the lane as she demonstrated to the major how her camera worked. The major's friendly greeting was met with a long, hard stare at the pair of them. Nell felt as if she were being hypnotised. Finally, she and the major were dismissed with a brusque nod.

"Curmudgeonly fellow, Harold Lejeune," Major Huckerby

had murmured. "I suppose one must make allowances. Believe me, grief hits a man hard."

And not only men, Nell thought grimly.

————

"Miss Grace!"

Nell was lost in thought. Once she got back to London, should she swallow her pride and try to enlist Rachel Savernake's aid?

"Miss Grace!" The voice became shrill. "Did you hear me?"

Nell swore. She'd thought she'd heard *disgrace*. That was the trouble with using an alias. It was so easy to forget who you were pretending to be.

Looking over her shoulder, she saw the rector's wife rushing towards her. Nell switched on a smile to compensate for her rudeness.

"Hello, there! Sorry about that, Mrs. Royle." The woman glared at her. "Daydreaming, don't you know?"

Judith Royle's golden curls were tucked out of sight beneath a brown hat as shapeless as her coat. She was as demure as a Madonna, but dressed dowdily, as if to apologise for her svelte figure. Stuck-in-the-mud parishioners no doubt disapproved of her on principle. Nell had pigeonholed Judith as a church mouse, cowering in the angular shadow of the Reverend Quintus Royle, permanently anxious and pathetically eager to please.

Not this afternoon. The delicate features were crimson with anger.

"Didn't you recognise your own name?"

Nell took a step back. This combative response was as alarming as it was unexpected.

"I'm sorry," she repeated. "I didn't hear—"

"It must be a peculiar experience," Judith Royle said through gritted teeth, "to accustom oneself to a false identity."

It wasn't in Nell's nature to remain on the defensive. Over the years, she'd faced down foes much more formidable than a rector's wife.

"You must excuse me, Mrs. Royle. I haven't the faintest idea what you're talking about."

"It's quite simple. You are not Cornelia Grace, are you?"

Nell frowned. "Indeed I am. Cornelia is my baptismal name. Though when I'm at home in London, everyone calls me Nell."

Judith Royle's mouth set in a stubborn line. In a low voice, she said, "I'm not a fool."

"Perish the thought. A simple enough mistake for anyone to—"

"Please, don't make this any more difficult. You're not the person you claim to be."

"Why do you say that?" Nell adopted a self-righteous tone. "I can only presume you're labouring under a misapprehension."

Judith Royle shook her head. Nell was perplexed. This woman wasn't the sort to say boo to a goose. What was going on? Better find out before matters got out of hand.

"Listen, it's chilly now the sun has gone in. Why don't you come to the Lodge? I'd love to repay the hospitality you showed me yesterday. We can have a natter over a nice cup of tea."

The rector's wife wavered. "I don't…"

"Please. Let me set your mind at rest."

"Oh, all right." Marriage to the rector, a joyless puritan twice her age, must have accustomed her to giving in. "But I can't be out long."

"Then we'd better get a move on."

Beyond the church, the lane turned and began its descent to the lower village. Nell and Judith Royle crossed over to an unmade track leading to an arched stone gateway. To the left of the arch was a high stone wall, on the right was the gatehouse.

Blackstone Lodge was in the Gothic style, irregular in construction and adorned with battlements. The effect was lopsided and disconcerting, as if the architect had indulged in a private joke.

"I always wondered what it's like inside," Judith Royle said.

Her voice was trembling and so was she. As Nell fumbled in her bag for her door key, she glanced at her companion. Sometimes seeing *was* believing. The expression on that pale Madonna's face spoke for itself.

Judith Royle was scared to death.

ABOUT THE AUTHOR

Martin Edwards has won the Edgar, Agatha, H.R.F. Keating, Macavity, Poirot, and Dagger awards as well as being short-listed for the Theakston's Prize. He is president of the Detection Club, a former chair of the Crime Writers' Association, and consultant to the British Library's best-selling crime classics series.

In 2020 he was awarded the CWA Diamond Dagger for his outstanding contribution to crime fiction. Follow Martin on Twitter and Instagram (@medwardsbooks) and Facebook (@MartinEdwardsBooks).